Cold Gold II

Dennis J. McTaggart

Publishers:
Inspiring Publishers
PO box 159 Calwell ACT 2905, Australia.
Email: inspiringpublishers@gmail.com

National Library of Australia Cataloguing-in-Publication entry

Author: McTaggart, Dennis J.

Title: **Cold Gold II**/*Dennis J. McTaggart*.

ISBN: 9781925346701 (pbk)

Subjects: Abalone industry–Australia–Fiction.
Detective and mystery stories, Australian
Short stories, Australian.

Dewey Number: A823.4

Contents

Teddy, from Then to When?

Edward Dennis McSweeny was born and raised in the western suburbs of Melbourne at a time when men were proud to work hard, using their hands. He lived with his two brothers: one older by three years and the other younger by three years.

Even as a child, he stood out as a larrikin. He had a happy and carefree air about him and had a wonderful childhood surrounded by love from his siblings and parents.

He was known as a Happy Little Vegemite. (Vegemite is a famous Australian spread. An advertising campaign started in 1954 used groups of attractive healthy children smiling and singing a catchy jingle, 'We're happy little Vegemites', to promote the spread.)

He went to school with all the new Australians and found them to be the same as everyone else was—a lot of good kids and a few dodgy ones, just like the Aussies.

There was food on the table every night, and each Friday night, even though they weren't Catholic, they had fish and chips for tea. One of the boys would run down to the Greek fish and chip bloke and buy them wrapped up in newspaper, run back, and open them up, and everyone would get into eating them.

His dad would have a bottle of beer and they and their mum would have a glass of lemonade. On special occasions, such as birthdays, one of the boys would take a couple of pots from the kitchen, go to the local chows (Chinese) takeaway, and bring back a pot of sweet and sour pork and fried rice. That was a rare treat as it was a more expensive meal than fish and chips.

Teddy often thought back to his happy childhood. Although the families in the street weren't rich, everyone was the same; all their fathers were blue-collar workers and honesty was a valued trait. You could leave your doors unlocked and the keys under the mat in your car, and nobody would steal anything.

On the few occasions when there was a blue between men, it was strictly one-on-one, and, at the end of the fight, the two men would shake hands and go and have a beer together. Teddy's father wasn't a heavy drinker, and Teddy had never seen him drunk or so drunk that he needed assistance. He was a happy man and had a happy family.

Before Teddy's father married the love of his life, he spent six years in the Australian Army in New Guinea, holding back the Japanese invaders who threatened the country he loved. His father never spoke of the atrocities that he and his mates witnessed.

Teddy wasn't much interested in school work. He was a bit of a dreamer, always looking out the window at the trees to see which way the wind was blowing. He could tell you, if you wanted to know, which would be the safest boat ramp to put your boat into the water and which way to go when you went fishing so as to get the smoothest ride home.

When Teddy was twelve, his dad bought a small, open wooden fishing boat that had a Seagull outboard motor on it.

The Seagull outboard, or more correctly known as the British Seagull, was an outboard motor that was manufactured between 1930s and 1990s. They were reliable two-stroke engines that were very simple to operate, and as long as you got the fuel mixture right, they would go forever. They weren't the fastest of motors and went out of production when the more modern outboard motors came into fashion. They didn't have a reverse gear. If you wanted the boat to go backwards, all you did was spin the motor 180 degrees round, until the tiller was facing backwards, and then accelerate. They were cheap and reliable, and Teddy loved that boat.

That was the end of any serious school work for Teddy. He spent as much time out on the water as he possibly could. Soon he was supplying fresh fish for his family and most of the street. His dad had a stern rule that he had to be home within an hour of the sun going down. This was because Teddy's mum worried a bit. The thought of having his beloved boat taken away, for even a day, was enough to make Teddy adhere to every rule.

There were plenty of abalone in the shallow water in Port Phillip Bay, and, equipped with a snorkel and face mask, he could easily get as much mutton fish (abalone) as he liked. But it was hard to sell. He often came across a crayfish, and that was welcomed into the family home. Teddy's family lived better than the rich people, simple pleasures are the best. Love and happiness make a great family, not wealth.

Teddy's elder brother became an electrician, and his younger brother went on to university and became an accountant. This was a big step-up for anybody from their street. When Teddy left school, he got a job down at one of the many shipyards that were on the waterfront at Williamstown. He soon became proficient at most types of mechanical and boat maintenance work.

Unfortunately, both his parents passed away when Teddy was in his twenties; it was a sad time.

The three brothers decided to sell the family home and try and set themselves up a bit. Teddy, who was no good with money, decided that the best thing that he could do was to buy a decent boat, and he found an old wooden fifty-footer and lived on that. He renovated the inside, made a spacious galley, and did up the wheelhouse. It looked old from the outside, but when you went inside, it was a real surprise.

Teddy mixed with all types of people, men mainly, from the wealthy boat owners who rarely used their vessels to the lower end of the scale—people who had always wanted to own a boat. Strangely, these sorts of people would come down of a night, after work, and muck about on their boats for hours at a time.

Teddy met and fell in love with the daughter of one of his wealthier clients, and they got married. But soon the magic disappeared. She wanted to be in the bright lights, and Teddy wasn't that keen on getting dressed up and mixing with the wankers as he called them. Teddy was happiest being with people who loved the sea. The married pair agreed to divorce, and as the wife had more money than the groom had, Teddy kept the boat and all his gear, and she kept everything that she had brought into the marriage. They parted and remained friends.

Teddy decided that, to increase his income, he would get stuck into abalone poaching big time. So he worked out a plan. It was simple. He would take out his big boat on an evening, steam over to a reef that was out of sight of land, and get a couple of hours in the darkness under the water, collecting abalone. At that time, the fisheries were more concerned with grabbing the New Australians for taking too many or undersized fish, and they never really bothered Teddy. He always worked at night and kept a low profile. He did a deal with a processor, and all went well.

Mixing with all the people in all the pubs in Williamstown, Teddy got to meet and enjoy the company of some shady characters from the Painters and Dockers Union. These were hard men who, more than likely, worked hard and played even harder. Once they realised that Teddy was OK, they didn't bother him. Like the old Beach Boys song goes, 'The bad guys knew him and they left him alone.'

Teddy was free to do his thing, and he made a lot of money, all tax-free. He was always on the lookout to make money. In the times before computers, there was always some shady bloke who worked in a factory and was able to get his hands on some stuff that had been missed in a stocktake, and Teddy was always on the lookout for cheap, often hot stuff.

He became friendly with the thieves and the stand-over men and the full-time crims. They were normal people as far as he was concerned.

Quite often, there would be fights in the pubs, and Teddy wasn't too bad at defending himself. He never started trouble, but if trouble came looking for him, he would accommodate it—no problem.

His younger brother, who did his tax, suggested that he sell the big boat and buy a smaller, faster boat and a small home in the western suburbs. Teddy decided to follow the advice, and the sale of the big boat went well, as it was well known around the waterfront.

He bought a small single-fronted house in Williamstown and placed it under an almost untraceable system that his brother, the accountant, had put together so as to make the ownership almost impossible to track back to Teddy.

He then took possession of a nineteen-foot Haines Hunter with a 115-horsepower Mercury motor. This boat really moved along, and when he considered all the time he had wasted before, by only going eleven knots, he laughed to himself. Yes, Teddy was away, wind in his face, and happy with life.

Teddy dated a few women and got on well with most of them. One day, he bumped into Rita. She was having lunch, sitting in the sun at an outdoor restaurant. He had spoken to her a couple of times at the library where she worked. He was a keen reader and had to change his address when he sold the boat, so she remembered him.

Teddy boldly walked up and said, 'Hullo, Rita, how are you this fine day? Do you remember me? I spoke to you the other day about changing my address from my boat to the house I just bought in Williamstown. My brother talked me into it as he said that it would be a good investment for the future. He's an accountant, so he should know, shouldn't he?'

Teddy was nervous, and the words tumbled out. He knew that he was talking too fast, but once he started, he couldn't stop.

Rita was a bit taken aback by the flood of words.

She smiled and said, 'Yes, mister, ah . . . '

Rita pretended that she couldn't remember Teddy's surname.

Teddy cut in and said, 'Don't go with the mister bit. Just call me Teddy. Everyone else does.'

Rita smiled and said, 'All right, it's Teddy, and, yes, I do remember you.'

Rita thought back to the books that Teddy read. You can tell a lot about people by what they read. Teddy read a lot of action fiction. His favourite authors were Wilbur Smith and Frederick Forsyth. Rita had at times ordered books in for him. She was comfortable with someone who enjoyed such authors.

Teddy blundered on. 'Are you on your own?'

Rita looked at the big bloke and saw that he was completely out of his depth.

She answered, 'Yes, I'm just having my lunch.'

Teddy asked, 'Can I join you? Do you mind?'

Rita looked at him and said, 'That's the best offer I've had all day.'

It took a moment to sink in that she had accepted his offer, and Teddy promptly sat down.

That was easy, he thought.

'Please keep eating,' Teddy offered and looked to seek out a waitress to get him something.

When the waitress came, Teddy ordered a pie and chips.

He looked at the salad that Rita was eating and exclaimed, 'I suppose that I should eat a bit more rabbit food, but it doesn't seem to fill me up.'

Rita smiled and said, 'I like salads.'

They talked for a while about the weather and the amount of people who were about—just small talk. Before Teddy realised, it was time for Rita to go back to work. So he walked her towards the library.

'I'm going this way anyway,' he explained.

Teddy left Rita at the library door and walked away.

Rita went inside and watched Teddy walk away, and she thought that he was a nice person.

I wonder how things will turn out, she thought. *He must like me or else he wouldn't have walked me back to the library.*

He was easy on the eye. Rita knew that Teddy had been married to an up-herself rich daddy's daughter and that he didn't have a permanent partner. In a small, end-of-the road suburb like Williamstown, word gets around pretty fast about who is available and who's not. Love-wise, things had been a bit quiet for Rita. Not a lot of available men came to the library. Her clientele were mostly older men and women and retired people who were all very nice but, like she said, old people.

Rita wondered what would happen next; maybe she was destined to be an old maid. The cranky old librarian, who always wore black, and the kids poked fun at behind her back, as they pretended to read books, and laughed when they looked up *fart* in the dictionary.

Teddy walked away and said to himself, 'Rita seems to be a nice sort of girl, but she's not the type who would like some of the lower pubs where I hang around. I want to bump into her again and have a talk.'

So next day, at lunchtime, Teddy staked out the library, and when Rita walked out, there was Teddy.

'Hi, Rita, are you heading off for a bite to eat?' Teddy asked brightly.

Rita looked surprised and answered, 'Yes, as a matter of fact, I am. I didn't get a chance to have a cup of coffee at 10 a.m., so I'm a bit hungry.'

Teddy asked, 'Are you going to have a salad?'

Rita smiled and said, 'No, Teddy, today I just might have a pie and chips, washed down with a coke.'

Teddy laughed, 'And would you let me shout you lunch as a special favour?'

'I keep saying it, but that's the best offer I've had today. Of course, you can,' she said.

Teddy thought that he fell in love that instant. He closely looked at her; she was trim and had a great smile and a great figure. And she was smart. She had to be if she worked in a library. They sat outside once again, and the warm breeze gently made her hair glisten in the sunshine. Teddy thought that she was beautiful.

They spent heaps of time together. Teddy met her parents, and, of course, they had heard of him. When he turned up for tea one night and brought a couple of two-kilo crayfish, he was welcomed into the family with open arms.

Everything was going well, and Rita agreed to move into Teddy's place.

By now, Teddy was a partner in a boatyard down on the waterfront in Williamstown. There wasn't a lot of money in it, but it paid their bills, and also Teddy got away on a night and did his abalone poaching.

He was approached by his partner and agreed to sell him some of his share of the boatyard business. On advice from his younger brother, Teddy retained a share of the property that the boatyard was on. His ex-partner and he agreed on a monthly rental, so Teddy had a bit of an income from that.

Things were going along well with the abalone poaching. He tried taking out other divers but found that they were all heavy drinkers or couldn't keep their mouths shut. So he stayed on his own and kept his eyes open for a team that he could use to make even more money than he was at the present time.

He had noticed three younger blokes who were poaching abalone and kept his eyes on them. He watched as they started to travel further away in their cars. Some of the blokes in the pubs started to buy crayfish off them, and a couple of those blokes mentioned them to Teddy.

So, one day, he approached them and said, 'Hullo, boys, I know what you have been up to. I've just bought a Shark Cat and I'm looking for a team to put together and really get stuck into getting a big quantity of abalone. We can start out in the bay and then move up and down the coast. I know all about this abalone-poaching caper, and I reckon that if we all stick together, we will make a good quid.'

Dean was the first to answer, 'What's the split-up? What do we get?'

'Mate,' Teddy said, 'this is how it's going to work. I'll supply the boat and compressors. You supply your own gear. I've got a processor sweet who will take what we can get for a decent price. I've got the connections, and we split it evenly up between us. If we make $10,000, then we split it four ways and we get $2,500 each.'

The three boys looked at each other.

Curly said, 'We will have to think it over. Can you give us a couple of hours, and we'll get back to you?'

'No problems,' Teddy laughingly said. 'But don't take too long, or I might change my mind. Here's my phone number. I'll talk to you soon.'

With that, Teddy walked away.

The three young men looked at each other.

Dean said, 'What the fuck! He's talking about splitting up $10,000 worth of abalone. Fuck me, he must know where all the reefs are, and he's got the markets sewn up.'

Curly agreed, 'That's a shit load of money. I would love to get my hands on that much.'

Tom said, 'I reckon that this Teddy is the real McCoy. I reckon that he has been in it for a while.'

The boys all agreed. Tom rang Teddy back and said, 'We are in. Can we meet up at a pub and have a talk?'

Teddy was happy with the result and suggested that they meet in the lounge bar in the Yacht Club hotel. This pub overlooked the bay, and they had cheap meals on the menu.

They all gathered there, and Teddy got a round of drinks. He gave them a brief history of himself, and they told him about their adventures. Teddy warned them not to say a word to anyone, as rumours would get about, and the next thing that you knew the fisheries would be on your back and the penalties were severe.

From the very start, the operation ran smoothly. Teddy could see that Dean was a gentle giant, Curly was an eager starter, and Tom, well, he was a whole different kettle of fish and was old-fashioned tough. Teddy thought that when the chips were down, then he probably couldn't get a better crew to be with.

On the first night of them all poaching together, they all met on time, down at the boat ramp. Teddy was impressed by how they all handled themselves. They weren't half-drunk, and they spoke quietly to Teddy and showed him respect. He explained how he was going to do things and how it would all work.

So they went to work. Teddy took the Shark Cat out into the bay and drove over to a reef. Then Dean and Curly went over the side and worked off a T-piece. Tom worked off another hookah (diving compressor) and stockpiled the abalone in a central drop zone.

This way, if the fisheries were to stumble across them, then they wouldn't have any abalone on board. Teddy gave Tom an underwater light that Tom placed on a net bag at the stockpile so he could see where the pile was each time he returned. When the distance between the stockpile and the divers became too far, they surfaced (after they turned their head-mounted torches off), and Teddy pressed the MOB (man overboard) key on his GPS to mark the spot.

Then they moved to another spot.

As this was their first dive, Teddy was only concerned about covering costs, but the attitude of his three new friends surprised him. They were all go—eager to get back into the water and get more abalone. This was a heartening attitude that they had.

After midnight, Teddy said, 'Well, boys, that is about all we can get as we now have to shuck them out and bag them up. Let's start to get them to the surface. Who wants to go down and start swimming them up to the boat?'

Tom immediately said, 'I'll do that. I'll swim them up two bags at a time.'

With that, Tom went over the side and started to swim the net bags to the surface.

After shifting the Cat a couple of times and going back to where the stockpiles were, all the net bags were soon on board. Teddy shifted the boat out into the middle of the bay.

After a couple of hours, all the abalone were shucked out of their shells and bagged up in clear plastic bags.

Teddy rang Tony, an Italian bloke, who took the abalone to the processors.

Tony was a disabled pensioner who was fit enough to do the running around for Teddy and was paid on cash-in-the-hand basis.

Teddy had previously told Tony not to introduce himself to the new boys as he wasn't sure if they could be trusted.

'Keep well back,' he told Tony. 'Let them unload the abalone and then pick it up and take it to the factory when we have gone back to sea.'

Teddy phoned Tony and headed towards the distant boat ramp. When they got close to it, a torch light shone out to them, and Teddy guided the Shark Cat into the boat ramp. The three boys piled up the bags of abalone on shore and jumped back into the boat.

Tom, Dean, and Curly were in awe of how Teddy operated. They couldn't believe just how smoothly things went. The fact that, for almost all the time, there wasn't any abalone on board was something new to them. For everyone to get in and shuck the abalone was a masterstroke. Then to have someone pick up the abalone at another boat ramp so that they could return to the boat ramp of their departure empty, it was all too much. No wonder, everyone thought that Teddy was a genius.

On their return to the boat ramp, Dean jumped out of the Shark Cat and backed Teddy's F100, with the trailer for the Shark Cat connected to it, into the water, and Teddy drove the boat up onto the trailer. Dean clipped the bow ring onto the hand winch and then pulled the Shark Cat out onto dry land. Teddy and the remaining boys climbed down.

Teddy said, 'Well, fellas, that's it for tonight. How did you think that it went?'

The boys were all stunned; they weren't used to things going this well.

Dean asked, 'How much do you reckon that we will end up with?'

Teddy smiled and said, 'I reckon that we ended up with 250 kilos of meat weight. That should get us about $10,000, so we should end up with $2,500 each. How does that sound?'

The boys were over the moon.

Curly said, 'Bloody hell, that's terrific. That's more than what we earn in a month.'

Teddy grinned and said, 'We've only just begun. It will take me a couple of days to organise the money. If you're short, tell me, and I'll be able to sub you some until we get paid from the processor.'

They all laughed and went their separate ways.

Tom said, 'If we do this once a week, then we will be rich.'

The others agreed. It was a time of great excitement for them.

Teddy arrived home, had a quick shower, and slid into bed.

His partner, Rita, asked, 'Did everything go as planned?'

Teddy smiled, kissed her, and said, 'Yes, love, it went really well. The new young blokes worked steadily throughout the night, and we ended up with about 250 kilos.'

Rita said sleepily, 'Well done, love,' and went back to sleep.

Teddy closed his eyes and went to sleep almost instantly.

Tony watched as the young blokes stacked the bags of shucked abalone in a pile, and when they had gone, he drove the van down beside the pile and quickly threw them into the van. He drove into the night, back to a processing factory. He had a couple of hours wait until they opened, and he wasn't happy. The processor was making sounds that it was getting a bit hot, accepting illegal abalone.

Teddy and Tony would have to start looking for another processor, one who was willing to fit in a bit easier with how they worked.

When the factory finally opened and Tony was able to weigh in the abalone, he rang through the weights to Teddy. Teddy made arrangements to meet the processor and was told that he couldn't get the money for three days. Teddy reckoned that the processor was just having a lend of him, but he didn't cause a blue; he just went along with it. The processor was a Jew and a very smart businessman. He squeezed out every cent that he possibly could.

Because of his background, of working on boats both big and small, Teddy got to know all the fishermen—the cray (lobster) boats, the shark boats, the scallop boats, and even the abalone boats. Most of the abalone boats were fast fibreglass outboard boats. The abalone divers who worked in Port Phillip Bay mainly stuck to themselves. A couple mentioned that a mate of theirs had just started to buy abalone off them and he was struggling to get enough abalone to export overseas. So they gave Teddy a knock-down to him. Teddy went with one of his mates and met Derek, the new processor.

He was a friendly sort of bloke, and Teddy saw that he had exactly what he was looking for, a place to unload illegal abalone. Both the men liked each other from the moment that they met. They agreed on a price and were both happy with the result.

In due time, Teddy went and picked up his money from the Jewish processor and told him that things were getting a bit hot, so they might give it a miss for a while.

The Jew looked at Teddy and asked, 'They don't know that you and I are working together, do they?'

Teddy smiled and said, 'No worries, mate, we don't leave any trails anywhere.'

The Jew looked relieved as Teddy drove away with the money.

Teddy invited all the boys round so that they could be involved in the whack-up. He had a fridge full of cans, and they all relaxed out in Teddy's backyard. When Teddy started to give them their money, they couldn't believe it—$2,560 each.

Teddy explained that he had picked up $10,240 in cash.

Dean looked at the money and asked, 'Who pays the bloke who picks up the abalone?'

Teddy looked at him and said, 'I do. Why?'

Dean said that the three boys had talked about it and they had agreed that they should each pay a bit so that it didn't all fall on Teddy's head. Teddy was a bit amused. These kids seemed to be really genuine and fair.

'All right, fellas, from next trip, we split up Tony's wages between us,' he said.

They all had another can and got going back to their homes. Teddy felt as if something was going to develop out of this.

Teddy rang Tony and said, 'Mate, I've got a new processor ready to take some abalone from us. I want to pick you up, and we'll go and meet him. His name is Derek, and he's just started to buy abalone off a couple of mates of mine who are legal abalone divers.'

They agreed on a time next morning.

When the three men met, Tony was happy to discover that whenever he wanted to unload the van, Derek would be there to weigh in the product. That meant as soon as Tony had grabbed the abalone, he would ring Derek and they would meet and weigh in. That was perfect.

Derek had also said that as soon as the abalone was weighed, boxed up, and in the freezer, he would get the cash out of the bank and pay straight away.

Everyone was happy.

Things were going well, so Teddy decided that he would ring his friend Dave in Bairnsdale. He had given Dave an untraceable phone that he had got some vagrant to buy for him. He let him know that he and his new crew were going to come up for a flying visit, and if the weather was right, they might get a couple of days diving in.

Teddy and Dave had been friends for a long time. In the 1960s, Teddy had decided to buy a New South Wales's licence to dive for abalone. At that time, the abalone licences were $2.00 each. So each winter, when the weather blew from the southwest, Teddy would tow a tinny up to Eden and dive for abalone up there.

It was a real treat to be a legal diver for a while. Teddy used to stay at Dave's place, which was a run-down farmhouse on the outskirts of Eden, and the pair got on fine.

Dave ended up getting a bad case of the bends, and Teddy looked after him when he was at his lowest. Dave was the sort of bloke who never forgot a favour. They were good mates.

So now whenever Teddy decided to do a bit of poaching up that way, he always got Dave and his brother Lee to get the abalone back to Melbourne for him. Lee had a smallish furniture van that they concealed the abalone in, behind a wall of furniture, so that they could freight the abalone to Melbourne undetected.

Teddy felt as if everything was starting to develop well. He thought that with the new Shark Cat and his new crew, the future looked great.

Whale of a Tale

Wallace (Piggy) Trotter, senior fisheries officer, was deep under cover, disguised as a wealthy grazier from the Monaro High Country. He was clad out in R M Williams gear from the boots up, and instead of a baseball cap, he had on an Akubra Stockman's hat that shaded his face and looked ridiculous.

He was drinking with a couple of down-and-outs in the top pub at Pambula, New South Wales. He was into his second week as an undercover agent.

He had been sniffing his way around all the pubs in the area and, at last, had come across a couple of dead beats, and he just knew that they were abalone poachers. One was an Aussie bloke called Gazza and the other one was of Italian heritage and called Louie.

Bastards, he thought to himself.

He was buying them middies of beer and getting to know them. He had told them that he was looking to buy some abalone for a friend's fiftieth birthday party which was in a couple of weeks. They said that it wasn't a problem, as they had done a bit of abalone diving and could put their hands on some. In confidence, they told him that they could get a few kilos of abalone meat and could deliver it to him whenever he wanted it. There was no problem at all; he just needed to have the cash ready.

Piggy was getting excited with the prospect that he would have these blokes wrapped up good and proper.

Then one of the bastards said, 'If you really want to get some weight together, then you should get onto the crew that comes down from Melbourne. They really get into it and get a tonne or two at a time.'

Louie said, 'My cousin works for them. He tows their Shark Cat around and does odd jobs for the one that's in charge.'

Piggy felt the hair on the back of his neck stand up. *Were these two morons talking about Teddy and his crew?*

'Who are they?' Piggy asked. 'Do you know anything about them at all?'

The two down-and-outs looked at Piggy and smiled.

'Mate, we don't know much at all about them. But we do know that they are the best poachers in Australia. They always get abalone.'

Piggy smiled and said, 'Surely they have been caught by the police or fisheries.'

The two men looked at Piggy, laughed, and said, 'Mate, the fisheries are so dumb that they don't know what day it is. Before the fisheries even hear about them, they are gone, gone but not forgotten.'

Piggy asked, 'How come you know so much about them?'

The two men looked at Piggy, and Louie said, 'Mate, we hear everything. My cousin keeps me informed about what's happening. Anything that happens around any fishing port eventually comes back to us. There is a network of people talking to each other, and word soon gets around.'

Louie was starting to speak as if he was part of the crew and that Teddy relied on his input whenever he did a run-up this way.

Piggy was beside himself with joy; maybe there was a chance of him being forewarned about when Teddy and those bastards were coming there for another run. If he was waiting and ready for them, then it was a piece of cake. He could grab them with their abalone, and they would get jailed. Yes, that would show them not to mess with Senior Officer Trotter. Piggy was well pleased with himself, and he got another round for his new chums.

Teddy and the boys were getting ready for another trip up to the Victoria-New South Wales border area. They were still basking in the success of their trip down to Pedra Branca. It had been a real winner, and they had all come out a mile in front.

But Teddy said, 'You don't beat a good horse to death. We'll keep shifting around, doing what we do, and keep under the radar so no one can see us. Keep cool.'

Everyone agreed with Teddy on that plan. That is what made Teddy so successful. You couldn't predict what he was going to do next or just where they were going to pop up next. It kept everyone on their toes.

As the summer season approached, the humpbacked whales started their long migration up to warmer waters in the north of Australia.

He was a young male humpbacked whale. He hadn't reached his sexual maturity yet as he was only six years old. Female humpbacked whales become sexually mature at about five years of age, and it takes the male another two years to reach theirs.

He had spent the first six months at his mother's side. He was roughly the same size as her head, approximately twenty foot (six meters) long, and he still suckled her pink milk. For the next six months, he would suckle and catch his own food until he was able to be on his own and not need his mother for food or protection.

The humpbacked whales' social structure is one of mainly solitary living. They may band together for a short time to feed. But they spend most of their time alone as they journey from the Antarctic Circle to warmer water to give birth and to breed. They don't eat while they are travelling or are in the warmer waters. They live off the fat stored in their bodies from the krill and small fish that they consume in the Antarctic waters.

Teddy decided that the weather was right for a trip into the New South Wales—Victoria border area. He rang Tom and said that they would be heading up north. Tom was happy to be getting moving and doing something as it had been a few weeks since they had fired a shot.

Teddy rang Curly and said, 'We are away in the next couple of days.' Curly was also happy to be on the move.

He got on to Dean, who seemed to be a bit interested, but as he had just had the love of his life (the beautiful Leckie) move in with him, he wasn't that happy about going away for a few days.

Teddy laughed and said, 'Will I have to throw a bucket of cold water over the pair of you to get you separated?'

Dean laughed and said, 'That won't be necessary. I'll be ready, and I'll let Leckie know what's going on.'

Teddy was happy for Dean. He seemed to be really in love, head over heels. It wasn't any wonder, as Leckie was one of the most beautiful women that Teddy had ever seen—a real Asian beauty. She was nice with it, and she had a real happy nature. *Let's hope that she can control Dean's gambling,* Teddy thought.

He then gave Tony a call and told him they were a day away from heading up the coast. Tony confirmed that all was in readiness and the Shark Cat was full of fuel and ready to go.

Teddy contacted his mate Beaver at the Wonboyn caravan park and asked if there was enough water on the entrance of the lake's bar to take the Shark Cat out there. Beaver told him that there was plenty of depth. So Teddy thought that he might go out from there, as it was a bit quieter there than at the boat ramp at Eden. There were not as many gigs, and, hopefully, there would be no fisheries present.

Dean looked at his new love. She was asleep in bed, and he thought that she was perfect in every way. He hated to leave her alone, but what else could he do? She wasn't the cheapest person to keep as she was determined to send money home for her family. Dean, in a drunken state, had said that whatever she wanted to send home, she could. The first money order was for $5,000. Christ Almighty, you would reckon that they could buy the whole village for that. Still, Dean reckoned that it was still cheap being with her. He looked again at her perfect face, smiled, and thought, *What a bargain!*

Tom told his partner Sandy that a trip was on the way and there wasn't a problem. Sandy accepted that Tom would be away from time to time and that's just how it was.

Curly mentioned to his mum that he would be away for a few days, and she started to pack him some clothes in a small leather case.

Hamm Nugent, the brothel owner, was bitterly disappointed when Dean had come and taken Leckie from the front desk of the brothel. He thought that he had lost face and that would have to be sorted out. He fumed to himself and thought of ways to make Dean and Leckie pay. He didn't want money; he wanted revenge. He had to show the rest of his workforce that he was a man not to be messed with and that it wasn't a wise thing to do: to mess with him.

Piggy was still deep under cover when he met up with Louie and Gazza again. They were once again at the top pub in Pambula, and Piggy was in the chair. He was shouting and still pressing Louie for some information. Piggy was aware of the old wartime adage, 'Loose lips sink ships'. The more beer he bought these dimwits, the more likely he was to learn about Teddy and his crew.

'So when do you reckon that those boys from Melbourne will be heading this way?' Piggy asked, trying to keep his voice low-key.

Louie said, 'I spoke to Tony's mother the other day, and she said that they were going away soon, within the next couple of days. She said that Teddy had rung up and told Tony to have everything ready to go as they were going to go up the coast real soon.'

Piggy was beside himself with joy. Those bastards were coming up here and he was already here, ready to pounce and arrest the bastards. This was too good to be true. Oh, sweet Jesus, how sweet it was!

Gazza asked Piggy if he wanted to buy some hoochie coochie (marijuana) for a bit of a smoke, but Piggy explained that he had a lung condition and he wasn't allowed to smoke anything. He bought his new best friends another middy, excused himself, and headed off. He had to get to the local fisheries and get them organised. He headed off towards Eden and the fisheries office.

The young humpbacked whale was returning back to the warmer waters where he would frolic and mix with other young whales. He swam past Tasmania and headed north towards the Victorian coastline.

Gazza and Louie wondered at the generosity of the grazier from the high country, but if he wanted to buy them some middies, then why not? He seemed to be a friendly sort of bloke and obviously had plenty of money. They had taken a bit of a shine to each other.

Gazza said to Louie, 'We should get him a feed of fish next time we put in the square hooks (illegal fishing nets).'

Louie said, 'Fuck him! He's got plenty. If he wants some fish, let him buy it like everyone else has to.'

'Yeah, that's fair enough,' Gazza said.

Teddy phoned Tony and told him they were going away. He said that they would put in the Shark Cat at the Wonboyn boat ramp and that he should get going as soon as possible. Tony was well on the way within an hour. Teddy decided to pick up the three divers on the way, and soon they were all heading out of Melbourne on the freeway.

They were in a Holden Commodore station wagon that Teddy had borrowed from a mate of his who owned a car yard. They drove along and listened to the radio. Tom kept looking for the right radio station.

Dean thought to himself, *I wish he would leave the fucking radio alone.*

No one else seemed to mind.

They had visited the Billabong Roadhouse, and Teddy wondered about the girl who did the night shift.

What a life, he thought, *serving petrol and flipping burgers all night!*

He wondered if she had a past and was working in the middle of nowhere for a reason. She was quite pretty in a tired sort of way.

Tony was well ahead of them and almost up to the curves at Mt Drummer. He was two hours' drive away from where he was going to launch the Shark Cat when his phone rang. He looked at the phone and saw that it wasn't a number that he had in his phone.

He answered, 'Hullo.'

The voice on the other end said, 'Hullo, Tony, it's Louie, one of your cousins. I spoke to your mum and she said that you are heading up my way.'

A brief recollection of Louie came to Tony. He was a loser and always seemed to be in trouble.

'How are you going, mate?' Tony asked with more enthusiasm than he felt.

Louie answered, 'I'm great, really good, mate. I thought that if you were coming up here to do a bit, then maybe we could get together and have a drink and a feed.'

Tony didn't like how this conversation was going. Firstly, he didn't want anybody to know just where he was, and, secondly, he didn't want anyone to realise that they were up there, poaching. He had a bad feeling about this. Something wasn't right.

He told Louie, 'Mate, I'll give you a ring when I know what I'm doing because at the present moment, I don't know how long we will be here and when I'm heading back.'

Louie answered, 'No worries, mate, I've met a bloke who wants to buy some abalone for a mate's fiftieth birthday, and I reckon that I could put him onto you and your mob.'

Tony was liking this less and less. What was this fucking idiot doing, telling everybody about what they were up to? He would have to tell Teddy and see what he thought about it all.

Something's not right. Something smells about the whole affair, he thought.

Tony disconnected from his cousin and rang Teddy straight away. He told Teddy that his cousin had just rung and said that he knew that they were on their way up the coast and that he had a bloke who wanted to buy some abalone off them.

Teddy said to the boys, 'It looks like someone's onto us. Tony just rang and said that his cousin Louie had rung his mum and she had told him that Tony was heading up the coast. Then this Louie has met a bloke who wants to buy some abalone from us. It's a bit smelly for me. The reason that we get away with what we do is because we don't let anyone know what's going on. That way, there are no surprise parties for us.'

All the boys knew that this could mean trouble—too many people knowing what they were after. This could all end in tears.

Tony kept driving towards Wonboyn Inlet. He knew that if there was a change of plans, then Teddy would get back to him. He slowed down and did a right-hand turn into the road that led into Wonboyn. He slowly drove past the entrance to the caravan park.

There were about twenty caravans in the park. Some were permanent holiday vans, where people came down and spent their weekends and holidays. These vans were also let out to people who wanted an overnight van, and the manager did a deal with the van owners. There were some people staying there on holiday or retired from work and looking for a quiet, peaceful place to put up their feet for a couple of weeks. On the other side of the road was an 'everything that you want' sort of a store, where you could get some gas, fuel, groceries, and daily papers, and after five o'clock in the afternoon, they did a great fish and chips.

Tony drove the F100 and the Shark Cat down the hill between the caravan park and the store, past the big grey kangaroos that calmly looked up at him as they nibbled the grass. Tony parked out of the way, down at the bottom of the hill, and waited. He got out of the cabin of the truck and started to untie the straps that held down the Shark Cat.

Teddy and the boys turned right, off the Princes Highway, and drove into the Wonboyn Township. It consisted of about twenty-five houses, some permanent, and the rest were holiday cottages. They drove down the hill, past the Caravan Park, and saw that Tony had parked the F100 and Shark Cat out of the way near the boat ramp. Teddy parked the Commodore wagon in the car park, and he and the boys got out and climbed up into the boat. All their diving gear was in the boat.

Tony and Teddy spoke for a short period, and then Teddy jumped up into the boat, and Tony reversed it back into the water. Teddy lowered the two motors into the water and started them up. They were soon ticking over smoothly. Teddy reversed the boat off the trailer and accelerated away down the lake. They headed out towards the ocean.

The bar at the entrance of the lake wasn't too bad. It had waves about three feet high—no problems for the experienced operator but a bit dangerous for the weekender.

Teddy manoeuvred the Shark Cat out into the breakers and then ran at a forty-five degrees angle across the face of the waves. This resulted in a smoother crossing, and soon they were out into Disaster Bay, heading south towards the Victorian border. The sea was slightly lumpy, and Teddy knew that, as they got further south, the waves would pick up.

They motored south and soon saw the lighthouse on Gabo Island come into view. They were well into Victorian waters. Teddy knew that there would be no abalone boats from Mallacoota out working, as the waves would have been too big on the Mallacoota bar for them to get out, and anyway, the abalone divers in Mallacoota were all millionaires and didn't need to work in bad weather.

The young humpbacked whale swam slowly up the Victorian coast, following an instinctive path genetically passed onto him from his mother. He was in no hurry, and he just cruised along.

Gazza and Louie hitched their tinny onto the back of Gazza's four-wheel drive and headed off towards Wonboyn Lake. On the way, they stopped and picked up their illegal net and hid it in the tinny under the floor. It was tightly folded and didn't take up a lot of room. It was better to have it out of sight, away from prying eyes.

They drove down to the boat ramp and saw a F100 pulled up at the shop opposite the caravan park. It didn't register to Louie that it might be Tony's F100. They put their boat in and took off up the lake towards the bar.

When they got close to the entrance, Gazza said, 'The waves look a bit big.'

Louie replied, 'No worries, matey, just hang on, and I'll get us through the bastards, no sweat.'

With that, Louie gunned the thirty-horsepower outboard motor, and they shot towards the waves. They hit the first one and were catapulted up into the air; the motor revved as it came out of the water. They hit the water with a sickening thud, and the gear started moving around the floor of the boat as they hadn't tied a lot of stuff down. Both of the men in the boat were winded.

The boat moved straight into the next wave, and straight into the air again, once again knocking the wind out of both the unfortunate duo. Thud! Back into the water! Louie had a look of sheer terror on his face as they hit the third wave. Gazza grabbed the side of the boat and hung on for dear life. Crash, into the air again, and they thudded back into the water. Loose objects started to fly around the boat, and the floor started to separate and come loose.

Then they were through the rough water and into the calm of the bay.

Gazza looked at Louie and asked, 'Do you have an encore?'

Louie regained some of his composure and said, 'No, mate, that's it. End of show! How did you like it?'

Gazza looked at the mess that was in the bottom of the boat and said, 'I'll be happy if I never go through something like that again. That was a bit tough.'

Louie didn't say anything but just laughed.

He thought to himself, *It wouldn't want to be any rougher than that.*

They went to their starboard side and stopped at the point across the bay, opposite the Green Cape lighthouse, and started to prepare their illegal fishing net. They were soon running it out from the point towards the Victorian coast. They ran it out at an angle from the shore.

The net was about fifteen feet deep and had a line of lead sinkers at the bottom. The top had a line of buoys that kept the net in an upright position. It started in shallow water and ended up in deep water—an excellent trap for fish.

The two poachers had fished this area before and always had good luck; hopefully, today would be no different.

Teddy and the divers were close to the coast on the Eden side of Gabo Island. As usual, Dean and Curly worked off a T-piece, and Tom transferred their full net bags to a central position at the bottom. They never brought their abalone onto the boat on their first day. If the fisheries dropped in on them, then the boat would be empty. The divers hit the water and started to take everything that was there regardless of size. Soon Tom was running back and forth to the deposit site; the bags were starting to mount up. They all surfaced, and Teddy helped them on board. There were ten bags at the deposit site.

It was starting to get a bit late in the afternoon, so Teddy hurriedly shifted the boat to another spot not far away, after marking the position on his GPS. Dean was eager to get back into the water as he didn't like diving at dusk or in the dark. He could still remember that white pointer taking out that seal at Pedra Branca; he felt a chill run down his spine.

'Let's get going,' he suggested.

They all got back into water and started to chip off abalone again.

Gazza and Louie set their illegal net and started to head back to the Wonboyn boat ramp. The waves on the bar were a lot easier to come in on than they were to go out through. It's easier to run with the waves than go against them.

They got the tinny onto their trailer and then started back to the top pub in Pambula.

When they walked into the top pub at Pambula, they were greeted by their wealthy grazier friend and accepted a couple of middies of beer.

Piggy enquired in a friendly manner, 'What have you two been up to?'

Gazza replied, 'We have been out, setting a net. We will leave it overnight and pull it tomorrow around midday or a bit later.'

Suddenly Louie said, 'That F100 parked outside of the store at Wonboyn, I reckon that it was Tony's truck. Jesus Christ, that means that Teddy and the boys are here already and are out working while we speak.'

Piggy almost had a heart attack. He was so close and yet so far away. *What to do now?* That was the question. First, he had to get some back-up—some other fisheries officers and a boat to get out and see what was going on.

He smiled and said, 'Jesus, is that the time? I must get going. I've got to meet someone in Eden.'

With that, Piggy got into his car and headed south towards Eden.

He rang the fisheries office in Eden and told them that the bastards from Melbourne were in the area and had possibly put their Shark Cat in at Wonboyn. They must be up the coast, past the Victorian or New South Wales border. He would have to get a team together so he could surround the poachers and get them when they came in with their abalone. *Get them red-handed.*

As the sun set in the west, Teddy and the boys finished up for the day. They had got another pile of net bags deposited in a heap. All in all, they had seventeen net bags ready to be pulled to the surface and shucked out. They were happy with their day's work.

Teddy decided to go back to the anchorage at Gabo Island and spend their night, lying on the anchor. There wouldn't be any traffic there.

The young, male humpbacked whale swam past Gabo Island and started up the coast towards the warmer waters. He noticed that he was swimming in blue water, not the green waters of southern Australia. He felt the temperature rise slightly as he headed north unknowingly towards the impending doom.

Piggy was in a war meeting. The room was full of fisheries officers, all eager for the kill, and their prey was Teddy and his gang of poachers.

Piggy told the assembled masses that he was sure that they were out there poaching as he spoke. And from what he could work out, they would stay out all night, get an early start, get the abalone, unload it somewhere, and then bring the boat back to some port somewhere, empty. The question was where they would unload their illegal fish. One of the officers suggested that they should stake out the Wonboyn boat ramp, and this suggestion was eagerly accepted.

Piggy had his doubts that Teddy would unload where he had put his boat in as it was too easy to guess.

No, Piggy thought, *Teddy will unload somewhere else, but where? That is the question.*

The assembled officers tossed around a few ideas, and, as they were locals, they suggested a couple of places. There was no chance of Teddy heading south as they wouldn't be able to beach their catch anywhere, as the sea was too rough. So it had to be a port somewhere reasonably close. There was Wonboyn, possibly Bittangabee Bay, Boyd Town (across the harbour from Eden), or Eden.

They all agreed that Teddy would have to unload somewhere. But where? That was the question: where?

The young humpback didn't suspect a thing. He was swimming along—not a care in the world—and then suddenly, he swam into the illegal net set by Gazza and Louie. He immediately stopped swimming, and the net wrapped around him.

He twisted and tried to shake it off, but it clung to him. He rolled over a couple of times, and the net cruelly enveloped him. He was caught fast.

He dived down to the ocean floor, and still it clung to him.

He tried to shake it off by launching himself into the air but all to no avail. He crashed back into the water with a splash and was well and truly trapped by the fine nylon net.

He tried swimming out to sea in a desperate effort to free himself but, alas, but all to no avail. He was starting to get tired.

Teddy and the boys dropped anchor in the still waters of the Gabo Island anchorage, and Teddy got a small meal ready. The divers had bought up a few crayfish. They weren't the typical southern rock lobster but a smaller version that was plentiful on the New South Wales shoreline. They were referred to as green crays. Teddy thought that they would make a fine supper after the main meal.

The next morning at dawn, Teddy and the boys were ready to go. They had a small breakfast and got into their dry wetsuits. Teddy took them back to where they had been diving, and, once again, they were in the water and working smoothly.

Although Piggy was out of Victoria and wasn't in charge of the New South Wales fisheries officers, he still was giving all the orders. He had marshalled all the officers together and given them his instructions. He sent some off to man the boat ramps at Wonboyn, some to go and set up a road block on the Chip Mill road, and some to go to the cliff overlooking Two Fold Bay with a pair of binoculars to watch for any boats that were in the area. Some others were to check every boat that entered the wharf area at the Eden Fishermen's Wharf. Piggy wouldn't put it past Teddy to hire a game fishing boat to meet them out at sea and transfer the illegal fish from his boat onto the other boat.

He was sure that he had everything covered.

◇ ◇ ◇ ◇

Tony was himself on a stake-out. He was parked down near the Eden Fishermen's Wharf and was keeping an eye on Piggy and the team of fisheries officers. He sensed that somehow they had got wind of what Teddy and the boys were up to. He racked his brain about how they could have been found out. The only thing that he could think of was that his cousin had somehow spilt the beans. He picked up his phone and rang his cousin. Louie answered the phone on its first ring.

'Yo, Cuzz, what's happening?' Louie asked.

'Well, I'm down at the Eden Fishermen's Wharf,' said Tony, 'and all the fisheries officers are heading out in different directions. There's a fisheries officer from Victoria heading the show. He's a sparring partner of ours, and it's just too big a coincidence that he's here and Teddy and the boys are here also. There has been a leak somewhere. I want you to meet me here and have a look around. Something's not right.'

Louie said, 'Sure, Cuzz, we are on our way through to Wonboyn to pick up a net. I'll be there in twenty minutes.'

Louie hung up and said to Gazza, 'We have got to meet Tony in Eden. It will only take a minute. Then we will piss off and pick up our net and be back nice and early for a beer with our new best friend.'

Tony watched as Piggy got everything and everyone arranged. It looked as if they were getting a fisheries launch ready to take to the sea.

Louie and Gazza arrived at the Fishermen's Wharf and saw that Tony was parked away from the wharf but in a place where he could see what was going on. Louie shook hands with Tony and introduced Gazza to him. Tony could see that neither of the men were rocket scientists. Tony pointed to a group of men who were standing together, talking between themselves.

'Do you recognise anyone in that group?' Tony asked.

Gazza and Louie quickly looked at the group of men and nodded. They both recognised the fisheries officers from the NSW Fisheries.

When they looked at Piggy, they both laughed and said, 'That's the rich grazier who wants to buy some abalone off you.'

Louie said, 'When he gets away from the fisheries officers, we will introduce him to you. You might want to do some business with him. He's got plenty of money.'

Tony took a deep breath and said, 'I already know the bloke.'

Gazza and Louie looked at Tony and said, 'Do you? Do you really know him?'

Tony looked at the two idiots and said, 'For fuck sake, he is Fisheries Officer Wallace P. Trotter, commonly known as Piggy. He isn't a wealthy grazier. He's a senior officer of the fisheries and someone who has sworn to put us all in jail, if it's the last thing that he does. What have you fucking idiots told him?'

Louie and Gazza were struck speechless, and both their minds raced back to them telling stories about what they were up to.

Louie was the first to speak, 'I can't remember what I told him. I think that I told him that I saw your F100 up at the Wonboyn store.'

Tony looked at his cousin.

He slowly nodded his head and said, 'He knows that Teddy is out at sea right now, does he?'

Louie nodded without saying anything.

Tony shook his head and cursed, 'Fuck me dead, you pair of halfwits have sold us down the drain.'

Louie whimpered, 'We didn't know that he was a fisheries officer. If we had of then, we wouldn't have told him anything. He kept buying us beers, and he seemed like a good bloke.'

'You are fucking idiots,' Tony exploded. 'I wouldn't go down to Wonboyn to pull your net.'

'Why is that?' Gazza asked.

'Well, for one thing, the fisheries will be down there, just in case we pull in and unload our fish there. And if you two turn up with a boatload of fish and an illegal net, that's the end of you. Just fuck off, and let me think. I've got to tell Teddy what is coming down on him.'

The two halfwits went and sat in their four-wheel drive and waited to see what Tony was going to do.

Tony rang Teddy.

The swell was starting to pick up, and Teddy had his eyes on the weather. His phone rang, and he saw that it was Tony. He answered the phone immediately. He knew that there was a problem as Tony never rang unless there was a problem.

'Tony, what's up, mate?' Teddy asked.

Tony said, 'Huston, we a have a problem (imitating that famous phrase from the moon mission).' 'My half-witted cousin has been conned into thinking that Piggy Trotter was a wealthy grazier from the high country, and he told Louie that he wanted to buy some abalone off him to give to a friend for his birthday party. So of course Louie told him about us and how he saw your F100 out at Wonboyn when he and his mate came down to set a net out in Disaster Bay. Piggy has put two and two together and realised that we are down here working. I'm parked outside the fisheries office in Eden, and Piggy has roused the troops and is getting ready to put to sea and intercept you blokes.'

Teddy took it all in and said, 'Well, at least we know that we are sprung. We haven't got any fish on board as yet, but we have got about twenty bags at the bottom. If we grab them and head out to sea and shell them, then we should be right to come back in at night. Stay tuned, and I'll let you know what we are going to do.'

The obvious thing to do was to haul arse and get out of the place, but Teddy knew that he should be able to outsmart the fisheries. He was pre-warned and had about an hour on his side. He gave the dreaded three tugs on Tom's air hose.

When a diver gets three tugs on his air line, that means that there is danger, from what or where it doesn't matter. Tom immediately stopped chipping abalone off the rocks and headed for the surface. Teddy was beside him when he surfaced.

Teddy leant out the diver's door and said, 'The fisheries are just leaving Eden. Piggy has worked out where we are and is on his way with the cavalry.'

Tom spat out his demand valve and asked, 'What are we going to do?'

Teddy had already worked out a plan.

'We will chuck on all the fish that we have deposited at the bottom, and then we will head out to sea and shell them. Then, under the cover of darkness, we will unload at a quiet spot up the coast. Tell the others and start to bring up the abalone.'

Tom swam down and signalled to Dean and Curly that it was time to get going. He clapped his hands in a sign to them that they had to get going fast. They both responded by heading for the surface with their net bags as fast as they could.

Teddy was waiting for them, and as soon as they got on board, he got them organised. They threw off their diving weight vests and started to pull aboard the net bags as Tom brought them to the surface. Soon all the net bags from the deposit site were on board. Teddy then went back to the first deposit site from the previous day, and Tom started to bring up the net bags.

Even though there was a lot of weight, the Shark Cat got up onto the plane easily, and Teddy headed out to sea. Soon the shoreline had disappeared under the horizon, and all the boys could see were the mountains that were behind the coast. Teddy had the GPS on, and he could tell that they were invisible to the naked eye.

Teddy kept going out to sea for another half an hour. Soon even the mountains disappeared, and they were on their own in the middle of the ocean.

As soon as the boat stopped, they all got into shelling out the abalone, and, after about four hours, all the abalone were bagged up and ready to be taken ashore. As it was still light, they relaxed, and Teddy started to take the boat north at a leisurely pace.

He rang Tony and said that all was well. Tony responded by saying that Piggy and another abalone boat had left the Eden harbour about an hour before.

Piggy was in full flight. He had a boat that was under his control and had even encouraged another abalone boat owned by a New South Wales abalone diver to join the team to track down the evil poachers.

'We've got the bastards this time. They won't expect us to pull up alongside of them. And we are the last thing that they will expect to see out there,' he said.

All those aboard kept a watch out for Teddy's Shark Cat. They were out of Two Fold Bay and past Boyd Tower. There was a slight sea on, and everyone felt good. Piggy relished the wind in his face and the motion of the boat as it sped towards what was sure to be a certain victory day for him.

Teddy and the boys were cruising along, just on the plane. The weather was calm, and the sea breeze hadn't come up yet, so there was no wind chop, just a slight swell that seemed to be dropping off as they went north.

Tom was looking through the binoculars and said to Teddy, 'There's something off our port bow. Looks like a dead whale. It's floating on the surface.'

'We'll go across and have a look,' Teddy said.

The young humpbacked whale was frightened and fatigued. He had become wrapped up in fishing net and was almost completely entrapped. He was unable to move his pectoral fins. His tail was weighed down by the lead weights that were at the bottom of the net and was about fifteen feet below the surface.

He heard and felt the boat approaching but didn't care. He was entrapped in the net, and after almost a day of trying to get clear off the net, he didn't know what to do.

He couldn't comprehend the trouble that he was in and could see no way out.

Teddy brought the Shark Cat up beside the stricken whale. It was almost twice as big as the boat.

Dean commented, 'You would get a few fillets off this bastard.'

Tom agreed, 'Yep. I would hate to have to carry it home in a wheel barrow.'

They all laughed at the notion of someone wheeling a whale into a fish and chip shop and selling it as fillets.

Suddenly the whale emptied its lungs of air and took in a fresh breath. The boys were suddenly caught up in a cloud of fine spray of salty, fishy air.

Teddy said, 'Bloody hell, it's still alive, and look, it's surrounded by fishing net. The poor bugger has got itself entangled. It must have swum into someone's gear, and it can't free itself. Let's see if we can give it a hand. Shouldn't take too long.'

All the boys agreed. Teddy got the boat nearer, and Dean reached over the side, and, with a boat hook, he snagged some of the fishing net and started to pull it into the boat. They could see that the pectoral fins were held by the net tight against the whale's body. Curly reached over and, with Tom's stiletto, cut through some of the net. The razor-sharp knife went through the net like a hot knife goes through butter.

Meanwhile, Tom had stripped off down to his underwear and pulled on his long johns from his diving gear.

He said to Curly, 'Give me the knife. I'll jump in and see what I can cut away from close up.'

He put on his face mask and a snorkel and went out the diver's door. Soon he was swimming alongside the whale.

'It's a big bastard,' Dean said.

Tom started to cut away the net, and, as he did so, Dean and Curly started to pull the net into the boat and store it up the front, out of the way. If they threw the net back into the water, then it would still kill fish.

After what seemed to be a long time, the boys finally got one of the whale's pectoral fins free. The whale, sensing freedom, started to swim away, towing the boat along behind it.

Teddy warned, 'Be careful of its tail. If it gives a big whack with that, it will sink us. The whale outweighs us by thirty tonnes.'

They all suddenly became aware of just how big the whale was and how insignificant they really were.

They started to haul in the net and kept cutting it away. Tom climbed back into the boat, and they worked non-stop for half an hour. At last, the other pectoral fin was released. All the boys were sweating, cutting, and pulling. Soon the front of the cabin was full of net.

Somehow the whale sensed that the boys were helping him and didn't start to try and free himself. The boys started to clear the enormous tail. One slap from its tail and the boat would be smashed to smithereens.

After nearly an hour of hard work, the whale was free, and, as if not really believing it was free, it slowly swam away from the boy's boat. When it was about 500 meters away, it suddenly exploded into the air and breached, up and back into the water with a huge splash, sending water into the air.

All the boys gave a cheer, laughed, and slapped each other on the back. They all felt really happy for the whale and pleased with themselves. They watched the whale for the next hour, and it would have breached about thirty times as if in an expression of thanks and happiness at just being alive and free. Its massive tail slapped the water, sending spray everywhere. The boys looked at each other and felt proud with the way things had turned out.

Teddy said with a smile, 'Let's get back to business. We'll get down the coast a bit and see what's going on.'

Piggy and his band of crime fighters were well into Victorian waters when they had the sinking feeling that they weren't going to stumble across Teddy and his gang of cut-throats.

They separated and went each side of Gabo Island, just to make sure that they didn't miss anything, but, alas, no sight of anyone. The New South Wales abalone diver had started to get a bit bored with the fruitless search and was eager to get back to the pub. He called up Piggy on the radio and told him he had had enough and was heading back to Eden.

Piggy, undaunted, said to his crew, 'Well, men, we may as well have a look around as they may have hidden in close to shore somewhere and we missed them.'

The fisheries officers had also started to get a bit sick of thumping around the ocean and were willing Piggy to call off the search and get back to dry land and a warm meal.

They turned and went back. They had a look in Disaster Bay and then Bittangabee Bay, all for nothing. Then they headed home. In a last desperate move, Piggy decided to call in close to Boyd Town, but, alas, there wasn't any action there.

They motored over the Eden Fishermen's Wharf and slowly climbed up. Piggy checked with the fisheries officers but all to no avail. No one had seen anything strange, and certainly no one had seen any abalone being put ashore.

Meanwhile, Teddy was slowly making his way north, forty miles out to sea. He was working off his GPS, and when he was offshore from Eden, he phoned Tony and asked if there was any action. Tony replied that Piggy and his band of officers had returned and were licking their wounds. All the fisheries officers were still on alert, but they hadn't worked out what Teddy and the boys were up to. Teddy asked if Dave and Lee were on hand with their furniture van, and Tony said that they were in position and waiting. Teddy thought for a moment and then told Tony that they would go into the mouth of the Jiguma River across the bay from the Merimbula Ocean Wharf.

Teddy told Tony to make sure that there wasn't anyone around there and for Tony to be ready with the F100 at Jiguma River as soon as they touched shore to be ready to unload the abalone into the F100 and then drive and meet up with Dave and Lee. Teddy explained that it should only take a few minutes to do the abalone changeover. Tony was to unload into the furniture van, then go and grab the trailer, and meet them at the Eden Fishermen's Wharf.

They would load the boat onto the trailer in front of Piggy and all the other fisheries officers, just to upset them.

Tony laughed at the thought of them driving Piggy mad.

Teddy disconnected and said to the boys, 'We are going to unload at the mouth of the Jiguma River. Hopefully, we will be on our own.'

All the boys nodded, and Teddy started to go in towards the shore, which was about forty miles away.

Dave and Lee had the furniture van parked up an isolated road, up in the hills behind Pambula. They had started to unload some of the furniture, so the polystyrene-lined tea chests could be removed and filled with the bagged abalone. Tony had let them know what was going on.

Tony slowly drove down the road to the mouth of the Jiguma River. There was no one around at all. As it had started to get dark, he felt that all would go well. As he could see a break in the fence that would allow him to get right down to the beach, he drove past and waited for the call from Teddy.

All was ready.

After the sun had sunk in the west, Teddy slowly piloted the Shark Cat in towards the bay that was not only the entrance into Merimbula but also where the mouth of the Jiguma river was, on the southwest side. He could see the lights of the mainly holiday and retiree residences shining brightly above the river at Pambula Beach and thought of the people who were sitting down for their evening meals.

Teddy phoned Tony who was waiting for them to arrive. As soon as Tony heard the sound of the motors, he shone his torch out into the darkness.

Teddy said, 'I've got you, mate. We'll come in on your torch light.'

Within minutes, the boat was in shallow water. Tony grabbed the first bag and put it on his shoulder. Dean jumped out through the diver's door, and Curly loaded a bag onto his shoulder. He easily carried it the short distance to the waiting F100. It only took a few minutes for the boat to empty and for Tony to be away into the darkness.

Teddy slowly backed the boat out into the bay and slowly motored off.

They were about 100 meters off the coast and heading out to sea when, all of a sudden, there was a mighty splash and the humpbacked whale they had cut loose from the illegal net breached beside their boat.

'What the bloody hell was that?' Teddy asked.

Tom looked out to sea and said, 'I think that is our mate the whale saying thanks, and he'll see us again somewhere out in the great wide blue yonder.'

Everyone on board laughed and felt happy for the whale.

Tony headed towards the furniture van. As soon as he stopped the F100, Dave and Lee started to pack the abalone into the tea chests and put them up the front of the van.

Tony drove off to get the trailer and then headed into Eden to pick up the Shark Cat.

Dave and Lee packed back all the furniture back into the van, completely hiding the abalone from prying eyes. They headed off towards Melbourne.

Dave rang Derek, the processor, and gave him an expected time of arrival. All looked good. They should be there in about seven hours.

Dave laughed to Lee, 'It's a good thing that we don't charge the people whom you are storing all the furniture for, for mileage.'

They both laughed at the thought.

Things weren't going all that well for Piggy.

He had realised that he had missed grabbing Teddy and his crew, unless they were still out there, waiting for their chance to come in.

He hadn't seen the F100 or that wog bloke who drove it for Teddy, but he knew that he would be around somewhere. He waited for something to turn up.

Tony connected the trailer to the F100 and headed into Eden. He was aware that Piggy and his crew of fisheries officers would be on the lookout for him.

He felt a bit self-conscious when he drove down the hill at Eden and into the boat ramp car park.

Piggy's mobile phone rang. It was a fisheries officer whom Piggy had sent up the hill overlooking the ocean. He reported a craft with full lights on, heading into Two Fold Bay at a great rate of knots. He thought that it might be the boat that they were looking for.

Piggy leapt into action, ordering people here, there, and everywhere. He ran down to the wharf and looked at the distant retaining wall just as Teddy came into view.

'There the bastards are,' Piggy roared out at the top of his voice. 'Get ready.'

At the same time, Tony drove down to the boat ramp and, with the reversing lights on, backed the trailer into the water. Teddy guided the Shark Cat onto the trailer. Tony clipped the boat to the winch strap, tightened it down, then jumped back into the F100's cabin, and drove the boat up onto dry land.

Piggy and his band of officers surrounded the trailer and boat.

With credentials at arm's length, Piggy bellowed, 'We are arresting you all on suspicion of abalone poaching. Climb down and let us search your boat.'

With that, Teddy slowly climbed down and looked at Piggy. 'Good evening, Officer Trotter,' he said. 'A pleasant evening to be out and about. You're looking well.'

Tom, Dean, and Curly slowly climbed down and went and stood beside Teddy. Piggy heaved his enormous frame in through the diver's door and looked around.

'So where are the bloody abalones, you pack of bastards?'

Teddy looked at Piggy and, with a smile, said, 'Mate, we don't know what you are talking about. You always seem to be looking in my boat for abalone, and there is never any here. We are recreational divers, looking to explore the wonders of the sea and just getting away from it all.'

Piggy seized the net and held it above his head.

'What's this then?' he asked.

Teddy smiled like a parent would when they are asked a stupid question by a child. Teddy explained that it was a net that they had taken off a whale that was entrapped by it and that they had spent all day cutting it off the unfortunate creature.

Piggy was determined to have a victory, no matter how small.

'I've got you. You pack of bastards. This is an illegal fishing net, and I'm charging you with being in possession of it.'

'Not so fast, you dickhead,' Curly spoke up and said. 'I've got some photos of us cutting the net away. We didn't want to leave it out in the ocean to go on killing fish. So we dragged it aboard and are going to destroy it, so it won't be a danger to anyone.'

With that, Curly produced his mobile phone and showed the deflating Piggy the photos of Dean and Tom cutting away the net, the same net that was in the boat.

'As you can see by the date on the pictures, it's the same net,' Curly said.

Piggy looked for support from his fellow officers, and, seeing that he didn't get any, he shut up.

'Well, we will confiscate the net and destroy it ourselves,' Piggy said in a last ditch effort to save some dignity. The fellow officers helped to unload the net and took it to a place where they could burn it.

Piggy slowly walked away, shoulders sagging.

He muttered to himself, 'I'll get the bastards, if it's the last thing I do.'

Tony started up the F100, and the boys jumped in. He drove them up the hill to the town and stopped outside a motel. Dean, Tom, and Curly booked in, and Teddy went with Tony, and they drove out of town, back to Wonboyn, where the station wagon had been left.

When Tony dropped Teddy off at the car park at the Wonboyn boat ramp, he turned towards Melbourne and headed off. Teddy got into the station wagon and headed back to Eden for a meal and a good night's sleep.

When Teddy arrived back in Eden, the boys were showered and ready for a meal and a few drinks. Teddy quickly showered, and they headed off to the Eden Fishermen's Club.

Hamm Nugent, the Asian brothel owner, had asked around at the gambling club and had spoken to some of the other waitresses and found out that Leckie was living with Dean. On the pretence of getting her address so he could forward her wages to her, he learnt that she lived with Dean in the suburb of Newport in the western suburbs of Melbourne. He drove over and staked himself out within sight of Dean's small rented property.

In Eden, news of Teddy and the boys' arrival had somehow got to Muddy, the bikie tough guy. He well remembered the last time that he and his gang had run into the group of divers. Although the memories of him and his crew getting soundly flogged had dimmed, he immediately sought out his gang and announced to them that this time, it was get-even time.

Tony's phone rang, and it was his cousin Louie. He said that he wanted to catch up with Teddy and make sure that there was no bad blood between them over his and Gazza's role in alerting the fisheries about what had happened. Tony gave Louie Teddy's number and told him to give Teddy a ring and see if they could sort things out.

Louie rang Teddy just as he was getting ready to step out with the boys.

Teddy said, 'Well, we are heading over to the Fishermen's Club. You can join us there, if you like.'

Louie agreed, and he and Gazza set off. Teddy and the boys were into their second round of middies when in walked Louie and Gazza.

Louie immediately walked up and shook Teddy's hand and said, 'Mate, we are really sorry for letting the fisheries know what you were up to. It was a stupid mistake, and we just tumbled in. We both honestly thought that the bloke we were talking to was a rich grazier from the high country. Mate, we are so sorry.'

Teddy could see that the concern was genuine, so he laughed it off and said, 'Louie mate, you have to be more careful than that. It's like the old story, mate. You don't trust anyone that you haven't known for ten years.'

Louie looked at Teddy and said, 'Yeah, mate, you're right. We should have been more careful.'

'Well, no harm done,' Teddy laughed and introduced Louie and Gazza to the rest of the boys. 'Why don't you have a bite to eat with us?' he asked.

Louie and Gazza accepted the offer, and, after a few middies, they went into the dining room, and all sat down for a meal. During the meal, Gazza said that they were off to Wonboyn to pull their net that they had set a day earlier.

Tom said, 'Was it a green gill net with lead sinkers and white styrene floats?'

Gazza confirmed that it indeed was one similar to that. Tom told them that they had cut one and the same off a whale that had wrapped itself up in it earlier that day.

Gazza looked at Louie and said, 'Fuck me, that's our new net gone.'

'Gone but not forgotten,' Dean quipped.

Curly produced his phone and said, 'Take a look and see if you recognise the net.'

Both Louie and Gazza looked at the stunning photos of the boys cutting the net off the whale.

'Yep, that looks like our net,' Louie muttered.

Teddy suggested that they had saved them a trip to Wonboyn. But that didn't cheer the two illegal netters up much. Not only had they lost their net, but they had also lost whatever fish were caught in it which would have brought them in money. They just shook their heads.

Dean said, 'I might wander over the road to the top pub for a drink.'

He knew that the temptation of the poker machines there would be too great for him to stay and not have a bet. They all agreed, and Gazza and Louie decided to go over with them and have a couple of more before they headed off. They all walked across the road and into the bar. They were confronted by a Maori bartender. He was built like a brick shithouse.

'Good evening, mate,' Teddy said with a smile.

The Maori smiled back and said, 'How are you, fallas. Do you need a middy?'

'Yes, mate,' Teddy replied, 'give us six of the best.'

'No worries,' the barman replied and started to fill them.

The boys all started to drink. Gazza and Louie were happy to be seen in the company of real hard doers. They felt that their credibility would go up, being seen in the company of these blokes. Another round was soon bought and consumed.

Louie said, 'We've got to drive, so we had better take it easy.'

Dean said, 'One more won't make any difference.'

Everyone nodded.

Hamm Nugent watched as Leckie walked the short distance to her local shopping centre, a small group of shops that included a fish and chip shop and a small IGA grocery self-serve store and bottle shop. He wondered what he should do next. Now that he knew where she lived, he felt that he should do something. 'But what?' he asked himself.

Muddy watched the group of men drinking in the pub. He knew Louie and Gazza and wasn't too worried about them, and he had seen Teddy and his gang in action and was sure that they could be sorted out.

Muddy didn't drink in the top pub as he wasn't a fan of Maoris. They weren't that easy to intimidate, and Muddy liked to stand over weak people. He had a plan, and that was to just storm in and belt the shit out of those smartarses and get away before the coppers arrived.

Go in, bash the shitheads, and go away. That is the plan— that easy.

A couple of Muddy's group remembered the belting that they had received the last time that they had tangled with these supposed poachers, and they weren't all that happy about another encounter. But Muddy had recruited four more bikers, and they looked as tough as they sounded. That built their confidence up a bit. There were ten of them and only six of the divers, not bad odds.

The front door of the pub burst open, and Muddy and his gang of desperadoes swaggered in. They had blood in their eyes and were looking for trouble. Their courage was strengthened by taking swigs of Black Jack bourbon.

When they all got in and confronted Teddy and the boys, Muddy asked in a menacing voice, 'Remember us you, arseholes?'

Teddy looked up and smiled and said, 'No, should we?'

Muddy was a bit taken aback but pushed on and said, 'We ran into you a few months ago.'

Teddy smiled and said, 'Now I remember. We gave you a real whipping and even sent you to hospital. I hope that you have got private health cover.'

'That was a sucker punch. I didn't see it coming,' Muddy insisted.

Teddy smiled and said, 'I bet that happens to you a lot, you fucking idiot.'

Dean said to the huge Maori bartender, 'Lock the door.'

Suddenly it was on. Teddy headed straight towards Muddy. Muddy saw him approaching and walked towards him. Dean whacked the closest biker, and he went down. Curly picked up a pool cue and broke it over another biker's head with a splintering sound; down he went. Tom hit a fat old biker in the guts, and he started to gasp for air. The fight was out of him for the night. Teddy strode up to Muddy, and Muddy shaped up.

Teddy said, 'This isn't Queensbury Rules,' and kicked Muddy in the balls.

Muddy hit the deck a little paler and started to groan.

Teddy gave the next biker an elbow to the throat, and it was all over for him. The monster barman from New Zealand had locked the front door and attacked the bikers from behind. His huge fist landed in the back of a biker's head, and he went forward into the back of another biker. He turned around just in time to see the Maori barman unload a savage roundhouse swing that probably would have killed him, only it didn't hit the spot; it only knocked him unconscious.

Teddy saw the Maori was on their side and thought, *That's evened things up a bit.*

The Maori, who was beginning to enjoy himself, looked around for another victim.

Gazza and Louie were on the side of the gods, for once. They belted a biker who wasn't all that interested in fighting anyway and moved on to another one. He was soon dispatched to the sickbay.

All of a sudden, it was over. As quick as it had started, it stopped. There were groaning and bleeding bikers all over the floor. The Maori barman gave one unfortunate biker a kick up the arse, walked across to the front door, unlocked it, and opened it to the night air.

He walked back behind the bar and said in a casual voice, 'Drinks anyone?'

Teddy said, 'Yes, thanks, mate. We'll have a round, please.'

The barman started to pour their beers.

Muddy staggered to his feet and walked gingerly towards the front door.

The barman said, 'You owe the pub 500 dollars for damages. Until you pay, you and your mob are barred.'

Slowly the rest of the group got to their feet and wandered off into the night.

'Jesus, all that happened fast,' Gazza said.

Teddy looked at him and Louie and said, 'Yes, lads, it was a bit quick. Thanks for the assistance.'

'No worries,' Louie said. 'I don't really think that you blokes needed any help, especially when the barman from hell jumped in to assist you.'

Teddy laughed and said, 'All help is gratefully accepted.'

The boys said goodnight to the barman and to Louie and Gazza and walked up the road to their motel for a good night's sleep.

Piggy was driving himself back towards Bairnsdale when he came up behind Tony driving the F100 and pulling the Shark Cat. Piggy overtook him. Tony didn't recognise the car as it sped past him.

Dave and Lee laboured up a hill. Lee saw the car approach him and didn't worry as at the speed that they travelled, almost everyone passed them. The car was trapped for a while but got an opportunity to pass and did.

Piggy was eager to get home and put his feet up and have a decent meal. He got stuck behind the slowly moving furniture van and thought, *Loser, imagine carting furniture around for a living. Well, I suppose that it's better than being on the dole.*

Hamm Nugent looked at the beautiful girl walking along the footpath. He thought about just driving up beside her and grabbing her off the street, but Leckie stopped and talked to an old man who was watering his garden. Leckie laughed at whatever the old fart was saying, and he seemed happy to see her. He had probably been waiting for an opportunity to speak with her. That made Hamm think that he would have to be careful with whatever he decided to do.

Dave rang Derek, the processor, again and let him know that they were just about at Bairnsdale, so they were about four hours away from Melbourne.

Into the night they travelled.

Teddy and the boys had a restful night and awoke bright-eyed and bushy-tailed. They had a cup of coffee and headed off towards Melbourne. A couple of hours later, they pulled into the Billabong Road House, filled up with fuel, and decided to have a steak and eggs for breakfast.

Teddy walked in and said to the bloke behind the counter, 'Gidday, mate, can you knock us up a feed? We haven't had brekkie yet.'

The bloke behind the counter said, 'No worries, I'll knock you boys up a steak, eggs, sausages, tomatoes, and toast.'

'That sounds good to me,' Teddy replied, and the bloke got about, making up their breakfasts.

Teddy asked, 'Hilda, your wife, isn't about. Has she knocked off for the day?'

The bloke behind the counter said, 'She's not my wife. She just works for me on the night shift.'

Teddy said, 'Sorry, mate, I must have misheard what she said.'

'No,' the bloke said. 'She just turned up here one day and asked if we needed a short-order cook. It's hard to get people to work here in the middle of nowhere.'

Teddy smiled and said, 'You're lucky, she's a great asset.'

All the boys sat down and started to eat their meals. They didn't say much and just concentrated on eating.

✧ ✧ ✧ ✧

Hilda was out the back of the roadhouse, getting some rest. She lived in a small unit that was reserved for the night short-order cook. It was comfortable enough, and it had everything that she needed. She ate in the roadhouse, so all she really needed was an electric jug, a fridge, a shower, a toilet, and a bed. All were provided and included in the wage package that she had worked out with Dan, the proprietor.

She had told Teddy and the rest of the blokes who asked her about her marriage situation that she was married to Dan, and that kept the flirting down to a minimum. She wasn't looking for a man.

Rather she was running away from a brute of a man—the man whom she was married to for what seemed an eternity. She didn't miss the black eyes and the bruising. In fact, she was happy for the first time in her life. There was just her to look after, no one else. All she had to do was look after the roadhouse in the evening, and that was all there was to it. She got on well with Dan.

He had lost his wife to cancer about a year before and was happy with the way things were going. Dan was fond of a young girl who lived on a farm about five miles away from the roadhouse, and he spent a fair bit of time at the girl's home.

Hilda was happy. She was thirty-five years old and had some money, not a lot, but some money of her own, for the first time in years.

The boys finished their meals, got into the borrowed car, and drove towards the city. They had about four hours to go. Tom drove, and Teddy got onto the phone and rang Derek, the processor. Derek was happy with the load and said that there was 1,400 kilos. He asked Teddy if he wanted some for the Vietnamese restaurant that Teddy dealt with. Teddy confirmed that he did want 100 kilos kept aside. Derek was happy with the result.

Teddy then rang Hung Lee (Henry) at his Vietnamese restaurant and let him know that he would bring around 100 kilos the next day. Henry got straight to work on the phone and sold off whatever he didn't need at a profit. He felt happy with the way things were working out. He wished that Teddy would go out and get some more green lip abalone as they were a lot easier to sell. But beggars can't be choosers.

Hamm Nugent started to make a plan. He would go around to Dean's house and talk to Leckie face-to-face. It was always better face-to-face as he had a way with words; that is sometimes lost when you are not looking straight into someone's eyes. Hamm was confident that he would be able to coax Leckie back into working with him.

Teddy dropped the boys off at their homes and drove over to Derek's processing plant. All the abalone were graded and boxed up and in the blast freezer. Derek was happy with the way things had worked out and told Teddy that if he wanted to wait, then he would get the money straight away. Teddy agreed, and they both headed off to the bank to pick up the cash.

Dean walked in and gave Leckie a big hug. He marvelled at how beautiful she was. He said that he would grab a shower and get into some clean clothes. He suggested that they might go out and have a meal at one of the better Chinese restaurants that evening after they had been over to Curly's place for the whack-up of the money.

Hamm decided to go over and have a chat with Leckie as he was sure that Dean was away. He got hold of Tiny, the Samoan security guard, and they set off. Hamm was confident that Leckie would be home on her own and if he needed back-up, then he had Tiny with him. Tiny was more than happy to get to see Leckie again as he missed her greatly.

Hamm said, 'Make sure that we have the opportunity to speak with her. We may have to point out to her that she could be here illegally and one call to the authorities would have her deported back to China. That's our ace up our sleeve.'

Tiny nodded and thought, *I know exactly how she feels.*

They pulled up outside Dean's place, and both walked into the front yard. Hamm knocked on the front door, and soon Leckie opened it. Dismay showed on her face as she recognised the two men standing there.

'Hello, Leckie,' Hamm said. 'We are here to talk about the short time that you worked for me.'

Leckie asked, 'What is it that you want with me?'

Hamm smiled an oily smile and said, 'I want you to come back and work for me.'

Leckie shook her head and said, 'My circumstances have changed. I no longer need to work for you. I am happy here with Dean, and I look after him and attend university to finish my classes.'

'What would happen if I was to ring the authorities and tell them that you are here illegally?' Hamm asked.

Suddenly Dean was at the door.

He gently moved Leckie aside and said to Hamm, 'Fuck off you dog, and take that coconut head with you. If I see either of you hanging around here, I'll bust your fucking heads open. Now fuck off and don't come back.'

The two men were a bit taken aback by Dean's appearance and aggression. He was clearly agitated, and they both felt fear slither up their spines.

Dean's hand came into view, and he had a baseball bat in it. As far as the two men were concerned, this was a game changer. They both turned on their heels and walked back to the car.

Hamm said to Tiny, 'I didn't realise that Dean was home. This is very bad. We are in a bad situation, and Dean will think that we are weak by walking away.'

Tiny wasn't too worried as he knew that Dean would have belted him first as he was the biggest main concern.

'Don't worry, we will catch up with him sooner or later,' he said. 'It's best not to cause a concern at the present time.'

They drove off.

With the money in a Target shopping bag, Teddy went over to Curly's house and went around the back into Curly's shed. Everyone was waiting there for him, and Curly handed Teddy a beer.

'How did it go?' Dean asked.

Teddy smiled and said, 'Like clockwork, smooth as silk.'

Teddy tipped out the money onto the pool table and started to pile the notes into four piles.

'There was $52,000, so that works out to $13,000 each, not a bad little earn.'

All the team knew that there was another 100 kilos to be delivered to Henry's restaurant and that $4,000 would go towards Tony's cut and Dave and Lee's slice.

Everyone was well pleased with the result.

Dean mentioned to the rest of the group about the run-in with Hamm Nugent, the brothel owner, and the coconut head. All the boys took in the information and waited to see what Dean was going to do about it.

Teddy said, 'Mate, we will have to be on the alert. If he wants to make trouble, then we'll give him all the trouble that he can handle.'

All the boys agreed.

The young humpbacked whale swam past the world-famous Bondi Beach.

As he moved closer to the warmer waters and to meeting up with the other whales, he was happy and relaxed.

Nature being what it was, he would make this trip many more times in his life.

Teddy and the Japanese Mini Submarine

Some twenty years after the Second World War, there was mention of a Japanese mini submarine, or the wreckage of one, being found by abalone divers off the southern coast of New South Wales close to the Victorian border.

It was mentioned in the local press that an abalone diver had swum over some wreckage and by chance had realised that it was a mini submarine.

The Australian Navy investigated. They engaged the abalone diver, who had discovered the wreckage, but after days of looking for a needle in a haystack, they gave up, and it was forgotten.

Akinobu Okumura looked up from the accounts which he was working on when his foreman came into his small office at the Tokyo Metropolitan Central Wholesale Market, commonly known as the Tsukiji Market.

'Yes?' he asked in an abrupt manner.

The foreman bowed slightly and said, 'I have inspected the abalone from Australia, and the whole shipment is correct in weight, and of the boxes I have opened, the quality is excellent.'

Akinobu nodded to his long-term employee and simply said, 'Thank you.'

The foreman bowed his head and left the office.

The Tsukiji market is the biggest fish and seafood market in the world and is also one of the biggest wholesale markets in the world. It is situated in central Tokyo. There are two distinct sections to the market as a whole. The inner market is the licensed wholesale market, where the auctions and most of the processing take place. There licensed wholesale dealers, about nine hundred of them, operate small stalls. The outer market is a mixture of wholesale and retail shops that sell Japanese kitchen tools and the like to restaurants and suppliers. Most of the shops in the outer market close in the early afternoon, and the shops in the inner market close even earlier.

Akinobu Okumura was a solidly set man in his early seventies. He had built, from the ground up, his successful seafood business. The last few years he had become more successful by taking a chance with a processing company in Melbourne, Australia, called Wild Ossie Abalone Company. He had become quite good friends with the owner Derek, a laid-back Aussie who always called him mate.

It was very hard to understand the Australian attitude, and it was definitely different from the formal way the Japanese did their business. Recently he had been getting more and more abalone from Derek and at a very reasonable price. Yes, things were looking up.

Akinobu was a few minutes older than Baku, his twin brother, and there was a great deal of amusement between the pair whenever they got together and drank sake, the fiery Japanese liquor distilled from rice. They were both married and had families.

Baku dealt in the shadowy world of the Japanese mafia known as the Yakuza. He was well up in the organisation and had full-body tattoos.

Baku believed that the Yakuza descended from honourable Robin Hood-like characters that defended their villages from roaming bandits and that they might even have descended from the Ronin samurai warriors who found themselves without a master in a time of political unrest. Others claimed that the Yakuza descended from the Kabukimono, the crazy ones, who were wildly dressed hoodlums who carried long swords, intimidated whole villages, and sometimes executed high-up village elders.

The truth is probably somewhere in the middle.

Akinobu was to meet his brother for dinner at a restaurant that, by chance, Akinobu supplied with seafood. When he arrived, he saw that his brother was already seated at a table and was being attended to by a beautiful young waitress. Baku was, as usual, dressed in a pinstripe suit that fitted him snugly. He was a bit thinner than Akinobu. He had a brightly coloured shirt on that screamed Yakuza and his handmade leather shoes were of the pointy-toed variety. The waitress immediately assumed that Baku was in the business (Yakuza).

Akinobu took a seat pad across from his brother and smiled at his twin.

'Well, little brother, what is it that you want to talk to me about?'

Baku smiled and said, 'Older and wiser brother, I feel the time is right to have the question that has been on both our minds for all our lives answered. Did our father die an honourable and brave death, or was he a coward and died the death of a weak dog?'

Akinobu looked at his younger brother and nodded slowly in agreement. 'I believe that the time is right, and as we are both wealthy men, we will try to discover what happened to our father, whom we never met.'

Both brothers knew that their father was a mini submarine commander and that he put to sea off the Australian coast. Some of his team-mates went into Sydney Harbour and were sunk. It was believed that the twins' father made his way down the coast and was sighted near Green Cape Lighthouse in southern New South Wales. They were bombed, and no sighting of them was ever recorded again.

The two brothers drank their sake and ate well. It was the only time that they could both relax, as you only can with close family, and they formed a plan. They worked out that Derek's run of luck and cheap abalone could only mean one thing: he was buying a lot of abalone from poachers. He must have a team of men who knew what they were doing and were avoiding the law.

Akinobu agreed to speak to Derek, and see what he could do for them, in the way of getting a team of divers to look for the sub and examine it closely.

The brothers parted and went their own ways. Akinobu went home to his wife, and Baku had business to attend to. His business started when it was dark and all honest men headed home.

Derek had got confirmation that the last load of abalone he had sent to his mate Akinobu had arrived and had passed its inspection by the importer. All he had to do now was quietly work away with his legal divers and wait until Teddy gave him the nod that he was going away again. He was a happy man.

A couple of days later, his phone rang, and it was his mate Akinobu, calling from his office in Japan. Akinobu, after a short discussion about how his business was going and asking Derek about how he was going, got down to business.

'Derek,' he said, 'I have a question to ask you, and if you refuse, then it will have no bearing on our business relationship or our friendship.'

Derek was all ears.

'My brother and I never met our father,' Akinobu continued. 'He died in the Second World War. He was a mini submarine operator, and, to the best of our knowledge, he was killed off the south coast of New South Wales in Australia. We are willing to pay for a team of divers to look for the wreck, and, if they find it, then they will photograph it and send us the photographs. We would then bring a priest to the site and bless our father's grave. We would then contact the official department that governs the area and have it claimed as a war grave in honour of our father and the men who served with him.'

Derek nodded to himself and answered, 'Akinobu mate, I'm sorry to hear that your father died in the war. I had a few family members who also didn't come back. It's very sad, very sad,' Derek said solemnly. 'Thank goodness that we have been relatively war-free for most of my life.'

'Yes, we are very fortunate,' Akinobu answered.

'Mate, I've got just the blokes you need to get this show on the road,' Derek said after a bit of quick thinking.

Akinobu translated what Derek had said and answered, 'Am I to understand that you will be able to do this for me and my brother?'

Derek replied, 'Yes, mate, no wukkers, leave it to me. What about these blokes getting paid? I will not accept a dollar myself, as this is the sort of things that friends organise for each other, just because we are mates.'

Akinobu thought that there was a possibility that he was the only person in Japan who could work out what Derek was saying and in a strange way felt a depth of pride and friendship that he could work it out.

Akinobu said, 'Derek, could you give me some idea about how much it will cost my brother and me?'

Derek was beside himself with joy; if he could get Teddy and the boys to do this, then Akinobu would be in his debt forever. This would really cement their business relationship.

Derek rang Teddy and said, 'Mate, a chance to earn an honest dollar.'

Teddy replied, 'Fuck that. That means that the taxman will be after us.'

'No, mate, this will be under the counter, no worries,' Derek said and went on to tell Teddy about the phone call he had just received.

Teddy was enthusiastic about the whole plan. He said to Derek, 'Mate, when I was a young diver, sometime in the early sixties, I worked out of Eden in NSW, and we all heard about the bloke who actually stumbled across a sub. He was a bit of an outsider and kept himself to himself. But the story goes that he went back and blew it to bits and sold it as scrap metal. I don't know if that's the truth or not, but I reckon that it's worth a try. I'll drive up there and have a talk to him. If I remember, he was a good sort of a bloke. How much do you reckon we can get out of it?'

Derek smiled and said, 'The bloke whom I sell all my abalone to is a pretty rich dude. He just pulls out however much I want. There's never been a problem, and he trusts me. That's always a good thing.'

Derek rang Akinobu and said, 'Mate, I've spoken to the divers whom I'm involved with, and they are eager to be of whatever assistance they can be to you and your brother. If they can't find the submarine, then nobody can. But they will need some money, some operating funds.'

Akinobu replied, 'I shall send you over some money, and they can begin the job of searching for our father's grave. I will send over $10,000 to begin with, and when you want more, then we will discuss it further with you.'

Derek agreed and hung up. He phoned Teddy.

Teddy replied, 'At the present time, we aren't doing anything. I'll jump into a car, drive up to Eden, and see if I can locate the good old boy whom I haven't seen for thirty years. I've seen his photo in the Australasian Hotel in Eden. It looked like him, like I say I haven't seen him in years.'

Teddy told the boys to meet him at Curly's shed in the next couple of hours, and they all agreed.

When Teddy got to the shed, all the boys were there, watching the 'Rolling Stones' on Sky pay TV. Mick Jagger was singing, 'Angie, I still love you, baby, and I guess I always will.'

'I love that song,' Teddy said; all the boys agreed.

Tom asked, 'What's the plan?'

Teddy said, 'An honest day's work for an honest day's pay.'

Dean said, 'Fuck that, if I wanted a job, I would go back to do what I was trained for.'

Curly laughed and said, 'We've been away from the tools for so long that we all would need retraining.'

Teddy went on to say, 'A couple of rich Japanese businessmen want us to find out where their dear departed daddy was killed. The only problem is that it was in a Japanese mini submarine and no one has a clue exactly where it sank or when. They only know that it was in the Second World War.'

All the boys showed a bit of interest.

Teddy, ignoring the good-natured banter, went on to say that when he was a young diver working out of Eden, he had heard about a diver who had found it. Teddy had never seen it and had only heard about it, and so he was going to travel up to Eden and try and find this old abalone diver and ask his help.

'That sounds like a plan,' Dean said.

All the boys agreed.

Teddy said, 'If I leave early, then it should only take me a day to go up and have a quick word, and I'll be back in time for tea.'

Dean said, 'If you are only going for the day, I might come with you and give you a bit of company as Leckie spends all day at university.'

'That sounds good to me,' Teddy said.

Bright and early the next morning, Teddy pulled up in front of Dean's house in Newport, a suburb close to where he lived, and Dean walked out and got into the car.

'Top of the morning to you,' Dean laughed.

'Yes, mate, it looks like the perfect day, a great day for a drive up the coast,' Teddy replied.

With that, they drove off and travelled over the West Gate Bridge. Soon they were in the traffic flow, and as it was early, there wasn't the normal amount of traffic, so they breezed along and were soon into the countryside.

Dean asked Teddy, 'How are you going to find this old abalone diver whom you haven't seen for thirty or forty years?'

'That should be easy,' Teddy said. 'We'll call into the Australasia Hotel in Eden, and I'll have another look at the photos on the wall. When I spot the bloke, I'll ask someone in the pub where he lives, and we will go on from there.'

Dean agreed that it was a good plan. Dean found another radio station as the city stations were getting out of range.

The old abalone diver whom Teddy and Dean were looking for was still asleep in his cabin, deep in the bush. When he woke up, he slowly got out of bed and stoked up his pot-bellied cooker-heater. The chill had been taken out of the air as the pot belly burnt all night. He walked outside and had a piss.

'There's nothing better than being able to take a piss in the open where no one can see you,' he said to himself.

He walked inside and thought about breakfast.

'Bacon and eggs for one,' he said out loud.

The dogs started to stir and bark a bit; it was normal. They wanted to be let off their chains. He would do that after he had breakfast.

Teddy and Dean drove past the Billabong Roadhouse, and Teddy wondered if Hilda was still working.

'We might call in on our way back,' Teddy suggested.

Dean agreed with a grunt; he was half-asleep.

The pair drove into Bairnsdale, pulled up at a service station, and filled up.

Dean said, 'Do you want me to take over the driving?'

Teddy agreed, and Dean got behind the wheel and drove off towards Eden.

About three hours later, they pulled into Eden, and Teddy and Dean walked into the Australasia Hotel. The barmaid, who had offered them advice to get going when they had had their dust up with the bikies, was on duty, and she recognised Teddy and Dean.

'Hullo, boys, do you want a couple of beers?' she said.

Teddy smiled and said, 'No, thanks, love, it's a bit early for us young fellas.'

She laughed and said, 'Well, what do you want? We don't do haircuts.'

Teddy laughed and said, 'We have come for a bit of information about one of your clients.'

The barmaid asked, 'Which one? There are a few of them.'

Teddy went to the wall, which had about 100 photos on it, and selected one. He showed it to the barmaid.

'It looks like an old mate of mine, but I can't remember his name,' Teddy said.

'Oh, that's Bill. Everyone calls him Billy Boy,' the barmaid replied.

Teddy studied the photo and said, 'Yes, that's it Billy Boy. Christ, he must be an age by now. He was an old fart when I was a kid.'

The barmaid smiled and said, 'He doesn't come in much. He keeps to himself.'

'Where does he live? Is he far away? We are passing through, and I would love to catch up with him.'

The barmaid smiled and said, 'That's nice. He will get a surprise. He lives out of town on the first road to your left when you reach the top of the hill heading towards Pambula.'

Teddy thanked her, and they got into the car and drove out of Eden. At the top of the hill, they turned and drove down a gravel road. They went for a couple of kilometres and came to a gate. The words 'No Entry' and 'Private Property' were roughly painted on a piece of corrugated iron that was wired onto the gate.

'He doesn't seem too friendly,' Dean commented as he got out of the car and opened the gate.

Teddy drove through and waited for Dean to get in after he shut the gate. They drove another couple of kilometres, and a small cottage came into view. There were dogs running and barking everywhere. They circled the car, barking furiously.

Suddenly a voice yelled out, 'Shut up, you bastards.'

Teddy and Dean looked to see where the voice came from, and they saw an old man standing on the veranda. He was very skinny and had the haunted look of a cancer victim. He had been sitting in the shade and was hard to see. The dogs stopped barking as one and stood looking at the car.

'What do you want?' Billy Boy asked.

Teddy got out of the car and said, 'Bill, long time no see, mate. Do you remember me?'

Bill looked at Teddy and said, 'No, can't say I do.'

Teddy laughed and said, 'Mate, I haven't seen you in thirty or forty years. Me and my mate Dean were in the top pub, and I recognised you in a photograph on the wall. I asked the barmaid, and she gave us your address.'

Bill looked at the big bloke with the gold chain and said, 'What's your name?'

'Mate, its Teddy. Don't you remember me?'

Recognition slowly came to Bill.

'Yes, I'm starting to remember. You dived out of a tinny, and you weren't too bad at the caper. What are you up to now?'

Teddy laughed out loud. 'Same old, same old.'

Bill summed up the situation and said, 'I bet you are poaching.'

Teddy laughed and said, 'I refuse to make a statement on the grounds that it might be used in evidence against me.'

Bill laughed and said, 'Now I fucking well remember. You always were a smooth-talking son of a bitch. Come up and have a coffee.'

Teddy and Dean walked up the three steps and sat in the shade on Bill's veranda. Bill brought out an old-fashioned coffee percolator that was steaming hot and placed it on a coffee table on the veranda. He poured out three cups of black coffee. Bill didn't offer any sugar or milk as he only drank his coffee strong and black and expected everyone else to do the same.

Dean took a sip, and it nearly blew his head off.

Bill got directly to the point, 'What are you after, Teddy?'

Teddy smiled and said, 'Mate, it's about that Japanese submarine that you found. A couple of gentlemen in Japan have contacted me through an associate. They want to see if someone can have a dive on it, as they think that their father may have been on it when it was sunk.'

Bill looked at his old mate and said, 'That fucking submarine has haunted me forever. I've had nightmares about it. I reckoned that when I found it, I would blow the fucking thing up and sell the scrap metal, but I couldn't do it. I knew that it was a war grave, and somehow that got to me. I decided that I wouldn't let anyone know where it was and that the poor souls could rest in peace for eternity.'

Teddy could see that Bill was getting upset at the mention of the submarine.

'Mate, you have got my word that if you tell us where it is, we will not disturb it for anything. The two blokes in Japan want to bring some sort of priest over and have the site blessed. All they want to do is to find the sub and have it blessed so that their father's soul can rest in peace.'

Bill looked at Teddy and said, 'It would be a great load off my mind. Let me get a map, and I'll show you where it lies.'

He returned with an old, tattered map, placed it on the table, and spread it out. He pointed to a section of coastline and said, 'There is an offshore reef that not many people know of. Do you remember how we used to find reefs in the old days?'

'Fuck me, I sure do,' Teddy replied.

He looked at Dean and said, 'In the old days, you would get a four-pronged grappling anchor and motor along in your tinny dragging it behind you at a speed that would allow the anchor to drag along the bottom. You could feel the anchor running over the sand, and when it hit rocks or a reef, you would be able to feel it jumping around. You would then swim down the anchor rope and see what was down there—that easy!'

Dean shook his head and had another sip of coffee.

Bill said, 'See the cliffs along there? Well, there's a reef just off that point there. It's about 400 or 500 yards straight off that point.'

Teddy looked at the map and nodded. 'I know that coastline like the back of my hand, but I didn't realise that there was a reef out there.'

'Yeah, no bastard did. I was the one that found it, and I never let on about it to anyone,' Bill replied.

Teddy said, 'Mate, I really appreciate your help. If there's anything in it, I'll make sure that you get a slice of the action.'

Looking at Teddy, Bill said, 'Mate, I reckon that there's a fucking curse on it. Ever since I found the fucking thing, I've had bad luck. I can't keep a woman, I can't even crack a fat any more, and now I've got the death sentence, fucking cancer. The only way I can ease the pain is through smoking about thirty cones a day. That's the only way I can get any peace.'

Teddy looked at his old mate and felt saddened. He remembered the fit and happy Bill drinking and laughing in the top pub more than forty years before.

'Is there anything that I can do for you, mate?' Teddy asked.

Bill shook his skeletal head and said, 'No, mate, my race is nearly run. I've got a daughter, but I've lost contact with her. I would like to see her before I die. She can have my property when I'm gone.'

Teddy tore the corner off the map, wrote his telephone number on it, and gave it to Bill.

'Mate, if there's anything that I can do for you, don't hesitate to give me a ring.'

Billy gave the map to Teddy and sat back. He was exhausted from the effort. He nodded and didn't say anything.

Dean and Teddy walked to the car and drove out. The dogs went into meltdown and ran around the car, barking. They drove to the gate in silence. Dean opened the gate, and Teddy drove through it. Dean closed the gate, and they drove towards Eden.

Teddy rang Derek, the processor, and told him that he had in his possession a map of where the submarine was. Derek was over the moon, and he rang through to Akinobu and told him the good news.

Akinobu was pleased with the results. He said to Derek, 'I am well pleased with the progress that you and your friends have made. I will alert my brother and tell him that you are making excellent progress. When can we expect to be able to come over and see the site for ourselves?'

Derek couldn't tell him exactly what time frame. He would have to discuss it all with Teddy and the boys. He told Akinobu that he would have to get all the people together and they would sit down and a talk.

Dean and Teddy had a bit of a look around Eden and started back towards Melbourne. When they got to Bairnsdale, he rang ahead to the Billabong Roadhouse and spoke to Hilda.

'We are at Bairnsdale and want you to put on a couple of steaks with all the trimmings as Dean and I will be there in about half an hour.'

Hilda agreed and smiled to herself. She thought that they were nice blokes.

Detective Jack Andrews was deep in thought or as deep in thought as he could get. He had his wife Hilda on his mind. They had been married for about six years, and just when he thought that he had the bitch under control, she pissed off and left him. Like his father had always told him, 'Women are like dogs. You have to show them who the boss is. A good smack around the ears on the odd occasion will keep them in line.'

Jack felt it sort of helped with the sex. There was nothing better than climbing on board when she was crying, snivelling, and shaking.

He laughed out loud. His old man was a country cop and knew all the lurks and perks. The butcher ran a book on the races, and so his old man never paid for meat. The pub also ran a book, so he always got a dozen bottles of beer and 100 dollars of a Friday night. That was a lot of money back in the old days. Yes, Jack was a carbon copy of his dear old dad.

Things had changed now. Jack was in Melbourne and was on vice. That had its perks.

When he and his partner spotted a new whore on the streets, they would grab her in an unmarked police car and take her somewhere nice and quiet and gang-bang her, sometimes two at once. The girls were usually young and needed the money for drugs. Yep, that was the way to start your shift off.

Half the brothels were giving them a sling just to make things run smoothly.

That slope head Hamm Nugent was getting bigger and bigger. He was starting to become a major brothel operator in town. Jack thought that he might get a bigger whack from the operation.

His mobile rang, and he answered, 'Detective Jack Andrews, how can I help you?'

The voice on the other end said, 'It's what I can do for you.'

Jack didn't know the voice, so he asked, 'What do you mean?'

'Mate, its Senior Constable Jim McDonald from Bairnsdale police station.'

'Gidday, Jimbo, what's the latest mate?' Jack asked.

'Well,' Jim replied, 'you know you said that you were on the lookout for a certain lady. Well, I've stumbled across her. The photo you showed us looks just like her. She's working at a roadhouse just out of Bairnsdale. I've seen her with my own eyes.'

Jack was instantly wide awake, and he sat upright in his chair.

'Where is the fucking bitch?' he asked.

'She is working at the Billabong Roadhouse about half an hour towards Melbourne from Bairnsdale,' Jim replied.

'Jimbo, you're a fucking genius, I might wander down there and have a little chat with her.'

Jim laughed and said, 'Mate, she might need a bit of smartening up. I'm sure she will be surprised to see you. I know her boss a bit, and we were talking. He told me that he had a new short-order cook. After a few beers, he let slip about her. So I took a drive out there and got some petrol and a Mars bar, and sure enough, it was her. She only works the night shift, and it's pretty quiet of a night. She is normally on her own.'

Jack thanked Jim and disconnected. He thought that he might need someone with him, and he started to think of a suitable punishment for the bitch. Yes, he would get a driver, and when he picked the bitch up, he would give her a four-hour thrashing on the way back. That should soften her up a bit. Then he would really give it to her when he got her home. He smiled and thought, *I'll never let the bitch out of my sight again.*

The sun was long gone when Teddy and Dean pulled into the Billabong Roadhouse. They were tired and needed a feed and a drink of coffee, although they were still strung out from the coffee that they had drunk at Billy's place. They walked into the restaurant and smiled at Hilda.

'How are you, luv?' Teddy asked.

Hilda smiled and said, 'I'm fine. Thanks. Your meals are almost ready. Can I get you a coffee?'

Both the boys agreed that a cup of coffee would be fine.

Hilda got to work and got the coffees ready.

✧ ✧ ✧ ✧

Detective Jack Andrews and his fellow detective friend Karl had parked their car away from the roadhouse and were watching it from the darkness. They saw Hilda doing a bit of cleaning up, and they saw Teddy and Dean get out of their car and go inside.

Karl said to Jack, 'What's the plan?'

Jack smiled into the darkness and said, 'They look like a pair of fucking hicks to me. They are probably from the bush, and when we show them our badges, they will shit themselves and run away. We will just go in and grab the slut. You drive, and I'll get into the back seat and let the fun begin.'

Karl said, 'Don't you reckon that it would be better if we waited until those two blokes have gone? Remember the old saying, no witnesses are good witnesses.'

Jack laughed and said, 'I can't wait. I'm so eager to take her away from all this. I just want to feel her soft throat in my hands. She is in for the trip of a lifetime, one that she won't forget ever.'

Hilda brought out the boys' meals, and they started to eat them; the steaks were delicious.

The boys had just started when the door burst open and in walked Jack and Karl.

'Hullo, my lovely,' Jack sneered.

Hilda paled visibility, the colour drained out of her face, and she felt dizzy and sick to the pit of her stomach.

She croaked, 'Jack, how on earth did you find me?'

'It was easy. When you have got as many friends as I have, all you have got to do is put out the word, and sooner or later, someone will stumble across you. And guess what? Someone did stumble across your pretty little arse. So here I am, here to take you back home. But first I will have to give you a good spanking for making me look like a fucking idiot in front of my friends.'

Dean looked at Teddy, and Teddy raised his eyebrows. They both put down their knives and forks.

Hilda was badly shaken but was defiant.

'I'm not going back with you,' she said. 'I'm not going to be badly treated by you or anyone else ever again. I'm happy here, and I'm not leaving.'

Jack looked at her; hate filled his face.

'You fucking whore, you will be doing what I tell you to. You are still my wife, and by the time that I have finished with you, you will be begging for me to do whatever I want with you.'

Teddy leaned back in his chair and asked, 'Hilda, could you be a good girl and grab us another couple of coffees, please, love?'

Hilda was suddenly brought back into the real world and carried over the percolator.

'Just leave it on the table. Thanks,' Teddy said with a smile.

Dean looked at Teddy and thought, *A weapon, that's what we need.*

Teddy asked Hilda, 'Is everything hunky-dory, luv?'

Jack said in a commanding voice, 'Keep your fucking head out of this. This has got nothing to do with you, and if you don't want a smack in the fucking mouth, you fucking halfwit, just sit there and shut the fuck up.'

Teddy didn't look as though he heard what Jack had said.

He gently asked Hilda, 'Are you in trouble?'

Hilda nodded her head without speaking; her eyes were fixed on Jack and Karl.

Teddy looked at the two men and said, 'You heard the lady. Now fuck off and stop disturbing our meal. I don't like loudmouths and bullies, and you seem to have both those qualities, so fuck off.'

Jack pulled his wallet out of his back pocket and showed his detective's badge.

He said, 'Careful what you say. We are both police.'

Dean spoke for the first time, 'You are both wankers as far as I can see. Like the man said, fuck off before you get yourselves hurt.'

Jack was a bit taken aback by the response of the two men. They weren't shitting themselves at all, and in fact, they were a lot more relaxed than the detectives.

Jack was a bully and used to people being afraid of him. This wasn't going as planned.

He put his wallet back into his pocket and said, 'I don't give a fuck. I'm here to take back what's mine, and I'll use force if I have to.'

Teddy looked at Jack and said, 'My advice to you is to just leave and let things work themselves out. I can't let you take her, as you have already said that you are going to bash her. So my advice to you is, go now and work things out when you have cooled off.'

Karl suddenly had a rush of blood and said, 'We don't need advice from some dickhead like you. We are here to do a job, and we will do it, so shut the fuck up and finish your meal.'

Teddy looked at Dean and said, 'Mate, I've lost my appetite.'

In one movement, Teddy picked up the percolator and threw the contents into Karl's face and chest. It happened fast. Karl was immediately scalded. He screamed and started to tear his shirt off. Dean was out of his chair, and, in the confusion, he struck Jack a solid blow across the face.

Anger boiled up in Jack, and he swung his fist at Dean. He wasn't afraid. There were only two things that stood between him and him getting his hands on his slut of a wife. They were both marked men as far as he was concerned.

Teddy saw Jack fight back at Dean. He looked at Karl and saw that he was almost out of the fight. Teddy slammed his fist into Jack's ribcage, and he thought he felt a rib crack. Dean smashed his fist into Jack's face again and again. Jack's face was puffed and swollen, his nose was broken, and soon the anger turned to fear as both the men concentrated on him.

Jack realised that he had made a mistake by not letting these two have their meal and go. He had been too eager to get involved to get his hands on the bitch.

Jack hit the floor. Karl was naked from the waist up, and his skin was a motley red colour. 'Help me,' he pleaded.

Teddy smashed his fist into Karl's face, and he hit the floor.

Hilda looked at the two men on the floor. She walked over to her husband and kicked him in the side.

'Bastard,' she said. 'He was going to flog me all the way back to Melbourne and then really get into me when we got home. He might have killed me for all I know. He is a savage brute. There is a chance that you have saved my life. Thank you very much. I don't know how I can ever repay the pair of you.'

Teddy smiled and said, 'First things first, we had better get you away from here. What are we going to do with these pair of bastards?'

Hilda said, 'The only place we can lock them in is the cool room. I can take off the inside release handle. They won't be able to get out then. I'll shut the place up, give Dan a ring, and tell him that I've had to leave suddenly. Can I get a lift somewhere with you two?'

Teddy nodded and asked, 'Have you got any friends whom you can stay with?'

Hilda shook her head and said, 'Jack knows all my friends. I will have to find a place to stay until things settle down.'

Teddy and Dean dragged the two detectives into the cool room and left them there. Hilda dismantled the inside opener, and she went and grabbed her few belongings—just two small bags. She closed the roadhouse, and as they drove off towards Melbourne, Hilda looked back and realised how much she had loved living and working at the Billabong Roadhouse.

After a couple of hours, she rang a sleepy Dan and told him that there were two detectives locked in his cool room and she had to leave. She explained that her life was in danger and that this was the only way out for her. She apologised that she was leaving, but there wasn't anything else that she could do. Hilda felt sorry for Dan as she knew that he would have trouble filling her position, but that's life.

Teddy drove into the night. He had a plan. He rang Bass Strait Barry and asked if Hilda could stay on board his seventy-foot boat. Barry didn't mind as it wasn't the first time that someone on the run had stayed aboard.

He told Teddy where the keys were and said, 'Let her sleep there, and I'll pop down there tomorrow and meet her and show her where things are.'

'Well,' Teddy said, 'that's your accommodation all set. You can sleep aboard Barry's boat. It's very comfortable. No one will know that you are there, and it's cheap.'

Teddy drove down to the marina and helped Hilda aboard.

He turned on the light in the main cabin and said, 'Home sweet home.'

Hilda couldn't believe the kindness that was being offered by Teddy and his friends. She could feel herself close to tears.

She looked at the two big blokes and simply said, 'Thanks for everything that you have done for me. I can't repay your kindness.'

The two men looked a bit embarrassed and awkwardly shrugged and said, 'Think nothing of it. We'll be in touch.'

Teddy asked, 'Are you right for money?'

Hilda nodded, unable to speak. The boys turned on their heels and walked back to the car, got in, and drove away.

The detectives Jack and Karl tried to force open the cold room door but found that they couldn't. So there was nothing else to do but wait until someone opened the door. The cool air was good for Karl's burns.

Dan, the owner, drove into the roadhouse and unlocked the front door. He saw the mess and the blood on the diner floor and walked over to the cool room door. He could see that there was stuff stacked against the door, so he started moving it.

Then he banged on the door and yelled out, 'I'm opening the door.'

With that, he swung open the door, and the sight of the two men was startling. They both had been savagely beaten. One's body was almost raw meat, and the other one's face was badly swollen and his nose was all over his face. They were both shivering and covered in blood.

'Bloody hell,' Dan exclaimed. 'What the fuck happened to youse two?'

Jack spoke first, 'I came to pick up my missus, and we got jumped by two blokes. The bastards surprised us and locked us in the bloody cool room. We might have fucking frozen to death.'

Karl's teeth chattered in agreement.

Teddy and Dean got to their homes and went to bed, and they slept soundly.

Leckie got up and looked at Dean's clothes. They were bloody. She looked at Dean and saw that he wasn't hurt, so she rightly assumed that it was someone else's blood.

Rita assumed the same when she saw Teddy's clothes on the laundry floor.

Derek was in his office when Teddy walked in with Billy's map.

'How did it all go?' Derek asked.

'As sweet as a bun,' Teddy answered. 'I caught up with an old mate who is just about rooted with bloody cancer. He gave me a map and X-marks the spot.'

'Well, let's make a bit of a plan,' Derek suggested. 'What are we looking at in the way of provisions and stuff?'

Teddy closed his eyes and said, 'If we take the big boat down and anchor on the reef, we might get lucky and find it in a day. If we don't find it, then we can stay until we do. We can stay at sea for weeks if we want to.'

Derek looked at his friend and said, 'It will be a while until the two brothers can get here with their religious friend to bless the site.'

Teddy answered, 'Let's try this. Barry will run down with the big boat, and Tony and I will tow the Shark Cat down. We dive on the reef, and when we find the sub, we contact the two brothers. They jump on the first available plane. When they get here, you pick them up at the airport and drive them here. I will shoot in to Eden in the Shark Cat, pick them up, and out to the reef we all go. We take a video camera down and swim around the wreck, and the two brothers watch it all on TV. Then the priest blesses the site, and they have a prayer meeting. Then away we all go. We charge them for our services, and away they go, happy in the thought that they have visited their dear old dad's grave.'

'That sounds like a plan to me,' Derek agreed.

Barry drove down to the marina and walked along the deck. He wondered what the girl would be like who had spent the night on board. He chuckled to himself; she would be ugly, fat, and lazy like most of the kids were these days, probably lying in bed still, and would have attitude. Well, he was just the one to give her marching orders.

He climbed on board and yelled out, 'Ahoy there, I'm coming aboard.'

He looked around the wheelhouse, and everything gleamed. All the windows had been freshly washed, all the surfaces were polished to a shine, and the wheel had been cleaned of all the blood and the dirt that had been transferred from his hands.

When he walked into the galley, there wasn't a thing out of place. Everything was clean; the whole place smelt of lemons instead of fish and sweat. The table was wiped down, and he could see his reflection in it. He went into one of the toilet or shower rooms, and everything was sparkling clean. He couldn't believe it was the same boat.

He and his usual crew Des weren't the cleanest of people, but for Christ's sake, it was a fishing boat, after all.

He was standing there amazed when a quiet voice startled him from behind.

'You must be Captain Barry.'

He swung around and saw this young woman standing there. She had on a pair of cut-off jean shorts and a T-shirt that was tied in a knot at the front. She was barefooted and had a great figure.

'My name's Hilda. Thank you for letting me stay here overnight. It's a lovely boat, and as I woke up early this morning, I decided to give the cabins a bit of a dust-off.'

Barry thought, *A bit of a dust off? The boat has never been this clean. It must have taken her all morning. So much for the fat lazy kid still lying in bed. This Hilda is a cleaning dynamo.*

'Pleased to meet you, and thanks for cleaning up.' Barry was a bit lost for words.

Hilda eased the silence by asking if Barry would like a cup of coffee.

Barry said, 'That would be great. I'll get it for you.'

Hilda smiled and shook her head.

'It's no trouble I know where everything is. I hope that you don't mind me cleaning up all the mugs and the plates.'

Barry couldn't believe his luck. 'Of course not, you've done a wonderful job. Thanks a million.'

'Can I explain my situation to you?' Hilda asked shyly as she started to make coffee for them both.

'Please go ahead,' Barry prompted.

'Well, my husband is a cruel and sadistic man. He would bash me for no reason, so I left him and ran away. He found me and tried to take me back, but luckily for me, Teddy and Dean were there, and they belted up my husband and his friend and took me to safety. It was easy for him to find me as he is a detective and he knows plenty of policemen all over the country. I don't want to cause you any trouble, and if it's your wish, I will leave the boat today.'

Barry muttered, 'Fucking coppers, I've had my fair share of run-ins with the bastards and never met a decent one yet. Hilda, you are welcome to stay on board as long as you like. You have done a great job, cleaning the place up, so just relax and kick back, and we will see what pans out.'

Hilda smiled and gave Barry a kiss on the cheek. 'Thank you for helping me.'

They sat there, looking out over the ocean, watching the seagulls and pelicans swimming around, looking for food, and slowly sipping their coffee.

Teddy was all go; he was trying to organise the trip.

He would get Barry and his boat to steam up towards Eden. He would drive up with Tony in the F100, tow the Shark Cat up, and put it in the water at Eden. He would then steam out to Barry's boat, find the reef, and have a dive on it to see if they could find the sub. He would keep the team together and take Tom, Dean, and Curly too. He would ask Derek for a grand a day for each of them and one grand a day for the boat, plus expenses.

Teddy rang Barry who was still on board. Teddy told him to get himself ready as they would be going soon in the next couple of days. He explained what terms he was going to ask for, and Barry agreed. Teddy disconnected.

Barry turned to Hilda and said, 'Do you feel like a few days away with Teddy and the boys?'

Hilda smiled and said, 'Just as long as I won't be in the way.'

Barry smiled and said, 'No worries, love. You will be put to work. You will have to earn your keep.'

Derek rang Akinobu in Japan and said, 'Akinobu mate, my mates are getting ready to head off and find your dad's submarine. They will be travelling up the coast in the next few days. You two blokes should get ready to fly over. Teddy said the weather's great and will remain so for the next week or so.'

Akinobu smiled and answered, 'Derek, my friend, I will alert my younger brother. He is waiting for me to get back to him. I will ring you when we are ready to leave.'

Derek disconnected and sat back; all was going well so far.

Teddy rang the boys, and they were all eager to have a look. Like divers all around the world, the yearning never stops for getting back into the water.

They prepared themselves for the upcoming trip.

Barry showed Hilda how to start the boat and gave her lessons on how to control it, how to moor the boat, and what ropes were for what. He found himself enjoying the company of the younger woman.

There's no fool like an old fool, a voice in his head softly whispered.

Barry had been on his own for a long time, and the thought of losing his wife, to a kidney disease, still caught in his chest. The hurt was always there.

Teddy told Derek that they were off the next day and that he and Tony would tow the Shark Cat up to Eden and put it in at the ramp there. Barry and the boys would take up the big boat, and they would meet on the reef.

Everything was set.

The next morning Teddy and Tony drove down the freeway, and Dean, Tom, and Curly headed for the marina.

Barry was waiting, and when the boys got aboard, Hilda started to untie the boat from the wharf.

Tom stated, 'What? No Des on this trip?'

Barry went a shade red and said, 'No, mate, he was a bit busy. He couldn't make it this trip. It's a good thing that Hilda was able to come along and help me with the cooking.'

Dean and Curly looked at each other, and a knowing smile passed between them.

They steamed out of the heads and turned south-south-east towards Eden.

Barry was busy showing Hilda how to navigate and how the autopilot worked, and Hilda was learning fast.

The boys sat in the galley and watched the ocean flow past.

Teddy and Tony stopped in Bairnsdale and got more fuel, grabbed a meal at McDonalds, and drove on. They had the 'best of' CDs on, and time flew.

Akinobu and Baku got out of their limousine at Tokyo International airport. With them was a Buddhist monk in ceremonial robes, and they walked quickly through the mingling crowds to the first-class lounge. Their fellow passengers gave way to them, and some even bowed slightly to the monk. They gave their passports and tickets to the officer at passport control and were quickly cleared. They took seats in the spacious lounge and helped themselves to a drink.

Soon the beautiful hostess approached them, and, with a bow, she quietly said, 'Your flight is ready to leave now.'

She handed the three men their tickets and once again bowed, showing great respect as she recognised the monk as a very important person and also that Baku was one of the honoured society. The three men boarded the flight and were soon speeding through the air towards Melbourne.

Des, Barry's occasional deckhand, walked out on the jetty of the marina and saw that Barry's boat was gone.

He asked a bloke who did a few odd jobs around the place for drinking money. 'Hey, sport, when did Barry go?'

The bleary-eyed odd-job man said, 'Ah, they left about four hours ago, I reckon.'

'Who's they?' asked Des.

The odd-job man, whose nickname was Slither, answered, 'Barry and the new girl he has on board and the rest of the crew, the normal blokes. Come to think of it, Teddy wasn't amongst them. One of them said to me that they were gunna go up to somewhere near Eden.'

Des grunted and said to himself, 'That bastard Barry has given me the arse, and he's got a Sheila on board. He must be rooting her. With all the crew on board, they must be doing a run. If it wasn't for me, then they would have been really in the shit when those two gangsters fronted them, bastards.'

He thought. *I'll get even with them somehow.*

Billy Boy was really getting crooker by the day; the cancer was killing him. He was sitting on his veranda, drinking the strong black coffee that he was accustomed to when the dogs started barking.

'Shut the fuck up. Don't you idiots know that it's the bush nurse? She's coming out to take my blood pressure, you fucking halfwits.'

The car pulled up, and a young woman got out and walked towards the house. She wasn't afraid of the dogs. They sensed that and quietened down.

'Hullo, love,' Bill said.

He noticed that she wasn't wearing the drab clothes that the nurses wore and wasn't carrying a briefcase.

She was suntanned and had long blonde hair. She was lovely to look at—a great figure and smartly dressed.

'Hello, Dad,' she said, 'how are you?'

Akinobu and Baku both looked down at the Australian coastline. From 30,000 feet, they could make out the waves breaking on the ninety-mile beach, and they could see the enormous expanse of wilderness.

Baku said to the monk, 'It looks beautiful.'

The monk smiled in a knowing way and said, 'Yes, the world is a beautiful place.'

The airliner flew directly over Barry's boat.

Des was on the drink. He was wallowing in self-pity about being left out of the action. He was complaining to a couple of dead beats that were the only people in the bar.

'Fuck Barry,' he said out loud.

One of the dead beats said, 'If he's cut you out of the deal, then maybe you should drop a dime, so to speak. Give the fisheries a ring, and let them know just what's going on.'

The notion festered in Des's addled brain, and, after a few more pots, he decided to do just that. He went to the phone and called 1234. The operator answered, and he asked for the toll-free fisheries dob-in number.

The call was answered by a fisheries officer who asked how he could help.

Des said, 'I want to dob in an abalone poacher and all his crew. They are steaming at this very moment towards Eden, and they will be in the water tomorrow.'

The fisheries officer was an old hand at this. He could hear the background noise of a hotel and knew that whoever he was talking to had been left out or short-changed on some sort of deal.

'Sir, we really appreciate your call. Can you give me more details?' he said.

Des was on a roll and spilt his guts. He told the fisheries officer everything—all about the trips that he had done with Teddy and the boys and about how they had run the abalone over of a night. The trained fisheries officer coaxed out of Des far more than he initially intended to say. When he was asked about the processor, Des couldn't tell him who he was as he had never met Derek. He tried to sound as if he knew what he was talking about, but the expert from the fisheries gathered that his informant didn't know who the processor was.

However, you looked at it, this information was pure gold for the fisheries.

Des said that he had to get going. The fisheries officer, who had recorded the whole conversation, tried to get more out of Des and even asked his name. But he pushed just a little too hard, and Des hung up.

The fisheries officer went through the information and thought about what he should do next. After careful consideration, he decided to transfer the information closer to where the illegal poachers were heading. He rang Wallace P. Trotter at the Bairnsdale office.

Piggy was relaxing at his desk. He had transferred some information about Gazza and Louie to his counterparts. They were the two dickheads whom he had brilliantly convinced that he was a wealthy grazier from the high country. He had almost caught those evil bastards, Teddy and his crew.

When his phone rang, Piggy answered, 'Yallow.' (Just like Homer Simpson.)

Piggy almost burst out laughing, but when the voice on the other end said, 'Is that Wallace Trotter? This is fisheries headquarters,' Piggy became serious.

The voice continued, 'We have just had a call from what sounds like a disgruntled abalone poacher or deckhand. He informed us that a boat is headed towards Eden with a crew of abalone poachers on board and someone called Teddy is going up to meet them by road.'

Piggy nearly fell off his chair.

He steadied himself and said, 'What other information do you have?'

When all was revealed and Piggy hung up, he started to make a plan.

Barry and the crew were making good time.

Hilda looked up and said, 'Oh, look, there's a plane travelling along the coast.'

'Yes,' Barry said; suddenly he was an expert of aviation and flight patterns. 'It looks like it's heading to Tullamarine. Maybe it's from some strange country filled with people who are eager to see our wonderful country.'

Tom looked at Dean and said, 'Fuck me, now Barry is an expert on air travel.'

Dean smiled and said, 'I think it must be love. He seems to have done his nuts over Hilda.'

Curly interjected, 'She's a lot better-looking than Des is.'

Tom laughed and said, 'Mate, I wouldn't be climbing over her to get to you.'

That remark made them all laugh.

Akinobu, Baku, and the monk exited first from the plane as is the custom when you are in first class. They made their way through immigration. There was hardly a wait at customs. Baku kept his left hand in his jacket pocket so that his shortened pinkie wasn't obvious to the immigration attendants.

Baku had lost the tip of his pinkie as punishment for one of his underlings doing the wrong thing during a job that they had done. Baku had taken full responsibility for his younger man's action. When the head of the crime syndicate passed a sharp knife and a piece of twine to Baku, he realised that he was to cut off the end of his finger. The twine was to staunch the flow of blood. Baku gave the wrapped fingertip to the boss as way of saying, 'I apologise for the behaviour of my gang.'

The origin of this practice dates back to the Samurai and now is mainly symbolic. When the katana (the samurai's long sword) is properly gripped, the pinkie is the strongest finger. So by losing the tip of the finger, that makes the grip weaker and, therefore, the user more dependant of his master for protection.

The three Japanese men walked out into the reception area and were greeted by a thirty-five-year-old man of Japanese descent, who was dressed in a dark business suit. He was taller than the three plane passengers and of a very solid build.

He bowed slightly and said, 'Greetings! My name is Chikara. I am your driver. Your limousine waits.'

The four men, after gathering the luggage, walked out the front doors of Tullamarine and walked to a 'no standing' zone where a black late-model Bentley awaited. Chikara pushed the trolley up to the rear of the Bentley and pushed a button on the key ring, and the boot popped open. He placed the three suitcases into the boot. He indicated that Akinobu sit behind him by opening the rear door, then walked around the car, opened the other side rear door, and indicated that the monk sit beside Akinobu. He then opened the front passenger door, and Baku got in. Chikara walked around the front of the car and got in the driver's seat. The motor started immediately and purred quietly. They drove into Melbourne through moderate traffic.

Akinobu gave Chikara the directions to Derek's factory, and Chikara punched them into the car's GPS.

Baku asked Chikara, 'How long will it take us to get to the factory?'

Chikara answered, 'It will take approximately half an hour.'

They all settled in for the ride.

The Yakuza is a powerful operation and is mainly in Japan, but its tentacles reach worldwide.

In Australia, the Yakuza is powerful, and its members are rich and influential. They are united, work together, and deal only in legal operations like construction, transport, and restaurants. Chikara's father was a member and owned a large, successful restaurant. When he was notified of Baku and his brother's imminent arrival, he chose his eldest son to chauffeur the men around. He told his son that he was to be on call twenty-four hours a day, seven days a week, and to do everything that was asked of him.

The four Japanese men pulled up in the yard of Derek's factory. Akinobu smelt the familiar smell of fish and smiled to himself.

He said out loud, 'No matter what country you're in, fish still smell the same.'

That broke the tension, and all the men laughed.

Derek saw the Bentley pull into his factory.

He walked out and said, 'Bugger me dead! No wonder you didn't need me to pick you up at Tulla. The car's worth more than me bloody factory.'

Chikara understood as he had been born in Australia, and Akinobu had a vague idea what Derek said, but the other two had no idea what Derek meant.

Akinobu translated.

Derek held out his hand and said, 'Are you Akinobu?'

Akinobu smiled slightly, bowed, reached out, and said, 'Yes, I am he. You must be Derek.'

'Bloody great to meet you at long last. We have spoken many times over the phone. Which one's your brother?'

Derek looked at the two Japanese men. One was dressed in an old-fashioned, pinstriped suit and pointy-toed shoes, and the other one was in robes.

Akinobu gestured towards Baku. Baku bowed slightly and put out his hand. He shook Derek's hand solemnly.

Derek thought, *That was a joke. It's obvious which one was the bloody priest or whatever.*

Derek smiled at the monk. He didn't know if he was allowed to touch him or shake his hand or what to do. Thankfully, the priest bowed and didn't put out his hand.

'Please come in and have a look around,' Derek insisted.

They all walked into the front of the factory that was also a fish and chip takeaway. One of the girls was serving a customer, and she emptied a frying basket full of dim sims and fish and chips onto a large sheet of white paper. She liberally sprinkled salt over the whole lot, wrapped it up, and gave it to a customer.

'There you go, love,' she said as the customer put the package under his arm and walked out the door.

They made their way out to the back, and Derek showed them the processing area and the storage area. He showed them the blast freezer, the holding freezer, and the cool room. All the men were suitably impressed.

They all went into Derek's office and sat, facing him at his desk.

'Do you want something to eat?' Derek inquired. 'I can get Carol to whip us up a feed of fish and chips, no problems.'

The men declined the offer, and Akinobu got straight to business.

'We would like to get going first thing in the morning. We will stay in Melbourne and leave first thing. Give us the directions, and we will go and get some rest.'

Derek explained that Teddy was waiting for them in Eden and that he would ferry them out to the wreck site as soon as they were ready.

They left Derek and made their way in to a city hotel, had a small meal, and tried to sleep off their jet lag.

Billy couldn't believe his eyes. There standing before him was his daughter, and he slowly got to his feet and gave her a hug.

'I can't believe that you are here, Olivia. It's wonderful to see you again.'

Tears started to run down his face.

Anything that had happened between him and her mother was suddenly forgotten.

Olivia hugged her father back just as hard.

'It's been a long time,' she said.

'I lost contact with you when your mum and I split up,' Billy said. 'I tried to get in contact with you, but I just couldn't keep up with what you were up to. What a waste of time! What a waste!'

Olivia laughed and said, 'Well, we are back together now. I'll look after you. You have lost weight it seems.'

'Fucking cancer,' Bill said. 'I've had the bastard for years, and now it's finally got the upper hand. It's gunna fuck me. I can feel it in my bones.'

Bill led his daughter into the small cabin.

'This is all I have. It's on twenty acres, and I own the lot. I don't owe a cent on it, and it's all yours when I pass away.'

Olivia smiled and said, 'I would rather have you fit and well than a cabin in the woods.'

Bill, for the first time, smiled back and said, 'It's something to remember me by.'

'It certainly is,' Olivia replied.

Bill got the coffee percolator out and poured a couple of coffees out. He suddenly felt bad about having no sugar or milk.

'Hope you like it black,' he commented.

Olivia smiled and said, 'Just as it comes is fine with me.'

One sip later, she instantly regretted saying that.

They talked for hours, and Bill finally got around to talking about the submarine that he had found. He told her how it had haunted him for years and how, out of nowhere, an old mate had turned up and wanted to know where it was because the children of the sub's captain wanted to view where their father had died.

'You know something?' Bill asked. 'I always thought that there was a curse on the fucking thing. As soon as I discovered it, things went bad for me. You and your mother left me. I never had any luck since the day I stumbled across it. Now, out of nowhere, a mate turns up, and I gave him the map, and suddenly things change. You turn up, and now maybe I'll have some good luck. Maybe I'll get better.'

Olivia looked at the broken man that was her father and thought that there wasn't much hope of improvement.

She smiled and said, 'Let's get you better first. I don't want to hear any more rubbish about you dying.'

Bill picked up his ever-present Bong and held a match to the small bowl. He inhaled a lung full of smoke, held it in for a few seconds, and then released it into the air.

'Do you want to have a go?' Bill asked.

Olivia looked at her father and said, 'There's something that I have got to tell you, Dad. I'm pregnant.'

'That's great news,' Bill responded, and then he thought for a moment. 'Are you married?'

'Sort of,' Olivia answered. 'We are going to be a two-mum family.'

Bill was confused for a moment.

'How does that work?' he asked.

'Well, my partner and I went through IVF, and I became pregnant that way.'

Bill looked at his daughter and said, 'Honestly, if you are happy that's all I care about. You can do no wrong as far as I'm concerned.'

Olivia hugged her dad and cried with happiness.

Teddy had given Barry a copy of the coastal map, and Barry was on position. He had turned on his depth sounder and picked up the reef. He dropped anchor just off the reef, and the current put him within reach of it. He rang Teddy and asked where he was.

Teddy was at the boat ramp and slid the Shark Cat off the trailer. He gave Tony the thumbs up and he headed off to sea. Tony drove away and booked into the pub for the night; he would wait on instructions.

Teddy pulled up the Shark Cat beside Barry's boat and climbed aboard. He smiled and said hullo to Hilda. She was as happy as could be, making herself useful on board.

Barry said, 'Mate, we are right over the wreck site. When do you want to have a look for it?'

Teddy said, 'We may as well have a look now as it's been down there for a while and will be covered in weed and growth.'

All the boys suited up, and Teddy and Tom went over the side on one T-piece. Dean and Curly followed them down on another T-piece.

Under the water, the visibility was good. The reef was about twenty feet high with deep grooves running right along it. It was roughly one and a half kilometres long and about 500 meters wide.

The divers started at the front and swam with the slight tide. The four of them swam in a line and looked at everything that was down there. They couldn't see anything that looked like a Japanese submarine, mini or not. As the reef was in deepish water, between seventy feet and possibly 100 feet, there was a question of how long they could stay at the bottom as they didn't want to end up with the bends.

The bends is a decompression sickness that will hit you when you stay too long in deep water. It is a constant worry for professional divers when common sense is overtaken by greed.

As the visibility was good, Teddy indicated to the other divers that they would swim up as close to the surface as was possible and still have a good view of the bottom. This is a known dangerous practice as white pointers and other sharks are known to take prey when it is on or up towards the surface. All the divers kept an eye out for sharks as they swam along. Once again, none of them saw anything that resembled a submarine, mini or not.

When they got to the end of the reef, Teddy gave them all the thumbs up, and they all surfaced. Barry was driving the Shark Cat, and they all clambered on board.

Dean said to Teddy, 'I didn't see any Jap sub down there. Neither did anyone else. I thought that it would stick out like dogs balls.'

Everyone nodded.

'What do we do now?' Tom asked.

Teddy replied, 'We start all over again. This time, we go right to the bottom and hit the rocks and any other thing that's down there with our abalone irons. Over time, the sand and weed will have covered it up. If we give the sub a whack, then we will hear a different sound.'

This sounded like a good plan. They decided to take shifts, and two would go down at a time and spend only half an hour down at the bottom. Teddy and Curly went to do the first shift. They slowly worked their way along the reef, jabbing their abalone irons into the rocks, waiting for a metallic sound. Nothing made that metallic sound. It seemed like only minutes when Dean and Tom swam down to take over the painstaking task.

Teddy and Curly slowly swam to the surface and climbed aboard.

Dean and Tom slowly worked along the reef. The divers had started at the deepest end and were slowly working up to shallower water. They kept this up for the rest of the day, and, when night fell, they hadn't heard the metallic sound of when an abalone iron hits metal.

They all went back to Barry's boat to discover that Hilda had been busy cooking up a meal of roast lamb with all the trimmings. All the crew were hungry, and they tucked into the delicious meal.

Hilda was as happy as any of them. It was good to see men eat heartily.

Meanwhile, Piggy was busy organising the New South Wales Fisheries. He had commandeered a fisheries vessel and talked a couple of local abalone divers into joining the hunt.

At first light, he would organise a light plane to fly down the coast and see just where the bastards were and radio back. Then they would attack. Piggy assured everyone that the plan was foolproof. Just wait, the bastards would get the shock of their lives. Sweet Jesus, it felt good to be alive.

The Japanese quartet rose early and headed out of Melbourne. The Bentley sighed almost silently towards the country.

It was quiet inside the car. Chikara drove and concentrated on his driving. The two brothers talked quietly in Japanese between themselves.

Baku said to his brother, 'I hope we aren't going on a wild goose chase.'

Akinobu smiled and answered, 'I want to be close when they discover our father's submarine. Derek has assured me that this team of divers is the best that we could hope for.'

The monk spoke, 'The country is very dry. The fields are not the same as back in Japan.'

Chikara spoke in Japanese and said, 'This year has been very wet. Normally, the country is much dryer than this. This is a very harsh land. It is very difficult for the farmers to get a good living off this land.'

They drove towards Eden in silence.

Teddy was first over the side next morning. He had decided to take a more substantial probe down. It was a jemmy bar, a tool that is sometimes used by people who dismantle buildings. Also he had seen something that didn't look right. When he swam down, poked, and prodded around, he discovered that, under a film of algae and sand in a wide crevice, there was something metal. He didn't want to get his hopes up as it could have been just sea junk, a scallop dredge, or some other rubbish. So he probed on, digging and scratching around until he was sure that what he was looking at was in fact a mini sub.

Tom swam down to relieve him, and Teddy motioned to Tom where he thought that there was something of interest. He slowly swam to the surface and told the rest of the crew that he was confident that he had found the mini sub.

He told Dean and Curly to swim down and help Tom to uncover what they could. Teddy also told them to look for anything that would indicate to them what had made the sub sink. Dean and Curly swam down and started to shift the decades of marine growth off the sub by scraping and fanning off the sand and algae.

Soon they could see what was obviously a mini sub.

When they were all on the surface, Teddy said to Barry, 'I'll go in and pick up the Japanese trio in the Shark Cat, and we'll make it back for the service.'

Barry decided to move the big boat directly over the spot where the mini sub was lying, and he held it in place with both a forward and a stern anchor.

Teddy rang the number that Derek had given him, and Chikara answered.

Teddy introduced himself and said, 'We have found the wreck site and haven't disturbed anything. We have begun clearing away the accumulated debris. By the time that you get out here, it will be exposed enough so that when you look, you will be able to see the submarine for yourselves on the TV screen. I anticipate that I will pick you up in two hours. Are you comfortable with that?'

Chikara consulted with his companions and said to Teddy, 'We are more than happy with those arrangements.'

Teddy said, 'I will meet you all down at the wharf in two hours' time. Goodbye.'

The two brothers were very excited about the fact that they would soon be standing above the site where their father spent his last few hours. But even so, there was a tension, as soon they would also learn if their father had died the death of a hero or a coward.

1942

On the deep reef off the NSW coastline, Youshio Okumura looked towards his crewman. He could see the terror in the man's eyes, even though the emergency lighting was dim.

'Be brave,' he commanded, even though he felt a little frightened himself.

His crewman looked at his leader and nodded. He couldn't see an ounce of fear in his face.

The mini sub had been hit by depth charges and maybe even a bomb dropped from a small fleet of dive-bombers who had spotted them. Youshio had dived, but the water wasn't deep enough to really hide them, so they were like sitting ducks. The power failed, and the emergency lighting came on as the sub settled at the bottom among some crevices.

Things were tough, and they were really in trouble. They knew that this was their last few minutes alive.

Youshio looked at a photo of his wife, who had recently told him that she was pregnant, and he thought about the fact that he would never see his baby. He silently prayed for his wife and as yet unborn child to have a safe journey through life and made the biggest decision of his life.

He decided to detonate the explosive device that would scuttle the sub and, therefore, they would not be taken prisoners.

He looked at his crew member and said, 'Thank you for your loyalty and service. We are going to our deaths as heroes and will be welcomed into eternity.'

Youshio saluted his crew member and detonated the explosive device. Water rushed in, and both men were soon drowned.

Calm settled over the reef, and the wrecked mini sub was untouched by human hands for the next sixty years. A vast array of sea creatures made the sunken sub a home and used it for protection or a hunting ground for their prey.

Present Day

The sleek Bentley made its way down to the wharf from the motel where the Japanese group had stayed the night. The four men sat inside as curious locals tried to peer into the interior to see who was in it and tried to work out what was going on.

Teddy steamed into the harbour and pulled up to the low wharf.

Chikara got out of the Bentley, walked down to the wharf, and said, 'Are you Teddy?'

Teddy laughed and said, 'I sure am. How are you going, mate?'

Chikara nodded and didn't say anything. He walked back to the Bentley, opened the doors for his passengers, and ushered them towards the wharf.

The locals stood and looked in amazement as the four Japanese walked slowly towards the Shark Cat.

Chikara got on board first and assisted the three men aboard.

Teddy introduced himself, and when they were all settled, he started the motors and motored away into the harbour. As soon as they were clear of all the moored boats, Teddy got the Shark Cat up onto the plane and headed away towards where Barry's boat was waiting.

Piggy and the other fisheries officers were all watching the carry-on with the Japanese and Teddy. Piggy wasn't sure exactly what was going on. It was a bit of a mystery to him, but that didn't curb his enthusiasm for the hunt.

So what, if there was a couple of Japs hanging around when he surprised them? He would lock those bastards up as well; fuck them. He would show them all who the boss was.

Piggy laughed to himself, 'Welcome to Australia! How do you like our jails?'

Yes, he would show the bastards.

Hilda watched as the Shark Cat made its way towards the big boat. She smiled to herself.

It's funny how things can change in your life. One day, you are flipping burgers in an all-hours roadhouse, and the next thing you know you are sitting in the middle of the ocean, waiting for a boatload of Japanese to come on board and say some prayers over the war grave of their father.

Hilda knew that Barry was enjoying her company more and more, and, in all truth, she was happy to be around Barry. He was much older than she was, but, if the truth were known, she enjoyed the company of older men. Well, let's face it. She enjoyed anybody's company rather that put up with her soon-to-be ex-husband's. She wondered just what he was up to, still looking for her, she supposed.

He was a monster, a giant moray eel (Gymnothorax javanicus). He was three meters in length; that's almost ten feet. And he weighed in at thirty kilos; that's sixty-six pounds.

When he came across the mini sub with the hole in the bow, he slowly made his way inside. Any human remains were long gone. The interior was perfect for him to hide his huge body, and he waited inside. Whenever a fish swam past, he would attack with lightning speed, and it was all over for whatever had gotten too close.

The moray eel's heads are too narrow to create the negative pressure most fishes use to swallow prey. Possibly because of this, they have a second set of jaws called pharyngeal jaws in their throat, which also have teeth on them. When feeding, morays launch these jaws into their mouths by opening their jaws wide, giving the appearance that they are about to attack. They are the only animal to use this sort of double-teethed action to catch their prey.

Teddy slowed the Shark Cat down and moved in towards Barry's boat. Chikara nimbly jumped aboard, and Teddy helped him assist the Japanese onto the big boat. When they were all aboard, Teddy introduced them to all the assembled crew.

Dean and Tom were to go down and take with them an underwater camera, and they would relay the pictures from the bottom onto a flat-screen TV that Barry had put in the galley.

Chikara requested that only the two brothers and the monk be with him in the galley as the pictures were relayed onto the screen.

Dean and Tom swam down and focussed the camera onto the sub. In the galley, the two brothers watched as the sub slowly came into view. Dean, who was in charge of the camera, slowly swam the length of the sub and gave the brothers a clear view of it. He swam around it and tried to show it from all angles. The brothers watched solemnly and felt a great sadness. They watched carefully as Dean ran the camera over the length of the sub.

Akinobu looked at his younger brother Baku and said softly, 'We can't be sure that our father died a hero or not. We must get the divers to see if they can find the hatch and see if it was opened or not. We can only assume that our father was still in the sub, if the hatch is closed.'

Baku agreed.

Chikara walked out of the galley and said to Teddy, 'We are not sure how the submarine was sunk. We need clearer pictures of the hatch to see if it's open or not.'

Teddy understood, and he and Curly started to get into their wetsuits.

When the two divers came to the surface and got out for a rest, Teddy said, 'We are going down to have a look at the hatch to see if it's open or not. If they want to see any more, then come down and tell me.'

With that, Teddy and Curly swam down with the camera.

The brothers watched; their faces gave nothing away. Teddy came to the hatch, and they could see that it was closed.

Both brothers nodded grimly to each other. The hatch being closed meant that their father had died in the sub and had not tried to escape. That meant that he was a hero with the others who had died for their emperor, and they felt a great weight lifted off their shoulders.

Curly summoned Teddy to bring the camera over as he had seen a hole in the bow of the sub. From the way the metal was pushed out, it was clear that the explosion had come from inside the sub and not from a bomb or depth charge outside.

Teddy swam the camera over towards the hole and looked through the lens. He got closer and closer.

Suddenly the huge moray eel exploded from inside the sub and grabbed the camera in its huge jaws and began shaking it around.

Teddy nearly shit himself, and he hung onto the camera for dear life.

Up on board, the four Japanese were crowded around the large flat-screen TV. Then all of a sudden, this monster from the deep suddenly shot into their vision. It looked like a creature from hell; the huge jaws opened, and they could see the second set of jaws frantically trying to get a hold of the camera. Both the brothers scattered backwards, knocking over the monk who gasped the equivalent of 'Fuck me dead' in Japanese.

Chikara instinctively took the stance of a ninja warrior.

Teddy remembered from the olden days someone saying that if a moray eel ever grabs you, don't pull back, as this will only make its teeth go deeper into your arm. Instead, push your hand further into its mouth and the gag reflex will make the eel spit out your arm.

Teddy collected his thoughts and gave the camera a shove into the huge shaking mouth of the eel. Whether or not that plan worked, or else the eel realised that what it had grasped wasn't edible, the eel spat out the camera and retreated into its hole in the mini sub with eyes blazing and mouth still wide open.

Teddy composed himself and pointed the camera at the hole in the sub.

Up on board, in the galley, the brothers had got to their feet and were looking at the picture on the TV. The monk waited for his heart to adjust back to its normal rhythm. Chikara relaxed his defensive stance.

They could see the hole in the bow of the sub, and it was clearly made from an internal explosion. It was obvious to the two brothers that their father had detonated an explosive device and died the death of a hero rather than be taken prisoner. They felt a sweet sadness. But now they knew it was true: their father had died the death of a hero and would be remembered as such.

When Teddy was sure that he still had all his fingers, he and Curly swam slowly towards the surface and were assisted onto the boat.

The boys helped them out of their gear, and Curly said, 'Did you see Teddy hand-feeding a moray eel down there?'

Everybody shook their heads and reminded Teddy that there had been a request that only the Japanese viewed the footage.

'Well, it was a bit hairy for a while,' Teddy said. 'There's a fucking moray eel down there, the size of a small train. And as I was filming around the area, the fucker came out and tried to grab the camera. It must live in the sub and thought that I was trying to broach its territory.'

Dean said, 'I believe that they are very territorial.'

Nobody else said anything.

The Japanese came out onto the deck, and Akinobu said to Teddy, 'Thank you for showing us the proof that our father died a hero. Were you frightened when whatever that was attacked you?'

Teddy smiled and said, 'It was very frightening. I realise just how much you and your brother had wanted to see the site where your father died, and as Derek is a dear friend of all of us, we decided that we would do whatever we could to help ease your pain.'

Akinobu was deeply moved.

He translated to his brother and the monk and then bowed to Teddy and said, 'We all appreciate you helping us. Thank you.'

Baku, the monk, and Chikara all as one bowed to Teddy and the crew.

Akinobu asked if they could then perform the ceremony for their father.

Barry agreed and asked if they wanted everyone off the boat or if they could show their respect to a warrior who had died the death of a hero as well.

Akinobu was so moved by the attitude of everyone that he allowed everyone to remain on board.

The monk had regained most of his composure, and when Akinobu explained that all the crew wanted to be present when the ceremony was being done, he agreed.

Baku removed his clothes and stood before them all in only a loincloth. His body was covered in the full-body tattoos of the Yakuza. Normally, the Yakuza wouldn't display their body sculpture. It had taken years of incredible pain and skill to have them put on, and Baku believed that his father would have been proud of him.

They all gathered on the deck of Barry's boat and stood in silence as the monk went about his business.

He chanted in Japanese, and, almost as if nature was aware of what was going on, the sea calmed to a tranquil, oily surface, and the slight breeze dropped. All the engines were off, and an incredible calm descended over the boat.

Piggy was raring to go. He had worked out that the poachers would have been working for long enough to have plenty of abalone on board. He gathered up his team of fisheries officers, and, with three other abalone boats, they set off in convoy towards where Barry had his boat anchored.

On arrival at the scene, he could see all the crew standing on deck. He indicated to the other boats to go in, with him in the lead boat. They pulled up beside the big boat, and Piggy clambered aboard, heaving his large body on board.

'You are all under arrest,' he bellowed. 'Where is the abalone?'

The four Japanese continued to do what they were doing and ignored the intrusion. The monk kept chanting, and Akinobu and Baku stayed at attention, eyes firmly clasped shut.

But Chikara was on the alert. He was ready to stop anyone who attempted to disrupt the ceremony.

Teddy put his finger to his lips in a shushing gesture.

Piggy stood with his mouth open, doing a pretty good impersonation of a goldfish.

Teddy said quietly, 'Show a bit of respect. These gentlemen are holding a ceremony to their dear departed father.'

Piggy was confused. 'What are they doing?' he asked.

Teddy answered, 'It's pretty bloody easy to work out. It's a funeral service for their father.'

Piggy was even more confused.

Everyone was looking for Piggy to come up with something to pull the proverbial rabbit out of the hat. All was silent apart from the chanting of the monk.

Everyone remained silent.

Suddenly the monk stopped chanting, and there was complete silence.

Akinobu said to Teddy, 'Thank you, the service has concluded.'

The monk walked away, and Baku turned to look at the people who had interrupted their father's funeral service.

He turned to Chikara and said in Japanese, 'What do these primitives want?'

Chikara turned to Teddy and asked, 'What do these people want?'

Teddy answered, 'They are fisheries officers, and they are looking for illegal abalone poachers. They think that we are being dishonest and are poachers. They will want to search the boat.'

Chikara translated the news to Baku.

Buka turned to Piggy and said in Japanese, 'You are a fool. We are here to show respect to our fallen father.'

Piggy looked at Chikara and asked, 'What the fuck did he say?'

Chikara politely answered, 'He said that he is sorry if we have caused you any inconvenience. We are humble people and want only peace between each other.'

'Well, that is better. No good having a bad attitude. Tell him we are fisheries officers. The people who are on this boat are abalone poachers, and we are here to arrest them,' Piggy said with confidence.

Chikara turned to Baku and said, 'You are correct. He is a fool. He is looking for illegal abalone and as far as we know there is none on board.'

Baku nodded and stayed, staring at Piggy.

Piggy began to feel uncomfortable under the direct gaze of Baku.

He began to recall some talk about the Japanese Mafia and how dangerous they were.

Teddy broke the deadlock and said, 'Mate, every time you come on board, you accuse us of being abalone poachers. It should be obvious to you by now we are not poachers. Have a look around and see if you can find any abalone. If you can't find any, then fuck off and leave us alone.'

There was nothing that Piggy could do but have a search through the boat and a look in the wells, and, as expected, no abalone to be seen anywhere.

Piggy slowly climbed back into the fisheries launch and headed back towards Eden.

Teddy's phone rang. It was a number that he couldn't identify, so he answered with 'Hullo.'

The voice on the other end said, 'You don't know me, but my name is Olivia. I'm Billy's daughter. I found your name on a bit of paper, and I thought that I would give you a ring. Billy is dying, and he's at the Pambula hospital. They don't think that he will last the night.'

'I'm sorry to hear that,' Teddy answered. 'Would it be possible for me to come and see Bill? I have some news on the Japanese sub that he found.'

Olivia said, 'If I was you, I would hurry, as I don't know how long that he has left.'

Teddy assured her that he would be as fast as he could.

Teddy explained to the Japanese that he would take them back to Eden as he had to go and visit the diver who had found the sub as he was dying and in hospital.

When they all arrived at the wharf, Teddy put the Shark Cat onto the trailer, and Tony tied it down.

Akinobu approached Teddy and asked, 'Would we also be permitted to see the man who discovered our father's war grave?'

Teddy replied, 'I'm sure that that won't be a problem. But be warned he is a very sick man. He is dying.'

Teddy and Tony unhitched the Shark Cat and drove away from the wharf area. They were followed by the Bentley, and they drove towards Pambula Hospital.

When they got there, they all walked into the reception area. The receptionist smiled and asked who they were looking for.

Teddy smiled and just said, 'Billy Boy.'

The girl behind the desk smiled and said, 'You must know him as only his friends call him that.'

Teddy answered, 'I sure did, many moons ago.'

The girl gave them directions, and they all walked into the room.

Bill was lying in the bed, his eyes were sunken, and he was barely conscious.

When he saw Teddy, he smiled and said, 'Hullo, mate, was it where I said it was?'

Teddy laughed and said, 'We dropped our anchor right on it, mate. It was exactly where you said it would be, but you didn't tell me about that fucking moray eel, the size of a fucking school bus that was waiting for me.'

Billy started to laugh, a throaty rasping laugh, and said, 'Mate, I swear I didn't know the bastard was there.'

Akinobu and Baku moved closer to the bed, and Billy gasped, 'I've seen your father. I can see his face in yours. He came to me in a dream back then. He smiled at me, and I somehow thought that he was happy that I didn't disturb the wreck.'

Billy had pulled himself up into a half-sitting position, and now he slowly sank back into the mattress.

Akinobu said softly, 'Both my brother and I thank you for the respect that you gave our father. Can we ask you to accept our blessings?'

Billy nodded, and the monk came over to the side of the bed and blessed Bill.

Olivia walked into the room and said, 'What are you doing?'

Teddy smiled at her and said, 'You must be Olivia. You are more beautiful than Bill said. I'm Teddy, and these Japanese are the sons of the man who died in the mini sub that your dad found and left in peace. These gentlemen have flown out here to bless the site where the sub lies. They also asked if their monk could bless your father as they are deeply indebted to him. If he had blown up the sub, then we might never have been able to find it.'

Olivia was taken aback. She nodded shyly to the two Japanese men, and they shook her hand.

Akinobu spoke slowly, 'We are deeply grateful to your father. We are happy to finally have found our father's remains and put them to rest. If there is any way of us being of assistance to you, then please don't hesitate to call.'

Akinobu gestured to Chikara, and he came over to them. 'Please leave your business card with Olivia. She is to ring you if she needs help in any way,' he said.

With that, the two men went over to the bed and bowed deeply to Bill.

'Goodbye, our friend,' Akinobu said quietly. The monk also bowed, and Chikara nodded. The four Japanese walked out, got into their Bentley, and drove towards Eden.

Teddy said to Olivia, 'It's wonderful that you and Billy made it back together. He was so low when I saw him, and he was desperate to get in contact with you. He really loves you.'

Olivia blinked back tears and thought of all the years that they had missed being together. She said to Teddy, 'Life is funny. You never know what it is going to throw up at you. I'm glad that I got back to Dad while he is still alive.'

Teddy nodded. What was there to say?

Barry steamed back towards Melbourne. When they passed inside Gabo Island, they pointed out where they had found the golden chalice.

Curly explained to Barry and Hilda how they had almost been goners and how it was strange, but sometimes the things that you wish for don't turn out to be quite as good as what you expected.

Teddy and Tony towed the Shark Cat back to Melbourne. On the way, he rang Derek, the processor, and told him the good news, how they had been successful in their attempt to locate the sub, and how happy the Japs were.

He told Derek that he wanted $5,000 for Barry, his boat, and crew, and a $1,000 a day for each of the four divers and $2,000 for expenses.

Derek was more than happy to accept the amount. He knew that Akinobu would be more than happy with the result. He wondered if the same would have applied if they hadn't found the sub. The good news is that they did find it.

Billy Boy was on the way out.

He looked at the one true love of his life and said, 'Thanks for being here for me.'

Olivia said, 'Dad, it's been a wild ride, but I wouldn't have missed it for the world. I love you.'

With that, Bill Boy closed his eyes and never regained consciousness.

A couple of days later, Teddy's phone rang.

Olivia said in a quiet voice, 'Hullo, Teddy, Dad's gone.'

Her voice broke, but she battled on, 'I was by his side. He was happy up to the end. I think that a great weight had been removed from his shoulders. The funeral will be in three days' time.'

Teddy admired her courage. She hadn't been around her father for a long time, but she had done all that she possibly could to make sure that Billy was comfortable in the end.

Teddy said, 'Olivia, you have done a wonderful job. You really are a beautiful person.'

With that, Teddy hung up.

Derek watched as the Bentley pulled into his factory. Inside were the four Japanese. They got out and walked inside. Derek walked towards them and held out his hand.

He said, 'I'm so happy that what you were seeking was finally done and your father can rest in peace.'

Akinobu formally nodded and said, 'We are pleased with the outcome, and we are indebted to you and your friends. Please tell me how much they require for their work, and I will give you a cheque.'

Derek started to list off who got what and what went where.

But Akinobu held up his hand and said, 'Please tell me the amount. This is no time for haggling.'

Derek said, '$19,000. You can make out the cheque to me, and I will make sure that everyone gets paid.'

Akinobu quickly wrote the amount down and handed Derek the cheque.

There was nothing else to do but shake hands and say goodbye.

Derek shook Akinobu's hand, and, on an impulse, he hugged him. Akinobu was amazed to see such an obvious act of friendship that he was a bit taken aback.

When Derek let him go, he said, 'Thank you, my friend. We all give thanks to you and your friends.'

Derek shook the remaining Jap's hands, and they left for the airport.

Billy Boy's funeral was a big one. Almost everyone within fifty miles of Eden came. Teddy and Dean were standing at the back of the church when four Japanese walked in. They were dressed in expensive tailor-made suits that fitted them snugly— silk shirts and black leather handmade shoes. They walked up to the coffin and bowed deeply before walking back to the rear of the church and waiting for the funeral service to begin.

After the service, Teddy walked up to Chikara and shook his hand. Chikara didn't introduce the other Japanese men. They were all quite tall and extremely well-built. They looked like bodyguards, Teddy thought.

'We are going back to the Australasia Hotel in Eden for a bit of a talk about Billy's life. Would you like to come?' Teddy asked.

Chikara answered, 'We will come, but only for a short time as we have to get back to Melbourne.'

When Teddy and Dean entered the lounge bar, the party was in full swing. People were already drunk or getting there fast.

Teddy walked up the bar and put 1,000 dollars down and said to the friendly barmaid.

'Let's have a drink on good old Billy Boy.'

She smiled sweetly and said, 'You've got a good heart.'

Teddy just smiled.

Chikara and his crew walked into the room, and the noise quietened down a bit.

Unfazed Chikara walked up to the barmaid and gave her a roll of 100-dollar bills. She thanked him and put them in the jar that was for drinks for Billy's friends.

Chikara then walked across to where Olivia was standing and said, 'Hello again, we are saddened by your loss. Your father was a man of principle and great courage. Please accept this as a token of our respect.'

He took a large sealed envelope out of his inner jacket pocket and offered it to Olivia.

Chikara went on to say, 'If you are ever in need of anything, don't hesitate to contact me.'

He bowed deeply and turned on his heel. As one, the four men walked out, got into their Bentley, and drove off.

Teddy walked over to Olivia and said, 'Pretty strange dude that one.'

'He gave me an envelope,' she said as she opened it and saw it was full of money and also a photograph of a young Japanese man dressed in his military uniform.

'He must have been the two brothers' father, poor bastard,' Teddy commented.

Teddy and Dean made their way back to Melbourne the next day. They were pretty quiet as they had really sent Billy off in such a great manner.

They drove past the Billabong Roadhouse and decided to keep going as they wanted to make up some time.

Barry steamed through the heads and headed for the St Kilda marina. Soon they were tied up, and the boys got all their gear together and left the boat.

Hilda and Barry were alone, and Barry started to clean up a bit.

Hilda said, 'I'll do that when you get off. It will give me something to do.'

Barry looked at Hilda and said, 'I don't want to get off. I don't want to leave you here on your own. Please come back home with me. I won't be able to just go home and sit there on my own. There are plenty of bedrooms. You will have your own space, and I won't crowd you.'

Barry had such a pleading look on his face that Hilda agreed to go back to Barry's place and give him some company.

Together they walked off the boat and down the wharf.

The Chase

*T*he human brain is unique in the fact that it doesn't seem to remember pain, or at least, as time passes, the pain you remember is not as severe.

Detective Jack Andrews and his friend Karl, also a detective, were sitting in an unmarked police car. They were still getting over the sound flogging they had received at the hands of Teddy and Dean at the Billabong Roadhouse a couple of weeks before when they had attempted to drag Jack's wife out.

They blamed each other for the fact that they received a flogging and had been locked up in the cool room for a few hours while Hilda and the two men escaped.

Jack was sure that he could have taken out Dean, and if Teddy hadn't thrown the hot coffee into Karl's face, then there would have been a whole different ending.

Karl reckoned if Jack had come to his defence when he was blindsided by Teddy, then there wouldn't have been a contest. There was no way two experienced detectives would have been overpowered by a couple of hillbillies.

Testosterone-filled confidence soared in the car as they planned a way to even up on the two strangers. It was the start of their shift, and they were looking for a young prostitute to have a happy start with.

✧ ✧ ✧ ✧

Hilda, Jack's long-suffering wife, had been at Barry's federation-style weatherboard house in Port Melbourne for a couple of weeks, and things were going really well for her.

She had her own room, a sunny north-facing bedroom. It had an open fireplace and room for a chair to watch the TV, but she found herself spending most of her time out in the good room, sitting with Barry, surrounded by old furniture and paintings, and watching TV and enjoying his company.

It was sad, but Barry still had all his wife's clothes and stuff all through the house.

Hilda had started to clean up the place but was met with a bit of resistance when it came to shifting his deceased wife's stuff. So she went easy on that front, but at the end of the two weeks, the house was sparkling clean. All the curtains were washed, and everything was shipshape.

Barry appreciated all that Hilda had done, but he was frightened that once Hilda had finished cleaning up the house, she might think that her job was done and she would leave. Barry was really happy to have someone in the house with him, but he knew that a young woman as pretty as Hilda would soon get bored around an old fart like him. So he strove to think of ways that he could keep her around.

He met Teddy in the beer garden of his favourite hotel in Port Melbourne and bought the subject up with him. Teddy understood his old friend's dilemma and suggested that Barry offer Hilda the deckhand's job that Des usually took on.

Barry said, 'I haven't seen Des since we went and found that Japanese submarine. He normally comes around for a beer and a bit of a chat. Maybe he feels like I left him out and he's a bit dirty on me.'

Teddy pondered the idea and said, 'Mate, you two have been friends for years, longer than most. I wouldn't worry. Maybe he's a bit crook. Give him a ring and see what he's up to.'

Barry agreed and decided to ring Des when he got home.

Meanwhile, Des was feeling down, really down. He couldn't believe that he had rung the fisheries and dobbed his best mate in. How the fuck could he have done such a low thing? What the fuck possessed him to pull a stunt like that? It was the piss, the beers, and those two low-life scum who had come up with the idea in the first place. Yes, it was their fault, all their fault. He would catch up with them and sort the pricks out.

The two detectives, Jack and Karl, hadn't been idle in their quest to find out about the two men who had belted them so soundly. They had spoken to the proprietor of the Billabong Roadhouse and learnt the two men had been there before and, in fact, stopped there on a regular basis to have a meal on their way back to Melbourne.

They also learnt that there were more than the two of them and that sometimes they were towing an abalone boat.

Dan, the proprietor, had been very helpful to the detectives as he felt that Hilda had let him down. Now he was without a night short-order cook. Dan was the sort of bloke who wanted to be as much help as he could to the two detectives.

In due course, they found out that the pair of hillbillies were in fact abalone divers. Not only that but they were also illegal abalone divers. Things were looking up for the two detectives.

They put two and two together and decided to get in contact with the Department of Fisheries. Soon they were on the phone to Senior Inspector Wallace P. Trotter.

As luck would have it, Fisheries Inspector Trotter was more than willing to tell all that he knew. He named the four divers and gave the detectives their home addresses. He also went on to say that he was on the verge of arresting them for taking abalone without the right licences. Piggy was in full flight, detective Jack had to slow him down as he was talking too fast to keep up with.

Piggy felt good; no, he felt better than good. He felt on top of the world. It looked as if he was going to join forces with Victoria's finest. How sweet it was! He was going to have all that could be summoned behind him next time he and Teddy clashed.

The two detectives sat and waited down the street from Dean's house. They saw Leckie come back from university and unlock the door, and later on, they saw Dean drive down the street, park his car, and go inside. They looked at each other and agreed that he was one of the pair they had their run-in with. They both smiled and decided to check out where Teddy was living.

The next morning, they watched as Teddy's partner Rita walked down to the corner and got on a bus to head to work. They waited until Teddy drove out, and they matched him as the other one of the duo who had belted them.

So they had them worked out. They would go and have a look on the police computer and see what was there on the pair.

They wasted a fair bit of time, looking up the evil duo. At the same time, they also looked up Tom and Curly, only to find that the four were all cleanskins. There was nothing on them at all; it seemed as if they were perfect citizens.

This made the pair of detectives step back and think. *If they had a crime file, then it would have been easier to act on them. They could have said that they were following up on them for some reason. That would have given them permission to pursue them on the computer, but as it stood, they didn't have a reason to follow up on them.*

The two detectives decided to see where the other divers lived and spent the rest of the day looking to identify them.

Believe it or not, the underworld and the police are closely connected. Whenever someone in the police force starts to take a particular interest in a person or a group, other members will soon find out. From there, it goes from mouth to mouth, and soon it is common knowledge. Every police station has its leaks.

Professional criminals all have some sort of link to information from the police force. It's one of those things that just happens.

A policeman might be at the Saturday Oz Kick with his son, and a known criminal might also be there with his son. The two start talking, and the criminal will groom the police force member. After a while, the criminal will take advantage of a situation. Then in some way, he will be able to do the member of the police force a favour—maybe grand final tickets, maybe a dozen bottles of the member's favourite Scotch whisky, or maybe introduce them to someone who can be of assistance to them somehow. Just as friend to friend. It can also take the part of a weekend barbecue at the criminal's house with his family. Soon the member of the police force feels that the friendship is solid, and they become firm friends. Both criminals and police know what is going on.

Such was the case with Ronny, Teddy's next-door neighbour. Ronny had worked on the docks all his life and had made a lot of acquaintances in the police force. One of them mentioned to Ronny that a couple of detectives had, had a run-in with some abalone divers. They had got a bit roughed up, to say the least, and one of the main offenders was his next-door neighbour.

Ronny was all ears. He listened eagerly when the officer went on to say that the two detectives were pulling out all stops to even up with the two divers.

Ronny knew that Teddy and his gang were poachers, and of course Teddy made a point to drop in some abalone and crayfish to Ronny on a regular basis.

So when Teddy arrived home on the evening when Ronny had learnt that there was an interest in him, Ronny made it his business to be there to talk to Teddy.

'Hullo, mate,' Ronny said to Teddy. 'What have you been up to? My mail is that you've been belting up coppers, or should I say detectives?'

Teddy smiled and said, 'Ronny mate, do I look like the sort of bloke who would do any harm to our boys in blue?'

Ronny looked at the big fellow and said, 'It must be a vicious rumour that's circulating amongst some of my dear friends in the police force.'

Teddy laughed and said to Ronny, 'Give me the mail, mate.'

Ronny came close and started to talk out the side of his mouth; his lips hardly moved. 'Well, Teddy, it's like this. This mate of mine who's been around the coppers forever reckons that you and a mate of yours were in a roadhouse when the detective went there to grab his missus. She didn't want to go with them, and you and one of your mates stepped in and belted the living daylights out of them. These two detectives are really dirty on you and are after you at full speed ahead.'

Teddy was silent for a moment and said to Ronny, 'Thanks for the warning, mate. I'll let the boys know and see just what we are going to do about the situation.'

With that, Ronny nodded his head and walked away.

Teddy said after him, 'I'll drop you off a couple of crayfish next trip.'

Ronny didn't look back as he walked away. But he waved his hand in the air as a way of acknowledging what Teddy had said.

Teddy started to think that if these detectives were after him, then they all could be in a bit of trouble. The last thing that all the boys needed was special attention by the police. If they realised that they were abalone poachers, then the police would have been in touch with the fisheries and Piggy would be the first one to tell them all he knew. They would get valuable information from him.

Teddy realised that now was the time to show extreme care.

The boys assembled in Curly's shed and sat down to discuss their problem.

Dean said, 'If they are on to Teddy and me, then we have got to assume that they also know about the rest of us. Hilda will be in real trouble if that crazy detective finds out that she is at Barry's place. We had better give him a ring and let him know that he could be in the firing line.'

All the boys agreed.

Teddy rang Barry and told him what he had learnt about the two detectives from his next-door neighbour.

Barry listened and said, 'It's probably only a matter of time before he realises that Hilda is staying here with me. So forewarned is forearmed. I'll be ready for the bastards when they show up.'

The boys and Teddy knew that Barry wouldn't take a step backwards, but he was one man against two youngish fit detectives, and that was a worry.

Through close investigation, Jack and Karl learnt that the divers were also involved with another fisherman called Barry and that he moored his boat down at the St Kilda Marina. They made their way down there and asked an odd-job man about Barry.

'Slither.' The odd-job man recognised them as coppers and was reluctant to talk to them. But Jack knew how to get around blokes like Slither.

He palmed him $50, and suddenly Slither was all talk. He told the two detectives everything that he knew about Barry, his sometime deckhand Des, and the new woman who Barry had taken on board. Jack felt his pulse quicken. He showed Slither a photograph of Hilda, and Slither immediately identified her as the woman who Barry had taken on board.

Jack and Karl were all ears. They looked at each other and smiled. They asked where Barry lived, but Slither didn't know. But he did say that Des drank at a local pub and that he probably would be there sometime that day.

The two detectives made their way towards the hotel.

Des was on his way to the hotel. He didn't know what to do about his despicable act of dobbing in his best mate. There must be some way he could get around it and make things up to his mate Barry.

Silence descended on the bar when the two detectives walked in. You could feel the hostility as Jack and Karl pushed open the door and entered the room. They looked around, and all they saw were hostile faces. The men who were in the barroom were all fishermen and tradies; none of them had a soft spot for the police or, as they were labelled by some, the filth.

Jack walked up to the barman, a balding, sweating, flush-faced veteran of years of alcohol abuse.

'Christ Almighty, it's dark in here,' he said.

The barman grunted.

'Give us a couple of sevens. Thanks, mate,' Jack asked loudly.

The barman looked back and muttered, 'I'm not your fucken mate.'

Jack just looked at him.

He leant over the bar and whispered quietly, 'You fucken moron. How would you like a police divvy van parked outside in your car park for a fucken month or more? You would have fucked all drinkers after that.'

The barman realised that the two police had the upper hand.

Jack smiled and said, 'That's better. That's a better attitude. Now we are going to get along just fine. Where's Des?'

The barman asked, 'Des who? I don't know any Des.' And he slid across two seven-ounce glasses of beer. Jack smiled and said, 'He's Barry's deckhand, or should I say Barry's ex-deckhand since Barry has got a new female one.'

The barman shook his head and said, 'I don't know about anything like that. I just pull the beers.'

Then the barman said quietly, 'Des will be here any time. When he comes in, I'll give you a nod. Just go down and sit at a table, and as soon as he comes in, I'll let you know.'

Jack and Karl sat at a table and slowly sipped their drinks. The other customers started to talk to each other again, and the pair was soon forgotten.

Des walked in and went up to the bar.

The barman slowly reached up with his right hand and slowly pulled down on his left shirt collar. This is a sign that there is danger looming and for the recipient of the gesture to take great care.

The barman got Des a pot and slightly nodded to the two detectives.

Jack and Karl made their way over to Des and sat either side of him at the bar.

'Gidday, Des,' Jack said with a bit of a smile. 'We need to have a bit of a word with you.'

'What the fuck about?' Des asked.

'Well, it's about your mate Barry and his new deckhand, the female,' Jack said with an oily smile.

'I don't know fuck all about any new deckhand. I only do the odd day away with Barry, and I hardly ever see the bloke,' Des answered.

'Well, we know that you did a trip over to the islands in Bass Strait with him and that whenever he does a trip, you go with him and his team of divers, Ted, Tom, Dean, and Curly.'

Des was gutted; he asked, 'Where did you find all this out?'

Jack smiled an evil smile and said, 'Some low dog phoned up the fisheries and told them everything because he got left out of their last trip. I wonder who would have done such an evil thing as that.'

Des was on the ropes. He didn't know just how much this detective knew or how much he was making up.

He regretted making that phone call to the fisheries even more. If only those two low dogs hadn't talked him into making that call. Teddy wouldn't be happy finding out that the fisheries and the police were hot on his heels; things were starting to hot up.

Des was scared and decided that he had better right the wrongs and catch up with Barry and Teddy.

He said to the two detectives, 'I don't know fuck all about what Barry is up to. He hardly ever talks to me. Every now and then, we go for a run in his boat, just to blow the cobwebs out, but that's all. Barry doesn't do any dodgy stuff.'

Jack said to Des, 'Mate, I know a lot more than I'm letting on about those abalone poachers, and I reckon that you are up to your fucking neck in it. But don't worry, we won't rest until you and your mates are getting your arse fucked in some low prison block.'

Des downed his beer and walked out.

Barry rang Des at home that night and asked if he was feeling OK.

Des replied, 'Yes, mate, I'm pretty good. I'm just getting older and grumpier. What about we meet up with Teddy and have a beer tomorrow arvo?'

Barry was happy that they were going to meet up as he missed his long-standing mate, so they arranged to meet up, and Barry hung up.

The next afternoon saw the three men sitting in the beer garden, talking quietly among themselves. Des told the two men about the questioning that the two detectives had given him. He said that they knew all their names and about the trip over in Bass Strait.

Teddy took stock of the situation.

He said, 'Well, it had to happen. Someone had to open their mouth and say something that the fisheries got onto. I suppose that belting those two detectives wasn't the smartest thing to do, but we had no choice. If we hadn't stepped in, they may have beaten Hilda to death.'

Barry said, not unkindly, 'I bet it was that bastard Slither. He would sell his own mother out for a couple of pots. If those coppers showed him a 20-dollar note, he would tell them all he knew. Poor bastard, the piss has really gotten a hold of him.'

Des felt a great weight lifted off his chest. Maybe, he thought, there was a way out for him here.

Barry said to Des, 'Mate, Hilda has spent a bit of time on the boat. She had nowhere to go after Teddy and Dean saved her from those two detectives, so she camped on the boat. She did such a good job of cleaning up the boat that I decided to ask her to stay at home with me and do a bit of cleaning up there. It gets a bit messy now that I'm on my own. I'm not rooting her or anything. She is just nice to have around.'

Des felt something shift in his stomach. He silently cursed himself for being such a fool and talking to the fisheries. Now his best mate was in the shit deeply.

Teddy, as always, was quite happy.

He said confidently, 'Let's not slash our wrists. This isn't the first time that we have been in the spotlight. In fact, we have always been under the hammer. We will just continue to do what we do best, and that is to continue to poach abalone. In fact, we may even go harder than before, just to keep everyone's minds off the possibility of the police and the fisheries really having a go at us.'

Barry and Des felt relieved that Teddy was taking such a defiant stand about the whole issue. Des, in particular, felt relieved that Teddy and Barry didn't put him in line for ringing the fisheries. Now there's a subject that Des hoped would never surface.

Dean was a changed man. He hadn't lost a cent betting since he had come back from his last trip. In fact, he didn't feel like sitting in a smoke-filled room and betting against Hamm Nugent and the likes.

Leckie had taken control of the finances, and she was more than happy. She had decided to send over $1,000 a month to her parents. This would ensure that they could buy enough food and even have some left over to maybe start one of her brothers in a small business. Everything was going along fine.

Tiny, the huge Samoan security bouncer, couldn't get Leckie out of his head. He wondered how she was. Was Dean looking after her? Was she happy? Could he ever see her again?

His partner in the security business, Jesse, laughed to himself when he saw his mate in such a position.

What a dickhead, Jesse thought. *How could anyone fall in love with a hooker?*

To Jesse, it just didn't make sense.

'Why don't we call in and see how she is going?' Jesse asked. 'You know where she lives. Why don't we just drop around and see if she is all right. We can say that you were worried about her after Dean and his gang dropped into the brothel and grabbed her.'

Tiny thought that that would be a good idea, but he wouldn't see her at Dean's place.

He would speak to her at the university she went to. They would be on even ground there. He would just bump accidentally into her, say hullo, and ask her if she was all right.

Yes, that was the plan.

Tiny started to work out how he was going to make the chance encounter happen.

Teddy and Barry started to work out a plan of attack or defence, depending on how it went. They knew that it wouldn't be long before the detectives got onto the fact that Barry and Hilda were living together. They both expected the detectives to make a move; the problem was how they could fight back.

It's suicide to fight a policeman as if that happens, the sky will fall on you. So they had to come up with a plan to keep Hilda safe and keep them all out of jail or, worse, keep them away from getting themselves killed. Both men realised that they were in danger.

Detective Jack Andrews spoke to his partner Karl, 'Mate, we are close to squaring up with those two dickheads who jumped us at that roadhouse. I reckon that we should just shoot the pricks. Why don't we arrest them and make it look like a random stop? Then they pull out a gun, and we have to defend ourselves. We can bring a throw-down and say that they were going to shoot us with it and that we had to fire in self-defence.'

A throw-down is a gun, usually a sawn-off shotgun or small calibre rifle, that the police have had for some time. They may have found it in a raid and failed to register it in the findings, or they may have gotten it off a friend or someone who just handed it in. When there is a shooting of a person, the police throw the gun down at the scene, after wrapping the victim's hands around it to make sure that their fingerprints are on it. They say that the victim was about to shoot them. So all they could do was shoot first. It's the oldest trick in the book, and it works.

In reality, most of the gangsters these days are so vain that they would consider it an insult to carry such a low-class gun. They would prefer to be seen with a nickel-plated .32 semi-automatic handgun, rather than something as brutal as a sawn-off, double-barrelled shotgun.

The two detectives schemed on.

Tiny, the Samoan security bouncer, walked the grounds of the university campus, and, sure enough, he bumped into Leckie. It had taken him hours to set up the surprise meeting.

'Hullo, Leckie,' Tiny said happily. 'I didn't know that you attended this university. I just walked my sister here as she has just started a course.'

The truth of the matter was Tiny's sister was back in Samoa in the village that they were both born in and could hardly read or write.

Leckie looked a bit concerned at Tiny's sudden appearance.

She smiled nervously and answered timidly, 'Hullo, Tiny, it's nice to see you. How have you been?'

Tiny smiled and said, 'Oh, I'm well. I was wondering how you were getting along. Are you well?'

Leckie answered, 'Yes, thanks, I'm really good. Dean and I are very happy. Thank you.'

Tiny said, 'I realise that Dean and I didn't get off to a good a start, but I'm quite worried about how Dean is treating you.'

Leckie answered firmly, 'There is nothing for you to worry about. Dean is a wonderful man, and he looks after me very well. I am very happy with the situation that I'm in. But thanks for thinking of me. I must go as I have a lecture to attend, and it starts in a couple of minutes.'

With that, Leckie started to walk away.

Tiny asked, 'Perhaps we could get a cup of coffee one day if I bump into you again.'

Leckie was non-committal and said, 'Let's see what happens.'

Then she walked away.

Tiny considered his options. There didn't seem to be any way he could get to her, but who knows, maybe one time she would drop her guard. He wouldn't give up; he would make sure that he was available.

Teddy decided that they should have a dive in the bay. It would have to be at night so there weren't any prying eyes about. There was a reef off Altona, a beachside suburb, which was famous because one of the former prime ministers lived there before she moved into the Lodge.

Teddy rang Tony and told him what he had in mind. He said that he would contact the boys and get back to him when he had it all set up.

Teddy started to ring around, and all the boys were happy to be getting back into the water. He arranged for them all to meet at a boat ramp on the other side of the bay.

Tony towed the boat to the ramp. All the boys climbed aboard, and Tony backed the Shark Cat into the water. Teddy started the motors, and they ticked over quietly. He backed the boat off the trailer, and they headed out into Port Phillip Bay.

It was wonderful to be at sea in the darkness. The salty, chilled wind whistled past, and all the boys were ready for the night's work.

Dean wasn't happy to be diving at night, but he was a lot happier to be diving in the bay than out in the middle of Bass Strait. He hoped that the water was going to be clear.

Curly was happy to be working, and Tom was the same. They knew that tonight would be a short night and that they would be back before dawn. So it was, be quick into the water, fill as many net bags as possible, don't worry about size, and get the heck out of the place.

They would work the same way as before: Dean and Curly would work together on a T-piece, and Tom would stockpile the abalone. At the end of the night, they would all shuck them out, bag them up into the clear plastic bags, and tie the ends up with wire twists.

Derek, the processor, had been notified and was ready to accept the shucked abalone when Tony dropped it in. Tony would then drop off the van, head down with the trailer to whatever boat ramp Teddy had brought the Shark Cat into, then take the Shark Cat back to his place, wash it out, and clean it up so it would be ready for the next trip.

Teddy checked the GPS and depth sounder, and when they were over the shallow reef, the boys entered the water and swam down. When they were close to the bottom, they switched on the torches that were strapped to their heads and started to look for abalone.

Abalone are a nocturnal creature, a bit like a snail. They will sit calmly in among the rocks and weed throughout the light hours, and when it gets dark, they start to travel about like a common garden snail. They travel up the weeds and generally move around.

It is illegal to dive for abalone at night, but that doesn't stop the poachers.

Teddy was careful not to have any lights on, and it was almost impossible to see the Shark Cat at night. The compressors were muffled as sound travels further over water at night. Teddy tried to keep as quiet as possible.

Tom wasn't having any trouble keeping up with the two other divers. He was filling his net bag and 'running the rabbit' back and forth to the stockpile with all their full net bags. All was going well. Tom had attached a small light onto one of the stockpile net bags to provide some guidance for him in the darkness.

As they were poaching, the boys grabbed any sized abalone, and soon they had all their net bags full, and Tom had taken them away to the stockpile. So after a couple of hours, they turned off their torches and came to the surface for a spell. They were all feeling good, and there were plenty of abalone at the bottom ready to be picked up and shucked out.

'How many bags are there at the bottom?' Teddy asked.

Tom thought for a moment and said, 'Six, I reckon.'

Teddy thought for a while and said, 'That's about $5,000 worth. Let's get a few more, and then we can call it a night. What do you reckon?'

As time was running out, the divers headed back into the water, and after they got a couple of more bags, they started for the surface. Tom and Curly went down and brought the stockpiled abalone up to the boat. Dean and Teddy dragged them aboard. Then they all commenced shucking them out. Soon all the abalone was bagged up. The boys got out of their wetsuits, and Teddy headed for a jetty that the fishermen used during the day.

Tony was waiting for them. Teddy saw the torch light that Tony shone out towards them and motored towards it. It only took them a few minutes to load Tony's van up, and he was off to the processor. Curly went with him to give Derek a hand to weigh the abalone up. So Tony could go and pick up the boys at another boat ramp.

Teddy and the two remaining divers casually motored over to the other boat ramp and waited until Tony arrived with the trailer for the Shark Cat.

Tony and Curly dropped off the abalone at Derek's factory, and Tony headed off to pick up the boys. Curly and Derek weighed the abalone meat. There was $7,200 worth. They both agreed that the count was right, and Curly rang through the weight to Teddy, who agreed that it was about what he had thought.

Teddy agreed to get the money off Derek after he had been to his bank the next day.

Curly got a taxi home, and Derek drove back to his place and went to bed.

Teddy hit the sack just as the sun was starting to rise. He fell almost instantly asleep.

Tom silently let himself inside his house, had a shower, and snuggled up to Sandy.

Dean got home, and Leckie was still awake when she heard Dean's key at the front door. Leckie asked Dean if he would like her to make him some breakfast after he had a shower.

Dean laughed and said, 'Leckie, I could eat a horse, hash browns, bacon, and eggs, if you don't mind. And about a gallon of strong coffee.'

Coffee didn't keep Dean awake.

Leckie got busy with the breakfast while Dean sang in the shower.

Tiny, the monster islander, waited for Hamm Nugent to arrive at the brothel that he and Jesse were guarding.

When Hamm arrived, Tiny said quietly, 'I saw Leckie this morning at the university that she attends. She is well and seems happy with her present situation. I don't think that she will be back here to work ever again.'

Hamm looked up at the big man and said, 'Time will tell. I have seen plenty of good relationships go bad. She knows that we will welcome her back if she finds herself in trouble.'

Tiny nodded his huge head and thought, *I don't think that she will be back.*

Teddy walked into Derek's factory and said with a smile, 'How did we end up?'

Derek laughed and said, 'You didn't do as well as normal, but then again, you were only away for a couple of hours.'

'A little longer than that,' Teddy replied.

Derek smiled and gave Teddy a bag with some money in it.

'I weighed in $7,200 worth of abalone meat. You didn't want any for Henry's restaurant?'

'No, mate, I'll give Henry a ring and sort him out next trip. I was amazed just how many abalone there were out on that reef off Altona. I dived there a couple of years ago, and it has really made a strong comeback.'

They shook hands, and Teddy walked out of Derek's factory.

The two detectives watched as Teddy walked out to his car and drove away. They noticed that Teddy was carrying a plastic Target bag, and they assumed that that was the pay-off for some abalone as this was a seafood-processing plant.

'There's the processor,' Jack said with confidence; his partner in crime agreed.

Jack continued, 'We should notify the fisheries and let them in on our little secret. We have, in a couple of weeks, discovered where the abalone gets processed. That's more than the fisheries have done in a year.'

Both the detectives shook their heads and laughed.

Teddy headed back to Curly's shed at his mother's property and walked in. All the boys were there, and they all had beers in their hands.

'How did it go?' asked Tom.

Teddy smiled and said, 'Like clockwork. Smooth as silk.'

He emptied the Target bag out onto the pool table and started to divide the money up.

'I'll give Tony $300 and take a $100 out for fuel, which leaves us with $6,800 to be divided into four. That's $1,700 each. Are you all happy with that?'

Everyone agreed that it wasn't a bad day's work, or should they say night's work.

Detective Jack Andrews called Wallace P. Trotter's number and smiled when he recognised Piggy's voice.

'This is Fisheries Inspector Wallace Trotter. How can I help you?'

Jack said, 'Hi, Wallace, it's Detective Jack Andrews here. I've got a bit of information that you might be interested in. It seems by chance my partner and I have stumbled across a processing plant that your band of poachers might be using to process their abalone. We have just seen the ringleader walk out with a Target shopping bag full of what we can only assume is cash. They must have been busy during the night.'

Piggy was flabbergasted. How did those two detectives stumble over what would be the hardest place to find? Could it be true? Could this be the place where Teddy and his team got rid of their abalone?

If it was the place, then all Wallace had to do was wait at the processing plant and arrest whoever brought in the abalone, and then trace it back to Teddy, and he had the bastard. Whoever was in charge of the abalone processing would buckle under the weight of the fine and make it easier for Piggy by rolling over on Teddy. Yes, that was the way it would work. There's no loyalty among the evil doers, none at all.

Piggy had never felt better in his life.

Barry and Hilda decided to go away on Barry's boat. They would stay away for a week or so, out in Bass Strait, and kill some time. It would be good to spend some time together away from the chance of Hilda's detective husband suddenly showing up and causing problems.

They were both relaxed when they made their way down to the marina. On the way, they met Slither, the odd-job man.

Barry asked, 'How are you, mate? There have been a couple of coppers asking questions around the place. Have they seen you?'

Slither looked Barry straight in the eyes and said, 'Barry mate, they were here and questioned me. I didn't tell them a thing. They tried to stand over me, but I was solid. I didn't say a word about you and your mates.'

Barry smiled and said, 'Mate, I know that you are as solid as a rock, and I know that you wouldn't spill your guts even if they offered you money.'

'No way known, mate!' Slither said. 'I wouldn't tell them a thing about your trips over to Tasmania with Teddy and the boys. No, mate, that secret is safe with me. You can trust me with your life.'

Barry laughed and said, 'No worries, mate, we are taking the boat out for a week or so and just having a look around, a bit of time off.'

'Good on you, mate,' Slither said.

He watched as Barry and Hilda untied and steamed off towards the heads.

As soon as they were gone, Slither got onto the public phone and called his new mate, Jack, the detective.

When Jack answered, he said, 'Barry and his new Sheila deckhand have just left the dock and are heading out into Bass Strait. I reckon that they are going to meet up with Teddy and his crew and do some more abalone poaching.'

Jack smiled to himself.

He said to Karl, 'This looks promising. That old fisherman and Hilda have just left the marina and are heading out into Bass Strait. The odd-job man reckons that they are going to do a bit of poaching with that Teddy. We should let the fisheries know what's going on and give them a bit of a surprise when they get back.'

Barry said to Hilda, 'You can't help but feel sorry for that Slither. The piss has really gotten hold of him. He would give up his mother for a slab of beer.'

'Do you think that he would have told my husband anything about me?'

Barry smiled and said, 'Hilda, one thing that I have learnt in my old age is that the people whom you help the most are normally the first ones to turn on you. I reckon that Slither would give anyone up for the price of a drink.'

They steamed out of the heads and headed towards Deal Island in the middle of Bass Strait.

Piggy received the news from the detective and started to make plans.

Teddy and his crew were going on a trip.

Piggy just knew that the bastards were going poaching, and with his new mates' help, Piggy would once again be hot on their trail.

Teddy knew that Barry and Hilda were going on a trip for a week or so, and that gave him a chance to think things out. He was worried that the two detectives would make life tough for Barry and Hilda, so to have them out of the picture was a relief. He spoke to all the boys in Curly's shed, and they discussed what they would do next.

Jack, the detective, was up and running. He knew that if he could get hold of Teddy while he was getting rid of some abalone, then he had him good and proper. He felt his temper grow. When he got hold of that slut of a wife of his, he would really sort her out.

His imagination drifted into a fantasy world of punishment he had in mind for her. He would break her spirit if it was the last thing that he did. He dreamt of strangling her and getting rid of the body. He wouldn't get caught; he was too smart for that. When he thought of all the dumb, lamebrained criminals, walking the street, surely he was too smart to get caught. He would enjoy beating her to within an inch of her life and then snuff it out—that easy. He would be in control right to the very end. He would show the bitch if it was the last thing he did.

Teddy rang Tony and told him about what was going on and how the police were on their tail, as well as the fisheries. He told Tony to make sure that the F100 and the boat and trailer were all completely roadworthy. They didn't want to be stopped on the road for a vehicle check.

Tony laughed and said, 'Mate, does that mean that we are in the spotlight? I didn't think that we were ever out of it.'

'Just be careful,' Teddy warned.

Tiny, the huge security guard was thinking more and more about Leckie. He couldn't get her out of his mind.

He wondered how she was and if she ever thought of him. He would continue to accidentally bump into her at the university and slowly wear her down.

Soon she might think that he would be worthwhile meeting for coffee.

✧ ✧ ✧ ✧

Piggy met with his superiors and outlined a plan. It would be simple. Instead of all the fisheries officers trying to apprehend Teddy and his gang of evil doers when they were at sea, they would simply wait at the processor's place. Then when Teddy and his gang arrived with the abalone, out of nowhere, the fisheries would appear and arrest the whole lot of them—that simple. They had been going about the whole thing the wrong way. It was easy to see their mistakes in hindsight.

Right now, all Piggy had to do was be there when the abalone was being weighed up.

The next day, Piggy was once again undercover, dressed in denim jeans, flannelette checked shirt, and elastic-sided steel-toe work boots. He made his way into the fish and chip shop at the front of Derek's factory.

He said cheerfully to the young girl behind the counter, 'Gidday, love. How are you? I feel like a feed of fish and chips for lunch. I'll have a piece of flake, four dim sims, and a minimum of chips, please.'

The young girl smiled and said, 'No worries, coming up. Would you like a drink with that?'

Piggy smiled and said, 'Ah, yes, love. I'll have a Diet Coke. Thanks.'

He made his way over to the glass-fronted double-door fridge that was stocked with every imaginable soft drink that was available.

'You've got plenty of stock in here,' he said brightly.

The young girl smiled and said, 'The boss always says that if you haven't got it, then you can't sell it.'

'It seems a big factory for just a fish and chip shop,' Piggy said, smiling.

The girl said, 'Derek also buys and exports abalone. He has a lot of friends in the industry. I think that he exports a lot to Japan. In fact, there were some Japanese men over from Japan a couple of weeks ago. They must have come over for a stickybeak at what Derek has here.'

Piggy knew exactly what they were doing over here. But he didn't let on that he had, in fact, bumped into them while they were over a reef where their father had been bombed during World War II in his mini submarine.

That piece of information truly sorted out that Derek and Teddy were in bed together. Piggy was feeling more and more confident that things were falling into place.

The young fish and chip cook asked Piggy, 'Do you work around here? I haven't seen you before, have I? Most of my customers are local. I see them every day or at least a couple of days a week.'

Piggy smiled and said, 'I've just got a start at the panel beaters around the corner, so you will see a bit more of me from now on.'

The young girl reckoned that the fish and chips were cooked.

She spread them out onto some greaseproof paper and asked, 'Would you like some salt on them?'

Piggy agreed hungrily, and she smothered the whole lot in salt before wrapping them up in a parcel and handing them to him. Piggy paid for them and walked outside. He paused to have a look at the factory and saw that it would be easy to keep an eye on it when night-time came. He would position himself out of sight and just see what went on.

Time would tell.

When the lunchtime rush started and the boss from the panel beaters came in for his lunch, the girl behind the counter said brightly, 'I saw your new panel beater earlier on. He came and got his lunch from me. He seems a nice sort of bloke.'

The panel beater said, 'I haven't started anyone lately. I wouldn't mind getting a couple of good blokes, but they are hard to find. If they aren't piss pots, they are druggies. I don't know what the world is coming to.'

The girl behind the counter looked a bit confused and said, 'Funny, I thought that he said that he was a panel beater and that he had just started with you.'

'No, luv, not me. I haven't started anyone lately.'

The young girl went on serving hungry customers and didn't think too much more about the confusion.

Piggy had a good look around the area and sorted out where he would station himself so that he could keep the processing factory in sight and not stand out like a sore thumb. When he found a place he was happy with, he opened his fish and chips and started eating; they were great.

Derek, unaware that he was now under the surveillance of one Wallace (Piggy) Trotter, went about his business. He sensed that the fish and chip shop was going steadily and he was waiting to be called in to lend a hand if the staff wasn't able to cope.

He had the young girl that was full-time, and another older woman came in at the busy times, but Derek enjoyed talking to the customers. He loved being involved.

It really was a lot easier now that he was exporting Teddy's abalone over to his mate in Japan. The money was rolling in.

Derek knew that none of his legal abalone divers would be in for a couple of hours, so there was no panic; he could relax and do a bit of book work.

Murphy, the security guard, was well into his sixties. He had worked most of his life in the security business, and it had treated him well. As a young man, he had worked on the front line at hotels and casinos and everywhere else. Now he looked for a quieter life. He was assigned to work the industrial area, where there was a heap of factories. It was a quiet job, and all you really had to do was just cruise around and make sure that there weren't any dickhead thieves about. You just had to keep your ears and eyes open, and if there was a problem, give the coppers a ring or call for back-up.

He started at 9 p.m. and worked right through to 6 a.m. He took an hour off for a break between 1 a.m. and 2 a.m. and had some sandwiches and a cup of coffee. It was a pretty good job. He didn't drink much—maybe a couple of cans to wind down after he knocked off. Yes, life was good.

He had a soft spot for Derek who would sometimes get a shipment of fish or abalone in late at night.

Derek said that he had a few mates who lived up the coast and that they sometimes got a load to him that arrived late. If they worked and processed the abalone, then Murphy would sometimes call in, and Derek would flash up one of the fish and chip cookers and cook them up a feed.

Derek made sure that he always called in the security guard, and he would have a meal with the workers in the factory.

Murphy was happy as a couple of times, he had been given a crayfish to take home. That used to make his wife happy. Hell's bells, he couldn't afford to buy crayfish; they were almost $100 a kilo. He hoped that there would be a crayfish for him around Christmas time. Yes, Derek was a good bloke, no doubt about that.

When Murphy saw the 4WD parked in an out-of-the-way spot, he realised that someone was on a stake-out. He had often seen the spot and realised that if someone wanted to watch the factory, then that would be the spot to watch it from. The first rule in security was picking the spots where someone would park if they were staking out a place. It might be to rob them or it might be a work care inspector waiting to take a photo of someone who had been claiming for a bad back. They could then get pictures of them working.

He rang in the number plate to his head office to see if it was a stolen vehicle and got the response that it wasn't. So it was someone who had an interest in whatever Derek was doing. He wondered what he should do. The safest was to do nothing and let it all pan out.

A little voice inside his head said, 'What about the crayfish at Xmas?'

If there was a problem and he did stand up and let Derek know that he was under surveillance, then he was sure that Derek would be more than willing to part with a big crayfish. Then just think how happy his wife would be.

He didn't think about it for long. He dialled Derek's number.

When Derek answered, he identified himself, 'Gidday, Derek, it's Murphy, the security guard. Sorry to bother you, but it's come to my attention that there is a 4WD parked where it can watch your factory, and it's very hard for you to spot it. Mate, it might be nothing, but I thought that I would let you know what's going on.'

Derek said, 'Thanks, Murphy. It's always good to know what's going on. Don't let on that you have spotted the watcher. Just let him think that he hasn't been seen, and I'll work out what's going on. And, mate, I'll tell the next lot of divers who come in that you want a couple of crays when they come across some.'

Murphy said, 'Derek, mate, don't be silly. There's no need for that.'

'Leave it to me,' Derek answered and hung up.

Derek rang Teddy and said, 'Mate, what's going on? There's a bloke parked in a 4WD, and he's watching the factory. It could be the fisheries or maybe it's one of those coppers that you bashed the other week. We had better check out just what the fuck is going on.'

Teddy was on the ball. He didn't think that it would be the two coppers. He reckoned that somehow the fisheries had got wind that they were using Derek's processing plant to export their abalone.

Teddy asked, 'Have you got anything going on tonight?'

Derek answered, 'No, mate, everything is cool, and nothing is coming in tonight. But the weather is clearing up, and the divers should get tomorrow in.'

Teddy replied, 'We will let whoever the fuck it is cool his heels for tonight and then we might see what pans out after that. Don't do anything. Just wait.'

Derek disconnected and thought, *Well, I'll stay alert and see what happens.*

All was quiet as Piggy kept the factory in sight. He was a bit hungry and needed a piss, but he didn't want to drive anywhere, so he got out of the 4WD and quietly pissed against the rear wheel.

Time dragged on. He didn't think that he dropped off to sleep but he may have.

Before dawn, a rubbish truck came and picked up a couple of bins, and the clattering surprised him.

When dawn arrived, he drove back to his motel and went to bed.

Derek arrived at his factory at about 7.30 a.m. and unlocked the door of the fish and chip shop. He made his way into the building and turned on the lights. The processing room was clean and dry, so he occupied himself with paperwork. At 8.30 a.m., he heard the young girl come in and start to get the fish and chip shop ready to open.

Derek walked into the front of the shop and said, 'Good morning, Carol. How are you feeling?'

Carol was happy and smiling. 'I'm good, thanks, Derek. How are you going?'

'Never better,' replied Derek. 'We had a good day yesterday. The takings were a bit up.'

'Yes, we had a couple of new customers. One bloke came in and said that he had just started at the panel beaters. But when I asked the boss, he said that he hadn't put any new people on. Funny that.'

Derek asked, 'What did the new bloke look like?'

Carol replied, 'I didn't take that much notice to be truthful. He was about medium height, a bit overweight, and he didn't look like a panel beater, more like an office worker.'

Derek was suddenly interested.

'What time did he come in?' he asked.

Carol thought for a moment and said, 'Just before the lunchtime rush, about 11.30 a.m., I reckon.'

Derek asked casually, 'Did he ask any questions about me or the factory?'

Carol said, 'Yes, he sure did. He commented that it was a big factory for a fish and chip shop. I told him that we weren't just a fish and chip shop, that we also exported abalone overseas to Japan, and that a few weeks ago, some Japanese came over to have a look at our operation.'

Derek smiled at her and said, 'That would have shut him up a bit. He thought that he was in a fish and chippery and there he was in an export factory.'

Carol kept busy with what she was doing. Derek went to check the hard drive on his security unit and had a look at the mysterious newly employed panel beater whom no one had ever heard of.

Derek saw Piggy Trotter walk in through the front doors and have a look around. He saw Piggy talk to Carol as she prepared his fish and chips, pay for them, and then head back out the front door.

He rang Teddy and said, 'Mate, I've got your sworn enemy come in and buy some fish and chips from us yesterday, one Piggy Trotter, senior officer of the Victorian Fisheries. He must have come in for a look around. He cased the joint, and Carol told him how we weren't just a fish and chip shop and that we also exported abalone to Japan.'

Teddy received the news and said, 'Thank Christ, we didn't lob at your joint last night with a load of abalone and walk straight into Piggy and a band of police and fisheries officers.'

Derek laughed and said, 'That would have taken a bit of explaining.'

Teddy agreed, 'We need to do a bit of planning for our next trip. I wonder how long Piggy is going to lie in wait for us.'

'That is the sixty-million-dollar question,' Derek agreed. 'I've got a couple of mates who own big freezers. One is a butcher, and the other one is the bloke who does my potato chips. I suppose that I could box up the abalone and get them frozen elsewhere. That would take a lot of pressure off the factory.'

Teddy agreed, 'Yes, mate, the fisheries are more concerned with you than us. They reckon that if they catch you with a load of illegal abalone, then you would be prepared to put us in rather than doing a stretch in jail.'

'That won't happen,' Derek assured Teddy.

'Let's hope not,' Teddy laughed.

Piggy was talking to a number of assembled fisheries officers, and he was laying out a plan. He had told them how he had spent the night on a stake-out and wasn't seen by anyone. It was all a matter of concealing your stake-out vehicle in a spot that didn't stand out. Somewhere you could spend the night completely unobserved and watch whatever went on. Then perhaps when the evil doers arrived and started unloading the abalone, you could take some photos that could be used in evidence against them.

Piggy made it sound easy.

Leckie mentioned to Dean about how she had bumped into Tiny, the security guard, at the university and how Tiny had been walking his sister to her classes.

Dean asked if Leckie had seen Tiny's sister, and when Leckie said that she hadn't, Dean immediately assumed that Tiny was on the make and it was no coincidence that she had bumped into him.

So Dean came up with a plan. He would lie in wait for the black bastard and belt the living daylights out of him. Then hopefully Tiny would take that as a warning that he should stay away from Leckie or Dean would properly fuck him up.

He realised that Tiny would be hard to scare, so he planned to take something along with him to make sure that the warning was heeded.

Dean started to plan the meeting. He looked at brass knuckles, a baseball bat, and even a revolver but settled on a sports bag with his baseball bat.

He placed it in the car and gave Leckie a ride to the university. He dropped her off at the classroom where her first lecture was being held and started to look for Tiny. He wasn't hard to spot.

Dean pulled up his hoodie; it almost concealed his face. He walked up behind Tiny, and when he had caught up with him, he took the bat out of his bag and swung it across Tiny's back. The impact of the bat almost knocked Tiny out. His breath rushed out of his lungs, and he gasped for air. He fell to his knees and put a hand onto the ground to stop himself falling head first into the footpath.

In a loud voice, Dean said, 'Bump into Leckie again and I'll fucking well kill you, you coconut head. I know what you are up to, you bastard. Keep the fuck away from her.'

Tiny tried to get to his feet.

He gasped, 'Hey, bro, I didn't mean any harm. I'm just being friendly.'

Dean said through gritted teeth, 'So am I. If I was serious, I would have killed you. Stay the fuck away from Leckie.'

Once again, Dean hit him over the back, and this time, Tiny collapsed onto the footpath, totally spent.

Dean drew back the bat to hit him again.

But a voice said, 'If you keep hitting him like that, you will kill him, and then you will really be in the shit.'

Glancing up he saw a young man looking at him. He was a student and had a wispy beard that looked as if the wind would blow it off.

The young man said, 'Calm down, I don't know what this bloke's done to you, but you killing him won't help your cause. You will end up getting life. You being locked up won't help anyone, especially this Leckie, whoever she may be.'

Dean cooled off. The mention of Leckie's name was enough to bring him back to the real world.

'Thanks,' he muttered and walked back to his car.

He looked back and saw that a crowd had gathered around the fallen security man.

Dean got in and drove away.

It was in the afternoon when Derek saw an abalone boat arrive at the side door of his factory.

He walked out, grinned, and said to the older diver, 'Hullo, mate, how did you go?'

'Not too bad,' the older man said. 'I reckon that I've got about 300 kilos of shell weight here. Not too bad! A day's work for an old horse like myself.'

'No worries, we'll get them weighed up and see what's there,' Derek said.

He began weighing up the abalone in the wire crates, and soon they had the correct weight. Derek wrote out a cheque to the diver, and, after a can of coke, the diver and his deckhand drove away.

Then Derek moved the abalone into the cool room for them to be processed the next morning when the abalone shuckers came in.

He knew that there would be more divers on the way as the weather was fine and the swell was down.

Piggy watched from his vantage point. He noted the car and boat registration numbers. They tied in with a legal diver, so that wasn't anything to do with Teddy and his gang.

Soon Piggy saw another abalone boat being towed into Derek's factory yard. He watched as Derek welcomed the diver inside, and as they spoke to each other, the diver's deckhand started to unload his abalone into wire crates and weigh them up. Piggy saw Derek write out a cheque and give it to the diver. The diver and his deckhand got into their 4WD and headed off.

More divers and their boats came in to unload their abalone. But there was no sighting of Teddy and any of his crew.

Piggy settled in for a long night.

Tiny rang Jesse, his security co-worker at the brothel, and told him he wasn't able to work that night as he wasn't feeling very well. Jesse asked a few questions, and Tiny admitted that Dean had bushwhacked him at the university campus and belted him with a baseball bat.

Jesse was a bit stunned as he realised that Tiny was a bit hard to get over. He felt a little bit of respect for Dean.

He said to Tiny, 'Mate, have a couple of days off, and when you're back on your feet, we might pay this Dean a visit and sort the bastard out.'

Tiny disconnected and thought, *Yes, we might just do that. This time, I'll be a bit more prepared.* He lay back in bed. *Boy, oh, boy, my back hurts,* he thought.

Detectives Jack Andrews and Karl hadn't been sitting on their hands. They had alerted Piggy Trotter that Barry and Hilda had left port and would more than likely run into Teddy and his crew and get some illegal abalone.

They had also been around Barry's house, had a look inside, and worked out that Hilda was living there. When they had got inside Barry's house, they could see what was going on.

Karl suggested that they trash the joint.

But Jack said, 'We don't want them to be aware that we know where they are. So we won't disturb anything. We can keep an eye on them without them knowing.'

It was a matter of wait and see.

Meanwhile, Teddy and Dean had spoken about Dean's run-in with Tiny. Teddy was disappointed that Dean had acted on his own.

He looked at Dean and said, 'Mate, we all stick together. When one of us is in trouble, then we all are in trouble. If you go running off on your own and something happens, then we are not there to back you up.'

Dean agreed and said, 'Yes, mate. I know, but it all happened a bit fast. I just acted on the spur of the moment.'

Teddy thought for a moment and said, 'There is a possibility that Tiny and his mates might try to square up. They know where you live. All they have to do is arrive one night, and you're in a bit of trouble, mate.'

Back at Derek's factory, under the surveillance of Piggy, business was going on as usual. Derek was weighing in abalone from the legal divers, and there wasn't a thing that Piggy could do about it.

The evening wore on, and as darkness descended, Piggy started to eat his evening meal.

After 9 p.m., Murphy, the security guard, clocked on and drove around and saw the 4WD was still there. He thought that it had probably just got there; he wasn't aware that Piggy had been there most of the day.

Murphy rang Derek's number and let him know that he was still under surveillance.

Derek laughed and said, 'Well, it will be a long night for the fisheries inspector. Let's hope that he's comfortable.'

The next morning, Derek opened up the factory at 7 a.m. The abalone shuckers came in and started to shuck out the abalone; there was about a tonne. When they were finished, Derek had about 300 kg of meat. This was boxed up into 10-kg shatter-pack boxes. This meant that between every layer of abalone, there was a thin layer of plastic. So if someone wanted just a couple of abalone, then all they had to do was drop the 10-kg box onto the floor. The abalone would separate, and they could easily take out what they wanted.

By 11.30 a.m., all the work was done, and everything was washed down and ready for that day's abalone to be brought in and weighed up.

Derek was happy; everything was going well. What he needed was a load of illegal abalone at the right price from Teddy, and everything would be apples. But he felt that, with the fisheries paying such close attention to him, maybe they shouldn't do too much until things cooled off.

Hamm Nugent arrived at the brothel and saw immediately that Tiny wasn't there.

He asked Jesse, 'Where is Tiny?'

Jesse said, 'Tiny had a bit of a fallout with that Leckie's boyfriend, and he ended up a bit knocked about. He rang and said that he won't be in for a couple of nights. Don't worry, I got another bloke to give me a hand. Everything is under control. There won't be a problem.'

Hamm grunted and thought to himself, *Things look like they are getting out of control.*

He went inside for a brief look around, then walked out, got into his car, and drove off.

'Things definitely are getting out of control,' he said to himself and shook his head.

He was just the man to get things back on track. It was time that he smartened some of these idiots up. He should concentrate on Dean and then get Leckie back under his control. How long would Leckie last without Dean's financial input—one week, two weeks, perhaps a month? He knew how important it was for Leckie to send money back to her family in China. He also knew that Leckie and her family would lose face if the money didn't come in every month.

All he had to do was put Dean out of action. Leckie would come crawling back to him and plead for her job back. Guess what, the receptionist's job would be well gone. All that was left for precious little Leckie to do was get on her back, start fucking, and guess who would be her first customer. Detective Jack Andrews, that's who.

When Jack had called in for his weekly payment, Hamm had asked what had happened to his face. Jack had said that he had been belted up by a couple of abalone divers and that one was shacked up with Leckie.

Giving her to Jack would be the way to get even with Leckie and Dean, Hamm thought. And he started to feel better.

He smiled evilly as he drove into the night.

Teddy wasn't a worrier, but he liked to have things planned out, and he didn't like the way that things were going with Dean and Tiny. Teddy feared that there would be some sort of payback from the security men. He didn't realise that Hamm Nugent and Jack Andrews were all connected. If he had, he would have been really concerned for Dean and Leckie.

Dark powers always seem to work better if there is more than one involved. So when Hamm Nugent, Tiny, Jesse, Jack

Andrews, and Karl all sat down and worked out how they were going to square up with Dean, the ideas flowed.

Hamm was happy to just have Dean beaten to a bloody pulp. If Dean was injured, then Hamm knew that Leckie would be defenceless and would be easy prey.

Whereas, Jack and Karl were more than happy to go the whole way and kill Dean. But the two detectives decided not to let on. They thought that the others might get cold feet. It's funny how people talk tough, but when the time for action comes, they go to water.

While all this was going on, Piggy was still on stake-out, keeping an eye on the processing factory.

So far, he had seen nothing out of the order, but he knew that he was onto something and all it would take was a little time.

Sooner or later, a truckload of illegal abalone would turn up and then he would strike and catch them all red-handed.

Piggy ate another doughnut, happy with the thought that soon he would have an arrest.

Teddy and the boys met up in Curly's shed. They were looking forward to another night's work. Teddy was a bit hesitant; he knew that they were under pressure from the fisheries. Also he was worried about Tiny and Dean. There was trouble brewing there, and something was going to happen, he was sure of it.

All the boys agreed that they had to be particularly careful and keep a sharp watch-out to see if there were any people following them.

They had to be aware of what was going on.

Derek, realising that the factory was under surveillance, began to make other plans about getting his illegal abalone processed.

He had a couple of mates who had blast freezers and freezer storage over the other side of Melbourne. They weren't licensed for exporting sea foods but would bring the abalone down to minus 30 degrees overnight, and that was all he really needed.

As Teddy always brought in abalone meat, there was very little processing. All they had to do was weigh it into 10-kg shatter-pack boxes and get them into the blast freezer.

Maybe Derek would send experienced people over to do it. So to the casual observer, there would be no difference in what was happening at his factory.

Derek got onto the phone and started to organise the processing deal with one of his mates.

The detectives, brothel owner, and two security guards started to plan how to go about getting even with Dean. They wanted to get him on his own and beat the living crap out of him. The detectives had darker plans.

Hamm put forward a plan to get Dean into the gambling den on the pretence that there was a card game on and the stakes would be high enough to attract big punters.

Hamm would tell the operators of the gambling den that he wanted to bring in some security as he had been threatened. So he would bring along Tiny and Jesse.

Jack and Karl would simply show their badges at the door; the doormen would shit themselves and let them in. If they said that it wasn't a raid, then they wouldn't even have to pay for a drink. This was one of the perks of being a copper.

They all agreed that was the way to go. Dean would be on his own, and there would be five of them.

Hamm thought that it was foolproof idea, one that would easily work.

Dean's phone rang. It was the manager of the gambling den.

He said, 'Mr Dean, Mr Dean, it is Frankie from your favourite place of excitement. My friend, you haven't been in for a while. Some of my better clients are having a big game tomorrow night, and I immediately thought of you. They are people with plenty of money and enjoy the skill of playing against the better players. You are one of the best players I know, so I thought that I might get you along. It will be a night that you won't forget.'

Dean was a bit amused by Frankie's call.

He did consider himself as a card player of some note. Dean remembered winning some big hands. As all punters are inclined to do, he completely forgot about the losing hands that had often sent him home completely bled out financially.

'Thanks for the invite, Frankie. I haven't had a game for a long time. I've been busy working and making some money. So I reckon that a couple of hands will brighten up my day. What time will it kick off?'

Frankie looked at Hamm and nodded, 'Dean, the players will all be here by 9 p.m., so any time after that will be good for you.'

Dean agreed and disconnected his phone. He thought that he wouldn't tell Leckie about the game as she didn't want him gambling all his money away.

He would say that he had to go and see Teddy and then tell her that they had got on the piss at Curly's place and that time had just slipped away—that easy.

Frankie, the manager, was happy with arranging for Dean to come to the gambling den. He was good friends with Hamm and thought that by doing something to help him, it would ensure his friendship.

Frankie was having an affair with one of the young drink waitresses.

After their shift finished, they had a drink back at Frankie's apartment. He confided to her about the upcoming trouble that would happen when Hamm and his friends got into Dean.

The waitress was also a friend of Leckie.

When Frankie had finished with her, she made her way home and decided to ring Leckie when she woke the next day.

It was late in the afternoon when Leckie's phone rang, and she was told of the impending trouble that Dean was walking into. Leckie realised that she had to do something or else Dean would be in trouble, but what?

Dean had already told her that he was going over to Teddy's place to have a talk with him and that they would probably end up back at Curly's shed and not to expect him home until late.

The only person that Leckie could turn to was Teddy.

She rang Teddy and said, 'I have just received news from a friend whom I used to work with that Dean has been invited to a card game. They said that there was going to be some big money players there, and I'm frightened that they are going to get even with Dean.'

Leckie was crying, and her words were running into each other.

'Whoa, whoa, slow down. What's the problem?' Teddy asked.

Leckie started to explain again, and, this time, the words came out at a better rate.

'Hamm Nugent and Tiny and some police are going to wait for Dean at the gambling club. Then they are going to hurt him for taking me away and for his involvement in bashing up the two detectives.'

Teddy said, 'Don't worry, I'll get the boys together, and we will even things up a bit. I'll give Dean a ring and have a talk with him. Don't worry, I'll send Rita and Sandy over to sit with you until all this unpleasantness is over.'

Ringing his partner, Teddy organised for her to pick up Sandy and go over to Dean's house and to wait until she heard from him.

Teddy rang Dean's phone, and it was switched off. So he rang Tom and Curly and filled them in on what was happening.

They got ready to help Dean.

As darkness descended on the city, Teddy, Tom, and Curly made their way towards the gambling club.

Dean was a lot nearer, and he felt good; he had missed the challenge of gambling. He was sure that one night's mucking about wouldn't make him fall off the wagon.

In the gambling club, Hamm, Jack, Karl, Tiny, and Jesse were all prepared and waiting for Dean's arrival. They were confident that everything was in place.

Dean climbed up the stairs and was confronted by the group, but then there was a smashing sound downstairs at the front door.

Just as Teddy and the boys pulled up outside, they saw Dean disappear into the door of the club. Teddy drove the car across the footpath and crashed the left side of the front bumper into the security door. The door sagged open.

They parked the car on the footpath, and all jumped out. Teddy put his shoulder to the door, which splintered off its hinges. Dean and Curly forced it open and pushed past the two security men.

Tom said to the startled pair, 'Fuck off if you know what's good for you.'

The two security guards bolted down the street, and the boys bounded up the stairs.

Jack said in a loud voice, 'Well, look who's here. It's the fucking hillbilly from the Billabong Roadhouse.'

Dean looked into the faces of the group of men and realised that he had been sold down the drain. He could expect no mercy from this group.

The door downstairs splintered, and Teddy and the boys ran up the stairs.

Teddy spotted Dean and said, 'Dean mate, do you need a hand?'

Dean was more than happy to accept anything that was going.

'What kept you?' he asked.

Teddy laughed and said, 'We got caught up in the traffic. Let's get this show on the road.'

The four divers moved as one across to where the five men were standing.

Teddy said, 'Here is yours, you fucking coconut head.'

And he drove his fist into Jesse's stomach. Jesse went down.

Dean swung at Tiny and hit him a glancing blow to the jaw.

Jack Andrews let a punch go at Curly.

Tom lined up Karl, who saw it coming but couldn't get out of the way. He saw stars and fell back onto the floor.

Teddy grabbed a chair and hit Hamm across the shoulders with it. The chair broke into firewood.

The staff in the club all got behind the counter. Some of the girls started to scream, and the men didn't want to get involved; the other customers looked on wide-eyed.

Jack landed a couple of blows on Teddy, but they didn't have much of an effect on him as Teddy was wired.

Tiny tried to grab Dean in a bear hug, but Dean slipped away and hit him hard in the face.

The big Samoan was a bit stunned, and when Dean landed a combination of lefts and rights, the sparkle went out of him. Tiny was hurt. He threw a right-hand punch at Dean, but Dean was ready and saw it coming. He easily swayed out of its path and replied with a smashing blow to Tiny's jaw. That was it for Tiny. It was goodnight nurse for him.

Karl was getting to his feet, and Dean, who was really getting going, was straight into him. He rained blows onto Karl, and, once again, Karl hit the deck this time and was out for the count.

With Tiny and Karl no longer in it, the odds were with the boys.

Jack realised that he had the throw-down gun in his briefcase.

Teddy saw him try and get to his briefcase and realised that he was going for a weapon. So Teddy headed him off by belting him in the side of the face. Jack's face went numb, but he was on course. He swung a couple of ineffectual blows in Teddy's direction. They merely bounced off Teddy and didn't do any damage at all.

Meanwhile, Hamm was feeling that he shouldn't have even been there. He was tough, but up against this mob, he needed a gun or a sword or some means of defending himself. Didn't these clowns realise that there were police involved? They weren't showing any respect for the policemen at all. He watched as Teddy slammed his fist into Jack's jaw, knocking the policeman to the floor. He looked at Teddy, Dean, Tom, and Curly, and they all seemed to be enjoying the fight.

The next thing he knew, Curly smashed his fist into his head, and he saw stars. Curly then lined him up with an upper cutter, and that was it. He saw it coming but couldn't get out of its way. That was all Hamm remembered.

Tiny was out to it, Karl was away with the fairies, Hamm was concussed and bleeding from the nose and mouth, Jack was unconscious on the floor, and Jesse was down with his eyes shut.

They were a sorry lot.

Teddy looked at his right hand and saw that he had fractured a knuckle, Dean was sporting a badly swollen left eye, Tom had grazes across his face, and Curly thought that he might have cracked a rib or two.

They were, by and by, in pretty good shape.

Teddy looked at the assembled group of bar people and said, 'We are off. Don't mention this to anyone or we will be back. If we have to come back, then you are all in trouble. Understood?'

Pale faces looked back at Teddy, some nodded, and others just looked at him in wide-eyed terror.

'Let's get this show on the road,' Teddy said. 'We will all meet back at Curly's shed.'

With that, they all walked down the stairs and out of the gambling club.

Teddy rang Rita and told her that they were all meeting back at Curly's shed. So she and the girls were on their way.

When they got there, all the boys were laughing and drinking beer.

When all was explained to them, they were angry at the boys for putting themselves in danger.

Teddy explained, 'You girls just don't understand. We don't let anyone get on top of us. If we let some dickhead stand over us, then soon everyone will want to start shoving us around.'

Teddy looked at the boys and said, 'It's one in, all in.'

All the boys lifted their beers and saluted each other.

None of them had ever felt better in their lives.

The girls were left wondering about what went on in those blokes' heads.

The boys started to work out how they would get on top of their current problems.

Teddy came up with a bit of a plan. He would talk to his next-door neighbour. He would see if Ronny could get word back to the two detectives' bosses that they were spending more time chasing Teddy than doing what they should be doing.

Tiny and Jesse were a problem too. They had to drop off or else the boys were going to have them sorted.

Then Hamm Nugent, no one knew what he was up to. Why would he be sticking his head in? Then there was Piggy on stake-out in view of Derek's factory. He was the least of their concerns until they did another abalone raid.

The boys had a couple of more and then headed home.

Dean and Leckie talked about the events that had occurred.

They didn't realise just how badly Hamm wanted Dean hurt so that Leckie would come back and work in the brothel.

It was all very confusing.

The ever-reliable Piggy was stationed in view of the processing factory. Not a lot was happening.

He started to realise that he couldn't keep watch twenty-four hours a day. He would have to have some sort of back-up. He thought that three 8-hour shifts would be the way to go. At the moment, if Teddy were to bring in a load of abalone in the middle of the morning, there would be no one there to arrest him.

Piggy started to work out a roster that he could show his bosses.

Teddy asked his next-door neighbour if he knew anybody who could put a bit of pressure on the two detectives.

Ronny said, 'Mate, I know just the bloke. He's a sort of policeman's policeman. He cracks down on the bent bastards, and this sort of thing is right up his alley. Let me talk to him, and I'll see what he can do.'

Teddy left it at that; he knew that Ronny would do all he could.

Ronny got straight down to business. He rang around and was soon invited to have a bit of a talk with some high-up police. They met in a bar in a part of town where none of them was known.

Ronny explained what had happened—how, by mistake, two of his friends had been in the wrong place at the wrong time, how they had fallen foul of two detectives, and how twice they had belted the detectives up. Ronny explained that the policemen were using their position against his friend and bringing the force into disrepute.

The two senior policemen listened and took down the evidence. This wasn't a one-off case. Plenty of policemen overstepped the mark and used their position to stand over the more gullible members of the public.

They parted and told Ronny that they would look into it.

Ronny felt as though he had achieved something positive.

The following day, Jack and Karl were summoned into their chief's office and were told to close the door behind them.

This was a bad sign.

They remained standing and when the senior policeman said, 'What the fuck have you two clowns been up to?' it was obvious that something was afoot.

Jack spoke, 'I don't know what you are asking us, sir.'

'What I'm asking you is, what have you to do with the attempted abduction of a woman from a roadhouse near Bairnsdale?'

Jack said, 'I don't understand.'

The senior officer sat back in his chair and said, 'You pair of fucking clowns went to the roadhouse where your wife was working, Jack, and you tried to drag her away against her will. Listen, this isn't some Arab country where they practice sharia law or somewhere that women have no rights. This is, in case you haven't noticed, Australia, and you aren't some tribal dickheads. You are officers of the law. You are supposed to uphold the law, not fucking well break it. What have you got to say for yourselves?'

Jack felt that they were losing ground.

'Sir, we went there to pick up my wife, and these two blokes jumped us. We weren't expecting anything. I went to have a talk with her, and Karl came with me for a bit of company. We are partners, and he wanted to help out.'

The senior officer looked at the two detectives and asked, 'What happened in China Town a couple of days ago? My advice is that you were involved in a scuffle in some upstairs gambling club with the same blokes. Only this time, they belted up some security guards and a brothel owner, as well as both of you. This has got to stop for your own protection before they really do you some damage.'

Jack was losing ground fast. He explained, 'These men are dangerous abalone poachers and feel that they are outside the law. They live by a set of rules that says they can do whatever they want and get away with it.'

The senior policeman looked at the two detectives and said, 'They don't appear to have any criminal convictions. As far as I can work out, they are model citizens. You should be chasing after druggies and sex-slave operators rather than a couple of fun-loving spear fishermen.'

Jack looked at his boss and said, 'There's a lot more to them than everyone thinks. They are bad bastards, and we should keep them under constant surveillance.'

The senior policeman rolled back in his chair and said, 'Look, you two. Do the job that you are paid to do and leave these blokes alone. If they are poachers, then the fisheries will take care of them. They always catch their man eventually. If I find out that either of you two blokes has even farted in the same suburb as them, you'll both be back in uniform, pounding the beat somewhere. I'm dead serious about this. Now get back to what you are supposed to be doing.'

Jack and Karl made their way out of the office.
They decided to keep their heads down for a while.

Ronny received a phone call from his mate in the police force and was told that the pressure had been put on the two detectives. They had been threatened that if they kept up their intimidation of Teddy and the boys, they would be back in uniform and on the beat somewhere.

Walking next door, he said to Teddy, 'Mate, I've just got news that the brakes have just been put on your two favourite detectives.'

Teddy laughed and said, 'Thanks, Ronny mate, well done. You seem to be in the know when it comes to the coppers.'

Ronny laughed and said, 'Mate, when you have been around as long as I have, you pick up a couple of tricks.'

Teddy smiled and said, 'That's one I owe you.'

Ronny smiled and walked away.

Piggy was the centre of attention. He was in a room surrounded by fisheries officers, and he had them all in the palm of his hand.

'Ladies and gentlemen,' Piggy said in a loud voice and waited until the talking stopped, 'as you are aware, my fellow officers and I have had a relentless battle with a group of abalone poachers. They are very smart and have had luck on their side, but I'm sensing that they are about to come unstuck. Through due diligence and hard work, we have discovered where they are getting rid of their abalone. I'm currently staking out the premises and realise that the job is too big to be a one-man show. So what I need is an around-the-clock surveillance team to be there on the alert so that whenever they unload at the factory, we will be there to arrest them.

It is my belief that they are currently away in Bass Strait poaching, and in the near future, they will be coming in to unload. I want us to be there then, and we will arrest them red-handed. There will be no escape.'

The fisheries officers listened intently; some felt like clapping as it had been an uplifting speech, and all present were eager to be among the team that finally put an end to this band of desperadoes.

Piggy said, 'Let's work out who can work on the surveillance team and what hours suit us the best.'

The gathering soon worked out times. Piggy felt well pleased with himself; things were starting to fall into place.

Murphy, the security guard, noticed the presence of a different car on the stake-out and realised that whoever was running the show had beefed up the surveillance.

He rang Derek and let him know what was going on.

Derek was appreciative of the information, and he rang Teddy and explained the situation.

Teddy said, 'Mate, they are really going out to get us. They probably think that because Barry has taken the boat out, we are out there and will be meeting him somewhere. And that we will be in with a load of abalone in the next couple of days. I reckon that this isn't the time to be bringing in abalone to your factory.'

Derek said, 'I can arrange with another factory to box up the abalone that you bring in. They have blast freezers, and the product will be as good as ever.'

Teddy thought for a while and said, 'Let's leave it for a while and see what happens. The fisheries will get tired of watching you weigh up abalone from legal divers.'

'I hope so,' Derek answered.

Teddy spoke to the boys and told them that as Derek's factory was under surveillance, they would take it easy for a while—maybe even have a couple of weeks off just until things cooled off a bit.

Hamm Nugent was hurt physically, and he burnt with a deep rage. Dean and his mates had made him look like an idiot. He couldn't understand how things had turned out so badly. He looked at his face in the mirror and saw a beaten man, and he swore to himself that he would get even. He made his mind up that he would kill Dean if it was the last thing he ever did.

He started to plan an attack. He had a gun. It would only take one bullet, and that was the end of Dean.

He would shoot Dean in front of Leckie. That would show her what he was capable of. She would see that he was the stronger one, and then she would be completely under his control.

The detectives Jack and Karl were being cautious.

They knew that their boss wasn't joking when he threatened to bust them back to uniform. That would be a bad blow to their egos, and the constant ribbing from the other detectives would drive them mad. But Jack still had to square up with that bitch of a wife of his. He schemed on.

Jack knew that Hamm Nugent was very upset that they had all been beaten up by Teddy's crew. He felt that together, they would fix Dean up.

The next time they met up for Jack's pay-off, they both decided that the sooner they killed Dean, the sooner they would save face.

Hamm thought that some of the girls who were working for him had started to lose some respect. It was nothing you could put your finger on, but they weren't the same. He had always prided himself on his appearance, but it was hard to look in control when your head was bandaged up in a turban.

The fisheries had Derek's factory under constant surveillance, but as yet there wasn't anything to report; everything was going as normal.

Derek was buying abalone off legal divers and not doing anything illegal.

Some of the fisheries officers thought that a raid on Derek's premises would be a good idea, but Piggy said that he didn't want to arouse any suspicion that Derek was in the hot seat.

One of the officers thought that Teddy had been away for a long time and that he should have been in with some abalone by now. So he and his partner decided to go around to Teddy's place, just to make sure that he was, in fact, away on a poaching trip. They arrived just in time to see Teddy reverse out of his drive and slowly drive towards Curly's shed. The pair of fisheries officers followed at a discreet distance and took up watch down the street. Teddy walked down the side of the house and into the shed; a couple of minutes later, they saw Dean and Tom also pull up and walk down to the shed. They looked at each other and realised that the time they had been staking out the processing factory had been a waste. Teddy and his gang of poachers weren't at sea, poaching abalone. They were in fact on land. The stake-out had been a complete waste of time.

Wallace P. Trotter was in hot water. It had been revealed that the information that he had received from the detectives that Barry had taken the big boat out to sea was correct, but that the assumption that it was a poaching trip was wrong. Barry had simply gone on a trip and taken his new deckhand out for a run.

Piggy was under pressure. He explained exactly who had given him the information and how he had come up with the thought that Teddy and his crew were out there poaching.

The stake-out on the factory was immediately called off.

The fisheries officers were put back onto whatever they were doing beforehand, and Piggy headed back to Bairnsdale where he faced plenty of questions from above.

'Hindsight is a wonderful thing,' Piggy reflected.

Perhaps they should have made sure that the poachers were away from their homes before they had staked out the factory and wasted all that time and money.

Hamm, Jack, and Karl were deep in discussion about the shooting of Dean.

'It will be easy,' Hamm stated. 'We will just whack him when he least expects it. We could ring him and tell him that Leckie has been involved in an accident at the university and that she isn't badly hurt but needs a lift home. He will come running. Then, when we can, bang. It's all over for Dean. I want to do it in front of Leckie so that she knows that it was me. That way, we will have supreme power over her.'

Jack said, 'I don't like witnesses. Any sort of witness is bad news.'

Karl interjected, 'Who is going to believe a hysterical slope-head anyway?'

He looked at Hamm and said, 'Sorry, mate.'

Hamm looked back at him, smiled slightly, and thought, *Moron.*

Jack said once again, 'I'm not happy with witnesses. If anyone says that we were there, then we are busted back to uniform. That's not going to happen. I can tell you that much.'

They plotted on, planning the evil event.

Meanwhile, Dean was going about his business, unaware that there were plans for his demise well under way.

He and Leckie decided to go and have a meal in the city. Dean had decided to keep away from the gambling club. He thought that he had been set up by the manager, Frankie. Some people were hard to understand; Dean thought that they were mates.

They finished their meal, Dean drove back home, he pulled into the drive, and they both got out of the car.

As they walked to the front door, they were confronted by Hamm. He had a revolver and pointed it at Dean.

Hamm simply said, 'Put your hands behind your head and walk around to the back of the house.'

Dean obeyed and started to walk down the side of the house.

Leckie said, 'What are you doing, Hamm?'

Hamm laughed and said, 'I should have done this before. I'm going to teach you a lesson. I'm going to kill Dean and force you back to work for me.'

Leckie was thinking fast; she said, 'I'll come and work for you. I miss me job.'

Hamm laughed and said, 'Your job as a receptionist is gone. You will work as a whore. You will service plenty of men a night and will take whatever I give you with no complaints. But, first, I will show you I am a man of power.'

Hamm brutally stuck the revolver into Dean's back.

As soon as Dean felt the weapon against his back, he quickly swung around and grabbed it by the barrel and forced it up and away from him.

The two men struggled to take possession of the weapon.

Dean was much taller than Hamm and much stronger, but Hamm's lower centre of gravity made it difficult for Dean to take control of the gun.

Both men struggled in silence.

There was a muffled shot; both the men stood frozen.

Dean slowly let go of Hamm who started to fall away from him.

Hamm had a patch of blood on the front of his shirt that was getting bigger and bigger. He tried to say something, but his mouth filled with blood, and it ran down the sides of his mouth. He made a strange bubbling noise and fell to the ground.

He was dead before he hit the grass.

Dean looked at Leckie and saw the horror in her face.

He put his arms around her and said, 'Don't worry, baby. It's all over. It's all over. He wanted to kill me so he could control you, and I couldn't let that happen. I would die before I let anyone hurt you.'

Leckie clung on to Dean's huge frame and knew that what he had just said was true.

She realised that Dean really loved her.

Dean thought fast.

He rang Teddy and told him what had happened.

Teddy and Rita ran to his car and drove straight over to Dean's house.

They both ran down the side of the house and saw Hamm's body lying on the grass.

Rita went inside with Leckie.

Teddy looked at his mate and asked what had happened. Dean explained, and as Teddy listened, he could see that it was a case of self-defence.

'We had better ring the coppers and tell them everything,' he said. 'I can see that it's a case of self-defence. It's obvious what happened. I'm just happy that you didn't get killed.'

'It sure was fucking close,' Dean admitted shakily.

The police came and then the coroner.

Then the ambulance came and took away the body.

Dean was questioned at the station, and Leckie had to give her account of what happened. Hamm Nugent was known to the police, and as Dean was a cleanskin, he was released on bail. Tom, Sandy, and Curly all came over to Dean's place and gave whatever support they could, but it was going to be a long night with little sleep.

When the news broke that Hamm Nugent had been killed by Dean, Tiny and Jesse decided that Melbourne was too small a town for them, and they hightailed it out of town.

Tiny suggested that they lose themselves in the Western Australian mines.

There were plenty of islanders working over there, so they wouldn't have any difficulty in getting work.

They left the next day.

When everything settled down, Teddy called all the boys together and said that they had better get ready for another trip away.

'Get all your gear together, and when the weather is right, we will be away,' he said.

New Zealand Star Bank

*T*he oddly named *New Zealand Star Bank* lies 11.4 km off the south-southeast coast of the Victorian shore in the Tasman Sea. It is situated between Little Ram Head and Wingan Point, almost straight out from Sandpatch Point, and is a haven for all breeds of fish and shark. At its shallowest point is about sixty-eight feet, so when you are diving, the time you would be allowed at the bottom is about fifteen minutes. Any time after that, you would have to decompress. It is rumoured to be chock-a-block full of abalone. They are, as divers say 'Back-to-back'.

Some time in the early Seventies . . .

Teddy had towed his aluminium dingy up to Eden from Melbourne as he thought that he might get in a week or two diving.

The weather was blowing from south-west, so it wasn't too good to dive in Victoria. But once you got round Gabo Island, then the weather was offshore and calm. He felt like a bit of time away from the hustle and bustle of Melbourne where he lived.

Some time before Teddy had bought a New South Wales abalone diving licence which only cost $2.00. So he was a legal diver in NSW, and that was a change for him as he spent almost all his time poaching abalone.

Whenever he went to Eden, he always stayed at his mate's place.

His mate, called Dave, was also a diver. They had known each other for years and enjoyed each other's company.

As it was a Wednesday afternoon, they had decided to take a run into Eden.

They were on the lookout for Big Jim who was a Maori and a giant of a man. He and his wife would go shopping every Wednesday, come rain, hail, or shine. When they were shopping, they would always buy a large cream sponge cake, and, if by chance, you were to drop around for a cup of tea on a Wednesday afternoon, then you would be offered a large slice of the sponge.

Jim and his wife were wonderful and generous people who would share everything they had with anybody.

Teddy and Dave soon spotted the large Ford Fairlane. Jim had one of the 1960 to 1962 models. It was heading towards Jim's home. This was a monster of a vehicle, a real Yank tank. It appeared as though every Maori in Australia owned one of these monsters at some time of their lives.

They pulled into the drive of Jim's house, and Dave yelled out a greeting, 'Hi, there, have you got the kettle on?'

Jim replied, 'Yes, it's about to boil any minute. Come on in and have a cuppa.'

Dave and Teddy got out of their car and walked up the garden path. The front yard was immaculate, not a weed or anything out of place.

The three men shook hands and relaxed, as you do with old friends. They all walked up the steps and into the neat and tidy house.

'Teddy mate, you're back here for a spell?' Jim asked.

'Yes, Jim, I'm here to do a bit and keep Dave in line while I'm at it,' Teddy replied.

Everyone laughed.

Jim's wife brought out the teapot and the cutlery. Dave watched her hungrily as she went to the kitchen and returned with the cream-filled sponge.

She smiled and asked, 'Can I cut you a piece of cake?'

'Yes, please,' they all chorused.

Teddy asked Jim, 'How have you been going, weight-wise?'

Jim looked towards the floor and said, 'Things are a bit tough here at the present time. The licences are so cheap that everyone is getting one, though some are only working on weekends. They have got a nine-to-five week job and just do abalone diving on a weekend. As there isn't any size limit, they take everything. There is no chance of recovery. You see them weighing in, and some of the abalone are the size of sparrows' eggs.'

All the boys agreed that it was time that some sort of size limit and licence regulations were brought in. They talked about how the industry was going and how tough things were.

Jim said, 'Meggsy Hall, and I reckon that we might do a dive on the New Zealand Star Bank.'

There was silence in the room.

Teddy said, 'They tell me it's deep out there, and it only breaks on rough days. You could do yourself a bit of damage out there.'

Jim looked at his friends and said, 'I reckon that the risk is worth it. If we land on abalone, we will be in and out in ten minutes with a boatload. We can shuck them out on the way back, and Bob's your uncle.'

Everyone laughed.

Jim's wife asked if they would like more cake, and both the boys declined the offer as they knew that Jim and his wife would give it all away; such was their nature.

Teddy and Dave drove away from Jim's place.

Teddy said to Dave, 'Mate, I'm worried that Jimmy and Meggsy are heading for trouble. That's deep and dangerous water out there, and they are a long way from help if they need assistance.'

Teddy shook his head. He always tried to stick to shallow water wherever he possibly could.

Dave laughed and said, 'You big fucking Sheila. You should hit the bottom like a real man and not splash about in the shallows. No wonder your wetsuit is faded. In fact, it's not faded. It's sun-bleached.'

Teddy ignored the banter from his mate. He knew that Dave was a deep diver and afraid of nothing that the ocean had to offer.

Teddy was a bit uneasy about his two mates going down into Victorian waters and diving on a reef miles away from shore. It was a well-known fact that white pointer sharks favoured offshore reefs as there were plenty of fish that lived on them and sharks were a real worry.

The elephant in the room was the bends, nitrogen narcosis, the dreaded sickness that could easily kill you, and it was a painful way to die.

Teddy and Dave spent the rest of the week working down the coast, abalone diving. They were going pretty well and making a good living. They were both hard workers and didn't drink a lot—just a few beers now and again and a wine with dinner.

Jim and Meggsy were preparing to do a poaching trip into Victorian waters and have a dive on the New Zealand Star Bank.

They were going out on a fifty-foot fishing boat. They planned on staying away for a few days as the reef was about 80 kms away from Eden. So it was a fair trip down there and back.

The boys dropped around and saw Jim, and as luck would have it, Meggsy was there also. They sat around and talked about the dangers that the two men faced, but like true thrill seekers, the divers just laughed at their concerns.

Dave admitted that if he had had more notice, he wouldn't have minded joining them.

Jim and Meggsy departed the next day and headed off towards the Victorian border.

The skipper of the fifty-foot boat watched the depth sounder as they cruised into position. He steamed around until he found the shallowest part of the reef and anchored so that the boat would sit directly above the top of it.

Jim and Meggsy suited up and got ready to get into the water. Down they swam.

It takes courage to descend into the murky depths, a long way offshore. But Jim and Meggsy had plenty of courage.

As they went deeper and deeper, they both searched for the bottom, but they couldn't see it. They still had a way to go.

They looked at each other and gave the thumbs-up sign; each could see that the other was grinning, and they were excited.

The bottom came into view.

It took them a few moments to realise it, but before them lay what looked to be an endless supply of abalone. And all the abalone that they saw were big. They both thought that there would be about three or four to the pound.

They started chipping off the abalone, and, in about five minutes, their bags were full. Meggsy indicated to Jim that he would take the bags up and for Jim to keep working and make a pile of abalone at the bottom. He would come down with a few more net bags Jim nodded his approval and continued chipping abalone off the reef.

Meggsy was soon back with six net bags for the abalone. He started to fill them with the abalone that Jim had stockpiled. Soon he was off to the surface with another two full net bags.

By the time he got back, Jim was going along like a steam train, filling bag after bag.

Meggsy, through signals, asked if Jim wanted to take some of the bags up and leave him at the bottom. Jim indicated that he was happy with the way that things were going and for Meggsy to keep doing what he was doing.

Time flew, and before they realised what was going on, Jim and Meggsy were well over the time that they were allowed to spend at the bottom. In fact, they were so far over their time that for them to get out safely, they would have to spend time on the anchor rope at varying levels, decompressing.

When Meggsy came up with yet another two bags of abalone, the skipper said, 'Meggsy, you and Jim had better call it quits. You've got a heap of abalone on deck. Give Jim the sign to get going.'

Meggsy swam down and signalled to Jim that it was time to go up to the boat. But Jim shook his head and kept on chipping abalone off the rocky bottom.

There were still hundreds of abalone to be seen. The fact that they were getting gradually deeper and deeper didn't worry Jim. There was money in front of him, and it was there for the taking.

Jim worked deeper and deeper.

Soon he was working in 100 feet of water.

Jim and Meggsy had both crossed the line; they were in trouble. But the lure of making a month's pay in a few hours proved to be a bigger hurdle than they had thought.

Meggsy was stuffing the bags fuller and fuller and swimming them up faster and faster.

The skipper started to worry as he had heard about this sort of thing happening to divers before—the divers getting greedy and not sticking to what they had planned.

He went to Jim's air line and gave it three sharp tugs, the signal to any diver that there was trouble and that he should get to the surface as quickly as possible.

Jim ignored the three tugs on his air line.

He thought that if he would get a couple of more net bags, then he would go to the surface.

Time sped by.

Jim gave no sign that he might go to the surface. He kept ploughing on chipping abalone, and Meggsy was swimming them to the surface.

Soon the effort began to show on the big fellow. His arm started to throb from the constant impact of chipping off abalone, and slowly it came to him that he had been down deep far too long.

He indicated to Meggsy that he was ready to hit the surface, and when his last net bag was full, he slowly made his way to the surface.

The skipper immediately told them both to go back and hang off the anchor chain. Suddenly they were both cold, freezing cold.

This should have been an indication to them that they were in trouble, but the nitrogen bubbles had already gathered in their spines.

They were getting sicker and sicker.

Jim slowly climbed aboard, and the skipper realised that they needed treatment.

Meggsy collapsed onto the deck.

The skipper started to panic; he raised the anchor and steamed, at full speed, towards the shoreline in the hope that he would come across another abalone boat, one that was faster, a runabout.

All the divers who worked out of Mallacoota used fibreglass runabouts.

They were very fast, and, of course, it was the fashion to have the biggest outboard motors that their insurance would cover.

As Jim and Meggsy's skipper headed towards shore, he got out his binoculars and scanned the shoreline.

He saw a diver's white runabout boat working in close to the rocky outcrop.

He steamed straight towards it and pulled his boat up beside the runabout.

He shouted to the startled deckhand that he had a couple of divers aboard who were suffering from the bends.

The deckhand immediately grabbed his diver's air line and gave it three hard tugs. The diver surfaced immediately, and the deckhand started to pull the diver in hand over hand by his air line.

When the diver got to his boat, he spat out his demand valve and asked, 'What the fuck is going on?'

The deckhand grabbed his half-full net bag of abalone and pulled it into the boat.

He then shut off the compressor, and silence descended over the boat.

The skipper shouted to the diver, 'I've got a couple of divers who are unconscious. They are bent to buggery. They will die if they aren't taken to the decompression chamber in Mallacoota as soon as possible.'

'Fuck me dead, pull up the anchor, and we'll get going,' the diver said without hesitation.

They got the unconscious men aboard the fast runabout, and, without a word, the diver and his deckhand headed back to Mallacoota; his diving was finished for the day.

The deckhand turned to the diver and asked, 'Do you think that they will make it back to Mallacoota alive?'

The diver saw that his deckhand was on the verge of panicking or breaking down.

He said, 'We will give it a fucking good shot. We are one of the fastest boats in port, and if anyone can get these boys back in time, we can. Just make them as comfortable as possible, and I'll try and dodge all the big waves.'

They sped across the ocean at their top speed. This was no time to dawdle. They swung around Bastion Point and came in across the bar at breakneck speed, not slowing down.

They ignored the speed restrictions in the channel and pulled up to the wharf.

There, the amazed crowd looked into the boat and saw the two men in a very bad state.

The two sick divers were rushed to the decompression chamber, but, alas, it was too late for them.

Jim was the first to pass away inside the chamber.

There was hope that Meggsy might battle on and live, but he also died in the chamber.

A great sadness descended over Mallacoota.

The news was soon conveyed to Eden, and the fishing and diving fraternity mourned two great blokes, who had been taken from them.

Everyone agreed that it was a terrible tragedy.

The news hit Teddy and Dave very hard, and they both mourned the loss of their two friends.

Teddy felt that he should have been stronger in his criticism about the reef.

But realistically, it would have been impossible to talk the two fearless divers out of the chance of a lifetime.

Present Day

Teddy, Tom, Dean, and Curly all sat together in Curly's shed.

It was their unofficial headquarters, and they all had beers in their hands and were laughing and joking.

Teddy said, 'Well, boys, we had better be getting our arses wet soon, or we will forget how to poach abalone.'

They all laughed at the thought.

'Where do you reckon that we will hit next?' Dean asked.

'I'm not sure,' Teddy said. 'There is good weather following this low, so we might shoot up to the Victoria-New South Wales border and see if we can't jag a load.'

All of them agreed; it had been a while since they had done any work.

As they always made a lot of money, they spent a lot of money, so the money had to keep rolling in.

Dean laughed and said, 'I miss the big boat and all its comforts. I must be getting old as I look forward to sleeping in a bed of a night, not curled upon the bottom of a Shark Cat.'

All the boys agreed.

They all thought that since Leckie had moved in with Dean, he was a different man.

Meanwhile, Barry and Hilda were getting along just fine.

They had gone out to sea for a few days, and, on their return, Hilda had begun to see about getting an intervention order against her husband Jack and his working partner Karl, just to give them some peace.

Barry realised that if he wanted to keep Hilda happy and with him, he would have to do a trip away with her, Teddy, and the boys.

What he needed was a plan, a plan that would suck in the team and they would be able to see that it was a good earner.

He had heard about the New Zealand Star Bank, off the Victorian Coast.

Barry had never fished it himself, but he had heard stories about it and how it was said to be loaded with abalone.

He vaguely remembered hearing back in the early seventies about two young abalone divers getting bent out there and dying from the bends, but he wasn't sure of the exact story.

Knowing that Teddy wasn't happy about diving deep, Barry knew that if all the precautions were taken, then it would be safe. He would have to be careful about how he went introducing the idea to the divers.

He knew that Tom wouldn't be a problem. He was as game as Ned Kelly.

Dean would be willing when he was told of the amount of money that it was possible to make.

Curly, well, he would stick with Teddy and go whichever way Teddy went.

Barry decided to go to the pub where Sandy worked and have a beer with Tom and plant the seed.

He and Hilda walked into the pub. It was a midweek afternoon.

Sandy smiled and said, 'Gidday, Barry, how are you? Hilda, I see that you are back from the trip on the love boat.'

Barry went a shade of red, and Hilda laughed out loud.

Hilda replied, 'Next time we go, we might take some kitchen staff as I had to do all the cleaning and cooking.'

Sandy smiled and asked what they would like to drink.

Barry ordered a pot, and Hilda asked for a gin and tonic.

'When does Tom come and pick you up after you knock off?' Barry asked.

Sandy said that it would be in about an hour's time. But she would give Tom a ring and he could come over earlier and have a drink with Barry and Hilda.

This is what Barry had planned.

He agreed, and Sandy rang Tom.

Tom said, 'I'll be there in ten minutes.'

When Tom arrived at the pub, Barry and Hilda were sitting up at the bar and talking to Sandy. There weren't a lot of customers as the evening rush hadn't started.

They got a table, sat down, and began talking.

After a few minutes of beating around the bush, Barry said to Tom, 'Tommy mate, I've come up with a plan that is too good to be true. It's a hit-and-run deal that involves diving on a reef, an offshore reef that doesn't break the surface. It's a bit deep, but I've been told that there are tonnes of abalone on it. It's packed back-to-back. Mate, it will be like taking corn off a blind chook.'

Tom was interested, more than interested. The lure of easy money was strong enough to take some risks.

'What does Teddy think?' Tom asked.

'Well, I haven't mentioned it to Teddy as yet. I wanted to know what you thought about it.'

Tom wondered if Barry wanted him to go without Teddy.

If that was the case, then Barry could belt the whole idea up his arse.

They were a team and only worked as a team.

Tom looked sharply at Barry and asked, 'Are you going to cut Teddy out?'

Barry quickly squashed that idea. 'No way, mate, Teddy and I go back a long way, and he's one of my best friends. It's just that Teddy doesn't like deep water, and this reef is deep, about 70 plus feet. It just keeps getting deeper and deeper. The sand line on it is probably 300 feet.'

Tom looked at Barry and said, 'Fuck me, even I won't go that deep. You need mixed gasses at 150 to 160 feet, and I'm not happy about diving on mixed gasses.'

'What I'm suggesting is for the whole team to go to the reef and anchor above it. I'll send down a wire crate about eight by eight by three feet. The four of you blokes hit the bottom and go like buggery and fill up the crate. If there are as many abalone down there as I've been told, then you should be able to fill the bastard in fifteen minutes. Then you all slowly come to the surface and wait for a while. Then we go through the whole operation again after a couple of hours. The key to it all is for you not to spend a long time at the bottom and make the ascent as slowly as possible. Don't pass any bubbles on the way up. It should be easy.'

Tom was interested. 'When are you going to tell Teddy about this planned trip?'

'Well, I wanted to see what you blokes thought about it. If you are keen, then I know that Dean will go for it. And if you and Dean are happy with the plan, Curly will also want to be in it. And the four of us could wear Teddy down.'

Tom looked at Barry and said, 'Mate, I'll tell you one thing. If Teddy doesn't go, then none of us will go. It's that simple—one in, all in, or one out, all out.'

Barry was relieved that Tom didn't think that he was going behind Teddy's back.

He knew that they were close, and he also knew that they were keen to get their hands onto some big money.

Barry felt that he had set the trap well, but time would tell.

Tom arranged to give the boys a ring and see what they thought.

He rang Dean who was all for it. Tom knew that if he was for it, then he had a chance with Curly.

When Curly was asked, he responded eagerly, but he wasn't that happy when told that Teddy hadn't been informed. He showed a bit of reluctance; if there was no Teddy, then there was no plan.

Now the big question was how to broach the subject with Teddy.

The next day, Barry invited Teddy and the boys to his favourite pub in Port Melbourne.

They all sat down and had a couple of pots.

Barry waited for them all to order a meal before he broached the subject.

'Teddy, mate,' he said, 'I've come up with a plan on how we can get our hands on a heap of big abalone. It's on a reef in Victoria, but it's in an area that is a bit deep.'

Teddy looked at his old mate and asked, 'Oh, yer, what's this reef called?'

Barry replied, 'It's called the New Zealand Star Bank.'
Silence followed.

Teddy looked up at Barry and repeated the name slowly, almost in a dream-like manner.

'The New Zealand Star Bank. That's a name that will always be indelibly written across my heart. Two of my mates died on that bastard. Two good blokes who thought that they had struck El Dorado, but it killed the pair of them.'

'What happened to them?' Tom asked quietly. 'Were they taken by sharks?'

Teddy looked at his friends and said, 'No, boys, it wasn't a shark attack. It was the bends. They were deep divers and afraid of nothing. They took one too many chances. Their luck just ran out.'

Silence reigned over the table as each man could feel the pain that Teddy was experiencing.

Barry spoke, 'It must have been hard on you when they died.'

Teddy looked at Barry and said, 'Mate, we have all lost friends over the times, but this was different. We didn't know the first thing about the bends or decompression tables then. We just got into it hard and fast, rip, shit, or bust.'

Barry nodded and said, 'Things are different now. If we went, we would be better set up. You wouldn't be swimming the bags up. You would just be gathering up the abalone and filling a crate at the bottom. Depending on how long you were down, you could decompress on the way up and then sit in the sun and get back in when your time was up.'

Teddy came back from wherever his mind had been and asked the other divers what they thought.

They all agreed to give it a go as long as Teddy went along with the programme.

Teddy nodded slowly and said, 'I can see that you have all given this plan some thought. I won't bullshit you. This is deep and dangerous work. If something goes wrong, then it's all over red rover. There is no coming back from this.'

The boys started to realise just how dangerous this trip was starting to sound, but they also felt the adrenalin start to pump through their veins.

This was what it was all about, the thrill of the chase. This was what they all lived for. This was why they did what they did.

Tom spoke for all of them, 'We are in, if you are.' We all agreed that if you said no, then we would all say no too. 'We are a team, and we don't work apart.'

Teddy said, 'Well, why the fuck not? It will be good to get back into the water again if only to show you girls how it is done.'

Everyone laughed, and they all quietly said in chorus, 'One for all, and all for one. One in, all in.' The camaraderie in the group was solid, and Teddy felt a sense of pride that such a close bond had been formed between them all.

Barry said that he would check out the weather map and get the boat ready.

They all left the pub happy; another adventure was about to begin.

Jack Andrews and Karl were still on the case. They were keeping their noses to the ground and asking around about Barry and Jack's slut of a wife, Hilda.

Jack was driven by a rage so powerful that he was finding it hard to sleep at night.

His drinking was out of control, and he hardly ever ate a home-cooked meal. He would grab a takeaway whenever he felt hungry.

He'd been pulled over in a random breath test a couple of nights before, and he told the young policeman that he was on the job. He told him his wife had left him and he was a bit of a mess. Luckily, the young copper took pity on him and said, 'Just pretend to blow into the breathalyser and get home as fast as you can. I'll cover for you.'

'That's one I owe you,' Jack replied.

Barry started to get the gear ready for the trip.

He made up three 8-foot square crates out of tube steel, with wire netting across the bottom and with about three-foot high sides. The wire netting was same stuff that they used on fences to keep people out of construction sites.

When he loaded them onto the boat, Slither, the odd-job man, came up and asked Barry what he was up to.

Barry told him that they were going out to grab some crayfish by sinking the crates to the bottom. They would put some bait in them, then pull them to the surface, and get a feed of crayfish.

Slither seemed happy with that explanation and wandered off on a mission to find someone who would buy him a drink.

Teddy rang Tony, the bloke who did all the running around for him, and asked him to get the gear out of the Shark Cat and take it all down to Barry's boat as they would be going away for a couple of days.

He told him to do it at night, as he didn't want the world to know that a trip away was about to happen.

Tony understood perfectly.

All the boys were excited.

They were going on a dangerous and exciting raid.

Secretly, they all were a little scared, but that just made it all the better. They were never going to die sitting behind a desk, pushing a pen around. If their number came out, they would die like men, with an abalone iron in their hands.

They prepared their women and told them they were going away for a couple of days.

They didn't go into the details.

Tony got all the gear down to Barry's boat, and he and Barry stored what they could below the deck. The rest they hid out of sight under a tarpaulin.

They didn't notice that Slither was watching their every move from a hiding place where he sometimes slept.

Slither was on the ball; for some reason, he didn't believe that the cages that Barry had loaded were for crayfish. He thought that something dodgy was afoot.

As soon as Tony and Barry drove away from the marina, he slowly went aboard Barry's boat and saw that all the gear that was needed for a poaching operation was stacked neatly in the wheelhouse.

Slither returned to the wharf and went to the local payphone.

Slither rang his new best friend Detective Jack Andrews and softly said, 'I've got some information for you about Barry and your ex-wife. What's it worth?'

Jack felt a surge of excitement.

He laughed out loud and said, 'Well, mate, that all depends on how important the information is.'

Slither sensed that he had his prey on the line.

He said, 'I want your guarantee that you will give me a spot tomorrow.'

Jack thought for a moment and said, 'If the news is good, then it's worth $100. Tell me what it is.'

Slither smiled to himself and said, 'That Tony who does all the running around for Teddy, the little wog bloke, he and Barry were down here tonight, loading up all the gear for the crew to go away for another poaching operation. I reckon that they will head over to Tasmania. They normally take the big boat away when they go to Tassie.'

Jack smiled and thought, *I'll let Wallace, the fisheries inspector, in on their little secret. That should burst their little bubble.*

Jack said to Slither, 'Well done, mate, I'll drop the hundred around to you tomorrow.'

Slither started to panic. 'Don't come down here to the marina,' he said. 'I don't want anyone to see me talking to you. I'll meet you at the public toilet block in the gardens in St Kilda. What time do you want me to be there?'

Jack knew of the toilet block that Slither referred to. It was a popular hang-out for poofters, druggies, and other weirdos.

Jack thought that he had better make it early as it really started to kick into gear when the sun went down.

'Let's make it at eleven in the morning,' he said.

'OK. I'll see you then,' Slither replied.

Jack hung up and thought for a while. It was handy having that old drunk on the lookout; at least, he knew what was going on.

Wallace Trotter was relaxing at his desk. He was going through a few reports on poachers whom he had outsmarted.

He had got a couple of school kids for taking undersized abalone, a family of Vietnamese for undersized bream, and a couple of drunken Aussies for overstepping their quota of dusky flathead. As far as Piggy was concerned, he was on the ball and keeping everything under control in his area.

He was feeling well pleased with himself when his phone rang. He hesitated in picking it up, as if you answer the phone too quickly, then the person on the other end would think that you were sitting there just waiting for it to ring.

'Fisheries Officer Wallace Trotter. How can I help you?'

'Hello, Officer Trotter, this is Detective Jack Andrews. I'm calling you to enlighten you to the fact that your favourite band of abalone poachers is on the move once again. They have just loaded their seventy-foot boat with diving gear and, as I speak, are getting ready to take off. My guess is that they will be heading over to Tasmania. They have done that sort of thing before I believe.'

Piggy was ready to rock and roll.

'Thanks for the information. Are you sure that they are going poaching. Last time we staked out a processing plant, and they weren't even out. They were all sitting home. It was me who was the mug sitting up all night with my dick in my hand and all for nothing.'

Jack had expected Piggy to be a bit defensive, as the last time had been a bit of a let-down. Luckily, none of the shit that hit the fan had landed on him.

'Well, my contact on the waterfront just rang and told me that they are ready to go. They will probably leave in the morning,' Jack said.

Piggy thanked the detective and disconnected—time to start organising people.

Turning around to the other fisheries officers, he said in a loud voice, 'Ladies and gentlemen, I have just been informed that that bastard Teddy and his band of desperadoes are about to hit the water and go on another poaching operation. They have loaded up the big boat at the St Kilda Marina and are, as I speak, preparing to head for the islands in Bass Strait. We will approach them on a number of fronts. Firstly, we will make sure that they have left their homes. Secondly, we will be looking for them from the air, and thirdly, we will try to apprehend them as they steam back into the bay. We will have the fisheries and the water police on standby. This time, they will not elude us. Now get yourselves ready for a few nights away from home. We will meet back here in four hours. Be ready to put in a few hard days.'

With that, the assembled officers started to make plans.

Barry contacted Teddy and said that they would be off in the morning.

It would take them a day to get there, so they should get into the water the next day.

Teddy asked Barry if the divers could be picked up at the Williamstown wharf, and Barry agreed.

Teddy rang the divers and told them that he would pick them all up at about 9 a.m. at the Williamstown wharf.

The next morning, an excited Slither was down at the wharf when Barry and Hilda arrived and got the boat shipshape—ready to cast off.

He asked Barry, 'What's up, mate? Are you heading off for another trip with Teddy and the boys?'

Barry smiled and said, 'No, mate, we are just heading out for a couple of days on the water, a bit of a holiday.'

Slither was a bit confused as he watched the boat head off.

He thought that Teddy and the boys would be on board, but they weren't.

Maybe Barry and Hilda were just going away for a couple of days. Or maybe Teddy and his crew would meet up with the big boat at sea, a bit like one of the trips that they did before.

It was a bit of a mystery. He wouldn't mention to Jack Andrews that Teddy and his crew weren't aboard when the boat left port.

He didn't want to jeopardise his $100.

Barry headed towards the Williamstown wharf, and as they were approaching, he could see the four men standing with their small bags on the wharf.

He pulled the boat up, and they lithely jumped aboard.

Barry steered the boat away from the wharf and headed towards the heads of Port Phillip Bay.

✧ ✧ ✧ ✧

Piggy was all go.

He had fisheries officers staking out Teddy's house and also Dean and Leckie's place.

When Teddy drove out onto the street, they followed at a discreet distance.

They followed as he picked up the other three divers and then drove down to the wharf at Williamstown.

They saw all the boys get out of Teddy's car and walk with their bags, out to the end of the wharf.

Teddy locked the car door and walked towards where he could see Barry's boat heading towards the wharf.

He had arranged for Rita to walk down from the library and take the car back home.

Piggy was up with all the latest information.

He knew that Barry had left the marina, that Barry had picked up the boys from Williamstown wharf, and that they were heading out and were probably going over to the islands in the middle of Bass Strait.

It was all too easy.

Did that Teddy really think that by leaving the marina without the divers and picking them up at another wharf would confuse Wallace Trotter?

Not a snowball's chance in hell. He was well onto them. They were in for a big surprise, and he was just the person to orchestrate such a cunning move.

Piggy smiled and thought about getting some food into himself.

Barry steamed out through the heads and started up the coast. Hilda started to get a bit of lunch going—ham and salad rolls—and the boys all ate hungrily.

Hilda was happy; she was really happy that life had taken a change and it was for the better.

Barry had explained to her that he was to receive 20 per cent of the overall money that they made on this trip, and, after he took out fuel and tucker, he would split what was left with her. Hilda tried to argue with Barry that the offer was far too generous, but Barry insisted and wouldn't take a step backwards.

Barry wasn't a fool. He knew that if Hilda was making money, then she was more likely to stay around.

He couldn't stand the thought of her not being with him. He was getting more and more dependent on her company.

Jack and Karl drove to the public toilets in the St Kilda gardens. It was a sunny morning, and there were a few people around. Karl asked Jack if he needed a bodyguard as the toilets were well known as a pickup spot for homos.

Jack assured him that he would be all right.

'Well, if you need a hand, just scream out loudly, sweetheart,' Karl lisped.

'Get fucked' was all Jack had to say.

'Good luck, tiger,' Karl laughed.

Jack walked towards the toilets and went inside. It was dark and cool in there, and they stank of piss. Jack tried not to breathe through his nose.

Slither was talking to a bloke who was obviously gay. They both looked up when Jack walked in.

The gay boy walked away, and Slither said, 'He's a mate of mine. I know him from the marina. I'm not a poofter. We are just friends.'

Jack didn't want to go into Slither's love life.

He abruptly said, 'Here's your money. Keep in touch, and let me know what's going on down at the marina. And let me know when they come back. OK?'

Slither nodded and clutched the envelope that Jack had given him. He had enough for a drink, but he would have to steer clear of the pubs that he owed money to.

He would go somewhere quiet and get some rum into him, and then he would get back to the marina and wait for Barry to come back.

This was a good little cash cow that he was on to.

Barry, Teddy, and the divers went through how they were going to get the maximum possible amount of abalone up on deck from the depths. Teddy didn't want anything to go wrong.

He knew one mistake could spell disaster. There could be lives lost, and that wouldn't happen, not if he had anything to do with it.

Even though he had, in his career, sunk five runabouts, he had never lost a deckhand or fellow diver in all the years that he had been diving. He wasn't going to get careless now.

Teddy agreed with Barry that they would drop anchor and lay above the shallowest part of the reef. They would attach parachutes onto each corner of the crates, and then they would throw them over the side. So if they wanted to shift them to a better position, all they had to do was fill the parachutes with air and that would render them weightless and easier to move.

Teddy reckoned that if the abalone were as thick as folklore said, then a diver could easily chip off ten kilos of shell weight in about twenty seconds.

If they could all do that and get the abalone into the crates, they should be able to fill one crate in about thirty minutes.

The thing that would slow them up was getting the abalone into the crates. If the crates weren't positioned in exactly the right place, then there would be time lost. They couldn't afford to waste any time at all when they were at the bottom. It would be hit the bottom, go like hell, and don't waste a second. But when you come up, do it as slowly as you can. Don't pass any bubbles, not even the tiny ones.

Piggy had organised a fixed wing plane to spot the desperadoes. He had given Teddy time to get wherever he was going, and, as the sun popped up from the horizon, Piggy and the pilot took off from Essendon airport.

They quickly flew above Melbourne and headed towards Tasmania via the Bass Strait islands. They skimmed around the islands but couldn't see Barry's boat. Piggy started to think that they were on the wrong track. They should have come across them by now.

They kept searching; surely they would see them soon.

After about two hours of flying around the islands, the pilot indicated that they were getting low on fuel, not dangerously low, but it was a bit of a concern.

He looked at Piggy and said, 'If we run out of petrol, we can't just get out and push it home, you know.'

Piggy asked himself why he thought that they had gone to Tasmania. Didn't Detective Jack Andrews say that they were going to head out into Bass Strait?

What made him think that they were going out into Bass Strait?

He rang Jack.

When Jack's phone rang, he was still in his dirty messy bed with a young prostitute, who looked even younger in the morning light. He was nursing a huge hangover.

He had vague memories of cruising the streets of St Kilda half pissed, looking for a root.

Shit, he was going to have to be careful.

He wondered who would be ringing at this hour. Maybe it was news about that bitch of a wife of his.

He looked at the screen and recognised Wallace Trotter's number. He thought about not answering, but he was awake now, so he might as well.

He put the phone to his ear and answered, 'Hi, Wallace, how are you going?'

The background noise made it difficult to hear what Wallace was saying. But Jack just heard him ask who had said that Teddy was going over to the islands.

Jack answered, 'It was my contact down at the marina. He seemed pretty sure that they were heading over to the islands.'

'Well, we can't see them. They don't appear to be here anywhere,' Piggy replied.

Jack asked, 'Do you think that they might have headed off the other way?'

Piggy was bamboozled. He replied, 'I'm stuffed if I know where the bastards are. I'll keep looking.'

Piggy disconnected and said to the pilot, 'We'll just keep looking around for as long as we can and then head home.'

Jack looked at the young girl or child's face and wondered what he was going to do with her.

A crazy thought ran through his drink-soddened mind that he should have a practice run, beat her, and kill her—just like what he was going to do with his wife Hilda. The young girl sensed that trouble was brewing.

She jumped up out of bed and said, 'Shit, I've got to get back and relieve the babysitter.'

She started dressing quickly and said, 'Where's my money? I'll call a taxi. What's the address?'

Jack told her.

She spoke to the taxi company and held out her hand. Jack put a couple of fifties in it.

The girl looked at the money, remembered he was a copper, and said, 'Hope you had a good time, love. You are really good in bed.'

She smiled and walked out to wait for the taxi. No way was she letting him have another root for only 100 dollars.

Jack heard the taxi pull up and drive off.

He shook his head and lay back in the smelly bed; his head pounded.

As the sun rose above the horizon, Teddy and the boys stirred. They were all excited.

Today was the day. How would it go? Would it be as a big a day as they all expected?

Hilda was in the galley, cooking up eggs and bacon and short black coffees. It was important for the divers not to eat too much as a full belly slowed you down.

Today they didn't want to be slowed down by anything.

The boys suited up, and Teddy organised the air hoses. Dean and Curly would work off a T-piece, and Teddy and Tommy would work off separate air lines. All the air lines were run out, and the divers were ready to hit the water.

They dropped a crate over the side in seventy odd foot of water.

Teddy laughed and said, 'Let's get this show on the road and belt a few of these little suckers off the bottom.'

With that, the four divers descended down into the depths. Down and down, they went. Suddenly they all spotted the bottom at once. Visibility was about forty feet, and the crate was sitting on the reef directly below.

They realised that there were abalone everywhere. They seemed to form a carpet, and their shells were almost touching each other. It was impossible to know where to start.

Tom swam ahead and started to chip off the abalone. He gathered about ten in his hands and was the first to put them into the crate. The boys broke out of their dream time and started to chip off abalone.

They each picked a side of the crate and started to work as fast as they could.

Teddy kept his eye on his watch. He had it set so that he would feel a vibration after fifteen minutes.

Everything was going smoothly, and the crate was slowly filling up.

When the time was up, his watch vibrated, and he went over to Dean and Curly. He pointed to the surface and slowly rotated his finger. They both took whatever abalone they had over to the crate.

Teddy swam over to Tom and gave him the thumbs up. Tom stopped chipping abalone and took his armful over to the crate.

Together, they all swam slowly upwards.

Barry explained to Hilda about how you could tell, by the bubbles, when the divers were coming up. He also explained how important it was for the ascent to be as slow as possible. Then he went on to explain how the nitrogen and oxygen separate in the diver's bloodstream and how on a rapid ascent the oxygen re-entered the bloodstream very easily but the nitrogen bubbles got bigger and bigger as the diver got closer and closer to the surface. The nitrogen bubbles would expand and cut off the supply of blood to the brain, rendering the diver paralysed and in a lot of pain. Hardly any diver survived a spinal bend.

If they did survive, they were badly affected for the rest of their lives. They were sometimes confined to a wheelchair and needed constant medical support.

Hilda started to realise just how dangerous what the boys were doing really was. She started to feel a deep concern for all the boys. They had shown her nothing but kindness and helped her in any way they could.

If it hadn't been for Teddy and Dean, she could quite possibly be dead and resting in a shallow grave somewhere.

She said a silent prayer for nothing bad to happen to them and for them to end the dive without any trouble.

Teddy and the three boys slowly made their way to the surface, making sure not to pass any bubbles. By doing this, they were sure that all the nitrogen bubbles would have time to re-enter into their bloodstream.

They broke the surface and made their way across to where Barry and Hilda were waiting. They got on board and were helped out of their diving vests by Barry and Hilda.

The boys were elated and on a real high, and they all started to talk at once.

Curly said, 'Jesus, Barry, you should have seen the bloody abalone down there. They are back-to-back. I reckon that there must be 100 tonnes of the bastards down on the reef. As we were coming up, we could see they just went on and on. It's amazing. I've never seen abalone like that before. It was like Pedra Branca only better. Lots more abalone down here.'

All the boys agreed; even Teddy, who thought that he had seen the lot, was amazed.

He said to Barry, 'Mate, I'm stunned. There are a lot of abalone down there. No wonder my mates went mad. It must have been a mind-blowing experience for them falling on that many abalone.'

All the boys nodded.

Teddy said to Barry, 'Mate, we have got that crate about half-full. I don't reckon that we will fill it up as I don't know if the winch is powerful enough to lift any more weight.'

Barry nodded and said, 'That's a good problem to have. It's a bit like saying that I've got no more room left in my wallet to put any notes in.'

Everybody laughed.

Hilda asked if anyone wanted anything to eat or drink. They all refused the offer as they didn't want to have full bellies when they went back in.

After an hour, the divers readied themselves to go back into the ocean. They manhandled another crate over the side, and it sank into the water. This time, the trip down wasn't as daunting as they had been there before.

They saw the bottom and the new crate. It was about thirty feet from the half-full one. They hit the bottom and started to chip at full speed; soon the new crate was half-full of abalone.

The abalone were so thick at the bottom that the divers had to clear a spot to kneel on, and as the crate was beside them, all they had to do was chip off maybe ten abalone and place them into the crate.

Soon all the area around the crate was stripped, and the divers had to swim away a few feet, chip off as many abalone as they could carry, then head back, and dump them in the crate.

Once again, Teddy's watch vibrated on his wrist, and, once again, he swam around the divers and gave them the signal to start towards the surface.

As a group, they started their long ascent.

When they got on board and Barry asked how it all went, Teddy laughed and said, 'We are definitely getting better at this caper. I reckon that we ended up with more in the last crate than we did on the first one.'

All the boys agreed.

They had a rest, and then it was time to hit the water again. So they carried the last of the crates over to the side of the boat and tossed it into the ocean.

The boys descended into the depths. They were starting to get a bit cold, and they all were happy that this was their last dive.

In their minds, they tallied up how much abalone they had so far. It was hard to estimate as they weren't putting them into net bags as they usually did. They would have a better idea when the abalone was shucked out and in the plastic bags.

They started to put abalone into the last crate.

Dean and Curly were working close together as they were on the T-piece. Things were going smoothly. Dean kept his eyes on Teddy and Tom, and he was amazed at how much abalone they all could get into the crate.

Their time at the bottom was almost over, and the crate was getting fuller and fuller.

Dean laughed to himself and thought, *What was it Barry said? 'It is as easy as taking corn off a blind chook.'*

He breathed out, and suddenly there was no air.

Fuck me, no air. What could possibly have gone wrong? He thought.

He frantically looked at Curly. *He's got no air either.* He had forgotten that he and Curly were on a T-piece.

Curly looked at Dean and ran his finger across his throat in a cutting motion.

They were both in real trouble. They were deep, and neither of the pair had any air in their lungs.

Curly swam across to Tom, and he saw that Tom still had air.

He spat out his demand valve, and, as he got near Tom, he pointed to his mouth and mouthed, 'Air'.

Tom immediately summed up the situation, dragged a large amount of air into his lungs, took out his demand valve, and passed it to Curly.

Curly sucked hungrily on the demand valve.

He breathed heavily until his breathing was under control.

Dean panicked. He could only think of one thing, and that was making it to the top. Leaving his useless demand valve, he struck out for the surface more than 100 feet above him.

Deep inside him, he knew that he wouldn't make it.

Teddy had been watching what had happened. He saw Curly frantically swim across to Tom and start to buddy-breathe with him, and he saw Dean strike for the surface and could see that he had panicked.

Teddy desperately swam towards Dean's air line and grabbed hold of that. He started to swim up towards Dean who was rapidly heading for the surface. Teddy started to pull himself, hand over hand, up towards the frantically swimming Dean.

Dean felt the weight on his air line and thought that somehow he had got his air line snagged on something. He started to take off his weight vest that the air line was attached to. This action slowed him down and allowed Teddy to catch up with him.

Teddy wrapped his arms around Dean. Dean realised that it was Teddy, and he could see in Teddy's eyes a determination.

Dean thought, *Teddy's here, and everything will be all right.*

Teddy took a deep breath and pushed the demand valve into Dean's mouth. Dean started to take big lungfuls. Teddy waited for Dean's breathing to slow down and indicated that he needed air. Dean passed back the demand valve, and Teddy took a couple of deep breaths.

On deck, Barry and Hilda were watching the bubbles and talking quietly. The noise of the compressors wasn't too bad, so they could hear each other.

Barry was telling Hilda about his life—how he and Des had been good mates and some of the tricks that they got up to.

Suddenly there was a loud popping noise and the sound of air rushing out.

Barry's face went pale.

'Fuck me dead, one of the compressors has blown a hose,' he said.

They rushed to where the compressors were and saw that the hose to the reserve tank was blown open.

Barry started to panic. *What the fuck can I do?* He asked himself. *I think that it's the T-piece line. That means that there are two divers in trouble.*

'Fuck me, keep an eye out for them. They might try to make it to the surface. If they do, they will need assistance to get to the boat,' he said to Hilda.

Barry grabbed a long length of rope and tied a bowline knot in it, forming a big loop.

He tied off the other end onto the deck railing and started to get out of his clothes.

He said to Hilda, 'When they hit the surface, I'll go over the side and swim to them. When I've got hold of them, you start pulling me in. I'll get them to the boat somehow. Fuck me, this looks bad, really bad. We are going to have some sick boys on our hands.'

Hilda could see that Barry was willing to risk his life to assist the divers. She realised what a good and decent bloke Barry was.

The pair of them waited, hardly breathing, to see what condition the boys would surface in.

Teddy knew that Tom and Curly would be making their way to the top. So he and Dean also headed upwards.

When they broke the surface, they saw Barry and Hilda looking anxiously towards them.

Teddy noticed that Barry was stripped down to his underwear and he had a rope around his shoulders. Teddy knew that Barry was on the verge of diving in to help them if they needed assistance.

Teddy gave Barry the thumbs up to let him know that they were all right.

Barry and Hilda started to pull in the air lines.

The boys got aboard, and they all started to talk at once.

Teddy asked Barry, 'What the fuck happened?'

Barry pointed to the compressor and said, 'The air hose from the compressor to the reserve tank blew out, and I didn't know if I should connect the air line straight to the compressor. I didn't know whether, if I released the pressure, then the weight of the water down there would try and squeeze you up the air line. I was worried that the difference in pressures would rip your tongues out.'

Teddy sized up the problem quickly.

'Connect the air line directly to the compressor. We will all go straight back down and decompress on the way up. We will come up the anchor chain very slowly.'

He faced the boys and said, 'Here's the plan. We all go down and swim to the anchor chain. I'll come up first, and don't any of you overtake me. It will take a while, maybe thirty minutes to complete the ascent. No short cuts. Do what I say.'

With that, the divers entered the water and swam to the bottom. They made their way to the anchor chain and slowly, hand over hand, Teddy worked his way towards the surface. It took a long time, and all the divers were cold, chilled to the bone, as they weren't used to the deep cold water. Finally, they made it up to the boat and got out of their diving gear. They were strangely silent.

Dean said, 'Thanks for grabbing me and stopping me, trying to get to the surface. I wouldn't have made it. I'm sorry for panicking. I don't know what came over me.'

Teddy laughed and said, 'Dean mate, I didn't want you to get to the surface and interrupt Barry and Hilda—whatever it was that they were up to. As it was, Barry was down to his underwear.'

Everybody laughed; even Hilda saw the funny side of it all.

Tom said, 'Bloody hell, you can imagine the fright that I got when Curly snatched my demand valve out of my gob.'

Relief flooded over everyone, and they all realised just how close they had come to being really in trouble.

Teddy said, 'I blame myself. We shouldn't have used the T-piece. From now on, everybody will have their own air lines.'

Barry said, 'Who's going to go down and hook onto the crates?'

Tom said, 'That's my job. I always swim the bags up, so I may as well do these three crates.'

Teddy said, 'I'll come along and give you a hand if you need it.'

Tom looked at Teddy and said, 'It's not a problem, mate. I'll do it.'

Barry got the boom on the mast and ran the wire rope through the pulley on the end. He let it slowly sink into the water. The wire was marked every fifty foot. When there was enough rope out to reach the bottom, Tom swam down and hooked up the four slings that were attached to the corners of the first crate. He gave his air line three hard pulls, and Barry started to winch the crate to the surface. Tom grabbed hold of the side and got a ride up. When the crate reached the surface, Barry winched it aboard and lowered it onto the deck. The boys took off the four slings that had lifted the crate and dropped them over the side. Tom swam down, picked them up off the bottom, and connected them to the next wire crate. He gave three hard pulls on his air line, and, once again, the crate was pulled to the surface. Barry lowered the crate onto the first one, and the boys undid the slings. Over the side they went, and down went Tom for the last time.

When all the crates were loaded onto the boat, they completely covered them with a tarpaulin. There wasn't any way anyone could tell that they had abalone in them. Barry up-anchored and headed out to sea. And the boys got ready for some food.

When they were about forty miles offshore, Barry turned off the motor and let the boat wallow in the oily smooth ocean.

In the silence, they heard the sound of a small aeroplane. They looked up and saw a small Cessna heading in their direction.

'I bet that's the fucking fisheries,' Teddy said.

Wallace Piggy Trotter had ceased looking for Teddy and his crew in the islands in Bass Strait. They returned to Essendon airport, and he told the pilot to refuel. If they hadn't gone that way, then they must have gone towards the New South Wales, Victorian border.

Piggy and the pilot scanned the area around the heads and then went up the coast. They were able to identify most boats as they had their numbers painted on the wheelhouse roof.

'There's no sign of the bastards yet,' Piggy complained.

The pilot agreed, 'I wonder where they have got to.'

They flew around the South Gippsland coast and up the Ninety Mile beach.

'Bloody lot of sand in that beach,' Piggy commented.

'Yes, I would have to count every grain,' the pilot confessed.

They flew past Cape Conran and towards Wingan Point. There was silence in the plane apart from the engine noise.

When they came to Wingan Point, the pilot asked Piggy, 'Do you want to have a look at the New Zealand Star Bank. It's about ten or eleven miles off the coast. It's bloody deep.'

Piggy thought, *Why not? Even if there is next to no chance that Teddy and his crew are out in the deep water.*

'Yes, OK', he said, 'but I don't reckon that they will be out there. These blokes are hit-and-run. They like to get in and out without anyone knowing what happened.'

The pilot swung the Cessna out to sea.

After a short time, he said, 'We should be above the reef now, I reckon.'

They both scanned the ocean and didn't see anything. Piggy looked further out to sea through his binoculars. Just for a split second, he thought that he might have spotted an object on the horizon.

'Shit!' Piggy yelled out. 'There's some boat way out to sea. Let's go out and have a look.'

The pilot guided the Cessna out to sea, and soon they had Barry's boat in sight.

'There the bastards are,' Piggy shouted in joy. 'I knew that we would find them sooner or later. They reckon that they can outsmart me. I'll show the bastards who's running this show. What's under the tarp? That's what I want to know. What have the bastards been up to? Circle the boat, and I'll take some photos of them. We will have to hurry as it will soon be dark.'

Teddy and the crew watched as the Cessna circled them.

Barry said, 'I'll bet you a million to one that the fisheries are in that plane, and I bet that they are taking photos of the crates that are stacked on the deck.'

Teddy remained calm and said, 'As far as they know the crates might contain anything at all, they might even be empty, and they can't see the abalone. So until they lift the tarp, we are safe. We will have to have a plan as to how we are going to unload, but apart from that, we are in the clear. We will wait until dark and then start to shuck out the abalone meat. Let's get some tucker into us.'

With that, they ignored the Cessna and went into the galley where Hilda had prepared a feast of roast beef and vegetables.

The divers were tired but relaxed. They knew that they had a big job in front of them, shucking out the abalone.

After the meal, Teddy said, 'Hilda, that was a great meal. We all really appreciate the amount of effort that you put into the cooking of our meals. Thanks very much.'

With that, all at the table raised their glasses. Hilda went a bit red and got embarrassed.

She said, 'If it wasn't for all your kindness, I wouldn't be here. So I feel that I'm paying you all back a little by cooking for you. Believe me, it's no trouble, no trouble at all.'

Hilda felt as if she was one of the team and that she was doing something useful. She hadn't felt this self-satisfaction in a long time.

Teddy laughed and said, 'Let's get into those little suckers.'

Soon they were all involved in shelling out the abalone.

Dean and Curly climbed up and started passing down bundles of abalone that had stuck together. As many as ten abalone were sometimes all stuck together.

Soon the first crate was empty.

The boys lifted the crate off, and Dean and Curly started to unload the second crate.

As before, the abalone were shucked out into drainage bins. The clear blood dripped onto the deck and ran in small rivulets into the ocean. Then the abalone meat was scooped into thick, clear plastic bags, and a wire tie was coiled around the top of the plastic bag tightly so that no blood would escape. Then the plastic bags were stacked at the stern of the boat, and a tarp was placed over them.

Barry said to Teddy, 'Mate, the fisheries are on to us. How are we going to get the meat ashore?'

Teddy had been thinking about little else while they were shucking out the abalone.

He said, 'Mate, I reckon that we head full speed towards Melbourne in the big boat, and I'll get Tony to meet us out at sea in the Shark Cat. We will transfer the abalone onto the Shark Cat. I'll go with Tony, and we'll beach the abalone somewhere around Phillip Island. The big boat will keep on going into the bay. With a bit of luck, the fisheries will be dead set sure that the abalone will be on the big boat. But we will run the abalone into Derek's processing factory and Bob's, your uncle.'

Slither, the odd-job man from the marina, was wallowing in the luxury of having enough money to get well inebriated. He was drinking pots of beer and having rum chasers.

Yes, there was no doubt about it. This job of his, spying on Barry and the rest of them, was a real earner.

He could see that it could go on forever. As long as Barry and Teddy were poaching abalone, then there was an earn in it for him.

He looked across the bar room and saw Des, Barry's old deckhand, sitting on his own.

Poor stupid bastard, Slither thought, *I might shout him a beer.* With that, Slither moved across the room and sat down beside Des.

Des looked up and asked, 'What's happening, mate?'

Slither announced proudly, 'I know that Barry and his new female deckhand have headed off for a few days away. They took some wire crates with then. The night before they left, that little wog bloke and Barry loaded up all the abalone poaching gear. They took all the divers gear away with them, but no divers got on board. Maybe they picked them up somewhere.'

Des looked at Slither. He had a pot of beer in front of him and also a shot glass of rum.

He knew that Slither was on the bones of his arse.

So Des asked, 'What happened to you? Did you win TattsLotto or something?'

Slither smiled a greasy smile that showed his blackened, broken teeth and said, 'I'm onto a new lurk, mate. I just keep my eyes open and see what's going on. Enough said.'

I bet Slither is giving up Barry and Teddy. The fucking dog, Des thought.

He completely forgot that he had made a phone call to the fisheries in a drunken stupor. That was when Barry left him out on the trip to New South Wales and took his female deckhand instead.

Des was suddenly overcome with a feeling of loyalty to Barry and Teddy. He abruptly told Slither that he had to go, stood up, and walked out, leaving Slither a bit dumbfounded.

When Des made it home, he immediately rang Barry's mobile phone.

Barry answered and said, 'Hullo, Des, what's up?'

Des answered, 'Mate, I don't know or care where you are, but I just had a drink with that bastard Slither, and he reckons that he's onto a new lurk. I reckon that he's been spying on you and reporting back to the same coppers that are after your new deckhand. He was pissed as a parrot and had a pocket full of money.

So, mate, I'm ringing to say that you are being watched and be careful when you come back as the fisheries are more than likely onto you.'

Des was talking so fast that he was breathless.

Barry said, 'Thanks for the warning, mate. Can you sit by the phone while I have a talk to Teddy and work out a plan?'

Des agreed, 'Yes, mate, I'm here. If you need me, just give me a ring.'

All the boys sat down and made a plan.

Barry explained to them that Des reckoned that Slither had sold them down the drain. There could be a reception committee waiting for them when they sailed into Port Phillip Bay.

Teddy had a plan and said, 'Here's what I reckon. Like I said to Barry earlier. We'll get Tony to tow the Shark Cat down to Phillip Island and put it in the water at Rhyll. Des can shoot across to my place, grab my van, and meet up with Tony at the ramp. Then Des can come out in the Shark Cat and grab the abalone meat off Barry's boat. I'll go in with Des and load it into the van while you and the rest of the crew steam back into Port Phillip Bay into the waiting arms of the fisheries and whoever else may be there.'

Teddy rang Tony and alerted him to grab the Shark Cat, drive down to Phillip Island, and meet up with Des, who would have Teddy's van. They would launch the Shark Cat and wait for further instructions.

When Tony's phone rang, Tony said to his wife, 'I bet that it's Teddy on the line. I reckon that he's in trouble and needs me to pick them up somewhere.'

He answered the phone and, on hearing Teddy's voice, gave his wife the thumbs up. He listened in silence and then repeated what Teddy had said to him.

Tony said to his wife, 'I'm off. See you when I see you.'

He was out the door and into the F100 and towed the Shark Cat into the night.

Teddy rang Des and asked if he could go over to his place, pick up his van, grab a mobile phone and the keys off Rita, and meet Tony down at the Rhyll boat ramp. He would then run the Shark Cat out to Barry's boat.

Barry had the boat out from Phillip Island. He knew that Des was on the way as Tony had given Teddy a ring to say that the Shark Cat was in the water and Des was on his way.

Barry looked at the radar and saw a boat approaching them. Barry had the lights on the top of the mast on, and Des saw the boat from a long way off.

He was soon beside the big boat.

The sea was calm, and the boys got in and unloaded the abalone meat from the big boat to the Shark Cat.

Teddy said to Barry, 'I'll go in with Des and get this back to Derek's factory. You continue on your way back to Melbourne.'

Barry felt a lot better now that the abalone was off the big boat. He gave Teddy a wave as the boats parted.

Teddy and Des made their way back to the boat ramp where Tony had the trailer in the water waiting. Teddy drove the boat up onto the trailer, and Tony pulled the laden Shark Cat out of the water and parked beside Teddy's van.

The bagged abalone meat was transferred into the van, and Teddy and Des quickly got moving towards Derek's processing factory.

When Murphy, the elderly security guard and recipient of many crayfish from Derek, came on shift, he noticed that there was a 4WD parked in a hidey-hole where the occupant could watch Derek's processing factory.

He thought to himself, *Well, look who's back. I'll give Derek a ring and tell him that our friend is back, watching him.*

Derek answered the phone, and when Murphy told him that there was a stake-out on the factory, Derek smiled.

He rang Teddy.

'Mate, we are in trouble. There's fisheries officers watching the factory. Thank Christ that the security bloke is on our side. You would have walked into a trap. I've made preparations for this. Take the abalone to a mate of mine's factory. He's called Bob, and he supplies me with pre-cut chips. I'll meet you there, and we will throw all the abalone into his cool room.'

He gave Teddy the address and then rang Bob to let him know that, as agreed, he would unload some abalone meat into his cool room.

Bob agreed, and they made a plan to meet at his factory.

Derek and Bob were waiting and having a cup of coffee when Teddy and Des pulled up at the cool room's sliding door.

Piggy was sure that he had the bastards this time. He reckoned that they had done a deep dive on the New Zealand Star Bank reef.

He thought he had driven Teddy and his band of desperadoes out into deep water. Surely this was a sign that Wallace P. Trotter had them on the ropes. *Bastards, victory at last,* Piggy thought to himself.

Piggy had already organised a stake-out at Derek's factory.

He alerted the water police that Barry's boat would soon be heading across Port Phillip Bay, and he wanted it apprehended and searched. He would be on that police boat and could feel the warm feeling of at last seeing Teddy and his band rotting away in jail.

As the day dawned, Piggy and a couple of other fisheries officers were sitting comfortably in the forty-five-foot police launch and steaming out into the middle of the bay.

The police had been alerted that Barry's boat had made its way through the heads and was on course for the St Kilda Marina.

As they came into view, Piggy shouted, 'There the bastards are. They have a tarpaulin covering up the crates of abalone. Faster, faster.'

Piggy was over the moon. The water policeman turned on the boat's siren and pulled up alongside Barry's boat. Barry dropped the revs and came to a standstill. Piggy and his fisheries officers scrambled aboard.

Piggy shouted, 'We are fisheries officers and demand the right to search this vessel and arrest everyone on board for the illegal taking of abalone.'

Piggy strode purposely down the deck and untied the ropes that were around the crates to hold the tarpaulin in place. With a flourish, he whipped back the tarp to be confronted by three empty crates.

There was a stunned silence as Piggy stared at the empty crates.

'What . . . what happened to the abalone?' Piggy gasped.

Barry asked, 'What the fuck are you talking about? What abalone? Mate, you've got to get a firm grip on yourself. I haven't got a fucking clue what you are talking about.'

Piggy's mouth was moving, but no words were coming out.

'The abalone, the abalone, where are all the abalone?' Piggy at last gasped. 'And where is that bastard Teddy?'

'Search the boat from stem to stern. They may have stowed the abalone somewhere,' he said to his officers.

With that, the police and fisheries officers started to look through the boat but, of course, came up empty-handed.

The sergeant of the water police said to Piggy, 'Well, mate, it looks like you are barking up the wrong tree. Did you see them with abalone on board?'

Piggy started to stammer, 'Yes, yes, I took photos of the boat with the abalone on board.'

Piggy had a sudden thought. Although he had taken photos of the crates, they were completely covered up. There could have been anything under the tarps. He knew that he had to catch them with the abalone or else there was nothing to take to court with.

'Where's Teddy?' Piggy demanded.

Barry said with a smirk, 'Teddy decided to get off and walk home.'

All the boys sniggered. Piggy went red and felt his blood pressure rise to an unhealthy level.

Piggy snarled at the water policemen, 'The bastards have unloaded the abalone somewhere. I'm not beaten yet. Take me to shore immediately.'

With that, Piggy and the others clambered aboard the police boat and headed back to shore.

He quickly got onto the fisheries officers who were on stake-out, watching Derek's processing plant.

He said to them, 'Mate, we are on board the boat, and there isn't any abalone here. They have unloaded them somewhere, and they should be arriving at the processing factory any time now. In fact, I'll come straight over and hopefully be there when the bastards arrive.'

Teddy, Des, Derek, and the potato chip man Bob quickly got the abalone into the cool room and closed the door. Teddy asked Derek what he was going to do.

Derek replied, 'I'm going to pack them into ten-kilo boxes and freeze them here. When the time is right, I'll take them over to my factory and put them into my stock. As luck would have it, the boxes of frozen chips are the right size for my abalone cartons. So we'll freeze them here and then deliver them in the chip boxes over to my place. Everyone will think that I'm just getting a delivery of chips for the takeaway.'

Teddy smiled and said, 'Mate, you're a fucking genius. Well done.'

Teddy and Des drove off.

On the way to Des's place, Teddy said, 'Mate, thanks for the tip off about Slither selling us down the drain. He's a prick. He would give up his mother for the price of a drink, poor bastard. At least, we now know that we will have to be careful around him.'

Des said, 'I'll keep my eye on him from now on and just see what he is up to.'

Teddy pulled up outside Des's place and pulled out a wad of 100-dollar bills.

He gave five to Des and said, 'Mate, thanks for your help. We all really appreciate you looking after us.'

Des took the money and said, 'No problem at all, Teddy. This will come in handy, maybe pay a few bills. Thanks, mate. I'll catch up with you and Barry later on for a drink.'

'That sounds good to me, Des,' said Teddy and drove off.

Piggy parked his unmarked fisheries 4WD behind the other fisheries 4WD and got out.

He got into the rear seat and asked the two fisheries officers, 'Is there any movement?'

They said, 'No, Wallace, nothing is happening at all. The girl has come in and is setting up the fish and chip shop. There is no sign of Derek or anybody else.'

'Don't worry, they will come. Sooner or later, they will arrive, and we will be here to grab them,' Piggy said.

In silence, they waited and waited. At about lunchtime, the fish and chip shop was busy with tradesmen coming and going. It seemed like a good business.

Piggy was hungry, so he sent one of the fisheries officers over to get them all a feed of fish and chips. As they were all in plain clothes, the officer fitted in with the clientele. He was served by the young girl behind the counter. He grabbed three cans of Diet Coke and his order and walked back to the vehicles.

Piggy, who was weak from hunger, greedily grabbed handfuls of chips and started to eat and talk at the same time.

Time dragged on. Piggy started snoring in the back seat. Both the other fisheries officers started to get tired; the adrenalin was wearing off, and they were just uncomfortable and tired.

They watched, disinterested, as a van with the name of a chippery backed into the loading bay and a young man started to unload boxes of frozen chips. He wheeled them in quickly and, after placing them into the freezer, got his docket signed and drove off.

Little did the fisheries officers know, but instead of just dumping the frozen boxes into the freezer, he pulled out all the existing boxes of frozen chips and stacked the new boxes of frozen abalone behind them.

The fisheries officers by now were sick and tired of the whole operation. They called for back-up.

When it arrived, they headed home for some rest, and Piggy sat with the new crew. They all watched the factory; not a lot happened.

Barry pulled into the wharf. He had dropped off Dean, Tom, and Curly at the Williamstown wharf.

Then he had steered the boat over to the other side of the bay to the St Kilda Marina.

He and Hilda tied up the boat and walked away towards the secured car park.

On the way, they met Slither. He didn't look the best as he was nursing a hangover and badly needed a drink.

'Hullo, mate,' Barry said, 'how have you been?'

Slither mumbled, 'You're back, aren't you?'

He kept walking with his head down.

'Have a look at the poor bastard,' Barry said to Hilda. 'It's sad to see a bloke end up like that.'

Hilda agreed. They got into their Ute and drove home.

Slither rang Detective Jack Andrew's mobile and stated, 'Barry and his deckhand are back. They seem to be happy, and so that means that they haven't been sprung yet. I don't know about you blokes. You don't seem to be on the ball at all.'

Jack didn't comment. He didn't want to get into a discussion about the ability of the Department of Fisheries. He told Slither to keep his eyes open and report back anything he saw.

Teddy got home, had a shower, and hit the sack.

When he awoke, he called Derek and asked how it all went.

Derek laughed and said, 'The fisheries officers are still watching the factory. We got the abalone load in disguised as potato chips. They are all in the freezer as we speak.'

'How much did we end up with?' Teddy asked.

Derek reported, 'There must have been some abalone down there as we ended up with 1860 kilos.'

Teddy laughed and said, 'Yes, I reckoned that would be about what was there. The boys and Barry will be happy. When can I grab the loot?'

Derek said, 'I'll drop it off to you. I don't reckon that you should be seen here at the factory, with the fisheries keeping an eye on the place. If you like, I'll drop the cash around to Curly's shed at four o'clock this arvo.'

That suited Teddy.

He called Curly and told him to tell the boys that the split-up of the money would be at Curly's shed at 4 p.m. that day. He also rang Barry and told him the same. Barry said that he and Hilda would be there.

All the boys were at Curly's shed, sitting down, having a beer when Derek walked in with a Target plastic bag full of money.

He emptied it out onto the pool table, and everyone felt good.

Derek said, 'Teddy, there's $74,400 there.

All you have to do is split it up, and I think I might grab a beer.'

Teddy started to work the money out.

Barry's 20 per cent worked out to be $14,880. Teddy counted that out.

He had paid Des $500, and he would give Tony $500.

That left $58,000 to be split four ways. That was $14,630 for each of them.

Teddy counted out the money, only stopping for a swig of beer.

Everyone was pleased with their work.

They had a couple of more drinks, and then they all headed home.

Meanwhile, Piggy and the other two fisheries officers were growing tired of playing the waiting game. They felt that nothing was going to happen.

Piggy was suddenly tired of waiting.

He said, 'Fuck them. Let's go and have an unofficial raid, more like a check-up. Derek's not there. There's only the two women in the fish and chip shop. We'll go in, show our badges, and have a look around the place. Just say that it's a routine inspection. We'll see what's in there.'

With that, the fisheries officers drove out of their hiding place and up to the front of the fish and chip shop. They wearily climbed down, and Piggy walked into the serving area.

'Hullo, love,' he said. 'We are fisheries officers, and we are here to do a routine inspection of your premises.'

Carol, the young girl behind the counter, smiled and said, 'Go ahead. You blokes haven't been around for a while.'

Piggy smiled back at her. 'It's just a routine inspection. We just want a look inside your freezers.'

Carol said, 'Help yourselves. We've just had a load of frozen chips come in. So the freezers are pretty full at the moment.'

Piggy and the two officers made their way out into the processing room. All was clean and dry, a sure sign that there hadn't been any action lately.

They opened the blast freezer and saw that it was empty. When they got to the storage freezer, they were met by a wall of frozen potato chip boxes. Piggy ripped one open and saw that it contained frozen chips. He looked at the wall of chip boxes.

He commented to the other two, 'Fuck me dead, they must go through piles of chips here.'

The others grunted and moved back away from the freezing air.

Piggy walked back into the fish and chip shop area.

He said to Carol, 'You seem to have a heap of chips in stock.'

Carol agreed, 'Like the boss says, if you haven't got it, then you can't sell it. I think that he does a deal and gets a bigger discount when he buys in bulk. He's a pretty smart bloke.'

Secretly Carol was a little bit in love with Derek.

Piggy smiled, 'Oh, well, love, we had better get going. I'll give Derek a ring and tell him we had a look and everything is under control.'

Carol looked at Piggy and asked, 'Have we met before? I think that I've seen you around in here or somewhere.'

Piggy smiled and said, 'I must have that kind of face. Quite often people say that they think they know me.'

With that, the fisheries officers walked out and drove off.

Detectives Jack Andrews and Karl sat in their unmarked police car.

Karl said to Jack, 'What's our next move? What are we going to do about Hilda?'

Jack, whose head was still throbbing from a drunken night, said, 'I'm not sure. We've to be a bit careful as if the boss finds out we are still wasting time, checking up on Hilda, we will end up in the shit good and proper. Let's just see how things pan out. Time is on our side.'

Piggy was once again on the carpet, explaining to his superiors about how he had missed Teddy and his gang again. He was running out of excuses, and there was a query about his time sheets and the expenses for the other officers.

His superiors were starting to get the idea that Wallace wasn't the man to catch Teddy and his gang.

One senior fisheries officers said, 'From now on, we must be alerted to all actions that you plan, so we can get an idea of what's going on. This well full of money is starting to dry up. I've been at the minister's office all morning, trying to explain why the fisheries budget has blown out so much in the last year or so.'

Piggy looked at the floor and said, 'Sirs, it's just been bad luck. Every time I thought that I had them cornered, they would come up with another plan. It's almost like there is someone telling them what I plan to do next.'

The senior officers looked sternly at Piggy, and one said, 'Are you suggesting that there is a leak in the department?'

Piggy was clutching at straws. All he was doing was trying to muddy up the water a little. He realised how close he was to the edge.

He said, 'No, sir, not for one moment. I'm not suggesting that we have a rat in the ranks. But it just seems odd that every move I make, they seem to be in front of me.'

The panel looked at one of their most successful fisheries officers and agreed that maybe they should put more into catching this band of abalone poachers, if only to make them look more successful in apprehending this gang.

'We have decided to give you a direct line to the advisor to the minister. Whenever you want something, you must run it past him. Don't hesitate to call him. You have twenty-four-hour access to this man. In other words, this is a step up for you. Use it wisely.'

Piggy nodded solemnly and walked out of the meeting.

He was a little confused. Was this a step up or a step down? Or maybe a step sideways?

Well, he would show the world. He would take it as a step up and a vote of confidence by his superiors.

The more Piggy thought about it, the more he felt it was a step up.

Right, let's kick some arse, he thought.

He was ready and willing to take on that bastard Teddy and his crew.

Just let them try and get one on Wallace P. Trotter.

Meanwhile, Teddy and his crew counted their money.

RIP Jimmy and Meggsy

Two Toms

Tom's father, Tom senior, smiled when Tom and Teddy walked into his messy, single-fronted Williamstown home.

Williamstown started off as a blue-collar suburb on the western side of Melbourne, but as the city expanded, it became a trendy suburb.

Since Tom senior's wife had died, he had let himself go a bit. He didn't shave every day; sometimes he didn't shave every week, and there were food stains down the front of his shirt.

Tom senior had named his son Thomas as had his father and his father's father before him. It was a family tradition.

Tom senior's nickname was Jock. Even Tom junior called him that.

Jock got his nickname on the first day when he started work at the Ford Motor company in Broadmeadows.

He was quietly talking to another Pommy when an Italian, Greek, or Maltese said, 'Fucka me dead, not another fucka Jock, soona we willa be over rana by theesa people.'

The person had mistaken Tom senior's East End accent for that of a Scotsman.

Tom looked at his new-found friend, shook his head, and said, 'Wogs!'

They smiled, and Tom's friend said, 'Well, that's it. From now on, mate, you are known as Jock.'

And from that day on, Tom senior became known as Jock.

Jock took a drag on his unfiltered cigarette. He had smoked two or more packets a day all his life.

He said, 'Tommy, me lad, my race is nearly run. The doctors have said that I've got pancreatic cancer. I've got about six months to live, or at least that's what they told me last week.'

There was no sadness in his voice. He said it in a matter-of-fact way, leaving no doubt to anyone that he was dying.

'I don't want to die in some hospital surrounded by strangers and other people who don't give a fuck about me and won't let me smoke and have two fingers of whisky. I'll check out when it becomes too hard for me. Everything is going to be left to you and Sandy,' he continued.

Tom looked at his dad and said, 'You look pretty fit to me. I reckon that you will last for years yet.'

Jock smiled and said, 'I'm not going to buy any green bananas, just in case I cark it before they are ripe enough to eat.'

Teddy and Tom smiled sadly.

'Jock, is there anything that we can do to make your life easier?' Teddy asked.

Looking at the big bloke with the gold chain, Jock smiled, 'Teddy, you have been a wonderful friend to us all. You and the rest of the lads are a great team, and since you have been together, you have all prospered. You all look after each other, and there has never been a problem. There's no jealousy amongst you, and you are like brothers. In fact, I reckon that you are closer than brothers in a lot of ways.'

Teddy nodded, 'Jock, it's easy. They are a good bunch of blokes.'

Jock nodded and said, 'I'll tell you what I've got in my mind. Now I don't want any arguing as I've made up my mind, and as Tom will tell you, when my mind is made up, then that's it. Nothing will change it.'

Tom and Teddy looked at the wizened old man.

He looked back and said, 'Those two dogs that raped Sandy, I'm going to square up, and I'm gunna knock them.'

There was silence in the room.

Tom and Teddy looked at each other; Tom was the first to speak.

'Dad, you can't be serious. Those are violent men,' he said. 'I can't see you lasting any time with them. They are both built like brick shithouses.'

Jock looked at the two men in front of him and said, 'The bigger they are, the harder they fall.'

Teddy replied, 'The bigger they are, the harder they hit more like it.'

Jock said, 'They didn't do too good when you got stuck into them, if I recall.'

Teddy said, 'Jock mate, that was a bit different. We were fit and ready for them. We took them by surprise and we outnumbered them.'

Jock laughed and said, 'I'm not going to engage in fisticuffs for fuck sake. I'll get up behind them and shoot the bastards in the back of the head. "Two to the head, just to make sure they are dead".' Jock quoted an old gangster rhyme.

Tom said, 'They may have Mafia connections.'

Jock replied, 'Like I told you a million times, lad, if the Mafia are so tough, why haven't they got head offices in Glasgow, Dublin, or Liverpool? They stick to their own. Don't be worried about the Mafia.'

Tom and Teddy looked at each other. They knew that Jock had made his mind up and there was no changing it. He would do what he had planned, with or without their help.

'What do you need?' Teddy asked.

Jock replied, 'I want a revolver, a .38. Don't worry about a silencer. I don't want any of those fancy guns. Just get me a revolver. Nothing can go wrong with a revolver.'

Teddy said, 'I can do that. I'll get it this week if that's what you want.'

Jock smiled, 'That's all I want for Christmas.'

They spoke for a while, and Jock told them about how he was going to do the deed.

He didn't explain exactly how he was going to do the killing, and he made up a story about how he would get away. He didn't want them to know the truth.

When it was time to go, Teddy said, 'Jock mate, I know that you have thought about this long and hard, but I can't help wondering if there isn't another way of going about it.'

Jock turned to Teddy and said, 'You know Tommy as well as I do, and we both know that sooner or later Tom will square up with those two. I don't want him spending his life in jail somewhere because of it. It's better that I do it as it's almost over for me anyway.'

Teddy nodded, and he could see that there was no turning Jock away from the course that he had chosen.

They said their goodbyes and walked out to their car.

Tom said to Teddy, 'He's a tough old rooster, and he can read me like a book. He knows that I'll get even with those two dogs if it's the last thing that I ever do.'

Teddy nodded and said nothing.

Mario and Nick's loan shark business was on the up and up.

There sure was a need for people to borrow money when they were desperate.

The brothers couldn't believe just how easy it was for them. Their biggest problem was people who didn't or couldn't pay them back. These people were dealt with in a vicious manner to prove to everyone that loan sharks weren't to be messed with and wouldn't stand being robbed.

When the person whom they had lent money to realised that they couldn't pay them back and went into hiding, well, then that's when the fun really began. Mario and Nick would go to the person's closest relative and demand to know the borrower's location. If it was a mother or other close relative, then the brothers would threaten them with physical violence or to burn down their houses.

When they finally caught up with the victim, they showed no mercy and gave them a good old-fashioned rough up.

The pair enjoyed the chance to frighten people. It was good to see the fear in people's eyes. It made them feel indestructible, and it made them feel like they were real men.

Mario said to Nick, 'Here comes a new one.'

The brothers were sitting at their normal table beside a bar at the casino.

They both looked up as a beautiful youngish Vietnamese woman walked up to their table. Having seen her around, they were on a nodding acquaintance with her.

'Hullo, Mario. Hullo, Nick,' she said quietly. 'I'm having a bad run, and I left my credit cards at home. I need a loan of a few hundred.'

This was the oldest excuse in the book. Everyone said that they had left their credit cards at home.

Mario rudely asked, 'How much do you want?'

'Would I be able to get a couple of hundred, maybe 500?' she asked in a pleading voice.

Mario smirked and said, 'Are you aware of our interest? It's 10 per cent on your money, and then 10 per cent a day after that. Sometimes we require a bit extra if you know what I mean.'

The Vietnamese woman had heard about the two brothers raping a girl and shuddered at the thought of these two animals touching her. But her need was great, so she put the idea to the back of her mind.

'What security do you need?' she asked.

'We want your driver's licence and your mobile phone number, and we want to know where you work,' Mario said.

'I work at a Vietnamese restaurant called the Lotus Inn in Little Vietnam, Richmond. It is run by a man called Henry and his family. They are very good people. Here is a card from the restaurant. I've written my mobile number on it, and here is my driver's licence.'

Mario took the business card and her driver's licence and read her name out loud, 'Lucy Wong. That's a nice name, Lucy.'

Lucy smiled and said, 'Thank you.'

Mario had money bundled up in his jacket pocket. He had bundles of $500, each with a rubber band around them. So if needed, he could pull out amounts of $500 at a time.

He quickly extracted one bundle and passed it under the table to Lucy, who took it quickly, and it disappeared into her purse.

'Thank you,' she said and walked away.

'Do you think she shaves her pussy?' Nick asked his brother.

'I'm fucked if I know,' Mario answered. 'The ones that I have been with all had smooth fannies. Maybe when women come from that end of the world, they don't have hair on their fannies. Maybe we will get the chance to find out.'

Both the brothers laughed and gave the subject some thought.

Jock was in pain. He was losing weight, and his clothes were starting to hang off him. One morning, he had forgotten to put on a belt and had walked halfway down the front path to get the mail when his fucking pants had fallen down. Thankfully there was no one about, he would have felt like a real dickhead.

He was thankful that Tom and Teddy had agreed for him to take out the two loan sharks. He knew, deep down inside, that Tommy would have squared up and this way there was no way that his son would end up in prison. He felt like a great weight had been lifted off his shoulders.

He thought about his deceased wife, the love of his life, and thought, *It won't be long now, Lassie. I'll be with you soon.*

Teddy knew a few people in the underworld. He was on good terms with some of the once-feared Painters and Dockers. Their motto was 'We catch and kill our own.'

They used to be a powerful force to be reckoned with, but sadly as time went by and drugs infiltrated the underworld, they were seen to be not as powerful as they once were.

Teddy walked from his home around the corner to a little pub called the Staggs Head.

He went into the front bar. It was dimly lit, and he knew a few people in there. He sat down on a bar stool and ordered a pot of VB. It was icy cold, and the bitterness was welcoming.

Teddy sighed and put the half-empty pot onto the bar.

'Fuck me, that tastes good. Now that they have got the recipe back to what it was, there's no beating it,' he said to himself.

The bloke beside him took a sip from an imported stubby and said, 'I don't know how you can drink the local brew. This beer comes from Mexico, and you put a slice of lemon down the top and drink through the lemon. You should try it someday. It's quite refreshing, you know.'

Teddy gave the bloke a smile and said, 'Yes, mate, I might try it one day.'

Here's another fucking wanker, Teddy thought. *I wonder if he knows my ex-missus.*

Teddy ignored the bloke and waited for some of his shadier friends to come in.

The door opened, and a tough-looking older man came in. He had a scarred face and heavily tattooed arms. Because of his age, his tattoos had sagged out of shape. He had a cauliflower ear; his name was Ken.

'Gidday, Kenny mate,' Teddy said. 'How's things going? Can I buy you a pot, mate?'

Ken looked at Teddy and remembered him. He had sold him some hot gear.

He liked Teddy and remembered him as a good bloke who always paid.

'Gidday, Teddy. Where the fuck have you been?' he said. 'Come to think of it, I was only talking to your next-door neighbour the other day, and he was saying how well you were going.'

'Yes, I see a bit of Ronny now and again,' Teddy replied as he indicated to the barmaid that he would have a couple of more pots. 'Mate, while I've got a hold of you, a mate of mine mentioned to me that he wanted to get his hands on a shooter. He wants a .38. It doesn't have to be anything fancy, just an old .38. I think he just wants it to take up the bush and shoot a few beer cans off a fence or something. I hadn't given it much thought, but when I saw you walk in, it suddenly struck me that you know your way around the place and you would be just the man to talk to.'

Ken felt pleased that Teddy considered him the man to talk to about such delicate matters.

He got closer to Teddy and spoke out the corner of his mouth; his lips hardly moved.

'Well, there was a bloke trying to get rid of one last week,' he said. 'But it's a bit dangerous because if the buyer gets caught with it, you just know them, rotten coppers. They will tell him they have tested the gun and it's one that has killed people. So then it looks like the new owner is going to be charged with murder. The bloke will shit himself and tell all. He will dob in whoever he bought the gun from.'

Teddy shook his head and said, 'The oldest trick in the book and the young dickheads tumble into it every time.'

Ken said, 'Mate, I'll see what I can do. You know that the price has gone through the roof. All these wannabe gangsters running around and they all want their own piece. They all reckon that they are *Scarface* or Robert De Niro. Fuck me, it's sad.'

Teddy laughed and said, 'Do the best you can for me, Kenny. I'll meet you back here tomorrow, same time.'

With that, Teddy left the bar, walking past the wanker. He was still drinking an imported beer with a lemon stuffed down the top.

Shaking his head, Teddy wondered what the world was coming to.

Awareness came back slowly to Detective Jack Andrews. It was the middle of the night, and he was still drunk.

He felt as if something was growing in his brain; the pain was intense.

Looked around the room, he realised that he was in his kitchen. Dirty dishes were stacked on every bench top, the sink overflowed with them, and there were plates of half-eaten takeaway food starting to go mouldy.

Everywhere he looked, there was mess. He had gone to sleep, sitting up at the kitchen table.

Jack gulped down a mouthful of warm beer in an effort to make himself feel better. It didn't work.

He had to get even with his runaway wife, and he schemed up a plan.

The plan was, he would go down and hide on that old fisherman's boat and wait until he came down to the marina. Then he would jump him and give him the father of a hiding. That would show the old fart who was boss. That was the only way to do it.

With that in mind, Jack Andrews drove down to the marina.

It was still dark when Jack got there. He slowly and quietly walked towards Barry's boat.

He climbed on board and pulled out a small jemmy bar—the sort people use in the demolition business.

Within seconds, the padlock that secured the wheelhouse door was broken open and Jack was inside. He had with him a small torch—the type favoured by burglars. He shone it around. He could see that everything was neat and tidy.

A woman's touch, he thought.

He settled in for a wait. He must have dozed off as he was awakened by the sound of someone jumping aboard the boat.

Fuck me, that must be Barry, Jack thought.

Barry jumped aboard and looked at the broken lock. *It looks like someone has been aboard. I hope the bastards haven't stolen anything,* he thought.

People breaking into boats and stealing stuff wasn't a common thing as there was usually someone around.

As Barry made his way aboard, he was on full alert.

Jack held his breath. He could see that Barry was being very careful about entering the cabin.

'Is there anybody about?' Barry asked in a soft voice.

Jack didn't answer.

Barry walked slowly into the wheelhouse.

Suddenly Jack swung the jemmy bar at Barry's head.

Barry reacted when he saw movement and flung his arm up to protect his head; the jemmy bar bounced off down his arm.

Jack was off balance, and Barry had the opportunity to swing an uppercut right into Jack's solar plexus.

The air whooshed out of Jack. He was stunned; months of drinking too much and bad food had taken its toll.

Barry took up the stance of the old Straight Back fighter from the days of his youth and let a combination rip into Jack.

Jack was in trouble.

Barry lined him up with a roundhouse blow that would have flattened a fit world champion, and Jack crashed into a corner of a nearby bench.

There was a dull, wet crunch—a bit like when you step on a lettuce—and Jack fell to the wheelhouse floor.

Looking at him, Barry could see that he had had enough. He wasn't moving at all.

Barry breathed loudly through his mouth and asked, 'Did you think you had the better of me, you fucking copper? I'm a lot smarter than you think, and I'm also tougher than you reckon.'

Jack didn't say a word.

He had died from the massive blow when his head hit the bench.

His eyes were open, and he stared at Barry.

'Fuck me,' Barry said out loud.

He had to think. What should he do?

Should he ring the police, or should he dump the body and not say a word to anyone?

The chances were that nobody had seen Jack come down to the marina.

Teddy—he could trust Teddy.

Barry rang Teddy.

Teddy's phone rang. He picked it up and saw that it was Barry's number.

'And top of the morning to you,' Teddy said to Barry.

Barry answered, 'Teddy mate, I'm in trouble, and I need a hand. Can you come down to the St Kilda Marina straight away? Don't fuck around, just get here as quick as you can.'

Teddy sensed that there was real trouble in the air.

He said to Rita, 'Love, that was Barry. He needs a hand to shift some gear off his boat, and Des must be on the drink. I've got to go over and give the old bloke a hand.'

'Rather you than me,' Rita laughed, still half asleep, and she rolled over and went back to sleep.

Teddy drove to the marina and walked out to Barry's boat. He stepped on board and went into the wheelhouse.

Barry was sitting on the captain's chair, and at his feet was a tarpaulin covering something up.

Even from where Teddy stood, he could see it was a body.

'What the fuck happened?' Teddy asked.

Barry looked at his mate and said, 'It's that fucking copper, Hilda's husband. He must have come aboard and was waiting for me when I came down early this morning, and he had a jemmy bar and almost took my fucking head off with it. It's a miracle that he didn't kill me.'

Teddy pulled back the tarp and looked at Jack.

He was as dead as a doornail.

'Right, we have two options,' Teddy said. 'One is to ring the police and tell them that you have killed one of their own and by the way his wife is living with you. That won't half look fucking suspicious! Or we tell no one and we sail out into the bay and dump the body.'

Barry had already thought of those two options.

Teddy asked, 'Which one is the best, do you think?'

Barry didn't take too long to make up his mind.

'Untie the boat, and we'll get going out to sea,' he said.

Teddy nodded his head and said, 'Let's go and dump this useless bastard somewhere where he won't ever be discovered.'

With that, the boat was untied, and the two friends headed out to sea.

Once they were in the middle of the bay, they pulled the tarp off the body and started to wrap it in chain.

Both the men knew what had to be done next.

Barry went inside, got a filleting knife, and made an incision from above Jack's pubic area up to the rib cage, opening up the abdomen. This would stop the stomach filling with gas and the body floating to the surface.

They both felt a bit sick.

Teddy said, 'We can drop the body here. It's pretty deep, and it's a well-known spot for sea lice. They will strip the body of flesh within a few weeks.'

'Let's hope that some angler doesn't hook up on it,' Barry commented.

Teddy said, 'It's too deep for pleasure boats to anchor here.'

They went through Jack's pockets and took out anything that could have been used to identify the body.

Teddy had Jack's car keys and mobile in his pocket.

He would dump the car at Tullamarine Airport that night.

Over the side went Detective Jack Andrews.

His body was gone in an instant.

Barry headed the boat for home. Teddy got a mop and a bucket and started to clean up.

When they got back to the marina, Teddy said, 'I'll come back tonight and grab Jack's car. I'll take it out to the airport and leave it in the long-term car park. It will be months before anyone realises that it has been dumped.'

Barry didn't know what to say and how to thank Teddy. He started to say something, but words failed him.

'Mate, I want to thank you for the help,' Barry started to say.

Teddy laughed and said, 'Barry mate, I don't need to tell you this, but don't tell anyone, not even Hilda. No one must ever know what happened here today.'

Barry nodded, unable to say any more.

He shook Teddy's hand.

They travelled back to the marina in silence, tied up the boat, and walked off the wharf together.

Their friendship was sealed by the secret.

Teddy walked into the front bar of the Staggs Head hotel. The usual crowd was there, and he ordered a pot from the barmaid. She smiled in recognition and placed a pot of beer on the bar, and he swallowed half of it down quickly.

He looked around and nodded to some of the older blokes that he had seen around the pubs.

Williamstown was a small area, and most of the people went from pub to pub, looking for friends and just relaxing. It was good to be able to have a beer and then walk around to another pub.

Most of the blokes had favourite barmaids, and every now and again, one of their favourites would shout them a couple of free beers. It was a pleasant way to spend their days.

Ken walked in, and Teddy saw that he was all business.

Teddy knew that he had sourced the gun that he had asked about.

With his lips hardly moving, Ken said to Teddy, 'Mate, follow me out to the shithouse.'

Teddy followed him out to the toilet, and, with a flourish, Ken whipped out a .38 from the back of his pants.

'How do you like this little beauty?' Ken asked with a smile.

Teddy held both his hands up in a mock surrender and said, 'I hope the bastard's not loaded!'

Ken laughed and said, 'Mate, I've got the bullets in a plastic bag.'

Teddy put out his right hand and said, 'Give us a good look at it. It looks like it's been around the block a few times.'

Ken said, 'My mate swears that it's clean, never done anyone any harm. There's no numbers on it, and it's impossible to trace.'

Teddy took hold of the .38 and looked down the barrel.

'Mate, it looks good,' he said.

He cocked back the hammer and pulled the trigger. There was a loud *click* as the hammer hit home. There was no slack or looseness in the firing mechanism, and everything went smoothly.

'How much does your mate want for it?' Teddy asked.

Ken said, 'Well, mate, he wanted $3,000 for it, but I told him that the bloke whom I was selling it to wasn't some sort of Shitman. He was one of us. So I managed to talk him down to two and a half grand. Mate, I can tell you that he could probably get almost twice that much if he sold it to some halfwit gangster, who wanted to walk around with it stuck down the front of his tracksuit pants.'

Teddy looked at Ken and said, 'Tell him I will give him $2,000 for it now, right now. I've got the money on me, here and now. No fucking about, here and now, and I'll also sling you a couple of hundred for your trouble.'

Ken looked a bit confused and said to Teddy, 'Wait a minute, and I'll give him a ring and see what he thinks.'

With that, Ken took back the revolver and went outside the hotel and made a call.

Teddy went back to his pot of beer. He drank it down and nodded to the barmaid for a refill.

Outside, Ken rang the supplier of the gun, 'Mate, this bloke wants the gun but can't come up with all the money. He said that he has $1,750. And, mate, I can tell you that that is all this bloke has. He's as solid as a rock, and it will never get back to you. I reckon that you should grab it while the money is there.'

On the other end of the line, the seller said, 'No worries, Kenny mate. Grab the money, and there's a hundred in it for you.'

'Thanks, mate,' Ken said.

He walked back into the bar and said to Teddy, 'Follow me out to the shithouse.'

When they were there, he said, 'Mate, it's all done. He accepted the two grand, and all is sweet. Give me the money, and the gun's yours.'

Teddy handed over the money and pushed the gun down the back of his jeans. His shirt covered the grip. He gave Ken the couple of hundred for his efforts.

Ken took the $2,000 and put that in a back pocket.

He gave Teddy a plastic bag containing twenty .38 bullets. He took the extra 200 and put that in a side pocket.

This was proving a great way for Ken to make money. He would give the seller $1,750 and would get a hundred back for his troubles and pocket the difference that Teddy had paid. All in all, it looked like Ken had made $550 for just putting people together and finding what they wanted.

Life was good.

Teddy wasn't an idiot. He knew that Ken would have got an earn from whatever he did. That's what those sorts of blokes did for a living, but it was the old story. You did what you had to do to keep everyone happy. That was the name of the game.

He had what Jock wanted—a gun to make sure that his son didn't end up in jail.

Teddy went over to Jock's house and walked up to the front door.

Through the door he could hear Jock coughing. It sounded as if someone was trying to crank over a T-Model Ford.

He waited until the coughing stopped. Then he knocked loudly on the front door.

Jock came to the front door and asked, 'Who's there?'

Teddy answered, 'Jock mate, it's Teddy.'

Jock opened the door and said, 'Fuck me, dead mate, you knock on the door just like a fucken copper.'

'I didn't know if you could hear me over all the noise you were making,' Teddy said with a bit of a laugh.

'These fucking cigarettes, I always thought that they would kill me, but it looks like the piss has beaten them to it,' Jock replied.

Teddy smiled and followed him up to the kitchen at the rear of the house.

They sat at the kitchen table.

Teddy pulled out the .38 from a plastic shopping bag and said, 'As promised, a .38. The bloke who I got it off swears that it's clean and hasn't done anyone.'

Jock looked at the gun and said, 'It's been around, just what I want. What do I owe you for it?'

'Mate,' Teddy said, 'the bloke who I bought it off is an old mate of mine, and he let me have it for a couple of hundred. Don't you worry about it, take it as a gift, and when you're finished with it, I'll dump it out in the ocean somewhere.'

Jock looked at Teddy and smiled, 'Are you sure that you don't want anything for it?'

'No, mate,' Teddy said. 'Relax and when you're finished with it, either just chuck it to the shithouse or give it back to me. OK?'

Jock smiled and said, 'Thanks, mate, can I get you a cuppa?'

Teddy laughed and said, 'I'm in a bit of a hurry. I just thought that I would drop it off and get going.'

With that, Teddy shook Jock's hand, walked out of the old man's house, and drove off.

Teddy rang Dean and asked him to drop him off at the marina.

When Teddy got out of Dean's car, he said, 'Don't worry about picking me up as Barry has to come over to my place, and, when we finish, he will drop me off.'

Dean asked, 'Do you need a hand?'

'No, mate, we'll be right,' Teddy answered.

He walked to the car park of the marina and pressed the door-opening button on Jack's remote control.

A Ford Falcon beeped into life as the doors unlocked.

Teddy glanced around, put on a pair of Riggers gloves, and then opened the driver's side door.

He had Jack's phone in his pocket. It had rung a couple of times, but Teddy had ignored it.

Driving out on the freeway, Teddy headed towards Tullamarine Airport and stopped at the ticket machine of the long-term parking site.

He took out a ticket and parked away from the exit gate.

Teddy walked into the airport, went up to a bar, ordered a beer, took it to a quiet corner, opened the phone up, and listened to Jack's missed messages.

There were a few from Karl, the detective, and a couple of ones from people seeking Jack. One Teddy recognised as Slither.

Teddy heard Slither explain to Jack how he and Barry had gone out to sea and tell him the time they had come back in. Teddy realised that it was Slither who was informing on them about their abalone poaching. He had been telling Jack all about what they were up to.

Teddy thought, *The poor drunken bastard! Well, that's one channel of information that has closed with Jack's demise.*

On his way to the taxi rank, Teddy dropped the mobile phone into a rubbish bin that was lined with a plastic bag. The cleaners never opened any plastic rubbish bags. They just tie them at the top and chucked then into a large rubbish compactor.

Teddy walked out, grabbed a taxi, and went back to Williamstown.

He got dropped off in the main street and walked home.

Karl, the detective, couldn't get hold of his partner Jack.

He had tried ringing him once again and decided to go around to his house. He parked outside and walked into the front yard; it was a mess. The lawn needed mowing, and the gardens were overgrown.

Knocking on the front door, there was silence from inside. He walked around to the back door and found that it was locked.

Karl carefully prised it open and said in a loud voice, 'Jack, you home, old mate?'

Silence greeted his question.

He made his way into the kitchen and saw that the place hadn't been cleaned, possibly since Hilda had done a runner.

Entering the bedroom, he saw the dirty bed and dirty clothes flung everywhere. Then he walked out into the living area and saw the same rubbish and mess all over the place. Karl felt sadness for his friend. Maybe he should have been more active in helping him in his time of need.

Karl walked out of the house and drove off.

Where would he look? Who would be the last person whom Jack had spoken to?

Slither needed a drink. No, he needed a couple of drinks. His hands shook as he waited for someone to come by whom he knew well enough to get a drink off.

He noticed that Barry's boat had gone out and returned with Teddy and Barry on board, no one else. He wondered what they had been up to.

It was obvious to Slither that they hadn't been poaching abalone. They must have just taken the boat out for a run just to keep things moving.

Slither decided to ring Jack, the detective, and report that Barry and Teddy had taken the boat out in the early morning for some reason.

When he dialled Jack's number, he got Jack's recorded message, so Slither left a message, telling Jack about them.

Slither hung up and thought he would give Jack another ring later on.

Karl was a worried man.

He didn't want to alert his superiors that Jack was missing in action, as there was a chance that Jack was holed up with a young prostitute somewhere and didn't want to be disturbed. But Karl couldn't cover up for him forever.

Karl thought that Hilda and the old fisherman might be involved, but he couldn't put two and two together just yet.

He was trained to work things out.

Karl decided to catch up with the old drunk down at the marina. He would talk to him and see if he knew anything.

Jock dismantled the .38 and gave it a good clean-out. By the smell, the gun hadn't been fired for some time.

Half the wankers who had them never had a shot out of them.

They were there just to scare off the lesser criminals.

Jock got six of the bullets out of the bag of twenty that Teddy had given him.

He placed them on his kitchen table and got out a large carving knife. He stood the bullet up with the lead pointing up to the ceiling and slowly allowed the sharpened edge of the knife to push down into the soft lead bullet, leaving a deep groove.

He lifted the knife off the bullet and turned the bullet around so that when he placed the knife on top of the bullet, the second groove he made was at ninety degrees to the first one.

Jock looked at the cross on the bullet and said out loud, 'That should make scrambled eggs out of their brains.'

What Jock had done was weaken the bullet to such a degree that when the bullet entered the skull of the intended victim, it would break into four smaller pieces, and they would bounce around inside the skull, doing unrepairable damage to the unfortunate victim.

This was highly illegal and the mark of a professional hit man.

No one ever survived such a lethal attack.

Jock continued his work with the air of a professional. He soon became engulfed in a cloud of cigarette smoke, and all the six bullets had the distinctive crosses in them.

He took the gun out into his backyard and loaded it up with a couple of bullets from the bag. Jock didn't want to waste the bullets that he had turned into dumdum bullets. He pressed the revolver into a couple of old cushions that he had gotten out of his garden shed and laid them onto his soft garden bed.

He pulled the trigger twice in quick succession.

Thump, thump, the revolver kicked in his hand. He hardly heard a noise.

None of his neighbours would have heard a thing.

'Well, the gun works all right,' Jock said to himself.

Walking back inside to his kitchen, he cleaned the gun and started to plan his next move. Pain rippled through his body.

He stiffly got up and went into the bathroom and swallowed a handful of pain killers.

It won't be long, Lassie. We'll be together again, Jock thought to himself once more.

Karl pulled up at the marina and saw the old drunk making himself appear useful, doing a bit of sweeping and picking up around the wharfs.

'Hullo, mate,' Karl said in a friendly manner. 'When was the last time that you spoke to Jack?'

Slither looked around him to see if there was anyone watching and said, 'I tried to ring him, but his phone was switched off. I haven't tried since.'

Karl smiled at the filthy drunk and said, 'Mate, Jack has been called away for a couple of days, and I'm running the show. So if you need anything or have something to report, just give me a ring. Here's my number. It's a toll-free number, the same as Jack's is. You can get in touch with me twenty-four seven, just like Jack.'

Slither took the card that Karl had given him and squinted at it.

'Well, I'll tell you what I had for Jack. I reckon that it's worth twenty dollars,' he said.

Karl was all ears. He reached into his back pocket and pulled out a twenty. He held it away from Slither.

'What news do you have?' he asked.

Slither had seen the money and was eager to help.

He stuttered out, 'Barry and Teddy came in just before lunchtime. They didn't have anybody else on board, and they must have taken the boat out for a bit of a run. There was no abalone gear on board.'

Karl handed Slither the money and said, 'Well done, if there is anything else to report, be sure to keep me informed.'

With that, Karl walked away towards the car park.

Jock had thought about where and how he was going to knock the pair of loan sharks.

He would get them when they were least expecting it. He would walk up behind them and 'bang, bang,' shoot them both in the head. When they were on the ground, he would shoot them both once again in the head.

Two head shots with dumdum bullets would be enough to stop an elephant.

Jock felt that he was moving at the right speed.

He knew that Tom would never forget the assault on Sandy and one day he would square up. Science being what it was today, he just knew that Tom would spend twenty years inside some low jail. His life would be ruined.

Jock knew that Tom had a heart the size of Tulloch, the famous Australian race horse, and he wouldn't take a step back.

Every time he spoke to Tom and Sandy, he felt a burning pride. Sandy was lovely. She was a real sweetheart, and they thought the world of each other.

Jock knew that she had a problem with the pokies, but she seemed to be getting along a bit better lately.

He started to get a bit sentimental as he thought of the way Sandy would often come around with a box of Johnnie Walker Scotch whisky. Jock was never short of a drink. He reckoned that Sandy got it at a bit of a discount from where she worked.

And most of the time, there would be a crayfish or two as well after a trip.

Yes, life was good. Jock loved Sandy like a daughter.

Jock thought of the first time that he had met his wife, Joyce. He was down at the local in the East End at a pub, not far from where he lived. He was with some lads, and one of them had mentioned that his cousin was coming down from Scotland for a few days holiday.

When Joyce walked in with her cousin, Tom senior was smitten immediately. He had never believed at love at first sight, until then.

They were introduced, and he found that she was easy to talk to and seemed to be attracted to him.

He bought her a drink, and they soon separated from the group and talked together. Tom senior told her of his plans for the future, and she explained about her life. They were the same age and followed different soccer teams, of course.

By the end of the evening, they had made plans to meet up again the next day.

And by the week's end, Tom had asked her to marry him and she had agreed.

A tear ran down Jock's cheek at the thought of his Scottish Lassie, remembering their son being born, how proud they both were of what they had achieved, their decision to come to Australia, and how Joyce had welcomed the challenge.

He thought back to how she had turned their first rented two-bedroom hovel into a home. When Tom senior came back from his first day at the Ford Motor Company and had told her that some European had mistaken his accent for that of a Scotsman, and that his new nickname was Jock, Joyce had laughed until she cried.

How proud she had been of their house in Williamstown and how the quaint suburb reminded them both of home.

Jock cursed himself for being so sentimental, but it felt good, in a sad way, to think of the past.

Lucy Wong was in trouble. She had lost the 500 that she had borrowed off Mario and Nick. The interest was mounting up day by day, and she was beside herself.

When she got paid, she realised that even with her pay, she couldn't repay the loan sharks what she owed; she was frantic with worry.

She was getting ready to leave Henry's restaurant when Henry asked, 'Lucy, you haven't been yourself the last couple of days. Is everything all right?'

Henry was concerned about Lucy's attitude.

Lucy tried to smile but missed by a mile; her face crumbled, and she said, 'Oh, Henry, I have been so stupid. I borrowed money off two loan sharks, and they have started to ring me and are demanding that their money, plus interest, is paid back to them. I already owe them 700 dollars, and it's going up by fifty dollars a day.'

Henry thought for a moment and asked, 'What if I give you the money now and you pay me back at 100 dollars a week. Would that make you happy?'

Lucy couldn't believe the generosity of Henry. She knew that he was a good man and an honest man and was always there to help people out. She nodded her head in agreement.

Henry went to the safe and got 700 dollars out.

He quietly spoke to his father and then placed the 700 dollars into her hand.

Lucy whispered, 'Thank you so much. Thank you.'

Gambling is addictive. Even when you are down to your last, you are still confident that there is a way out by keeping on gambling.

Lucy walked into the casino. She kept well away from the area where the loan sharks would be sitting at their table and went across to a roulette wheel.

There were a few people around the table, but it wasn't as packed as sometimes.

She manoeuvred her way into a position where she was close to the spinning wheel.

Pulling $300 out of her purse, she threw it onto the table and said, 'Fifty dollar chips, please.'

Lucy was always courteous to the croupiers as she believed in the karma that if you were nice to people, then nice things would happen to you.

The croupier swiftly produced her chips and spun the wheel; he threw the white ball in the opposite direction to the way the wheel was spinning.

He said in a loud voice, 'No more bets. Thank you.'

The ball rattled its way to a stop, and the wheel spun its way to a standstill. The croupier announced, 'Zero. Thank you, ladies and gentlemen.' He proceeded to rake in all the losing bets.

Lucy felt her panic grow. She still had plenty of the $700 left, but she knew that she wouldn't be able to walk away from the table.

Jock walked out of the front door of his house and got into the taxi. The driver was some sort of Arab or Indian.

He said, 'Gidday, mate, can you take me to the casino, please?'

The driver replied with a grunt and started his journey.

'Nice evening for a bit of a punt,' Jock said.

He was a little bit drunk, and although the weather was warm Jock had his overcoat on.

The taxi driver grunted something and thought to himself, *Fucking Aussies! They are always drunk and spend all their money gambling.*

The driver was happy to be taking people to the casino, but sometimes when he took people away from there, they had no money and they would do a bolt.

He looked sideways at his passenger and thought. 'I could catch this old man. He looks half dead to me.'

At the brightly lit casino entrance, Jock got out of the taxi and gave the driver a 50-dollar note. 'Keep the change, mate. I reckon that if you are saving up to buy a personality, you'll need a fucking lot more than what I've given you.'

The taxi driver didn't understand. He took the 50-dollar note and studied it under the dash light.

Jock walked into the casino and was amazed at how many people were up and about at this time of the night.

He headed up to the bar and ordered a Johnnie Walker Scotch whisky, no ice. He took the drink and watched the two loan sharks. They were talking to a Chinese or Vietnamese. Jock couldn't tell the difference.

The elder loan shark walked into the toilet area, and the oriental followed behind him. The loan shark came out, went back to his table, and said something to the younger one. They both had a chuckle.

Jock looked around the area. Everyone was concentrating on whatever way they were losing their money.

He saw the young people losing their deposits for a home, and he saw the pensioners losing their kid's inheritance.

Pain ripped through his body. He swallowed the last of his painkillers with some Scotch, and soon the pain retreated back into where it was waiting to attack him again.

He got himself another Scotch and sat down. He was sitting behind the two loan sharks.

They had watched him walk stiffly past them and had ignored him as they hadn't remembered seeing him before.

Jock had been to the casino once before and had watched the two men. He didn't want to shoot the wrong duo.

He got up and walked to the bar. He placed his glass on the bar and walked towards the two men. The barman, seeing him put the glass down, took no more interest in him as he obviously didn't want a refill.

Jock walked up behind the two men, pulled out his .38, and said, 'This is for Sandy, you fucking dogs.'

He shot Mario in the back of the head.

Mario fell forward onto the table.

Nick started to look around, and Jock shot him in the side of the head.

Neither man had the opportunity to get to his feet.

Jock shot Nick once again and then aimed at Mario and shot him in the back of the head.

There was silence in the gambling room apart from the constant bells and whistles from the banks of poker machines.

Time stood still.

Jock looked at the bank of faces, all with their mouths open, and said, 'They were rapists. They got their right whack.'

Jock put the barrel of the revolver into his mouth. It tasted smoky and oily.

'This one is for our Tommy, my Bonnie Lassie,' Jock said around the barrel of the .38 and pulled the trigger.

The bullet exploded into Jock's brain and separated into four smaller pieces, and they bounced around inside his skull.

Lucy wasn't going all that well. She had had a few pickups but was almost 200 dollars down when the first gun shot rang out.

Bang! It was very loud.

The croupier had spun the roulette wheel and had just cast the white ball in the opposite direction.

Bang! Another shot echoed out.

Lucy looked up and saw that the croupier's attention was directed away from the spinning wheel. The little white ball jiggled over the rungs on the roulette wheel and stopped.

The white ball landed on twenty-three red.

Lucy looked at the croupier and saw that he was intently starring at whatever was happening. She slid out two 50-dollar chips and put them directly on the twenty-three.

Two more shots rang out.

She heard someone say, 'They were rapists. They got their right whack.'

There was another *bang*. This one sounded a bit muffled, and then silence.

Everyone stood still. No one spoke.

Then security came from out of nowhere.

Twenty burly uniformed security guards surrounded the lifeless bodies.

The pit boss quietly said, 'Pay, everybody, and get the game moving as quickly as you can.'

The croupier obeyed. He said in a loud voice, 'Number twenty-three. Thank you, red, twenty-three.'

He whisked away all the losing chips and then pulled Lucy's chips towards him.

He looked at her and asked, 'What nomination do you want your chips in?'

Lucy answered, 'I'll have seven 500-dollar chips, please.'

The croupier got them and pushed them with his rake over to Lucy.

She put them into her purse and walked away from the table.

As she walked towards an exit that was far away from where the bodies were, a security guard asked her to stop as she might have been a witness.

Lucy shrugged and said, 'I must go as I'm late for work. I didn't see anything.'

Lucy was desperate to get out because she knew that the security cameras would have picked up her placing her bet after the white ball was in its position.

She just hoped that in the confusion, the security people would be behind in their viewing.

Lucy walked out and hailed a taxi.

She was away and well in front. She still had $400 of the $700 that Henry had given her and was up $3,500. She was down $200 when the commotion had started, but, all in all, she was well in front.

She decided that she would give Henry back his $700 and never set foot in the casino again.

Lucy smiled as she sped towards her apartment.

When the news got out that it was Tom's father who had killed the loan sharks and had put an end to his own pain, all the boys were distraught.

Teddy said to Tom, 'Mate, I never thought that Jock was going to knock himself. Please, mate, forgive me for getting hold of the .38 for him.'

Tom looked at Teddy. He could see that his friend was beside himself with grief.

'Teddy mate,' he said, 'don't blame yourself. When my dad made his mind up, there was no way of stopping him. He would have got a gun from somewhere and still done exactly the same.'

Teddy nodded, unable to speak.

Tom said, 'He did it for me and Sandy, mate. That was his way of us squaring off and me not ending up in the nick.'

All the boys were saddened by Jock's passing. After the funeral, they all held a wake for the old fellow.

They held it in Jock's favourite pub in Williamstown.

There was free beer all day and into the night. Many tears were shed, and many stories were told.

In the millionth of a second before his life was snuffed out, Jock was transformed into a young man. He found himself standing in front of the little pub in the East End of London.

He looked up at its familiar front door, and he could hear the sound of laughter and people talking. He made his way up the steps and opened the bar door.

The first person he saw was his wife Joyce.

She was young and beautiful, and she smiled and ran into his arms.

'Tommy, my love, you have saved our wee bairn Tommy from all that misery. You are a real man. You are the man I love and will always love.'

Joyce kissed Tom on the lips.

Tom looked around, and he knew everyone in the room.

Everyone there was happy and laughing, and they were all welcoming Tom into the start of a new life.

They had all previously passed away.

Tom knew that he had been reborn into eternity.

Muddy Hits a Snag

Muddy, the self-proclaimed terror of southern New South Wales, slowly regained consciousness.

He roughly pushed aside the whore whom he had spent the night with. He was amazed at how a woman's appearance could differ in only a few hours.

Last night, she had looked hot; now she looked terrible. Her make-up was smudged, and her lipstick was a mess. He could tell that she was still alive because she was snoring.

They had been on a huge bender, had mixed drink and drugs, and ended up in a coma-like state.

Muddy had been unconscious for hours, and he needed a piss.

'Fuck me,' he said out loud and wondered just where he was.

He looked around the darkened room.

All the blinds were down, and there were empty Jim Beam and Coke cans and drug-taking paraphernalia littering the floor. Pizza boxes were scattered around—some filled with half-eaten pizzas. It was a real mess.

Checking that it wasn't a jail cell, he went looking for the toilet.

When he found it, he lifted up the lid and almost gagged at the smell and sight.

It all slowly came back to him.

The crew had ridden up from Eden to Sydney and met up with their chapter in Sydney.

He remembered the endless embracing and handshaking and the smell of unwashed bodies.

The resident 'old ladies' who were drunk or high made sure that he and his crew were looked after.

Old ladies were the women who didn't have a permanent root and went with anyone who was available.

Muddy recalled the endless lines of cocaine and the sculling of shots of anything and everything.

It was funny, but once you had snorted a couple of lines, then you could drink anything.

You just kept rolling along, just like Old Man River.

His nose itched and was crusty from the snorting of coke, and he scratched it as he pissed. Wondering where his crew were, he thought he would look for them as soon as he was done in the toilet.

He was in the chapter's clubhouse which was in an industrial area in the Western Suburbs of Sydney.

Muddy remembered arriving and he and his crew being welcomed with open arms from his fellow group members and open legs from the women in the clubhouse. They got stuck into the drugs and the piss and then got stuck into the whores.

He remembered his fellow bikies telling him about their protection business. It all sounded so easy.

All they did was walk into a business in full club colours.

They would say to the proprietor that the kooris were getting out of control and the police were overworked, so they had decided to offer protection services to those smart enough to see that this was the easy way out.

They would say that for 200 dollars a week, the business would be trouble-free. Then they would let everyone know that the business was under their protection and there wouldn't be any trouble.

If the proprietor decided that it wasn't worth the money being asked, then all the bikies had to do was chuck a brick through the front window. As soon as the window was replaced, then they would do the same, week in, week out.

If the business still didn't want to join up, then it would be a Molotov cocktail that followed the next brick.

Soon the proprietor would realise that it was just too much trouble and sign up for the protection offered by the bikies.

Once the businesses were hooked, you slowly increased the rate until they couldn't afford you, and then they went broke.

That didn't matter as another sucker would come along, and it would start all over again.

Muddy zipped up and went into the main clubroom. Some of his members were still entwined with the women on offer.

He opened the fridge door, and it hit the wall behind loudly. He got out a can of beer and opened it.

The noise he was making woke up his fellow bikers.

Muddy said loudly, 'Let's get this show on the road. We won't get anywhere sitting around here.'

His crew groggily got to their feet.

The women looked on, most of them not moving from where they had spent the night. They knew that whatever had been promised the night before was forgotten.

They were used to such treatment. It was all part of the life that they led. They were mostly homeless and addicted to drugs. Prostitution was the lifestyle they were accustomed to, and they would remain prostitutes until their looks and figures deserted them. Then they would be on their own.

If they got lucky, one of the bikies would look after them. But they knew that they weren't going to end up in a cabin with a white picket fence, roses, children running off to school, and happy Sunday dinners with the family, like you see on the television. But that was their lot in life. They had never known any different.

From an early life, they had associated sex with need. There wasn't a lot of love involved.

Muddy located his crew, and they assembled out the front of the clubhouse and said their goodbyes.

In ear-splitting thunder, they took off back towards Eden.

Billy Boy's daughter, Olivia, had given birth to a son.

She and her female partner Danni were thrilled.

They were a family, and they were convinced that they would be a happy family.

Olivia had given some thought to moving away from Sydney and going somewhere so they could all live and be happy without the hustle and bustle of the city life.

Her father, Billy Boy, was the diver who had stumbled across the Japanese mini submarine that Teddy and the boys had then re-found many years later. They had shown the Japanese brothers that their father had died there.

Billy had left her a cabin in the country when he died. It was just out of Eden.

She spoke to Danni, and they decided to give it a go, living there.

The girls sold the house that they had in Sydney and moved out, so they were cashed up.

They moved into Billy Boy's cabin and were happy. They both loved the countryside and the feeling of freedom. They got some chooks and a couple of dogs and relaxed.

But it didn't take long for them to realise that they were too young to retire.

While they were in Eden, one day they saw a shop that was for sale. It had been a coffee shop and takeaway and had a big backyard.

It was licensed as a food preparation area and had a good feel about it. It was in the middle of the main street near a grocery store and opposite a post office. They both agreed that the position was perfect.

They would open a place where people could sit down and have a cup of coffee and a sandwich. Also they would turn the backyard into a plant nursery and serve coffee out there. It would be a wonderful place to relax and look at the plants which were for sale.

Both the girls felt that it would work.

They bought the shop and started to plan what they were going to do.

After they cleaned up and repainted it, they put modern furniture in the cafe and outdoor furniture in the backyard; it looked wonderful. They were happy with the results.

They advertised for staff and found that there were a lot of young mums who were willing to work after they dropped their kids off at the school and were happy to knock off and pick their kids up when school came out.

They built a couple of hothouses by their cabin in the hills, with the idea that they would bring on the plants in them.

When they were ready to bloom, they would take them into the cafe where they would sell easily.

It was a great idea.

There was always someone in, looking at the plants and having a cup of coffee.

They decided that they would open at 9.30 a.m. and close at 5 p.m.—no evening meals and breakfast all day.

The hours suited them fine.

They had only been open about three months when Muddy walked in around lunchtime.

The cafe was almost full.

Muddy swaggered up to the counter and said, 'Who's running this show?'

Olivia wasn't overawed by Muddy's appearance.

She looked him straight in the eye and said, 'I am, love. How can I help you?'

Muddy was confident. 'It's not what you can do for me. It's what I can do for you, blondie.'

Olivia looked back at Muddy and said, 'I don't reckon that there is a lot that you can do for me.'

Muddy was a bit taken aback by her attitude.

He was a man to be feared, after all.

'Let me explain,' Muddy said with a leer. 'We can offer you protection from the kooris. They run wild around the place. They could do a lot of damage to your little shop after you close.'

Olivia had heard from other shop owners that the bikies had been demanding protection money and if you didn't pay them, then your front window would be broken until you saw sense.

'I'm not sure that the kooris are a problem this end of the street,' Olivia answered.

Muddy smiled and said, 'Well, they won't be if we are involved, let me tell you.'

Olivia pretended to give it some thought and finally said in a quiet voice, 'Why don't you fuck off? We don't want your protection, and we don't want your custom. Just get the fuck out of here and leave us alone. You should shout yourself a bath. You stink worse than a pig.'

Muddy was a bit taken aback by the venom in her voice.

He didn't know what he could do to wrest control of the situation.

Glaring back at Olivia, he thought, *Fucking bitch, doesn't she know who the fuck I am?* Well, he would show her. He would show the lesbian bitch who was running the show.

Muddy looked at Olivia and said, 'Bad move, blondie. You know where we are if you need us.'

With that, Muddy walked out into the street, got on his motorbike, and roared away.

Olivia thought to herself, *That wasn't probably the smartest thing to do. But fuck him. I'm not going to bow down to some dumb fucking bikie.*

When she closed the cafe, she spoke in length to Danni. They agreed that they wouldn't bow down to the threat because people would hear that they hadn't acted as strong as a man would have.

Both of them realised that they had to be strong and take a stand.

They took the baby and went back to the cabin and their hothouses and started to prepare the plants they were going to take into the nursery the next day.

Muddy was at the bikies clubhouse. He was pretty pissed off with the way that Olivia had given him the bum's rush.

He was determined to make an example of her and her pussy-eating partner. He would show them he wasn't to be fucked with.

The bikies schemed together.

After midnight, they left in a Holden Commodore.

They made their way downtown and went behind Olivia's shop. They forced open the back gate and entered the yard.

Then they started quietly tipping plants out of their pots and scattering them all over the place.

Muddy forced open the rear door of the cafe and went inside. They opened the fridge doors and threw everything that was inside them out onto the floor.

The bikies then emptied food bins and threw the food against the walls of the cafe.

It was a real mess.

They let themselves out and drove off.

One of the bikie geniuses suggested that they break the front window.

But Muddy said, 'That's our next step. We will do more than that if those two lessos don't pay up.'

They all laughed at their daring as they drove back to their headquarters.

A good night was had by all.

The next morning, Olivia drove the van into Eden and parked it around the rear of the building.

She noticed that the back entrance had been tampered with. She slowly got out and walked into the backyard. There was rubbish everywhere, and most of the plant display was ruined. Olivia noticed that a lot of pot plants had been tipped out onto the ground and trodden on.

Making her way into the cafe, she saw that the walls and windows were covered with food that had been taken out of the fridges and cool room. It had been splattered everywhere.

Olivia felt like bursting into tears. She was heartbroken at the thought that someone would do such a thing.

She phoned her partner, and as soon as Danni picked up the phone, Olivia burst into tears. Sobbing, she told Danni what someone had done.

Danni immediately said, 'Ring the police. I'm on my way. I'll be there in ten minutes.'

Olivia rang the police, and a sergeant answered.

She began to cry again, and the sergeant said that he would be there in a minute.

The police and Danni arrived at the same time.

The sergeant looked around and saw that there was a big mess but not a lot of damage.

There had been a spate of damage done to shops in the area over the last few weeks.

He was in constant talks with the koori community and found them to be reasonable and generally well behaved.

Sometimes the young bucks would play up; normally when they got a few charges into them. But by and by, they weren't a bad mob.

The sergeant had his own idea about who was behind the damages to the shops.

He laid the blame on the motorbike mob who handled most of the drugs in the area.

Olivia had calmed down, and, on the policeman's advice, they started to take photos of the damage for insurance purposes.

He took a few notes, and Olivia mentioned that a bikie had come to the cafe and suggested that they pay them protection money. Maybe their refusal was the reason that they had been targeted.

The sergeant thought that Olivia was probably correct, but he didn't say too much.

He wasn't in a position to expand on his theories.

'It doesn't look too bad,' he said to the girls. 'A bit of elbow grease, and it will be shipshape again.'

Danni offered him a mop and said, 'You're right. If we all get into it, it should be back to normal in a couple of hours.'

The sergeant shook his head and said, 'Unfortunately I have heaps waiting for me back in the office. I would love to get stuck into it with you two, but, alas, I just don't have the time.'

With that, he walked out of the cafe, got into his car, and drove off.

As the news got around, some of the women who worked part-time in the cafe turned up to help clean up.

Soon there were a dozen women toiling away.

Olivia decided that they wouldn't open that day as all their food had been destroyed.

They put up a sign in the front window that said,

We will be open for business at 9 a.m. tomorrow.

When the cafe was spick and span, the girls all sat down and had a glass of wine.

The discussion soon turned to who would have done this.

Olivia spoke about how the bikies had come in and offered protection from the kooris.

One of the girls said, 'I know most of the kooris, and I don't reckon that they would have done it. I reckon that it would have been the bikies.'

Another woman spoke out and said, 'You will have to be careful. They are mean, and they always attack in a group, never one-on-one. They attacked my husband one night. He didn't do anything. He just looked at them the wrong way. They all attacked him and his mate and put both of them in hospital. We were lucky that they weren't killed.'

Another woman said, 'You should get those mates of your dad, the abalone poachers, to give you a hand. Rumour has it that they have belted the living daylights out of those bikies on a couple of occasions. They seem to have their measure.'

Olivia and Danni put their heads together, and they thought that they would see what happened next.

If they were left alone, then they wouldn't do anything. But if a problem arose again, then they would do something.

They all left and decided that they would open again the next morning.

Teddy sat beside the pool table in Curly's shed.

All the divers were there.

He said, 'I reckon that it's time to have another run at the New South Wales-Victorian border. We should be able to go up there and knock off a tonne or more in a couple of days.'

As the weather was blowing from the southwest, it was cool in Melbourne. There was a high coming up from the south, so it looked as if they would get a few days in the water on the border.

Dean said, 'Yes, it's time that we did a bit. Put our noses to the grindstone or more correctly our abalone irons to the rocks.'

Everyone laughed.

Tom said, 'We are going to have to be careful as that copper, Jack Andrews, will be hanging around. I reckon that he and Piggy are working together.'

They all murmured agreement.

Teddy and Barry were the only two people on earth who knew that Detective Jack Andrews wasn't still in the game. They and they alone knew that the good detective was slowly getting eaten away by sea lice deep in the waters of Port Phillip Bay.

'All right, I'll let Tony know that we will be off in a couple of days,' Teddy said with a grin. 'We'll put the Shark Cat in at Wonboyn and head out from there. We should be away for a couple of days.'

All the boys felt the surge of excitement course through their bodies. This was what they lived for, the feeling of excitement and the feeling that they were going together on another adventure.

They felt good.

Teddy looked around at the boys. It was good to see the youthful excitement on their faces.

For the first time, since Tom's father had shot the two loan sharks and ended his own pain-filled life, Tom felt the adrenalin kick in.

This was how life should be moving all the time. He and Sandy had gotten over most of the pain of losing Jock. They both realised just what he had done to make their lives easier.

Sandy blamed herself for getting raped. If she hadn't starting gambling and gone to the loan sharks, then none of this would have happened.

But Tom said, 'Sandy, what's done is done. You can't put the shit back into the donkey,' quoting Tony Soprano. 'There is no undoing what happened. My dad saw a way out, and he took it. Believe it or not, he died a happy man. He gave us the greatest gift anyone could give.'

Teddy rang Tony and told him to get ready to tow the Shark Cat up to Wonboyn.

Tony assured Teddy that all was in readiness.

Ringing his mate, Beaver, at the Wonboyn caravan park, he asked if there was enough water so they could get over the bar.

Beaver said, 'Mate, there's plenty of water on the bar. It's been wet up here and the bar is deep.'

He then rang Derek, the processor.

When Derek picked up his phone, Teddy said, 'Mate, we are away for the next couple of days. With the problems that we are having with the fisheries, what do you reckon we should do about the drop-off of the abalone meat?'

Derek was prepared for this question.

He replied, 'Mate, we will use the potato-processing factory that we used last time. I have got the boxes worked out. We'll pack them into potato chip boxes at the potato factory and then drive them to the blast freezer at my place. Then transfer them into abalone boxes just before we ship them out.'

'That sounds fair to me,' Teddy replied.

Teddy alerted his mate Dave that they would be up for a run any day soon.

Dave rang his brother Lee and told him that they had a trip coming up to Melbourne with some abalone hidden in the back of the truck.

Meanwhile, Wallace (Piggy) Trotter was being his normal vigilant self.

He and another fisheries officer were down at the boat ramp near the Bemm River.

They were at a lake that was made popular on the Sunday morning football show by two Australian rules football legends Jack Dyer (Captain Blood) and Lou Richards (Louie the Lip). It was a favoured fishing spot in Gippsland.

They were waiting out of sight of the boat ramp and were spying on a group of men who were trying to get their boat onto a trailer. They had been out fishing, and Piggy reckoned that they might have a lot more dusky flathead than they were allowed.

New restrictions had been brought in, and Piggy was making sure that they were followed.

The men were having trouble getting the boat onto the trailer. The boat ramp was open to easterly weather, and there were three foot waves banging into the pontoon jetty.

Pontoon jetties were a wonderful invention in calm water as they floated up and down with the tide. But in a situation like the fishermen were experiencing, they became dangerous. With one pontoon going up and the other pontoon going down, the chance of getting your hand jammed between them was a constant danger.

There were no handrails, so when the weather was rough, you were in for a wild ride.

The fisheries duo watched from afar as the men battled the weather and conditions.

Finally, the fishermen had the small aluminium dingy on the trailer. The driver of the 4WD was given the thumbs up, and the dingy was towed up out of the water.

This was what Piggy and his fellow officer were waiting for. There was no escape, and they pounced.

The dynamic duo leapt out of the fisheries 4WD. They had parked it in a position that blocked the fishermen's 4WD.

Piggy swaggered towards the group of men.

'Hullo, gentlemen, we are from the fisheries and want to check your fish for size and for quantity. Please let us have a look around.'

With that, the two fisheries officers started to look in the boat and rummage through all the Eskies and bags of fish. Soon all the catch was laid out on the boat ramp.

'Are you aware of the size limits and the bag limits and everything else?' Piggy asked, glaring at the assembled men.

A couple of them mumbled something, and Piggy moved in for the kill.

'Well, what have we got here?' Piggy asked, running his tape measure alongside a large dusky flathead.

'The size limit is 55 cm, and this one is clearly over that size, and what about this lot? They are all oversize. Don't you blokes know that these are the breeders and if you take out these, there will be no more fish?'

The group of men all looked guilty. They had been sprung!

Piggy then started to count out the smaller flathead.

There were seventy-five fish.

Putting his hands on his hips, Piggy said, 'You blokes have really blown it now. The legal limit is five. I'm going to ring the police and confiscate your boat and your vehicle. I'm sorry, but you have left me no other option.'

The fishermen began to show a bit of hostility towards the fisheries officers.

'Don't start any trouble as the police are on their way. I'm sure that you don't want to be charged with assaulting a fisheries officer,' Piggy said.

The offending fishermen spoke among themselves and seemed to accept their fate.

The police arrived. The men were read their rights, and charges were laid. The boat and vehicle were confiscated.

Piggy was beside himself. He assured his fellow officer that this was the way to do things. Proper planning was essential. Being in a position where they could observe but not be observed was the key.

With a happy heart, Piggy and his offsider headed back towards Bairnsdale.

On a straight stretch of highway, Piggy saw a Shark Cat being towed towards them.

'Well, I'll be buggered,' Piggy said with a sense of disbelief. 'That's those bastards, Teddy and his gang. I bet they are heading up towards Eden where they will put in and come back down to Victorian waters and get stuck into some poaching.'

What to do? What to do? Piggy thought of a thousand things all at once.

Due to the new rules put in place for him, anything that he wanted to do would have to be okayed by his superior.

Piggy drove on and kept watch on the Shark Cat in his rear-vision mirror.

He waited until the Shark Cat went around the corner and was out of sight, and then he slowed to a stop.

Piggy rang through to his head office and spoke to his superior's secretary.

She informed Piggy that he was busy in a meeting and couldn't be disturbed. That was all the information that Piggy needed; he was on his own.

He swung the 4WD around and started to head in the same direction as the Shark Cat.

The chase was on.

Teddy and the boys were heading towards the New South Wales border. Teddy was driving, and the other three were doing it easy.

Teddy's phone rang.

It was Tony. 'Teddy, I've just past the fisheries in a 4WD. I reckon that it was Piggy at the controls. How far are you behind me?'

Teddy replied, 'We are about twenty minutes behind you, I reckon.'

'Well, if you don't pass a fisheries 4WD, then I reckon that it is a certainty that they are on my tail. What do you want me to do?'

Teddy said, 'Mate, just keep it going. We don't care who sees us put the boat in. It's when we pull it out that's the worry.'

Tony kept going.

Olivia and Danni, with the baby, opened the cafe bright and early the next morning.

A lot of women came in and asked what had happened and why they weren't open the day before.

Olivia explained what had happened, and all the customers gave them great encouragement to keep going.

In fact, it was turning out that their business was improving. The good people of Eden were showing their support.

Everyone knew somebody who worked in the café, and all the people felt that what had happened was a direct affront to all good, clean-living local people.

Meanwhile, Muddy and his gang were quietly congratulating themselves on the destruction that they had created. Muddy said, 'Well, boys, it won't be long before those lessos will be ready to join the club. I wouldn't mind rooting the blonde one.'

One of the gang replied, 'Who knows, mate, if she gets a bit of dick into her, she might switch back.'

All the crew sniggered and laughed.

'I reckon that it's time for a drink!' someone suggested, and the fridge was opened and cans of beer were handed around.

Tony drove down the road into Wonboyn and pulled up the F100 in the parking lot beside the boat ramp.

He started to untie the Shark Cat. It had towed beautifully, and he had hardly known that it was behind him.

Piggy was watching from a concealed spot in the bush.

He said to the other fisheries officer, 'I bet that bastard Teddy is somewhere near. I bet they are going to launch out of Wonboyn. Where will the bastards unload the abalone? That's the million-dollar question.'

A few minutes later, he said, 'There they are. There the bastards are.'

Teddy and the boys pulled up in a station wagon that Teddy had borrowed off his mate in the car yard.

It was important not to use a car registered in the name of anyone who was involved in poaching. The fisheries would be able to confiscate the vehicle if they could prove that it was used in the illegal taking of abalone.

They all got out and walked around the boat.

Tony had all the straps untied, and the boys climbed up into the Shark Cat, so Tony backed the trailer into the water.

Teddy lowered the pair of 200 horsepower Mercury motors deep into the water. Both motors started immediately and ticked over smoothly.

Teddy slowly backed the boat off the trailer and swung the bow around towards the open lake.

He gave Tony the thumbs up and started to accelerate down the lake towards the bar.

It was a great feeling, cruising down the lake. It was like gliding across a mirror.

The water was flat, and the reflections on the water from the foliage that lined the shore made it almost impossible to tell exactly where the water ended and the shore started.

The powerful boat motors threw up rooster tails about twenty feet high behind the boat.

As they approached the bar, Teddy didn't bother to slow down at all.

Suddenly they were in the middle of the choppy water in the midst of the bar.

Small waves crashed into the twin-hulled vessel.

They didn't need to cut across the bar on a forty-five-degree angle as there wasn't any swell to speak of.

Once out in Disaster Bay, they quickly headed towards the Victorian border.

They sped around the corner where the two down-and-outs Louie and Gazza had run out the illegal net that a humpbacked whale had got tangled up in. Teddy and the boys remembered how they had saved it from death by releasing it.

On they sped towards the border.

Teddy had the GPS on and saw when they had crossed the border.

They headed for a reef that was offshore but in shallow water.

It was the same reef that an abalone diver had been grabbed by a curious white pointer. It had spat him out when he jabbed his fingers in its eye.

He was one lucky boy. He had the sense to keep his wetsuit on to hold himself together for the frantic trip back to Eden where he ended up with over 100 stitches in him.

Piggy watched as the Shark Cat slid across the mirror-like surface of the Wonboyn Lake heading for the bar.

He asked the younger fisheries officer, 'I wonder where they are going to unload their abalone.'

Piggy was deep in thought.

The younger man volunteered, 'It will be somewhere near here unless they take it back to Melbourne.'

Piggy looked at the young man and said, 'Melbourne is just too far away to be running their Shark Cat there. I reckon that they will unload it and transfer it by road. In the past, we have put road blocks in place, but somehow we never catch the bastards.'

The younger officer screwed his face up in a thoughtful expression.

He said, 'Well, if you are sure that you have found out where they are processing the abalone, why don't we wait there and grab them when they least expect it?'

Piggy nodded his head, 'Yes, that's the plan. That is exactly what we will do. We will arrange for someone to lie in wait there and see what happens.'

Piggy and his underling drove their 4WD out of Wonboyn and headed back to the Bairnsdale office.

Teddy slowed the Shark Cat to a stop and looked at the depth sounder.

'It looks good here,' he said.

The boys didn't appear to hear what he had said. They were busy getting into their wetsuits.

Teddy got whatever gear they needed and said to Dean and Curly, 'After the near-death experience we had on the New Zealand Star Bank, you will all have your own air lines. So if you run out of air, just grab the bloke next to you and get his demand valve. But don't forget to let him have a few breaths.'

They all laughed heartedly.

Tom said, 'Last time I let Curly grab my demand valve. I thought that he was going to suck the compressor down the bloody hose. If I see him coming my way, I'm off.'

Everyone laughed again, but they all realised just how lucky they had been when things went foul out on the New Zealand Star Bank.

The boys went over the side and swam down into the clear water. There was a fair weed cover on the rocks, and it took a while to spot some abalone, but, like always, when you saw one, you saw another one, then another one, and then you realised that they were everywhere. The boys got stuck into getting abalone.

Tom soon started a stockpile of net bags on a sandy spot.

Between filling his bag, he ran the two other divers' bags back.

Soon the full net bags began to pile up.

Teddy drove the boat and kept a lookout for any sort of trouble.

He saw a runabout go past inshore, but he didn't know if it saw them or not. Maybe they did but were another poacher. Who knows?

The divers came up, and Teddy pressed the MOB (man overboard) button on the GPS to mark the position of that pile. They moved away from that stockpile, and the boys started to relax.

They knew that they would have about half an hour, a bit of a spell, and then they would be back into it again.

When they were rested, Teddy drove over to another spot, and after consulting the depth sounder, he said, 'This looks OK. We haven't worked this area before. Let's see what's down there.'

With that, Teddy started up the compressors, and the boys went over the side and swam down. Like before, they didn't spot any abalone at first, then they saw one, and then they saw plenty.

As darkness settled over the ocean, the divers called it quits for the day.

They swam up and got into the Shark Cat.

Everybody was pretty happy, and as they changed into dry, warm clothes, they started to talk about how much weight they had piled up at the bottom.

Tom said that they had about twelve net bags in the stockpiles. That should give them about 360 kilos of meat and that should work out to about 15,000 dollars—not bad for an afternoon's work.

Tomorrow would be a big day as they would start early and finish late.

Teddy headed into the anchorage at Gabo Island.

They dropped anchor and were preparing to have a meal when into the anchorage came another abalone boat.

In it were a couple of divers and their deckhands from Mallacoota.

These men had been diving for years out of Mallacoota, and they knew every crack and crevice around the place. They pulled up beside Teddy's boat and looked inside.

Teddy gave them a smile and asked, 'How are you going, fellas? Is everything OK?'

They didn't appear to be too talkative.

One of the divers said, 'We are on the lookout for poachers, and we want to know what you blokes are up to.'

'That's easy,' Teddy replied. 'We are a bunch of shipwreck hunters, and we have been looking at areas where we think there might be a few wrecks. It's what we do to burn off a bit of steam, our way of relaxing.'

The divers looked at them, and seeing that there was no abalone on board, there wasn't a lot that they could do.

One of the deckhands said, 'If we run into any poachers, we are going to belt the fuck out of them.'

Teddy smiled and said, 'You know what Confucius said, "Man who goes looking for trouble usually finds more than he bargained for". So you want to be careful.'

The divers looked at each other, puzzled, and backed their boat away from Teddy's. Without a word, they left the anchorage and headed back to the boat ramp at Mallacoota.

Tom laughed and said, 'Did Confucius really say that?'

Teddy smiled, 'Fucked if I know. He probably did. He said every fucken thing else.'

All the boys agreed.

They started to prepare their dinner.

When Muddy and his gang realised that the girls were back in business, they planned another attack.

This time, they would get serious. This time, they would show the girls that they weren't to be fucked with.

They would break the front window and then torch the joint. That would show the bitches once and for all.

Muddy walked into the cafe and saw Olivia behind the counter.

'Hi, there, blondie, had a bit of trouble, did you?'

Olivia looked at the bikie and saw a pathetic example of a human being.

She spoke to Danni, 'Looks like this clown has got the wrong address. All the blokes with small dicks are meeting over in the back bar of the pub across the road.'

Muddy was stunned; his mouth opened, but nothing came out.

'Come on, love, spit it out. What are you trying to say?' Olivia asked with a smile.

He closed his mouth and said, 'Get fucked,' and walked out of the cafe.

Danni was laughing so hard that she thought that she might wet herself. 'Jesus, you were a bit rough on that poor bastard, weren't you?'

Olivia said, 'He's the bastard who wanted protection money. I reckon that he was one of the people who trashed our cafe.'

Danni stopped laughing and said, 'We could be in a bit of trouble. I reckon that we had better ring the police and tell them what happened.'

Olivia nodded and rang the police station.

When the sergeant heard what had happened, he assured Olivia that he would be on guard and keep an eye out for the bikies.

Night fell as Piggy got back to his Bairnsdale office.

He told all those around him that Teddy and his gang were, at this very moment, poaching abalone. Instead of lying in wait for them to return to a port, he would have his Melbourne colleagues stake out the processing plant and arrest anyone who turned up with a load of illegal abalone meat.

That wasn't as good as Piggy being there, but he still found the thought of Teddy and his crew getting locked up to be pleasant.

He rang his plan through to his superior in Melbourne and assured him that all was under way and that he had actually seen Teddy and his crew head off out to sea.

So forewarned is forearmed, so to speak.

Piggy hung up the phone and said loudly to all the rest of the fisheries officers in the room, 'Now all we have to do is be alert. I have put everything in place, and I feel that victory will be ours.'

Everyone in the room felt good within themselves.

Muddy and his crew had a plastic Coke bottle three quarters full of petrol. They then poured half a bottle of washing-up detergent into it. Muddy explained that the detergent would make the petrol stick to the walls and make the fire bigger.

All the bikies were amazed at Muddy's knowledge of such matters. They didn't know that Muddy had only learnt of this development when he was in Sydney.

They all had a couple of swigs of Jack Daniels as heart starters, got into a Ute, and headed away towards the main shopping area and the girls' cafe.

They pulled up alongside the front window.

As Muddy was sitting in the back of the Ute, he put out his hand and accepted the fire bomb from the front window of the Ute.

He turned it upside down, and the cloth wick was immediately soaked with petrol.

Muddy lit the wick and with a whoosh, it ignited.

He was a bit taken aback by the savageness of the burning wick. Maybe he should have soaked the wick in something less flammable such as kerosene.

He quickly tossed it up in the air towards the top of the cafe window; the bottle didn't break as a glass bottle would have done. Plastic bottles are not recommended for use as Molotov cocktails as they don't shatter on impact.

The coke bottle ricocheted back into the rear of the Ute, where the wick popped out and petrol poured onto the still burning wick.

With a whoomph, the entire back pan of the Ute was in flames.

Muddy, in fear of his life, leapt out of the burning Ute.

He and his fellow arsonist's motorcycle boots had been saturated by the leaking petrol and were alight too.

They both started stamping on the ground to try and put out their boots.

Muddy shouted, 'For fuck sake, drive, drive.'

The driver had no idea what was going on, so he tramped his foot on the accelerator.

The Ute, with the back completely consumed in flames, took off, leaving Muddy and his fellow arsonist on the footpath, doing what could only be described as an odd version of the once popular stomp dance of the early Sixties.

Muddy was badly singed. He smelt of burnt hair, and his face hurt.

His fellow arsonist was also a bit smudged.

'What the fuck happened?' he asked.

Muddy slowly shook his head and watched as the fire ball of the Ute headed out of town.

'I don't really understand at all,' Muddy confessed.

The police sergeant, who was watching from a distance, started to wonder just how bright these clowns were.

He thought that they were smarter than that.

Shaking his head, he decided that all the fun was over for the night.

He might as well head home and get some sleep. He started to laugh, and by the time he got back to the station, he was almost beside himself. He had to shut up or else his wife would think he was off his rocker.

✧ ✧ ✧ ✧

As the sun rose above the horizon, Teddy and the boys got ready to start the day.

Dean said, 'I sure miss the big boat and the luxury of a comfy bed.'

All the others agreed.

Teddy said, 'You blokes are getting soft. When I was your age, we used to swim out from the shore. We didn't have the luxury of a boat.'

Tom said, 'For fuck sake, don't get him started on how tough he had it as a kid, or we will never get into the water.'

All the boys laughed and got in.

Down they swam. As always, it was hard to see the first abalone, but once you saw one, then you saw plenty, and the divers saw plenty.

They started to gather them up, and, as always, Tom started a stockpile and the bags mounted up.

✧ ✧ ✧ ✧

The white pointer sensed that the divers were there from the signals through the water.

It realised that there was a lot of aggression coming from the divers.

The white pointer was the same one that had bitten the abalone diver years before and nearly killed him. It remembered the taste of the diver's weight vest and also remembered that it wasn't a good thing to eat.

So it gave the divers a wide birth and went on its way to find something more palatable.

✧ ✧ ✧ ✧

Before they knew it, it was time to hit the surface and have a bit of a spell.

Teddy asked, 'How many bags have you got stockpiled down there?'

Tom replied, 'We have got about eight full net bags.'

Teddy nodded and said, 'Well done, lads, we should get about twenty by nightfall with a bit of luck.'

The divers got ready to get back into it.

Piggy was on the phone, organising the team of fisheries officers who were going to stake out the processing factory in Melbourne.

He was excited, and it rubbed off.

The officers were ready to hit the street.

They decided that they would get to the stake-out point as soon as possible and get into their routine.

The officers drove their fisheries 4WDs to the same spot that they had used previously. They were aware that this time, surprise would be on their side.

As far as they were concerned, Teddy didn't have a clue about the fact that they were on to him and his team.

As ever, Murphy, the security guard, was alert. He spotted the 4WD as soon as he started work.

'Well, well, our snooping friends are back on the job, aren't they?' he said out loud.

He decided to give Derek a ring, just to fill him in.

Derek, who by now had Murphy's number in his phone, picked his phone up on its first ring.

'Murphy, you old bastard. How the fuck are you?' he said.

'Gidday, mate,' Murphy replied. He was happy that Derek and he got on so well.

'Mate, our friends are back, and they are watching your factory. There's a fisheries 4WD in the same spot that they used before.'

Derek smiled to himself. *It's amazing what a couple of crayfish will do for you,* he thought.

'Thanks for the info, mate,' he said. 'I'll tell the divers that I want a couple of crays for you and your missus. How is your good lady wife by the way?'

Murphy was flattered that Derek had asked about his wife.

He smiled and said, 'Mate, she's as happy as Larry and she wants to thank you for the crayfish. She really enjoys a feed of them every now and again. I can't thank you enough, mate.'

'Don't mention it, mate.' Derek said. 'I appreciate you keeping me in the loop.'

Derek disconnected and thought to himself. *Those bloody fisheries are hot on our tails. It's a good thing that I'm using my mate's potato chip factory to pack the abalone in.*

Word somehow got around town that the bikies had tried to set fire to the girls' cafe.

There were a lot of people concerned that sooner or later, they would really get going and do something stupid.

It was a situation that the girls fought to control.

Danni suggested that it would be easier to pay their demands and just get on with a carefree life. But Olivia was sure that if they buckled, then the bikies would want more and more. Soon they would be working for them and not themselves.

Olivia had a framed photograph of a Japanese mini sub commander on the wall of the cafe. Teddy and the boys had been employed by the warrior's sons to find his long-lost mini sub. The two sons had flown over from Japan to perform a burial ceremony above the sunken site.

Olivia often admired this photo.

She remembered that the Japanese driver or bodyguard, who had been with the sons and their priest, had offered help if ever they needed it.

Turning to Danni, she said, 'That Japanese driver, Chikara, said to me if I ever needed help, I shouldn't hesitate to ask him for it. That is due to the respect that they have for my father. I am sure they would be of assistance to us now.'

Danni said, 'It can't hurt to give him a ring.'

Olivia dialled the number that Chikara had handed her on the day her father, Billy Boy, was buried.

Chikara was at his desk in the Japanese restaurant that his father owned.

It was a big room and expensively furnished. One wall was a see-through mirror, so whoever was in the office could see how the restaurant was going.

The restaurant was almost full. The head waiter was escorting an obviously well-to-do customer and his partner to a secluded table.

Chikara knew the rules. While they were waiting for the entrée, Chikara would walk up and greet the man, like a long-lost brother. The partner would be suitably impressed, and all would be well.

His phone vibrated in his pocket. He looked at it and didn't know the number.

He answered, 'Chikara speaking. How can I help you?'

Olivia started speaking too fast, 'Hullo, Chikara, you probably don't remember me. I met you when you drove the two Japanese brothers and a priest up to Eden so they could have a ceremony over their father's grave site. My name is Olivia.'

Chikara paused for a moment, and the memory flooded back to him. 'Of course I remember you, Olivia. I also remember the great debt of gratitude we owe your father for telling us where the submarine was.'

Olivia felt better after hearing those words.

'Well,' Olivia stumbled on. 'My partner and I have moved to Eden and started up a cafe and plant nursery. It's a good little business, but we are being stood over by a biker gang. They are demanding protection money. We haven't paid them, so they broke into our cafe and made a big mess. We had to close for a day to clean up. Then the other night, we are told they tried to burn us down.'

Chikara asked, 'How can I help you?'

'I know it's a big ask. But could you give them a ring and have a talk to them and get them to leave us alone?' Olivia answered.

Chikara thought for a moment and said, 'Let me get back to you. Can you give me an hour, please?'

Olivia felt relief flood through her. She said, 'Of course, take as long as you like. Thanks for your help.'

She hung up and said to Danni, 'He is going to help us. I feel so much better now.'

Danni said, 'I wonder what they are going to do.'

'Probably give those bikies a ring and scare the shit out of them,' Olivia suggested.

Chikara spoke to his father and told him about the phone call from Olivia.

His father nodded slowly and said, 'My son, we owe the departed girl's father a debt of honour for helping Baku and Akinobu find the site where their father was killed in the war. I want you to handle this personally. I will ring Baku immediately and tell him what is going on.'

With that, Chikara bowed slightly and started to make plans.

The first thing that Chikara did was ring a friend who ran a gym that specialised in martial arts. He said that he needed him and two others, preferably martial arts instructors, for a couple of days, no more than a week. He explained that there was a job that needed to be done interstate. He would pick them up at the gym at eight o'clock the next morning.

Chikara rang Olivia and said that they had everything under control, that she shouldn't worry but leave everything up to him, and that he would speak to her shortly.

Olivia said to Danni, 'Well, I bet that dumb bikie is in for a shock.'

The next morning, Chikara pulled up in front of the gym. He was driving a Hummer, which is the civilian version of the High Mobility Multi-purpose Wheeled Vehicle (HMMWV), commonly known as the Humvee.

Three extremely fit, tall Japanese-Australian men were talking quietly amongst themselves. When they saw the Hummer, with the blacked-out windows pull up, they immediately got inside.

Chikara drove off towards Eden.

It would take them about seven hours to get there.

The three men whom Chikara had picked up were named Tomoya, Kenta, and Tatsu.

They were Australian born of Japanese parents and had Australian names. In each other's company, they always reverted back to their Japanese names.

They had been friends since childhood and had been to school together. They had stood side by side through the years of bullying and name-calling.

Their parents had insisted that they take up karate from an early age and learn the ways of the Japanese ninja and the ronin. The young boys were very good students and learnt to defend themselves quickly. Soon the bullying stopped, and they were left in peace.

Chikara explained about Olivia and her father, who had found the Japanese submarine, and the problems that she was facing due to her refusal to be stood over by the motorbike gang. He explained how he had met Teddy and his crew of abalone poachers, how they had found the mini submarine and how he and the others had nearly shit themselves when a moray eel had attacked the camera while Teddy was filming the submarine and they were watching it all on a TV monitor on board. Everyone found the story funny.

Soon they were in Bairnsdale.

They pulled into the Noodle Bar in the main street, had some lunch, and then went on their way.

Teddy and the boys were doing what they did best. They were poaching abalone. The day was nearly over, and the net bags were stacking up.

The boys were in the boat, having a spell when they saw a boat heading towards them.

It was the same abalone boat that had come into the anchorage at Gabo Island the night before. The same four men were in the boat.

Teddy had let the boat drift away from where he had pressed the MOB button.

He decided that another approach was needed.

'What the fuck do you pricks want? Can't you leave us alone?' Teddy asked heatedly.

One of the divers said, 'Mate, we just came to tell you that a white pointer was seen down the coast, about three kilometres away, and it was swimming this way.'

Teddy said, 'Thanks for the warning, but we aren't scared of white pointers.'

The four men peered into Teddy's boat and saw that there wasn't any abalone on board, so they backed off.

Without another word, they headed back to Mallacoota.

Tom said, 'Fuck me, they had a good look to make sure that there wasn't any abalone on board.'

'Yes, it would appear that they are keeping an eye on us. We will have to be careful when we do get the abalone on board, and I don't reckon that we will do it in daylight,' Teddy added.

Dean said with a smile, 'Good one, Teddy. We aren't scared of white pointers. Like fuck we aren't. It's all right for you, you prick. The fucking thing would have to grow arms and legs and climb into the boat to get you. Yer, that's fucking right. What you should have said is, "I am not scared of white pointers, you prick".'

All the boys laughed.

It was four o'clock in the afternoon when Chikara walked into the cafe.

Olivia was doing some washing up, and when she turned around and saw Chikara, she couldn't believe her eyes.

'Chikara, well, I didn't expect you to come all this way. Danni, Danni, come here and meet Chikara.'

Olivia walked around and gave Chikara a hug.

Suddenly she felt safe.

Danni came up and said, 'How do you do? Are you tired from the long drive?'

Chikara smiled and said, 'No, it's an easy drive. I enjoy driving through the forests.'

Olivia said, 'You will have to stay with us. We live a short distance from town.'

Chikara said, 'There are a couple of us. We would prefer to stay close to the cafe. We will stay in the motel down the street. In fact, my friends are settling in, as we speak. We will watch the cafe until your problem is solved. Trust me, it will only take a few days.'

Olivia smiled and said, 'I can't tell you how much we appreciate all the trouble you are going through. Is there any way that we can repay you?'

Chikara thought for a moment and said, 'Breakfast in the morning will be a great way to start the day.'

With that, he walked out of the cafe and went to the motel.

Muddy and his co-arsonist had gotten over nearly burning themselves to death.

With renewed vigour, they had decided that they would do a bit of damage to the cafe that night after the pub had closed.

They would go around, kick the door in, make a proper mess inside, and then smash the front window. Surely that would convince the two lessos that it was a lot easier to pay your friendly biker gang and live in peace than have your front window broken every night.

Chikara and his friends had a light dinner and relaxed.

They thought that if there was going to be any trouble, it would be after the pub closed at ten o'clock that night, so they lay back and watched TV.

At ten o'clock, they all changed into tight, black tracksuit-type gear. With black balaclavas ready to be put on, they made their way down the back lane behind the motel and stopped at the back gate of Olivia's cafe.

They settled down and waited for some action.

After about an hour and a half, they saw a car without headlights pull into the lane.

Four bikies got out and made their way over to the rear entrance of the cafe.

They had a short discussion, and two went to walk around to the front.

Chikara suddenly appeared in front of Muddy.

Muddy wasn't prepared to be confronted by a figure, taller than he was, dressed in black and wearing a balaclava.

'What the fuck?' Muddy exclaimed.

Chikara drove a stiffened hand into Muddy's beer belly.

Muddy was winded, and he staggered back. Chikara slashed at Muddy's face with the edge of his hands. His hands were toughened by years of hitting into solid bags of sand.

Muddy was out for the count. He hit the ground face-first.

While Chikara was belting Muddy, the others went into overdrive. The hapless bikies were set upon by the martial arts experts. With hardly a sound, they struck.

The only sounds were the striking of fists and the odd groans from the bikies.

Soon they were all on the ground unconscious.

Chikara looked at them and said, 'I will dial triple zero and tell the police where to pick up these amateurs. You all go back to where we are staying and relax. Something tells me this is going to be easier than I thought.'

The three men walked away into the night. Chikara dialled the triple zero and told them where the bodies were.

There was great excitement in town the next day.

The story got around that Muddy and some of his gang had got beaten up and had spent the night in hospital. Everyone was wondering who could have done such a thing.

When Olivia got to work the next day, the cafe started to fill, and soon everyone was talking about what had happened.

When the four Japanese-Australian men walked in and quietly sat down at a table, Olivia walked over and said, 'Did you have a comfortable night, and did you sleep well?'

Chikara said, 'It took us a while to settle down, but we all slept soundly once we got to sleep.'

'I'll get you some breakfast. You can have the house speciality,' Olivia said.

Olivia went to prepare the meal.

Muddy looked at his face in the mirror.

He almost didn't recognise the battered and bruised face that looked back at him. His face resembled a meat lover's pizza with double tomato paste.

When he and his crew had been admitted to the hospital from the ambulance, they were immediately taken to the operating theatre and had the gravel removed from their faces.

The iodine antiseptic that the doctors and nurses had put on made them look a whole lot worse than they actually were.

Muddy had released himself and his crew.

As they drove towards Eden, he started to plan.

He had no idea who or what they were up against, but they all knew that for them to be beaten so badly, there must have been twenty attackers. As they talked among themselves, the number of the winning team escalated.

Muddy knew just who to ring; it would be his mates and fellow bikies in Sydney.

Muddy rang and spoke to The Tsar.

He was the leader of the chapter in Sydney.

The Tsar told everybody that he was a Russian, but, in fact, he was from a neighbouring country. But whenever he tried to explain to someone just where he was from, they shook their heads and said, 'Never heard of it, mate. You sound like a Russian.'

So that was it. He referred to himself as of being of Russian descent.

When The Tsar heard Muddy asking for help, he started to wonder just how tough Muddy and his crew really were. Like, what the fuck could they be up against in Eden?

To him, it was a little shithole full of dumb fishermen, a couple of koori families, and a few Maoris.

To The Tsar, that didn't seem like a lot to get over.

He told a grateful Muddy to sit tight and he would come down with a couple of brothers and sort things out.

They would leave in an hour and should be there just after dark.

The Tsar decided that he would take a team of ten bikers down. That should settle the natives.

He got his crew together, and they left within the hour. Soon they were streaming down the highway side by side.

The four Japanese-Australian men were confronted by four platters of food.

They took up the whole table.

Chikara looked at his three friends and said, 'I told you I would shout you breakfast.'

Kenta said, in Japanese, 'There is enough bad fat in these meals to kill half of Japan.'

Tatsu suggested, 'They didn't need to drop a bomb on Japan. They should have sent us over some breakfasts like these. That would have slowed our imperial army down.'

They all agreed and started eating.

Down went the bacon, eggs, hash browns, tomatoes, baked beans, toast, onions, and mushrooms.

Olivia started to pour out cups of steaming coffee. They all had their coffees black.

Soon the platters were empty, and the men were full.

Chikara said, 'Let's walk down to the Fishermen's Wharf and have a look at the fishing fleet, that's if they are in at the moment.'

As they strolled down, they were under the watchful eyes of the sergeant of police.

He thought to himself, *There's a bit of new blood in town. They arrived yesterday in that blacked-out Hummer. They are staying at the motel, just up from the girls' shop. And last night, Muddy and a few of his henchmen ended up in hospital as a result of getting flogged by unknown assailants.*

The sergeant put two and two together and came up with the thought that Billy Boy's daughter must have a few connections somewhere in Melbourne.

He wondered just how all that came about. He would make some calls and see if he could find out more about these four men. He decided to let things work their way through. He would be there to pick up the pieces.

Muddy and his crew were licking their wounds in their clubhouse.

It wasn't like the chapter house in Sydney. Muddy's was in a run-down house in the back streets of Eden. It looked as if the place hadn't been painted for years and the front lawn was a jungle.

There were Harley Davidson motorbikes parked all over the yard, and Muddy was holding court in what was once a living room. The rest of his crew were there as Muddy and the other three bikies explained to them how they were ambushed by a far larger pack of dangerous men.

They explained how they had put up a gallant fight but were overcome by sheer numbers. Next time, they would have a full contingent of fit and healthy men and it would be a different outcome.

The Tsar and his crew came down the hill to Eden from the Sydney side.

They had made good time. They cruised through the industrial area and headed into the main shopping centre. They glared at the locals and wolf-whistled any female they saw. They were doing a pretty good impersonation of Marlon Brando in the *Wild One.*

They rode down the hill to the Fishermen's Wharf.

On the way down, they passed four fit-looking Japanese men who were jogging up the hill towards their motel.

The four men smiled at the group of bikies. The bikies snarled and glared at the men who jogged on.

The Tsar pulled his Harley Davidson onto the front yard of Muddy's house.

He gave it a rev and turned it off.

All his crew did the same, and silence descended on the street.

Muddy's crew all came out and welcomed the ten riders. They were tough-looking in their leathers.

Beers were passed around, and all the bikies went inside.

Chikara watched from a distance as the group went inside.

He said to his three companions, 'We might pay them a visit tonight, just to let them know that we are around. I would hate for them to think that they rode all this way for nothing.'

The four men made their way back to the motel where they had a light meal and relaxed in front of the TV.

The Tsar and Muddy were in heaven.

They were in the middle of about twenty of their henchmen and about six willing young ladies (a term used loosely for biker molls).

One of The Tsar's men and a young lady were having sex on the couch. The biker had rolled her over, and they were going for it doggy style, much to the amusement of the fellow bikers.

There were bikers snorting Coke and shooting shots.

Everyone was on a high.

The Tsar looked at Muddy and said, 'It's good to be king!'

They both laughed.

Chikara and his three friends, completely dressed in black, made their way across town to where Muddy and his crew were celebrating.

They cruised silently in the blacked-out Hummer and stopped up the street from Muddy's house.

Chikara said to the three men, 'Here is the plan. We will run a steel wire through the rear wheels of their motorbikes. Then we will hook it up to the Hummer and tow as many as we can away down the street and leave them in a mangled heap. That should take their minds off sex. I believe that this type of men hold their motorbikes in very high esteem.'

The three men all nodded and got out of the car.

The street lighting was poor, so they moved easily in the shadows towards the house where things were really starting to get going.

Tomoya had the 100-meter coil of strengthened-steel wire. On one end, there was an inch loop and on the other end was a three-inch loop.

He gave the end with the smaller loop to Tatsu, and he slowly walked into the front yard, bent down, and started to thread the wire through the rear wheels of the Harleys.

Kenta stealthily made his way to the door to stand guard.

Chikara waited with the engine quietly ticking over.

Soon the wire rope was threaded through all the rear wheels of the Harleys.

Tomoya then passed the smaller loop through the bigger loop and slowly pulled up the slack until the wire rope was reasonably tight.

He flashed a small LED torch towards Chikara, who slowly moved the Hummer forward.

Just as Chikara got opposite to the front gate, the front door opened, and one of the Sydney Bikies came out to get something from the saddlebags on his motorbike.

As he walked out, he saw the wire rope and could just make out Tomoya standing with the wire in his hand.

'What the fuck is going on? What are you . . . ?'

That was as far as he got.

Kenta slashed across his throat with one hand and drove his other stiffened hand into the biker's solar plexus. He crumbled down the front steps and lay unconscious on the front porch.

Tomoya placed the loop over a towing hitch on the rear of the Hummer, and the three men got on board.

Chikara accelerated slowly until the slack was taken up, and then he floored the accelerator.

The weight took up, and, all of a sudden, the motorbikes were smashed together and were dragged off their stands.

They were pulled backwards together and started to mangle against each other, smashing mirrors and hand controls. They smashed against the front gate and ripped the already leaning gateposts out of the ground.

Chikara headed up the road.

The huge engine of the Hummer took to the challenge eagerly.

At the first corner, the mangled bunch of bikes swung wide and smashed into a front fence. Bits of motorbike were being flung into the air.

Petrol was flowing everywhere from the ruptured tanks on the motorbikes.

Chikara drove the tangled mess into the night.

Suddenly a spark ignited the spilt petrol. With a whoosh, the mess of mangled motorbikes went up in flames.

Chikara kept driving for a short distance until they were clear of any residential buildings.

He then stopped the Hummer, and Tomoya jumped out.

Chikara crept the Hummer back a couple of feet, and Tomoya unhooked the wire rope.

He jumped back into the Hummer, and the four men drove away from the scene of devastation.

The Tsar and Muddy looked at each other when they heard the noise of the bikes being crunched together.

There was a second when their drink-addled brains were working overtime to comprehend what was going on.

'What the fuck?' Muddy asked anybody.

'Our bikes, what the fuck is going on?' The Tsar asked.

The entire room of bikies ran out onto the front lawn just as their motorbikes were dragged across the lawn and out onto the street.

The sound of a powerful motor was just audible above the metal screeching on the sealed road.

Some of the bikies started to run after the tangled mess that was once their beloved motorbikes.

They saw the tangled mess get dragged round the corner and then the flash of light as it ignited.

Muddy and The Tsar jumped into the almost burnt-out Ute and drove towards the fire.

Some of the more alert members had jumped into the back of the Ute.

They pulled up beside the tangled, burning mess that was once their gleaming Harley Davidsons.

There was disbelief in their faces.

How could this have happened?

In minutes, their world had been destroyed.

One minute, they were drinking, doing drugs, and rooting a couple of old ladies.

The next minute, they were standing beside their destroyed bikes.

Who the fuck was responsible for this? How did it happen?

Earlier that night, Teddy and the boys had waited until the sun set in the west, and then they headed back to the position where they had stockpiled the first lot of abalone.

Tom, as usual, swam down and started to bring the abalone up to the boat.

It was quickly stored up in the bow, and Teddy piloted the boat up to the second stockpile.

Soon all the abalone was on board, and the boys started shucking it out; the meat was all sealed into clear plastic bags with the air squeezed out and the tops sealed by wire ties.

They kept watchful eyes on the radar and the darkened ocean in case the abalone boat from Mallacoota was prowling about.

Teddy took the boat over to where the remaining abalone was stockpiled, and Tom swam down again.

Soon all the abalone that the boys had bagged up was in the boat.

Tom started to get out of his wetsuit, and they all got into shucking out the abalone.

After a couple of hours, it was all shucked out and bagged up.

Teddy had arranged for Dave and Lee to wait in Eden until he rang and told them where they would unload.

He thought that Wonboyn would be out as that was where Piggy knew that they had put the boat in.

He knew that Piggy would be on the lookout for them and would be aware that he would be bringing in the abalone somewhere in the area.

So it was with some concern that Teddy decided that, this time, they would unload onto the sheltered beach at Boyd Town.

There was an old inn there called the Boyd Town Seahorse Inn.

Teddy had been in there for a few drinks over the years.

He knew that it would be quiet, especially at 3 a.m. in the morning.

The only thing that would upset them would be an early morning fisherman or something like that. But the risk was worth it.

Little did Teddy realise, but Piggy was in bed, sleeping the sleep of the totally satisfied.

All the pressure had been taken off him since he had been demoted—not so much demoted but put in a place where before he made a decision, he had to check with the minister for fisheries or his secretary. They were the ones who had decided that it was a waste of time and money trying to track down and arrest the poachers when they were in possession of illegal abalone.

What the powers to be had come up with was, catch the bastards at the factory when they came in to weigh up. It was that simple.

And since they knew where the poachers were selling their abalone, all they need do was stake out the processor's factory and seize all the abalone. Then they would put so much heat on them that they would roll over and give up the poachers.

That would be it, another fine piece of work.

It all made sense really, and of course the minister would take all the back slaps and wallow in the fact that he was really much smarter than the fisheries inspectors and, of course, the evil abalone poachers.

Teddy rang Dave and Lee and told them where to pick up the abalone. He told them to keep their eyes open.

He rang Tony and told him that they would load the Shark Cat onto the trailer at Eden at first light.

Tony told him that there had been a bit of excitement in town, and it looked like Billy Boy's daughter, Olivia, was somehow involved. Tony said that he would fill him in when he found out more. Teddy told him to find out all he could. He sent Tony into Boyd Town to have a look around and see if there were any fisheries or anyone else about and to report back to Dave and Lee.

The security guard, Murphy, had kept Derek in the loop.

He had told him that the fisheries 4WDs were in position and that they were still keeping their eyes on the processing plant.

Derek was glad that Dave and Lee were taking the abalone to his mate's potato chip factory and there it would be boxed up in chip boxes for delivery to his processing factory when things quietened down.

Back in Eden, the fire brigade arrived with lights flashing and sirens going at full power.

Those residents who weren't already up and watching the fun were soon awakened from their slumber, and the crowd built.

The Tsar, Muddy, and the bewildered bikies slowly came to the assumption that they had been singled out by someone, but who?

Who could they take out their frustrations on? Someone had taken them to task. Someone wanted to show them that they weren't as big and tough as they had once thought.

The Tsar asked Muddy to go over what he had done and who he had had a run-in within the last few days.

Muddy racked his brains.

All the people whom he was standing over weren't brave enough to do something like this. They were in their boxes. There were no heroes there.

The volunteer fire brigade hosed down the smouldering pile of worthless rubble, and the police sergeant ran a tape around it, which proclaimed it a crime scene, and he left a constable on guard duty to protect it from treasure hunters.

Muddy and the rest of the gang slowly walked back to the house and decided that they had a big problem. There was somebody in town who wasn't afraid of them. That was a situation that rarely occurred. It would take some working out and some deep thought.

The Tsar asked about the condition of the Ute and how it got to be burnt.

Muddy dismissed it as a job gone wrong, involving two lesbians.

He was sure that they were as weak as piss and that they would be in the net soon enough.

The Tsar realised that you didn't have to be the sharpest tool in the shed if you were the hammer. He told Muddy to think again about who had the balls to pull a stunt like this.

Muddy admitted that it was a mystery.

The Tsar then asked more about the two bitches. Were they paying him protection money?

If not, then why not?

Muddy explained that he had been a bit busy and hadn't got around to getting back to them.

The Tsar asked where they had been when they got their faces turned into mincemeat.

Muddy said that they were at the rear of the lessos' cafe. It was almost midnight. They were attacked by a large group of unknown assailants.

They did a great job of defending themselves but were overwhelmed by the sheer number of people they were fighting.

It was easily two or more to one, Muddy added.

The Tsar said, 'Let me get this straight. You broke in and trashed the cafe. Then when you tried to burn it down, you fucked up your Ute and nearly burnt yourselves to death. Next, you went back and tried to fuck them up again and were met by an army of men who put you all in hospital. Now all our bikes are fucked.

I'm starting to think that maybe these fucking lessos may be stronger than you reckon. We had better look at them a bit more closely. What happened tonight wasn't done by some weak-kneed pussy lickers. I reckon that we are dealing with a team of professionals. I think that these are dangerous people whom we are involved with.'

The Tsar got on the phone and rang Sydney.

He said that they needed some back-up and some bikes.

Nearly all the bikies had a back-up bike that they kept for emergencies.

The second in command asked, 'Just what the fuck have you got yourselves into down there in sleepy hollow?'

The Tsar replied, 'I'm fucked if I know. There seems to be a presence in this shit-heeled town that needs some taking care of. Grab a few more blokes. Grab the truck, put the spare bikes in it, and be here as soon as you can.'

With that, he hung up and said to Muddy, 'We'll put our heads down for a couple of hours, and then we'll see just what the fuck these lessos are up to.'

Teddy spoke to Tony, 'Mate, all clear?'

'Clear as a bell,' Tony replied.

'Are Dave and Lee ready on the foreshore?' Teddy asked.

'Yes, mate,' Tony replied. 'They will shine a torch out to you as soon as they hear you coming.'

Teddy slowly piloted the Shark Cat into Boyd Town beach.

He saw the light shine out towards him and slowly raised the two Mercury outboards.

The boat came into the beach broadside.

As soon as the hulls touched the sandy bottom, everyone started to unload the abalone.

Dean and Curly started to run the clear plastic bags up the beach and stacked them up at the rear of the van. There Tony handed them up to Dave and Lee, who loaded them into tea chests and packed them into the front of their furniture van.

Within fifteen minutes, the van was loaded and Lee and Dave were away.

They drove slowly out on the Boyd Town road, and soon they were starting their long drive to Melbourne.

Teddy and the boys relaxed a bit.

Tony said, 'Your mate Billy Boy's daughter, Olivia, and her partner have set up a little cafe in Eden. It looks like some fucking bikies have been trying to stand over them. I don't know just what the fuck they were doing, but the bikies have been burnt and bashed, and earlier on this evening, all their Harleys were set fire to and dragged up the fucking street.'

Teddy looked at Tony and said, 'What the fuck! That Olivia looked as if butter wouldn't melt in her mouth. I can't see her doing all that. She is a sweet thing. We had better drop by and make sure that she is all right.'

All the boys nodded.

Teddy said, 'Why don't you blokes get a bit of shut-eye and Tony and I'll go and grab the car out of Wonboyn? We can put the Shark Cat onto the trailer at Eden and then go and catch up with Olivia.'

With that, the boys jumped into the Shark Cat, drove it out into the middle of Twofold Bay, and settled down for a spell.

Tony and Teddy drove down to Wonboyn, and Teddy picked up the station wagon.

By the time they got back to Eden, the sun was up.

Tony backed the trailer into the water at the boat ramp, and Dean drove the Shark Cat up onto it. All the boys climbed down, and Tony secured the boat to the trailer.

Tony said that he wanted to get going as it was a bit slower towing the Shark Cat and he would feel better when he was home and the Shark Cat was hosed down.

Then he could relax.

Teddy and the boys drove up to the main street and parked outside what they thought was Olivia's cafe.

They were sitting in the station wagon when they saw Olivia drive up the street in her van and go around to the rear.

When she had unlocked and was starting to get things ready, Teddy knocked on the front door. Olivia came to the door, and when she opened it and saw Teddy, she was taken aback.

'Teddy, how are you?' she asked. 'What are you doing here in Eden? When did you arrive?'

Teddy said, 'Hullo, love, how are you? You look terrific. How is your cafe going?'

Olivia looked at the big bloke and felt a real sense of friendship.

She laughed and said, 'Oh, we are all right. We have had a bit of trouble with some dumb bikies. But guess what? I rang Chikara, and he and three of his mates came up and said they would sort it all out for Danni and me. They think that they owe me a debt of gratitude for Dad telling you where that submarine was.'

Teddy smiled and said, 'Chikara, well, that was decent of him. Is he still about?'

Olivia said, 'Yes, he and his mates will be in for breakfast. They come in every morning as way of payment.'

'That really sounds good to me,' Teddy said. 'How about lining up four breakfasts for me and the boys?'

'I'll start on them right away,' Olivia said.

The three boys came in and greeted Olivia.

It was good see that she was happy.

She told them about Danni and their new son and how happy they had been until the bikies started to make things hard for them.

Teddy said, 'We have run into them ourselves. They are real dickheads.'

Teddy started to organise the coffees, and soon the breakfasts were placed in front of the hungry men. They all started eating, and no one spoke.

'That's what I like to hear when people are in the cafe. Silence! That means they are enjoying their food,' Olivia said brightly.

'We sure are,' Teddy said.

The Tsar and Muddy were parked away from Olivia's cafe but had good vision of the front window.

The Tsar said, 'Looks like business is good. There's a chance that you will get them for 500 a week.'

Muddy looked again and saw Teddy and the boys were inside, eating.

'Fuck me. That's them, abalone poachers. That's the bastards who bushwhacked us. I wonder what they are doing here.'

The Tsar asked, 'Do you know them?'

Muddy answered, 'Yer, we've run into them a couple of times and smacked their arses. We gave them a good old thrashing.'

The Tsar asked, 'So you are on top of them then?'

'On top of them, yer, we are on top of them. Ha, they will shit themselves if they see us,' Muddy volunteered.

'Well, that will be on our side. We will go in and confront them now and let the owners see that we aren't meant to be fucked with.'

Muddy started to get a bad feeling about this. He had seen Teddy and his crew in action.

He started to say to The Tsar that perhaps they should get reinforcements as they were only a couple of minutes away. But The Tsar was chock-full of confidence as Muddy had said that he and his gang had already given these mugs a belting.

He got out of the car and, with Muddy trailing behind him, made his way across to the cafe.

Curly sipped his coffee and said, 'Looks like we have company. It looks like that dickhead bikie and one of his mates are on their way in.'

Olivia said, 'The one lagging behind is the one who has been demanding money off me and Danni.'

Teddy looked around and said to Olivia, 'Hope that you have got a mop and bucket because I think that there is going to be a bit of blood spillage very soon.'

The Tsar walked into the cafe and glared at Teddy.

Teddy looked back and smiled, 'Yo, dickhead, what's up?'

Muddy wasn't feeling too good; this didn't sound right.

Curly looked at Muddy and asked, 'Do you still want me to suck your dick?' referring to the first time that the two groups had met in the pub in Eden.

Olivia asked in an innocent voice, 'Is this where you ask me for protection money and I tell you to go and get fucked?'

Teddy put down his coffee cup and said, 'I'll make it easy for you. Fuck off and don't ever come back, and we will only give you a bitch slapping. Hang about, and we will belt the living fuck out of you. It's your decision!'

The Tsar started to realise that these blokes weren't all that afraid of Muddy and his gang. The second thing that he realised was that they were outnumbered. The third and probably the most important thing was that while they had been talking, two of the four men had got behind them and their exit was blocked. All these things went through his brain in a split second.

Teddy stood up and said, 'Time's up, dickhead,' and swung a blow at The Tsar's head.

The Tsar fended it off but couldn't stop Teddy's left fist crashing into his belly.

He staggered back and crashed up against the counter.

Olivia was waiting with a solid old-fashioned frying pan, and she swung it at his head with a loud resounding gong.

The Tsar went down on his hands and knees.

Muddy had his own problems. As soon as Teddy had swung at The Tsar, Curly had run at Muddy and grabbed him in a bear hug, giving Dean a clear shot at his head.

Dean slammed a fist into Muddy's already battered face.

Blood started to run down his cheeks.

Once again, Dean hit Muddy a vicious blow.

The only reason that Muddy was still standing was that Curly had hold of him.

Teddy grabbed The Tsar by the scruff of his neck and stood him up.

Tom gave him the old one, two, three, and The Tsar had had enough.

Teddy and Dean frogmarched them out of the cafe. They footed the bikies up the arse, propelling them out the door.

They both stumbled and fell in the middle of the street.

Teddy said to Olivia, 'Well, that was a lot cleaner than I thought it would be. It's obvious that they aren't bleeders.'

Olivia said, 'Yes, it's good that there isn't any mess.'

The Tsar and Muddy got back to their car and headed off back to Muddy's house.

Soon all the bikies came in and started talking about what had happened the previous night and how most of their Harleys were destroyed by an unknown group.

Soon everyone in town had heard about the two bikies getting kicked out of the cafe by the four abalone poachers. In fact, everyone knew that the boys were poachers, but they weren't concerned because they didn't take from NSW fishermen.

Chikara watched as the bikies were ejected from the cafe.

He said to his friends, 'Looks like Teddy and his crew are in town. I wonder what they are here for. Maybe they have been poaching somewhere around here. I will give Olivia a ring and see what's going on.'

Chikara spoke to Olivia.

He asked to be put on to Teddy.

Teddy answered the phone, 'Hullo, mate, what's doing?'

Chikara smiled when he heard Teddy's voice. He said, 'Teddy, it's good to see you again. How about we meet up and have a talk? We can meet at our motel if you like.'

Teddy agreed, and soon they were sitting on chairs and beds in the small motel room.

Chikara explained why they were there in Eden and what they had done so far.

Teddy laughed when he heard about the mangled motorbikes and said, 'Boy, you really know how to hurt a bikie—damage his motorbike.'

Chikara asked, 'What do you think they will do to retaliate?'

'Well,' Teddy answered, 'it's a shoe in that they will reckon that it was us who fucked their bikes up, so they will come after us. I reckon that they will bring in more reinforcements and get more motorbikes. As I see it, they still don't realise that you are here, so you can be our backstop. They will come for us, and suddenly up you pop. You've seen them in action. They are as weak as piss. For Olivia's sake, we want to really slow them down. Really fuck them up, or else they will just be back into the protection racket with her as soon as we leave.'

Chikara agreed with everything that Teddy said.

Dave and Lee made their way to the potato chip factory in their furniture van.

After a bit of furniture manipulation, they got the bags of abalone meat into the factory where Derek, one of his men, and Bob, the factory owner, all got into weighing up the abalone.

The meat had to be trimmed up a bit, and any guts still on the foot had to be removed.

It was difficult to process cleanly at sea. So there was a bit of work to be done before the abalone was drained and boxed up in shatter-proof chip boxes. But it didn't take long.

A couple of hours later, all the work was done and the abalone were in the blast freezer.

They would be brought down to minus 30 degrees in twelve hours.

Another night's work was done.

The fisheries were still staked out with Derek's processing factory in view.

Piggy was sleeping the sleep of the innocent.

Murphy, the security guard, was as alert as ever keeping his eyes on the watchers.

The Tsar and Muddy talked briefly together before they fronted their crews.

Now was the time when a decision had to be made. It was obvious that those poachers had destroyed their motorbikes and, for that, they must die. It was as simple as that—no other way to think.

If the bikies didn't make an example of those four dickheads, then it was all over for them in the protection racket, and they could kiss goodbye to their drug business.

If they were seen to be weak, some other biker group would come in and take over their territory, and then it was all over for them.

The leaders explained to their men just what was going to happen.

As soon as the reinforcements turned up, they would track down the poachers and get into them.

The Tsar was insistent that it be him who was going to take out the leader of the poachers.

He felt that he had to set an example and save a bit of face. He looked at Muddy and the three members who all had gravel rash on their faces and wondered just how much help they would be.

Thank Christ, he had a team coming down from Sydney.

He got onto the phone and rang to see where they were. Above the road noise, he was told that they were two hours away. He hung up, satisfied that all was going to plan.

Teddy and Chikara sat and talked together.

They reminisced about their adventure together with the Japanese submarine and how stupid Fisheries Officer Trotter was.

Slowly the talk turned to their next problem.

He explained that there would be a fight. If they were lucky, it wouldn't be out in the open. If they were able to surprise the bikies, then they had a chance of sorting things out. It was all about timing.

Teddy decided that he and the boys would go into the public bar of the Australasia Hotel and have a couple of beers.

Word would soon spread that they were there, so the motorbike mob would arrive and it would be on.

Once it started, Chikara and his team would come in from behind, and the two groups would surround the bikies. That would make for some interesting moments.

The reinforcements for the Sydney bikies came down the long hill to Eden and passed through the industrial area.

There were ten bikes leading a large van that held the replacement motorbikes for the now de-biked bikies.

They passed the motel where Teddy, Chikara, and the men were waiting.

Teddy said, 'Here's the cavalry. Let's hope that they had a quiet time on the way down. We'll give them an hour to settle in, and then we will make our way over to the pub and have a quiet beer and relax.'

Everyone laughed at that. There wouldn't be any quiet beers or relaxing.

The police sergeant had been watching what was happening in his town. He thought he knew what was going on. He knew that the two bikies had been thrown out of the cafe earlier on this morning and that ten other bikies had come to town with a van big enough to hold a heap of bikes.

The sergeant knew that they would be replacement bikes for the ones that had been destroyed.

He had seen the poachers come in and put their Shark Cat onto the trailer. He knew that the Japanese men were at the motel, and he thought that the poachers and the Japs had got together.

As he worked it out, there were eight of them and maybe twenty bikies. He knew that the poachers had given the bikies a bit of a hiding a couple of times.

He didn't know about the Japs, but they looked as fit as Malley bulls. (The Malley is an area where farmers fatten up their livestock. So to say someone is as fit as a Malley bull is to say that they are in very good condition.)

He radioed for back-up and called all his constables in.

What he wanted was a show of strength. He wanted as many police vehicles as possible to be there when the shit hit the fan, and he just had that old copper's feeling that it was going to happen.

Teddy and the boys walked across the street and went into the hotel.

As usual, the bar maid whom they had gotten to know was on duty.

When she saw the boys, she said out loud, 'So it's true, is it? You boys have been playing up and you've got the local bikies all stirred up. I don't know if I should let you drink in here. As soon as "you know who" finds out you are here, he and his gang will be straight down. I saw a group go through town an hour ago. I reckon that they are here to give them some back-up.'

Teddy gave her a smile and said, 'Geez, love, we are just a group of thirsty fishermen looking for a cold middy of the finest beer in Australia.'

The barmaid shook her head and said, 'OK, I'll let you have a drink. But I don't want any trouble.'

Teddy smiled and said, 'If we see any trouble, we will run away and hide.'

The barmaid got four middies and passed them across the bar.

'It's against my better judgement,' she said.
The boys settled in and slowly sipped at their beers.

Muddy's phone rang His lookout said, 'Them poachers are in the bar at the Australasia Hotel. There are four of them. They don't seem to have any back-up. They are just sitting in the bar drinking.'

Muddy looked at The Tsar and said, 'Those four poachers are in the bar. Let's get down and have a crack at them.'

The Tsar said, 'The main man is mine. All right, everyone, let's get going.'

With that, Muddy and his crew and the Sydney reinforcements drove towards the hotel.

Muddy and The Tsar got off their bikes and, with about ten others, walked into the bar. A hush settled over the patrons. Everyone knew that there was going to be trouble.

Teddy looked around and said, 'Well, well, here's *Dumb and Dumber.* Haven't you blokes got sick of being belted and kicked up the arse? Do the dickheads with you know that we already gave you a smack around this morning?'

The bikies looked at Teddy, Dean, Curly, and Tom; nobody made a move.

Suddenly one of the out-of-town bikies said, 'Let's get this show on the road.'

He made a plunge towards the four men. He had his fists up, and Teddy gave him a kick in the balls. Down he went and lay on the floor, groaning.

The three other divers quickly ran at the assembled bikies and started punching them.

The bikies were a bit taken aback by the swiftness of the attack.

They were used to people standing back and being frightened of them.

Dean hit one with a roundhouse swing that sent him staggering back into a wall of leather-clad bikies.

Due to the limited amount of room in the bar, the bikies couldn't rush the four.

They could only come with a line of four abreast.

That suited the divers fine.

Teddy swung and connected with a biker and moved onto another one.

The room was filled with the sounds of striking flesh and groans from the injured men.

Tom and Curly were fighting side by side. Tom wished he could get more room to manoeuvre in.

Dean and Teddy were still out in front, belting anyone who was in their way.

The Tsar said to a member, 'Get the rest in right now.'

One of the Sydney bikies ran out to call in the rest of the gang but was met by a black-clad figure who, in a swift move, knocked him unconscious in a single blow.

Chikara and his three men went to where the rest of the biker group were waiting to be called into the hotel.

He smiled and said, 'Don't go in. You'll get all the fighting that you want right here.'

With that, the four Japanese-Australian men started belting into the astonished bikies.

They were completely taken off guard.

They were waiting to be called in as a surprise attack but were in fact being surprised themselves.

Chikara and Tomoya went straight towards the nearest two, and, in an instant, they were on the ground, groaning in pain.

Kenta and Tatsu quickly moved onto another pair of unfortunate bikies and drove their fists into them. The men were left gasping on the ground.

The four Japanese men took to the remaining group without missing a beat.

Meanwhile, inside the hotel, Curly was in trouble.

A couple of bikies had singled him out as he was the smallest of the divers. One hit him a jarring blow to the side of the head. Curly hit the deck. He was on his hands and knees when the other assailant started kicking him in the ribs. Curly rolled himself into a ball for protection.

As always, Dean had kept his eye on his lifetime friend.

When he saw the bikies start to kick Curly, something in Dean's brain snapped.

The blood drained out of his face, and it contorted into a mask of rage.

He hit the biker in front of him with such force that he dislocated his jaw. He swung around and in an instant was beside Curly.

In a fit of superhuman strength, he grabbed the two bikies who were kicking Curly by their throats and lifted them off their feet.

He took three steps while holding the bikies out in front of him at arm's length.

Both the bikies grabbed hold of Dean's arms in a futile attempt to release the chocking grip. Dean slammed them up against the sidewall of the bar.

The sound of the two skulls hitting the wall was sickening.

Dean once again smashed their heads into the wall.

Both the men were unconscious. Dean let them drop to the floor.

He stopped for a second and looked at Curly. 'Are you OK, mate?' he asked as he helped his friend to his feet.

Curly nodded and said, 'Thanks, mate, that was in the nick of time.'

Dean threw himself into the swarming mass of bodies again.

Teddy had seen Dean go to Curly's aid.

He was worried for a moment that Dean would kill someone, but as soon as Dean realised that Curly was OK, his face had lost that 'I'm gunna kill you' look, and he was back on an even keel.

With Curly back on his feet, the odds were getting better all the time.

Muddy and The Tsar made their way through the mass of fighting men towards Teddy.

The Tsar grabbed Teddy by the arm as Teddy swung at a biker.

Using Teddy's momentum, he swung him around.

Muddy got the opportunity to hit Teddy a telling blow to the side of his head.

Teddy's face went numb, and he saw stars.

The Tsar took the opportunity and let go a couple of blows into Teddy's body.

They really hurt Teddy. He covered up and fended off blows that had started to rain on him from Muddy.

The lefts and rights from Muddy lacked much power and simply bounced off Teddy, but he was starting to tire.

Tom could see that Teddy was in trouble but couldn't do a great deal about it.

Dean tried to make his way over, but a couple of bikies were starting to concentrate on him, so he had his hands full.

Meanwhile, out in the car park, the reserve bikies had been overwhelmed by the Japanese and lay, bleeding and nursing fractures on the ground among their Harleys.

Chikara said to his three companions, 'Quick, we have to give Teddy and the boys a hand.'

With that, the four men ran into the bar. The scene before their eyes was hard to take in.

There were bikies everywhere. Some were lying on the floor, but the rest were locked in a battle with the divers.

Chikara could see that Teddy's race was nearly run.

He was getting a hammering from the two biker leaders and was in a bad way.

All the divers had their hands full.

Chikara and his men attacked from the rear. They started hitting the bikies from behind with devastating effect.

Teddy sensed that the tide was turning.

Just in time, he thought.

Chikara drove the heel of his hand into a biker's nose, and the biker fell to the floor.

He moved on to Muddy, who was hitting Teddy.

This left Teddy and The Tsar facing each other.

'Things are a bit more even now, you weak prick,' Teddy said.

He hit The Tsar a hard blow to the face.

The Tsar was rocked.

Teddy moved in for the kill.

He hit The Tsar with an uppercut that threw the biker's head back, exposing his throat. Teddy smashed his fist into The Tsar's unprotected throat.

He went down, making gasping sounds.

The fight was out of him for the day.

Teddy turned to Muddy and said, 'Mate, you are in more shit than a Werribee duck.' (Werribee is the site of the Melbourne sewerage treatment plant.)

Teddy unloaded onto Muddy.

Muddy was soon dispatched to the floor and rolled under a table.

Teddy looked around. The fight was over.

There were bikies lying all over the floor—some completely unconscious, some dazed, but all in a bad way.

Dean was leaning up against a wall; there was blood on his face, and his fists were bloody. Curly was moving stiffly, and Tom was standing hunched over with his hands on his knees. There wasn't a lot of fight left in them.

Teddy said to Chikara, 'Mate, thanks for your assistance. You and your mates evened things up a bit.'

Chikara smiled and said, 'You should see the car park. The rest of the bikie gang are out there.'

Teddy looked concerned and said, 'What? Are they waiting to come in?'

Chikara laughed and said, 'Well, they are out there, but I don't reckon that they are waiting to come in. We had a bit of a battle with them. I reckon that they are ready to go home and clean themselves up a bit.'

Teddy said, 'There were more waiting outside?'

Chikara nodded.

He said, 'When we were waiting to come in and give you a hand, we noticed that the group had split in two. So we decided to slow up the second group so they couldn't rush you.'

Teddy nodded. 'Well done, mate,' he said.

Chikara said, 'We had better get down to business. Do what we came here to do.'

Teddy and Chikara walked up to the two biker leaders, and Chikara said to them quietly, 'Listen to me, you two pieces of shit. The reason that we are here is because you fucking halfwits tried to stand over some friends of ours, the two girls who have the little cafe and nursery. It turns out that they are owed a great debt by some very dangerous men in Japan. If you or your gang of fuckwits ever do any harm to them again, then we will come back and kill you. Do you understand?'

Muddy and The Tsar both understood.

They were in a very bad situation. They were at their weakest; they had been beaten. They still didn't know how many of their men were injured, but they were sure that all the bikies had lost interest in fighting.

The Tsar looked at Teddy and asked, 'What about our bikes?'

Teddy said, 'I don't know anything about your motorbikes. We had nothing to do with anything that happened to them.'

The Tsar and Muddy looked at Teddy and said, 'Who fucked with our bikes then?'

Teddy looked at the two bikies and said, 'You have my word that it wasn't me or any of my crew.'

Chikara remained silent.

Muddy looked at The Tsar and said, 'Who the fuck could it have been? Maybe it was another biker group trying to make headway into our area.'

The Tsar remained silent. Everything hurt.

The police sergeant sat ready for action.

He had his men assembled around town.

One word from him, and they were poised to attack.

The sergeant had seen the Japanese men run into the waiting group of bikies and literally belt the living fuck out of them. It all happened really quickly.

He had hesitated to bring his constables into the battle as he wanted to keep casualties down in his ranks. There was just too much paperwork when an officer got injured. So he had waited.

Suddenly it was all over.

He had seen the biker come running out of the pub door, and he had seen the Japanese man down him with some sort of karate punch, more like a flick of his wrist. The biker was still down. He was groaning, so at least he wasn't dead.

All the rest of the bikies from the mob outside were either lying on the ground or holding onto their bikes for support. A couple of the smart ones had bolted and were, at this moment, hiding away out of sight.

The sergeant thought to himself, *Thank Christ, there were no guns involved. It would have been a lot worse if some of these halfwits had produced a sawn-off shotgun and started firing.*

A thought flashed through his mind about once when there had been a shoot-out among rival bikie members and innocent people had been killed. *Thank goodness, that didn't happen here.*

He marshalled his troops and sent the back-up back to Bega. He knew that he and his crew could handle any problems that arose from now on.

The bikies, with as much dignity as they could muster, decided to call it a day and go back to Muddy's place. They had done quite enough for one day.

They rode off on their Harleys to have a drink and tell each other how they had held up their ends. There wasn't quite as much laughing and clowning about. They had some serious drinking to do.

Teddy and Chikara went into the girls' cafe.

Chikara said to Olivia, 'We sat down and talked to all the bikies, and they agreed that they didn't want any money off you. They had a change of heart.'

'Yes,' Teddy said. 'I believe that they are going straight from now on.'

Everyone laughed.

Olivia asked Chikara, 'How can I ever repay you?'

Chikara said, 'How about breakfast in the morning before we leave?'

Olivia smiled and said, 'Our pleasure. What about you and your boys, Teddy?'

Teddy laughed and said, 'We had better get going. The lads are eager to get home to their loved ones. We will leave tonight.'

Teddy and Chikara walked out onto the footpath.

'Well mate,' said Teddy. 'We had better hit the road. When are you going to head off?'

Chikara said, 'We will leave after breakfast tomorrow. We will stay tonight just to make sure that there aren't any heroes about still wanting to bother the girls.'

Teddy nodded and shook Chikara's hand. 'Great to catch up with you, and thanks for the hand. You and your mates are a good mob to have around in a scuffle.'

Chikara laughed and said, 'There are three Australian karate champions in my team.'

Teddy said, 'No wonder you went through that bunch of bikies like a dose of salts.'

Chikara smiled. 'Luckily there were no guns as even we struggle against bullets.'

Teddy and the boys drove out of Eden towards the Victorian-New South Wales border. They had only driven a few kilometres when the police sergeant drove up behind them and turned on his siren and flashing lights.

Teddy pulled to the side of the road.

The sergeant walked up to the driver's window. Teddy slowly lowered the window.

'Good afternoon, officer,' Teddy said, smiling.

The sergeant looked into the car and asked Teddy for his driver's licence. Teddy produced it.

Looking at it, the sergeant handed it back and said, 'You boys certainly stirred up those bikies.'

Teddy answered, 'Officer, we were attacked and had to defend ourselves. By rights, we should have called the police, but we realised how busy you are.'

The sergeant looked at Teddy and asked, 'Did you and your mates smash up those bikies' bikes?'

Teddy looked the sergeant straight in the face and answered, 'I give you my word that we had nothing to do with that.'

The sergeant thought for a while and said, 'I believe you, which leaves only the Japs.'

'Don't ask me,' Teddy said.

'Are you boys heading back to Melbourne?'

Teddy answered, 'Affirmative.'

The sergeant nodded his head and said, 'Have a safe trip.'

He walked back to his car.

Teddy and the boys drove off towards Melbourne.

The fisheries officers still had Derek's factory staked out.

They hadn't seen anything out of the ordinary happen. It was a busy takeaway, and plenty of people came and went—no action at all at night.

They watched as a delivery of frozen chips was unloaded into the rear of the factory. They watched as the young bloke ran a trolley back and forth. It didn't take him long, and all the boxes were unloaded. He took care to make sure that the stock was put at the rear of the freezer. They watched as Derek gave him a hand. It didn't take too long.

From Bairnsdale, Piggy checked in with the fisheries officers who were staking out Derek's factory.

They had nothing to report.

He got a report that the Shark Cat was seen passing through Bairnsdale, so that must mean that the divers had finished their work and would soon be back in Melbourne.

The sixty-million-dollar question was, where was the bloody abalone?

Piggy knew that it was either on its way to Melbourne or still in New South Wales.

He spoke to the NSW Fisheries, and they confirmed that Teddy and the other divers had put the Shark Cat onto the trailer at Eden and that it had been empty.

Piggy concluded that they must have unloaded somewhere, but where?

That was the question—where?

The Tsar and Muddy nursed their wounds. They were filthy on the fact that they had been beaten, even though they had the numbers on their side.

The Tsar looked at Muddy and asked, 'What are we going to do about the two lessos at the cafe?'

Muddy thought for a minute and said, 'What the fuck do you reckon? That Jap said if we go back and annoy them, then he and his crew will come back and kill us.'

'Do you reckon that they would do that?' The Tsar asked.

Muddy started to think that The Tsar wasn't that bright.

He said, 'Mate, they have just beaten the living fuck out of us. Our bikes have been wrecked, and everybody in town will now think that we are as weak as piss. I myself am sure that if we fuck with those two girls, then they will come down and kill us.'

Secretly this is what The Tsar wanted to hear.

He said, 'Well, if you're not prepared to stand up to them, we may as well go back to Sydney.'

Muddy nodded and said, 'Mate, I'm just going to have a few days quietly, getting over my injuries. I'm a slow learner, but I reckon that those two lessos are to be kept away from. Every time that we have had a go at them, we have ended getting the shitty end of the stick. I'm fucked if I know what's going on.'

The Tsar said, 'Well, if you're not going to do anything, then we'll fuck off back home.'

Muddy nodded. 'I reckon that's a good move.'

The Tsar marshalled his troops, and, with some doubling up on their Harleys, they quickly left town. They were beaten, and they knew it.

Muddy reflected on what had happened.

He looked at his face in the mirror and said, 'Fuck me dead, I'm lucky to be alive.'

The next morning, Chikara and his team went into the cafe and had another artery-clogging breakfast.

Olivia spoke to them as they were eating, 'We can't thank you enough for the help that you have given us.'

Chikara smiled and said, 'We were lucky that Teddy and his crew were here, or it might have been a different story. I'm sure that the bikies won't trouble you again. But if they do, give me a ring.'

They finished their breakfasts, and Chikara gave Olivia a hug and a kiss on the cheek.

He simply said, 'Take care of each other. We are always here if you need us.'

With that, the four Japanese-Australians walked out, got into the Hummer, and drove off towards Melbourne.

Henry and the Silver Eagle

Teddy's mate Henry was in his element.

He was now at the front of house at his family's restaurant.

The restaurant was very successful due to the long hours and hard work that Henry's family put in. They worked from early morning to late at night.

It had taken years, and the restaurant was booming.

Henry's abalone business was also booming, thanks to a steady supply of abalone from Teddy and his crew.

He had a list of buyers, and as soon as Teddy rang, he would contact them to say that another shipment was about to come in.

Henry was very strict about his clientele. He sold only to those whom he trusted and who paid upon delivery.

It was true that he was sometimes accused of profiteering, but that's what being the middleman is about. And his prices were less than half the retail price from the wholesalers.

As Henry pointed out, it was his contact and he ran the greatest risk because he was the one who had, at times, all the abalone at his premises.

If he was raided, he would lose everything. All the others had to do was produce a legal receipt, and they were in the clear.

So Henry had advised all his abalone customers to have a receipt. No matter how old it was, it would be enough for the fisheries as you could keep frozen abalone for a long time.

If the fisheries raided your restaurant and found abalone, all you had to do was produce a receipt, and all was well.

It was that simple.

Every nationality has its bad people. The Chinese have the triads. The Italians have the Mafia. The Japanese have the Yakuza, and on it goes.

Henry was aware of the evil ones in the Vietnamese community.

They hadn't bothered his family's restaurant so far.

As the restaurant became more popular and busier, the evil ones started to take notice.

One of them particularly was starting to take notice of Henry and his family.

Van Leong was known to many as the Silver Eagle. He was a short, swarthy, and extremely violent Vietnamese man. He watched as Henry's family started to show signs of wealth.

He learnt from jealous people that Henry's restaurant was a thriving business and that he was starting to become a big operator in the distribution of illegal abalone.

The Silver Eagle thought that now was a good time to get in on the ground floor and become a partner. He had plenty to offer; he would become a protector for Henry and his family.

They would never feel fear from the bad people if it was known that the Silver Eagle was by their side.

He decided it was time he made himself known to Henry and his family.

Van Leong or the Silver Eagle had come to Australia as a boat person with his parents.

That's where the similarity between his family and Henry's ended.

Van's father was a drunkard and his mother, although a good woman, realised that the easy way out was for her to get away from the drunken abuse.

She would leave Van's father and find another man who would look after her. She wanted a man who would not want to spend his life drunk and gambling away any possibility of a new start in life.

She left without a glance back.

Van stayed with his father in the housing commission unit that they had been given by the government. He became accustomed to physical and mental abuse from his father.

He soon became involved with like-minded Vietnamese youths and formed a gang.

The gang started to do a bit of small-time robbery—mainly drunks and women on their own and a bit of stand-over.

They stuck to small businesses that were run by Vietnamese.

Slowly his reputation grew.

There were about twenty in the gang, and they got involved in the distribution of drugs.

Van came up with a plan.

He would get a member of the gang to start buying off a dealer and slowly ask for bigger quantities. Then they would say that they had a big buyer who wanted a large amount.

When the dealer came with the larger amount, then Van and his gang would suddenly appear and rob him. They would take all the drugs and anything else of value that the dealer had on him, and they would pretend to assault their member as well to make it look like a genuine robbery.

One time when they decided to rob a dealer, he had bought some back-up with him in the form of three heavies. When the gang started to assault the dealer, the three heavies appeared. Van, who had been watching, leapt into the fray, wielding his machete.

Soon the heavies were lying on the footpath, bleeding heavily.

Van looked at the dealer and said, 'Give me all your money and drugs, or else I will kill you.'

The dealer quickly submitted, and Van and his gang escaped into the night.

Making their way back to Van's father's unit, they weighed up all the drugs. These were then sold on the streets. The money flowed in.

The gang realised Van's potential and appointed him their leader.

Van realised that he needed a special name to frighten people.

He decided to call himself the Silver Eagle. He felt people would think of him as a powerful bird of prey.

Having seen a show on TV, in which a bad-arsed American-Indian had called himself the Blue Duck. Van was sure that the name Silver Eagle would frighten people more than a duck's name.

It wasn't long before all the Vietnamese were talking about the Silver Eagle with fear and awe.

He was approached by some of the Aussie dealers, and they showed the proper respect towards him.

Mind you, at times, it was hard to tell if they respected him or not, as their attitude was so casual. They didn't seem frightened of him.

He sensed that they used him to open up new markets for themselves.

Van was happy because they didn't sell to his customers in his areas.

They let the Vietnamese sell to the Vietnamese.

Everybody had their own clients, and everything went smoothly.

But as we all know, life is never easy and nothing stays the same.

Van wanted to get even bigger to branch out into big-time stand-over and into the distribution of illegal abalone.

He set his sights on Henry, knowing that like himself, Henry and his family had come out as boat people.

Knowing that at times their restaurant was very busy, he also discovered that Henry was a large supplier of illegal abalone.

Van thought that he and some of his gang should go and have a talk to Henry and his family. Then Van could explain to them how beneficial it would be for Henry to accept Van as a partner.

He had heard from other restaurant owners that Henry would only supply some restaurants with the cheap abalone. If Van was a partner, then he could reorganise the distribution of all the abalone.

In the long term, Van would talk to the abalone poachers and get them to supply him directly. He would cut out Henry and have the whole operation to himself.

Van arranged to go and talk to Henry at his restaurant with four of his gang members.

The five Vietnamese walked into Henry's restaurant. There was a sense of menace about them.

Henry was standing behind the 'Please Wait to Be Seated' sign.

Van walked up and asked, 'Do you know who I am?'

Henry looked at the five men, smiled, and said, 'No, but I know you have excellent taste. That is why you have chosen this restaurant to dine in.'

Van was a bit taken aback by Henry's attitude.

He said, 'We want a table for five, and I want to talk to you about a matter of great importance.'

Van was being very gracious.

Henry smiled and said, 'Certainly, please walk this way.'

With that, Henry ushered them towards a table at the rear of the dining room.

They moved past tables of people who were eating.

Many of the Vietnamese saw Van and looked away quickly. They recognised the Silver Eagle and felt a bit afraid.

The Aussies at the other tables didn't seem to notice the five men at all.

Henry sat them down and gave them menus. He asked if they wanted tea as a lot of Vietnamese don't drink alcohol, and they all accepted.

Henry went off to organise a waitress to serve them.

Speaking to Lucy Wong, Henry said, 'That table of five looks like trouble to me. The one with his back to the wall asked me if I knew who he was. I told him I didn't, but I think that he may be the man who calls himself the Silver Eagle. Be very careful what you say to them and get them whatever they want.'

Lucy took their tea to them and smiled. She poured out their teas.

Van looked at Lucy and asked, 'Have I met you before? You look familiar.'

'I'm not sure, sir,' Lucy said with a smile.

Van asked, 'Do you go to the casino?'

She replied, 'I have been many times. Perhaps you have seen me there.'

Nodding slowly, Van said, 'Maybe you are correct. It could have been there.'

Lucy stood patiently at the table and waited for their orders.

Van said, 'We will have five serves of the abalone.'

Looking at Van, Lucy asked, 'Would you like an entrée first? I'm sure you know that the abalone takes a little while to prepare.'

'Yes, we will have five serves of chilli prawns as an entrée while we are waiting,' Van replied.

Lucy smiled and said, 'Yes, sir, I will get your entrées.'

With that, Lucy went and placed the orders on the 'waiting orders' list.

When Henry saw the order for five abalone dishes, he said to his father, 'Father, there is a table of five men, and I think that they are criminals. I think that they are here to offer us protection. They have ordered abalone meals, and I don't think that they are going to pay for them.'

Henry's father looked at his son and could see that there was no fear in his son's eyes.

He prayed to an ancient god for protection for his family, and he said to Henry, 'My son, as far as we know, they are customers, and we will treat them like good customers. We must let things work out for themselves, and then we will do what we must.'

Looking at his father, Henry saw a man of great wisdom and courage.

Henry realised that all they had was due to his father's strength and strong work ethic. He knew his father was right.

Walking from table to table, Henry talked to the diners. He knew most of them by name, and the ones that he didn't know, he introduced himself to and asked them how they were enjoying their meals.

He could see that the Vietnamese were worried by the presence of the table of five but reassured them all that everything would be all right.

Van and his table drank their tea, noisily ate their entrees, and then started on the abalone main courses.

The restaurant started to empty as people went to see a show or go home.

Henry knew that usually there would be a quiet period until the movies ended and then there would be a mini rush as people got a late-night feast, and then it would all be over. Henry and the staff would sit down and have a meal together.

Then they would all head home or out for a bit of entertainment to finish off the night.

Henry's mum had already left and gone back to look after his two younger sisters.

As the restaurant cleared of customers, Henry knew that he had no other option than to go and sit with the table of five and see what they wanted.

He wondered what they had in mind.

The men had finished their meals and were sipping tea.

'I hope that you all enjoyed your meals,' Henry said brightly.

Van replied, 'Have you worked out who I am yet?'

Henry smiled and said, 'I'm sorry, but I can't place you. Are you a movie star or perhaps a politician or someone famous?'

Van smiled and said, 'I am the Silver Eagle, and these are a small number of my associates. We have come to make you a deal of a lifetime, one I'm sure that you won't refuse.'

'Please tell me more,' Henry asked.

'Some of my friends are unhappy about the fact that you are not sharing your good fortune with them. They think that they should also be offered the illegal abalone that you are receiving. They are talking about cutting you down to size. What we are offering is a partnership. We will distribute the abalone and also offer you protection against the evil ones. None will touch you when they find out that you are protected by the Silver Eagle.'

Henry looked at the Silver Eagle and thought, *What a stupid name!*

He said, 'Surely the people whom I sell to is my business. And as for protection, I'm not sure that we need any.'

Van stared dully at Henry and said, 'We are making it our business from now on. We will be 50 per cent partners in your abalone business, and, for additional cost, we will protect the restaurant.'

Henry looked at the Silver Eagle and felt a trickle of fear run up his spine.

He knew that these were unpredictable and dangerous men and likely to do anything. He had to stall for time. He thought that he must contact Teddy. He would know what to do.

Henry said, 'My friends, I need time to think. I already have a partner in the abalone business. I will need to talk to him. He is an Australian and a very important man. It is he whom you should be talking to, not me. As for our restaurant, it only makes money because we all work for a small amount of money. If we had to pay you money, then we would have to close.'

Van knew that Henry was downplaying the restaurant. He had expected that. All these hard-working fools said that they weren't making money, but when you squeezed, money dripped out of them.

What he hadn't expected was that Henry had a partner and he was an Aussie.

Having met many Australians, Van thought they all seemed to be a bit laid back and lazy. They all drank a lot of beer and seemed happy.

Everyone feared death, but the Aussies all seemed to say, 'Fuck the consequences. If you fuck with me, then I'll fuck with you.'

They seemed to be sure of themselves. They looked you square in the eye as if to say, 'Here I am. If you don't like me, then bad fucking luck.'

Van had never quite worked out the Aussie way of life.

He gathered himself together and said, 'Well, we had better meet your partner. When can I talk to him?'

Henry stared at Van and said, 'I will let him know that you want to meet with him. How can I let you know when he is available?'

Van was on the back foot.

Suddenly Henry had put him on the side of the one who was waiting. He felt he was losing control.

He angrily said, 'You tell your partner I will tell him when I want to speak to him.'

Henry realised that he was in the box seat and said to Van, 'I have told you he is a busy and an important man. He doesn't have time to wait for you to call him. He will tell me when he can see you, and you will only have that time to talk to him. If you miss that opportunity, then you miss out altogether.'

Van realised that he had been outsmarted. He had let himself be the one that was waiting to be summonsed.

Henry pushed his advantage. He suggested, 'Give me a number that I can call you on, and I will set up an appointment for you,'

Van gave Henry the number of a phone that was used in their drug business.

Henry asked, 'Can I get you something else to eat or drink?'

'No, we will go now and not cause any trouble. We will fix up for the meal when we meet your partner,' Van retorted.

Henry looked into Van's eyes and asked, 'Are you sure that you don't want to pay for the meal now?'

Van replied, 'You are lucky that you found me and my friends in good humour. Be thankful we didn't wreck your little restaurant. Don't push your luck.'

'As you wish,' Henry answered.

With that, Van and his men walked out.

Van wasn't sure if he had come out in front or not.

They had eaten a meal for nothing, but Henry hadn't been afraid of them. That could only mean that Henry was convinced that his partner could handle Van.

He would have to be careful of Henry's partner.

As soon as Van and his men had left the restaurant, Henry spoke to his father.

He told him how the meeting had gone and how Van was known as the Silver Eagle. He explained that Van wanted to be a partner in the abalone business and how he wanted to offer them protection for the restaurant.

Henry's father was silent for a minute. 'I have heard talk about the Silver Eagle. Some say he is a dangerous man. He has a group of men with him who are to be feared and will do harm to people who don't pay them.'

Henry waited in silence.

'How do you think that Teddy will react to having to meet this dangerous man?' Henry's father asked.

'I don't think that Teddy will be worried about the Silver Eagle. He isn't a man to be easily frightened. I don't think that Teddy will do any business with this man. I'm sure that he won't cut us out,' Henry replied.

Henry's father nodded.

Henry said, 'Do you notice that when I give Teddy the money for the abalone, he doesn't count it? He trusts us.'

Henry's father smiled and said, 'Yet this Van, this Silver Eagle, and the first time he comes to our restaurant, he doesn't pay. Teddy has always paid. He has never asked for a free meal, ever.'

Henry said, 'I'll give Teddy a ring and talk to him. He will know what to do.'

Teddy's phone rang. He was sitting at home, watching TV with Rita, sipping on a glass of Scotch and soda.

'Hello, Henry mate,' Teddy said with a smile. 'What can I do for you?'

Henry immediately felt reassured when he heard Teddy's voice.

'Teddy, I have a problem, and I need your help.'

'Mate, you sound all worked up. What's the matter, mate?' Teddy asked.

Henry started to tell Teddy about Van and his threats.

Teddy said, 'Whoa, whoa, Henry, slow yourself down, mate. Then tell me what's the problem, and we will see what I can do to fix it.'

Henry took a deep breath and explained slowly how Van and some of his gang had come into the restaurant and demanded protection money and how he now wanted to get into the illegal abalone business.

Teddy listened and said, 'Henry mate, when I do a deal with someone, it stays a deal with that someone. I don't like some dickhead coming in and trying to make changes. It's up to you. If you want this dickhead to be part of your operation, then that's up to you. But we haven't had a problem in all the time that we have been operating, and I reckon that there is no room for a freeloader. If you want me to tell this bloke to fuck off, I will. It's that simple.'

Henry immediately felt a surge of relief wash over him.

He said, 'Thanks, mate. When can you meet with him?'

Teddy smiled to himself.

He said, 'What about before you open, not tomorrow, the day after tomorrow in the morning. I'll get the boys together, and we will meet with them bright and early. What do you say about 8 a.m.? Let's see if Van's gang are bright-eyed and bushy-tailed at that hour.'

Henry didn't have a clue about what bright-eyed and bushy-tailed meant. He was just happy that Teddy wasn't worried about the meeting.

Henry answered, 'Thanks, mate, and I'll see you then.'

After he hung up, he told his father when Teddy was coming.

Then he rang the number that Van had given him.

Van answered, and Henry told him when Teddy was available. Van wasn't at all happy.

The meeting was at 8 a.m. in two days' time, and he wasn't a morning person.

He had a bad feeling about early morning meetings. He tried to change it, but Henry, who was very confident, just said, 'Take it or leave it. If you want to talk to my partner, then be here at 8 a.m.'

As an afterthought, he added, 'Don't keep my partner waiting. He is not a man to be kept waiting.'

Henry hung up.

He suddenly had the upper hand. It felt good.

Teddy gave the boys a ring.

He arranged to meet them at Curly's shed the next morning at about lunchtime.

They all agreed.

Rita asked Teddy what was going on.

Teddy said, 'Henry has a bit of a problem. Some Shitman is trying to stand over him. He's asked us to go down for a bit of back-up. No problems, it's an early start. We should be through by 9 a.m.'

Rita said, 'Be careful, there are a lot of bad people out there.'

Teddy smiled and said, 'Well, maybe they are the ones who have to be careful.'

With that, he laughed, 'I'm hitting the sack. Are you coming?'

Rita smiled and said, 'I may as well. There's nothing on TV.'

Van sat with his gang. They had been busy, trying to find out who Henry's partner might be. They hadn't come up with anything as yet. No one had any idea.

He thought to himself that the partner was probably some 'suit and tie' investor—someone who had always wanted to be a gangster and someone who talked tough but, when it came to the crunch, would go to water.

Van convinced himself that Henry's partner would be weak when confronted by a real gangster. He laughed when he thought of standing over this weak businessman.

How he would squeeze every last dollar out of him.

Van was confident he would come out in front.

Teddy met all the boys in Curly's shed at lunchtime the next day and explained what was going on. He told the boys that he had been busy finding out all he could about this Van Leong or, as he called himself, the Silver Eagle.

He had found out, through various contacts, that he was a self-proclaimed gun for hire.

Van insisted that he would kill anyone for $5,000.

He boasted to anyone who would listen that he was a killer.

Teddy discovered that in fact, he was a paper tiger as far as anyone in the underworld could find out.

He stuck mainly to the Vietnamese community and mostly around the western suburbs of Melbourne.

As far as Teddy could work out, this was his first foray into the Richmond area.

Teddy explained all his findings to the boys, and they made a plan.

They would get there early the next morning and go in through the rear entrance of Henry's restaurant.

He and Henry would meet Van and his gang at 8 a.m.

If a problem arose, then Dean, Curly, and Tom would rush out from the kitchen and get stuck into them.

Teddy explained to the boys that it was more than likely there was going to be a problem as he was going to tell Van and his gang to keep the fuck away from his partner and dear friend Henry. And that if Teddy was to see Van or any of his gang anywhere around Henry's restaurant, then they would never be seen again.

Dean laughed and said, 'Well, I bet he's not going to like that a real lot.'

Tom added, 'Fuck him, I'll stick my knife into him that should let a bit of hot air out of him.'

Everybody laughed.

Teddy said, 'Like I've said before, try not to kill anyone. Just knock them about a bit.'

All the boys were happy.

They had a couple of more beers and headed off. They had agreed to meet at Dean's place at 6.30 a.m. the next day.

That night in Henry's restaurant, Lucy said to Henry, 'I have asked around, and I've found out that the Silver Eagle is a very dangerous man. He and his gang have done many bad things. They are to be feared.'

Henry smiled and said, 'We are having a meeting. Van and his gang are coming to have a talk with me and my friend Teddy. I'm not worried at all. Teddy will bring some friends of his. We will not be in any danger. My friend Teddy is a very capable man, and his friends are equally able to protect themselves.'

Lucy was very worried as she felt a deep affection for Henry.

He had shown her compassion when she was in debt to the two loan sharks who had later been shot to death in the casino. Lucy had paid Henry back the next day and hadn't been back to the casino since.

She knew that she could never go back as she had cheated the casino by slipping two $50 chips onto the winning number while the croupier was distracted when the two loan sharks had been shot.

Bright and early the next day, all the boys assembled at Dean's place.

They all got into Teddy's car and drove in silence to Henry's restaurant in Richmond.

Apart from Teddy, they were all armed.

Tom had his stiletto, Dean had his baseball bat, and Curly had his leather cosh.

Teddy didn't carry a weapon. He relied on his strength and quickness for safety.

They pulled up at the rear door of Henry's restaurant.

Henry's father opened the door.

'Hullo, Tiddy,' he chanted.

Teddy smiled at the mangled attempt of his name.

'Where is my girlfriend?' Teddy asked. He always referred to Henry's mother as his girlfriend.

Henry's father answered, 'She is home as we think that there might be trouble here this morning.'

Teddy laughed and said, 'Don't worry, old mate. If there is trouble, then we will sort it out.'

They walked into the restaurant.

'Let's have a look at the set-up,' Teddy said to Henry. He was familiar with how the tables were set up as he and the boys had eaten there many times. He told Henry to set up a table for two against the rear wall, between the *in* and the *out* doors to the kitchen.

Teddy would sit with his back to the wall.

He told Henry to make a clear way down the centre of the room so he could watch Van and his gang as they walked towards him.

Teddy told Dean, Curly, and Tom to stay out of sight, so if Van had someone watching the place, that person wouldn't know that they were there.

Telling Henry to lock the front door, Teddy looked at his watch and saw that it was almost 8 a.m.

They waited.

Van and four of his gang drove up to the restaurant.

They walked up to the door and found it was locked.

Van gave the door a good rattling.

He looked in and saw Henry sitting at a table talking to someone.

Henry got up and unlocked the front door.

Out the back in the kitchen, Henry's father had an evil-looking stainless steel cleaver.

As the boys watched, he ran it down his almost hairless arm.

Tom nodded; he could see that it was razor-sharp. Curly softly hit his leather cosh into the palm of his hand. Dean tapped his baseball bat into his hand.

Silence filled the room. The boys were ready.

Tom slowly tapped the point of his stiletto on the stainless-steel-topped preparation table, making a tic, tic, noise.

Teddy heard the tic, tic noise and knew that it was Tom's stiletto. He had heard the noise before.

He knew that his back-up team was ready.

Henry opened the door and stood aside as Van and his gang made their way down the centre of the restaurant to where Teddy was sitting.

Van looked at the big man who was sitting, looking at him.

He noticed that he had a thick gold chain around his neck. Van thought that he might get one the same.

'Are you Henry's partner?' Van asked.

Teddy had watched the group walk towards him, and he could tell that Van had a weapon stuffed down the front of his pants. *Probably a .38 revolver,* he thought.

He could see that the gang was armed with weapons, machetes, and knives.

No problem so far, Teddy thought.

He saw Henry lock the front door.

That would stop them running out and would also stop any more of their gang members coming in as back-up.

Teddy looked at Van and didn't say a word.

Van looked at Teddy.

This wasn't what he was expecting.

He had expected some fat-necked, flabby-bellied older man in a suit, who would be scared of him and his gang.

What he was confronted by was a fit man in his late fifties; it was hard to tell exactly that the man didn't seem to be worried about him at all.

'Do you know who I am?' Van asked.

Teddy looked at Van and said, 'No, mate, I haven't got a fucking clue who the fuck you are or what the fuck you want. Perhaps you could elaborate.'

Van was a bit taken aback by the attitude of this fool.

'I am the Silver Eagle. I'm a killer and a gun for hire. My gang and I are to be feared, and we are afraid of no one.'

Teddy looked at Van and said, 'The Silver Eagle, that doesn't sound too threatening to me. I reckon that you are more like a yellow chicken.'

Van gathered himself up to his full height of five feet two inches and said, 'Many people are afraid of me and my gang. No one stands up to us. We are to be feared.'

Teddy looked at Van and said, 'You and your gang look like pieces of shit to me. Let me make it perfectly clear, right from the start. I don't want to do any business with you, and Henry doesn't want to do any business with you. Henry doesn't want you around here any more. Now what I want you to do is get the fuck away and don't ever come back. If I see you or any of your baggy-arsed Shitmen again, I'll put you all into hospital. Do you understand? There is nothing here for you and your gang.'

This wasn't how Van had planned it to go.

Teddy was doing all the talking and clearly wasn't frightened of him.

Van sat down at the table and smiled.

He pulled out an enormous revolver from the front of his trousers and laid it flat on the table, pointing at Teddy.

'You have not met my other two friends, Mr Smith and Mr Western,' Van said smugly.

Teddy looked at the handgun. It was a Smith and Wesson .357 magnum.

It was a gun made famous by Clint Eastwood in his *Dirty Harry* movies and a must-have for any wannabe gangster.

It looked huge in Van's childlike hands.

Teddy said, 'Actually it's Mr Smith and Mr Wesson, not Western, and little boys like you shouldn't be playing with big guns like that. You might get hurt.'

Van felt that he was in charge again.

He said, 'I'll do more than hurt you. I will kill you.'

Teddy was within arm's reach of Van across the table.

He quickly reached with his left hand, grabbed the magnum by the barrel, and drove his right fist into Van's face with a sickening thud.

Van was completely taken by surprise.

His vision blurred as his eyes watered, and his nose was flattened against his face.

Teddy forced the gun up towards the ceiling and jammed his thumb behind the trigger so Van couldn't shoot it.

He hit Van again with a hard straight right to his already bruised and broken face.

As soon as Teddy hit Van, the two kitchen doors burst open, and the entire assembled group rushed into the restaurant.

Dean hit a hapless victim to the ground with his baseball bat, and Curly hit his target with his cosh.

Both the Vietnamese were out of it.

Tom and Henry's father rushed out, looking for blood.

Tom hit a Vietnamese with a right cross, and Henry's father belted another one with the side of his cleaver.

Meanwhile, Teddy had ripped the magnum out of Van's hand.

He grabbed Van by the hair and reefed his head back. Van was semi-conscious, and his mouth hung open.

Teddy shoved the barrel of the huge magnum into Van's mouth, knocking out two of Van's front teeth.

'All right, you bastards,' Teddy roared out, 'if you don't want your mate's brains blown all over the front windows, rest easy.'

Van's gang could see that they were beaten, and those who could gave up.

Teddy looked at Van and said, 'This is the answer to your questions. We don't want your protection. We don't want anything to do with you or your gang. Fuck off. If I ever see you or your gang again, I'll shove this gun up your arse and pull the trigger. Do you understand? You're a fucking halfwit.'

Van tried to nod but found it difficult with the .357 magnum jammed in his mouth.

Teddy said, 'Henry, unlock the door.'

Henry ran to the front door, unlocked, and opened it.

Teddy walked Van backwards towards the door.

When he got there, he removed the magnum and spun Van around.

He gave him a shove out the door and kicked him up the arse, propelling him across the footpath.

Van sprawled full length in the gutter.

'Fuck off, and don't bother us ever again,' Teddy ordered.

All Van's gang who were able quickly helped Van to his feet. Blood was spraying out of his mouth whenever he breathed out.

Van and his gang quickly disappeared.

Teddy turned to Henry and his father and asked, 'Do you think that they will ever bother you again?'

Henry's father spoke, 'I'm not sure. You made a fool out of Silver Eagle. Maybe he will be back to try and save face. I really don't know. I do know that at all times we must be prepared for them to attack.'

Teddy said, 'Well, Henry mate, we didn't have a choice. This way, we have shown them that we are a force to be reckoned with. The Silver Eagle will know that if he fucks with you, he fucks with us. We will just have to see what happens. Time will tell.'

With that, Teddy and the boys made their way home, satisfied that they had done a good morning's work.

Van and his gang retreated back to Van's father's housing commission flat.

They were greeted by Van's father.

'Look at you', he cried, 'it's still morning and you are already beaten. You young fools. You think you are smart but you are not. You think that the life you lead is easy, but it is not. You go into battle without taking time to sum up your enemy. This is why you are so easily beaten. You leave, sure that you will win. Then you come home like small children, with your teeth knocked out and your tails between your legs. Let's pray that our ancestors can't see you.'

Van was angry at his father, but he couldn't argue as he had done just what his father had said. He had gone into battle without summing up his enemy.

That was a foolish thing to do.

The Aussie criminals were different from other kinds of criminals. They seemed to be half-asleep, but like the dragon, they could suddenly breathe fire.

Van concluded that he must be more careful in the future. He must look for the weakest link in the chain.

He put his father's drunken ramblings behind him and swallowed a handful of painkillers. His mouth hurt.

Henry asked his father what he thought about the morning's events.

His father answered, 'We have made a powerful enemy in the Silver Eagle. We have shown him that we are not alone. We have strong friends, and they are willing to stand beside us in our times of need. I feel the Silver Eagle will come at us again but from a different angle, from where I don't know.'

Henry agreed with his father. They had to work out which direction the attack would come from.

All they could do was wait and see what happened next.

Word spread quickly through the Vietnamese community, and soon the Silver Eagle's failed attempt to extort money from Henry and his family was on everyone's lips.

The stories grew from teller to teller. Soon it was declared that anyone who was being stood over by the Silver Eagle and his gang had only to seek Henry's help and all would be well.

Van was beside himself.

It looked as if all his hard work had been for nothing.

He felt that he had to spread fear into everyone's hearts again. He must show that he hadn't lost face. He must do something to show people that he was in control once again.

Then he came up with an idea.

Henry's family would be an easy target.

After asking around, he found out that Henry had two younger sisters who attended a private school in the rich side of town.

That was a sure sign that the family had money.

He watched as the girls were dropped off and picked up from their private school.

Van decided that the right time to attack would be when there were only women and children about.

It had to be done fast, or else he would lose all credibility.

He must make no mistake. He must do it himself.

Then once again, people would fear him.

He waited and watched early in the morning when the children were dropped off at school and then later in the afternoon when the mothers came to pick them up and to take them home.

He watched as the two girls ran, laughing to their mother, shouting over each other, telling her what they had learnt and done all day at school.

Van decided that the best time to attack was in the afternoon when the girls were being picked up.

As they walked towards their mother's car, he would strike fast like the viper.

He would splash liquid into their faces and tell them that it was acid.

That would be a warning that no one could ignore.

Van would say to the mother, 'Tell your husband and son to pay what I demand.'

They would see that Van wasn't a man to be messed with.

He smiled an evil smile and thought, *I will show all who the dangerous one is.*

The next afternoon, Henry's mother drove carefully across Melbourne towards her daughter's private school.

She thought, not for the first time, how sad it was that Henry hadn't gone further with his education. She had tried talking Henry into furthering his education, but Henry was headstrong and insisted that his time was better spent assisting them in their restaurant.

He was a great success there and was very popular with the clientele.

Her husband was a fine chef. They worked hard, and the restaurant was a great success. Life was good, and they wanted for nothing.

She saw her two daughters talking and laughing with friends.

When they saw her, they started to walk towards her car.

Smiling, she wondered how long it would be before they were too big to show such affection towards her.

The girls started to run towards her, and she could see that they were full of excitement and hope. They wanted to tell her about their day.

Suddenly a short Vietnamese man was between them. The girls stopped running, and confused looks crossed their faces.

The mother leapt out of her car and dropped her handbag.

Time stood still. She ran towards her daughters. She was sure that something was wrong, very wrong.

'No, no,' she yelled at the top of her voice. 'Please no!'

Van opened the jar and splashed the two girls in their faces.

He yelled in Vietnamese, 'It is acid, acid. You girls will never look the same again.'

Both the girls started screaming and started to try and wipe their faces.

Their mother arrived and saw liquid running down her girls' faces.

'Mummy, Mummy, we have acid on our faces. Help us,' the girls were screaming.

The mother did the only thing that she could think of.

In a desperate act, she started to lick their faces. She tasted the sweetness of soft drink.

She shouted to her girls, 'It's nothing. It is lemonade. The man was playing a trick on you. Look, I'm licking it off your faces, and I'm not hurt. Look at Mummy.'

And she kept licking the girls.

Van ran off to a waiting car.

The fracas had been seen by other mothers, and they came running.

Some had bottles of water, and some had wet wipes and other cleaning gear.

Soon the two girls were calm again. The other mothers formed a protective wall around the mother and her two daughters.

Teachers came out, and the police were alerted.

When they arrived, the girls' mother was a little afraid of them, but the other mothers weren't.

One blonde woman with breasts the size of watermelons took charge.

She protectively put her arms around the mother and two daughters and started to berate the officers about the lack of safety mothers were afforded as they picked up their children and how no one ever bothered about the speeding cars at the children's crossing.

When the officers finally got to the mother and her two daughters, they had all calmed down a bit.

One of the mothers returned the handbag to her.

The girls' mother told the police that it must have been a case of mistaken identity, and they seemed relieved and headed off to fight crime in another part of the city.

The blonde woman with the massive breasts took charge and said, 'There is nothing to worry about. You are safe and will always be safe. All the mothers will protect you and your daughters.'

Things started to return to the calmness that was normal for pickup time at the school's front gates.

With that, the mother and her two daughters headed back to the restaurant.

When she arrived, she sent the girls out into the restaurant to fold napkins in the dining area. She called her husband and Henry into the office.

It was only then that she allowed herself to break down and cry.

Henry and his father looked at each other, puzzled. They both knew that she was tough and it would take a lot to upset her.

She told them everything—how the girls had been walking to her when a short Vietnamese man had got in between them and had thrown what he said was acid into her little girls' faces. She said that she noticed that he had two front teeth missing.

She explained how terrified she had been and how she had licked their faces and tasted the sweetness of some sort of lemonade. Then she went on to describe how frantic her daughters had been, how all the other mothers had come to their aid, how a blonde woman with the big breasts had got between her and the police, and how that woman wasn't afraid of them. She had even got angry with the police and defused the situation.

Henry's father looked at Henry.

They both knew who the Vietnamese man with the two missing front teeth was.

It was Van, the Silver Eagle. This was a warning.

He would strike them through their family.

Everyone feared for their family; it was always the weakest link.

This was a problem that would have to be sorted out. They both realised that.

Both men knew that Van had signed his own death warrant when he threatened their family.

They both knew that they had to move and move fast.

When the last group of diners had left the restaurant, Henry got busy on the phone and rang around some trusted friends.

It didn't take long to find out where this Silver Eagle lived.

Henry discovered that he lived with his father in a multi-storey block of housing commission units in Footscray in the western suburbs of Melbourne.

They realised that he wouldn't be home. It was much too early in the evening for Van to have finished whatever he was doing.

They drove over and parked in the unit car park.

The father and son made their way to the elevators. The elevators stank of stale urine.

Henry looked at his father and shook his head.

The stench of urine was a sign that people had given up and pissed where they stood.

Getting out on the fifth floor, they made their way to Van's father's unit.

Henry knocked on the door.

There was no noise from inside the unit. Henry knocked again, louder this time.

From inside the unit, an angry voice said in Vietnamese, 'What do you want?'

Henry said in a desperate voice, 'Please, sir, I need to see Van urgently. I have money, and I want to buy off him.'

Van's father cursed and roused himself off the couch where he had passed out.

'What am I now, a doorman for my useless son?' he asked out loud.

He opened the door and saw a well-dressed young man who said in a pleading voice, 'Please, sir, I am in need. Van told me that if I was ever in need, all I had to do was knock on his door. Sir, I have plenty of money, plenty of money.'

With that, Henry pulled out a thick roll of money and held it against the fly-wire door.

Van's father looked at the roll of notes and thought that there might be a possibility of him getting his hands on some of it.

He released the catch and started to open the door.

Henry pulled open the door and rushed inside, knocking Van's father onto the floor.

His father followed closely.

'Where is your dog of a son?' Henry's father asked.

Van's father was winded.

'I don't know,' he gasped.

'Today your stupid son threatened my children. He pretended to throw acid in their faces. For that, he must die,' Henry's father spoke softly but with great menace.

Van's father said, 'I know nothing of such evil. I have nothing to do with anything that my son does. He is an outlaw. He is not like us. I have tried to bring him up the right way, but his mother left us, and I am a sick man. I did the best I could. It's not my fault that he turned out like he did.'

Henry's father helped him to his feet and nodded to Henry.

Henry got behind Van's father and slid the loop of a leather belt over his head. He pulled it tight around Van's father's neck.

Van's father tried to get his fingers under the belt, but the pressure was too great.

His eyes bulged, and his tongue protruded from his mouth. His face turned a shade of deep red.

Henry turned around, and, with the belt over his shoulders, he leant forward, making Van's father's feet lift off the ground.

All of Van's father's weight was hung from his neck. His bladder released itself, and a smell of urine filled the room.

Henry kept the weight on the belt, and soon there was no movement from Van's father.

They both carried Van's father into a bedroom.

Henry's father took the weight of the body, and Henry placed the belt over the open door. He pulled down on the belt, and Henry's father lifted the body up until its feet were off the floor, and it was suspended by its throat from the top of the door by the belt.

Henry tied a knot in the belt so it wouldn't pull through the door jamb, and they closed the door, leaving Van's father hanging on the inside of the door.

Anybody coming across the body would think that it was a suicide, another drunk offing himself. It happens all the time.

The pair went into the lounge room and waited for Van to come home.

Van was one happy little Silver Eagle.

He thought that he had put terror into the hearts of his enemies once again. He felt he was on top of it all.

He bet that Henry and his father were sitting somewhere shitting themselves, waiting for his next move.

When he demanded money and some of the action from the illegal abalone business, they would fall over themselves, giving it to him.

Yes, he was a man to be feared.

He got out of the taxi.

The dumb Indian driver didn't have a clue about who he was.

How he would have quaked in fear and prayed to whatever god that he prayed to if he'd realised that in the back of his taxi was the Silver Eagle.

Van gave the driver $20.00 and waited for his change.

The idiot slowly counted out his change, gave it to him, and drove off.

Fucking slope heads. They never tip, not like the stupid Aussies, the taxi driver thought to himself.

Van got into the lift, and the smell of urine assaulted his senses.

He thought that when he became powerful, he would outlaw people pissing in the lifts.

It must be those black bastards, dirty from birth, not like him.

He wondered if his father would be still awake, probably asleep on the couch in a drunken stupor—the old fool.

Van opened the screen door. It was unlocked.

How many times had he told his father to keep the screen door snibbed?

He quietly slid his key into the door lock.

If the old fool was asleep, he didn't want to wake him up and listen to a tirade of how smart his father was and how stupid he was.

He quietly opened the door.

The room was in darkness. His father must be in his bedroom.

Van clicked on the light switch. Nothing happened.

Bloody light bulbs, the new energy-saving bulbs that they had gotten for nothing didn't last as long as the old ones.

He moved silently into the room.

Suddenly a torch blinded him.

'What are you doing, you old fool?' Van asked harshly.

Henry spoke softly, 'Just evening things up a bit. You scared my sisters. You have stepped over the line. You are the fool.'

With that, Henry's father hit Van with a baseball bat that had been standing against a wall in the unit.

Van didn't feel a thing.

Both father and son picked up Van and walked towards the door.

They checked to see if anybody was about.

When the coast was clear, they took Van's unconscious body over to the waist-height wall on the side of the walkway and rolled it over the edge.

Henry's father said in Vietnamese, 'Fly, Silver Eagle, fly.'

The already unconscious Van plummeted to his death on the concrete fifty feet below.

He landed with sickening thud.

The pair calmly walked away and got into the lift.

They went down to the foyer, walked to their car, got in, and drove away.

Henry's father said to Henry, 'Say nothing to your mother about what happened tonight. We will tell your sisters that everything is taken care of.'

Henry nodded. They pulled up at their home and walked inside.

Teddy was watching the morning news. He was only watching it to see the weather map to see what was going on weather-wise.

A perfectly groomed newsreader came on and mentioned that what looked like a murder-suicide had happened in the Footscray housing commission flats.

It appeared that a father and son had fallen out and the father had thrown the son off a walkway on the fifth floor and then had committed suicide.

Teddy thought that it was sad that these people had come to find a new life but how things went wrong.

Henry and his father got to work and started to prepare for another busy day.

His father had told the girls that it had all been a silly joke and the man who had scared them wasn't right in the head. He told his daughters that the police had locked the man up and he wouldn't be around ever again.

The girls were uncertain, but when he told them that either he or their big brother would be there to pick them up, they were satisfied and soon had forgotten all about what had happened.

Henry said to his father, 'Father, I am surprised that you were prepared to kill someone to keep our family safe. I thought you would have rather taken a different approach.'

Henry's father looked at his son.

He said, 'Son, there is a lot that you don't know or understand about me. When you were born, I promised our ancestors that I would protect your mother and all our family to the death. There is a time for talk and a time when talking is not enough. Sometimes you must act quickly and there is no time for talk.'

Henry was silent for a minute.

Then he asked, 'You travelled across the ocean so we all could have a better life. You took a gamble and risked much danger. How could you protect us from the perils of pirates and rebel fishermen?'

Henry's father smiled at Henry and said, 'When I sold everything and we boarded the boat to come to Australia, I bought a hand grenade. I kept that grenade with me at all times. If we had been boarded by pirates, I was going to clutch my family in my arms and detonate the grenade. I would have killed us all and maybe taken out some pirates, but I couldn't let you, my young son, be killed and my wife raped and killed by pirates without putting up a fight. If we were to die, it would be on my terms.'

Henry slowly nodded his head.

There was a lot about his father that he didn't know or understand.

The police delved deeper and deeper into the deaths. The more they investigated Van, or the Silver Eagle, they found more people who were involved.

It became obvious to them that the Silver Eagle was running a stand-over operation, as well as being a major player in the drug business. The more questions they asked, the more they were faced with dead-end results.

They hoped that some information would filter down somewhere along the line.

When Teddy and the boys heard that it was Van and his father who had died, Teddy summed it up.

He said, 'The Vietnamese have been at war for ever, first with the Chinese, then the French, and then with themselves. I'm sure that the Silver Eagle knew what he was getting himself into. He just tried to stand over the wrong bloke.'

Tom asked, 'Do you reckon that it was Henry?'

Dean added, 'I'm not sure that Henry has got killing in him.'

Curly said, 'Henry's old man might have something to do with it. I reckon that he would be a tough nut to crack.'

Teddy said, 'Maybe. If you put the two of them together, you don't know how things might end up. But I don't really care if

Henry and his dad did do it. It's none of our business. We'll still sell to them.'

The four friends relaxed and sipped their beers.

Dean asked, 'How does the weather look?'

There was silence in the room.

They all knew that there was good weather coming, but they always left when they were going to work up to Teddy.

Teddy said, 'I'll give Bass Strait Barry a ring and see if there is a window of opportunity for us to go out among the islands in Bass Strait.'

The next day, Henry's mother stopped their car outside the entrance to the private school.

Normally, the other mum's didn't say much to her, but today all the mothers were there.

The big-breasted blonde woman asked, 'Are your daughters both OK?'

Smiling, the girl's mother said, 'Yes, thank you, it was a joke gone wrong. Thank you for all your help and concern yesterday.'

All the mothers smiled and insisted that she was welcome.

The blonde said, 'It is a mystery about the father and son dying over in Footscray last night.'

Silence descended on the group.

The girls' mother looked at her and said, 'I know of no such thing happening.'

'Maybe a coincidence,' the blonde smiled.

She put her hand on the girls' mother's shoulder and said, 'What had to be done was done.'

The mother looked confused and watched as her two daughters ran towards their classmates, laughing, and thought to herself, *Life is so good.*

Karl and His Missing Mate

Detective Karl was in a quandary.

His partner and friend Detective Jack Andrews was missing.

Jack was more than simply missing; he had seemingly disappeared from the face of the earth. When he didn't show up for work, Karl thought that he might be on the piss somewhere with a skinny young hooker.

Jack had a taste for the young ones.

Karl thought that it might have been their thin childlike bodies. It certainly wasn't their innocence. He knew that by the time they started to hawk the fork, they were generally well experienced in the ways of the world. They had usually been sexually abused by a trusted family member. That favourite uncle or grandfather would have run his hand up their dress or groped their breasts. It was all downhill from there.

It became obvious in their office that Jack wasn't coming in of a morning.

Karl was called into the boss's office and given a grilling by Detective Inspector Ray Boyd.

Ray didn't muck about.

'Look, Karl,' he said, 'I know you and Jack are partners and like a fucking idiot you were with him when he went up to Bairnsdale and tried to drag his wife back to Melbourne. That was a monumental lapse of common sense. When was the last time that you saw him?'

Karl hesitated. He didn't want to dump his mate Jack into the shit.

Ray sensed that the bond of loyalty was strong between the two detectives.

He said, 'Mate, is there anything that you can tell me that might give us a clue to where he is or what happened to him?'

Karl opened up.

'Sir,' he said, 'I haven't seen Jack for more than seven days. I went around to his house and had to break in. The place was a mess. There were dirty dishes everywhere, and it didn't look like Jack had been there for a couple of days.'

Ray Boyd looked at Karl and slowly shook his head.

'You didn't think to raise the alarm earlier?' he asked.

Karl looked at his shoes and mumbled, 'Sir, I didn't want to cause Jack any trouble. I thought he might be holed up with a girlfriend or something.'

'Does he have a problem with the drink?' Ray asked.

Karl looked up and said, 'Not really, but he went downhill when his missus pissed off. He wasn't expecting it.'

Ray looked at Karl and thought, *Good mate or not, this bloke has acted out of misguided loyalty.*

Ray was an old-time copper, and, for him, the force came before anything, before his wife, before his family. It was always the job first.

He was a thief taker, and he always got his man. He had done time in the armed robbery squad when the crooks were fair dinkum, not like they were today. These days' smart-arsed druggies were making more money in a month than he was in a year.

He remembered one time asking a new Australian where he was on a particular night and that Shitman had answered, 'I think that was the night when I went around to your mother's place and she sucked my dick.'

Ray had belted him and knocked him out of his chair, and the little prick had put in a complaint against him. He was dragged before a police committee and ordered to take counselling. It was lucky the other policeman there lied and said that the crim had slipped and fallen. But Ray realised that his days of belting crims were over.

The police force as he knew it was gone.

He was an ancient relic, a person whom time had left behind.

Word soon got around that he was losing it.

Ray looked at Karl and felt sorry for him.

It really did look like Jack had gone missing.

He said to Karl, 'Start asking around. Go to Jack's snouts and see what they can tell you. Find the last person whom he talked to. I'll put an alert out on his car.'

Karl nodded and walked out of the office.

Where was he going to start?

Bass Strait Barry and Hilda were getting along fine; they worked together well.

They were sitting in the sun in the backyard, having a coffee when the doorbell rang.

Because Hilda still thought her husband Jack was looking for her, Barry answered the door.

When he saw Karl standing there, Barry asked, 'What the fuck do you want?'

Karl was unfazed by Barry's hostility.

He looked at Barry in the face and asked, 'When was the last time you saw Hilda's husband, Jack?'

Barry smiled and said, 'I've never seen the shithead. Why do you ask?'

'He's gone missing,' Karl said, 'No one has seen him for almost a week.'

'The dumb prick has probably got lost. He'll wander home when he's hungry,' Barry exclaimed with a smile.

Karl slowly asked, 'You haven't done him a mischief, have you?'

Barry shook his head. 'Mate, I'm an old man. I can't do myself a mischief. You're barking up the wrong tree.'

Detective Karl wasn't convinced that Barry was telling him everything.

He asked, 'Can I speak to Hilda?'

'Hilda who?' was the reply.

Karl was starting to lose his temper.

'Look, you old fool. I know that she is living here with you. Bring her out, or I'll ring up and get a search warrant.'

Hilda was suddenly at the door beside Barry.

'What do you want?' she asked.

Karl was a bit taken aback by Hilda's appearance.

She looked a lot different from the last time that he had seen her at the Billabong Roadhouse near Bairnsdale. She looked well, and her skin glowed. She looked years younger.

'When was the last time that you saw Jack?' Karl asked.

'The last time I saw Jack was when you and he tried to drag me back to Melbourne. Have you got over your injuries yet?' Hilda enquired smugly.

Karl didn't answer her question.

He went on, 'Well, he's missing. No one has seen him for over a week.'

'Have you been around to his house and looked there?' Hilda asked.

'Yes, and it hasn't been cleaned since you left,' Karl replied.

Hilda looked at Karl and said, 'I have no idea where he could be, and I don't really care if he never shows up. He's dead to me.'

Karl saw Barry give the ghost of a smile.

He thought to himself, *This bastard knows something. I'm sure of it.*

'You will be hearing about this matter again. I won't stop until I find out what has happened to Jack,' Karl said as he walked away.

Barry said to his back, 'Fuck off and do some proper work. Find some murderers or something.'

Karl stopped, turned, and looked at Barry.

He said, 'I think that's exactly what I'm gunna do, find a murderer,' and got into his car and drove away.

Hilda looked at Barry and said, 'Jack's gone missing. I wonder where he could be.'

Barry looked back and said, 'Don't worry, love, if he turns up, I won't let anything happen to you.'

Hugging Barry, Hilda said, 'We had better keep our eyes open, just in case he pops up sometime.'

Barry laughed and said, 'I don't reckon that there is any chance of that happening.'

Hilda looked at him in a knowing way.

They went back inside, and each got another coffee.

Karl headed down to the marina. He was looking for Slither.

Slither was doing a bit of cleaning up and wondering where his next drink was going to come from. Karl pulled up, got out of his car, and walked towards him.

Slither knew then where his next drink would come from.

Walking up to Slither, Karl said, 'Hullo, mate. When was the last time that you saw Jack? He's gone missing and no one's heard from him.'

'The last time I spoke to Jack was at the St Kilda public toilets. He dropped something off to me,' Slither answered.

'Yes, I remember,' Karl said. 'He went missing some time after that.'

'He must have come down here later on as I saw his car parked here one day,' Slither commented.

Karl was suddenly interested.

He asked casually, 'What day was that?'

Slither screwed up his face in an attempt to concentrate, 'Ah, fuck me, I can't remember. I do remember that it was here all or most of the day. It struck me as a bit odd, why would he leave his car here all day? The next day, when I came in, the car was gone.'

Karl got out a $20 note and gave it to Slither in silence.

Slither continued, 'I can't remember exactly what day it was, but I do remember the car being here all day.'

'Try and remember what day it was,' Karl asked.

Slither said, 'It was the day that Barry and Teddy took the boat out for a run. They went out and came back in. They were only away for a few hours. I don't know what they were up to.'

He realised he had gotten all he was going to get from Karl that day.

'Give me a day or so,' he said. 'And I'm sure that I'll come up with more information.'

Karl nodded and walked away.

Slither tried to work out how he could string this out and how much he could end up getting.

Barry waited until Hilda was out of earshot and then rang Teddy.

'That bastard copper Karl was around. He knows that Jack, his detective mate, has gone missing. He asked me when I had seen him the last time. I told the prick that I had never laid eyes on him.'

Teddy replied, 'Mate, don't be worried. No bastard knows that we dumped Jack out in the middle of the bay. His body will be almost gone by now. Those sea lice are good at getting rid of stuff like that.'

Barry answered, 'Mate, I'm not worried. There is no way that any shit can come back onto us.'

Teddy laughed and said, 'You know what happened to Jack and I know what happened to Jack, and as far as the rest of the world is concerned, he has done a runner.'

Ray Boyd wasn't head of his section by chance. He had worked his way up to the very top by never taking his eye off the ball.

He knew that Jack had gone missing. He wasn't as dumb as they all thought, and he started to put two and two together.

Ray had known Jack's old man. In fact, he had been a bit of a mate of his in the old days. When he saw Jack come through, he gave him a bit of a hand up. Nothing anybody could point to; he just did a bit behind the scenes. He made it a bit easier for Jack, for his old man's sake. He knew that Jack and Karl did a bit of sampling what they should have been arresting, and He reckoned that he got that from his old man. Jack's old man only got to be a sergeant of police in some shit-heeled country town.

That wasn't for Ray. He wanted to climb to the top, to become something. Now it looked like Jack had gone missing. That wouldn't look good—him losing a copper under his command.

Ray started to think; he would do a bit of sniffing around himself. It would be good to get back into the harness and do a bit of good old-fashioned police work rather that sit behind a desk all day.

He would show these youngsters a thing or two about police work.

Putting an alert out for Jack's car, he told them to check out all the normal places, crowded car parks, hotel car parks, and, especially, the airport. Crims always dumped cars out at the airport.

Ray then got onto the phone company and did a trace on Jack's phone.

It would take a while, but they would tell him where the phone was used last.

Modern times, he thought to himself. *It's a lot easier now than in the old days.*

He secretly thought that the crims were getting dumber.

In the old days, you could tell a crim by the shape of his head.

These days, even the kid who delivered the papers could get his hands on a computer and print off some 100-dollar notes. Who knew what half the population were getting up to on their home computers?

He reflected that maybe they weren't getting dumber; there were just more of them, and, with the help of modern-day equipment, the police were actually getting smarter.

✧ ✧ ✧ ✧

Barry and Hilda were doing a bit of cleaning up on Barry's boat. It didn't really need any cleaning as Hilda kept it spick and span, but Barry enjoyed just mucking around on boats.

A stupid thought came to him from the kid's book *Wind in the Willows. There's nothing, absolutely nothing better than mucking about with boats on the water all day.*

He thought that it might have been Mole who made that grand statement.

Barry smiled to himself.

'Do you want a cup of coffee, love?' he asked Hilda.

'Yes, why not?' she replied.

Barry made himself useful, getting some water boiling.

He looked up and saw Slither looking at him through the wheelhouse window.

'Hey, Barry,' Slither shouted out. 'A copper was down here, asking about that Jack, the detective, who used to come down here. He wanted to know when I last saw him. He reckons that he has gone missing. I told him that I couldn't fucken well remember. But I mentioned his car was in the car park the day when you and Teddy took the boat out for a run for a couple of hours. Can you remember what day that was?'

A shudder ran up Barry's spine.

Barry screwed up his face and said, 'Fuck me, mate, I can't remember what day that was. You say we were only out for a couple of hours?'

Slither said, 'Yeah, mate. I didn't see you go out, but when I was here doing some cleaning up, you and Teddy pulled back into port.'

Barry scratched his head and said, 'Mate, I'm fucked if I know just what day that was.'

Slither continued, 'Well, I reckon that his car was here all that day. I didn't see Jack around anywhere, and when I got in the next morning, I'm sure the car was gone.'

Barry shook his head and said, 'Ah! Fuck me. My brain is getting worse and worse. I can hardly remember what I did yesterday, let alone a couple of days ago.'

'Yer, it's tough. Next time that you are talking to Teddy, ask him. He should remember,' Slither requested.

'Yes, mate, no worries,' Barry replied.

With that, Slither walked off as if on some mission of great importance.

Hilda asked, 'Did Jack leave his car down here the same day he went missing?'

Barry looked at Hilda, 'Seems that way, love.'

'And you didn't bump into him?'

'No, love,' he said.

Hilda slowly sipped her coffee.

Barry seemed to be interested in a spot on the distant horizon.

The seagulls and pelicans looked for food and preened themselves.

Calmness settled over the water.

It didn't take the police long to discover Jack's car at the airport. It was brought in by truck, and the forensic people went through it. There were no obvious signs of anything wrong. No bloodstains or bullet holes.

Ray Boyd read the report.

It appeared that Jack had dumped the car and got on board a plane and headed off somewhere.

He put up Jack's name on the travel computers, and nothing came up.

Since 9/11, it was almost impossible to fly under a false name, so it appeared that the car had been dumped.

By who, was the big question.

Ray learnt that Jack's wife had moved in with Barry, an older fisherman, who had been around the traps for years.

On closer inspection, he discovered that Barry wasn't completely out of his depth in doing things the illegal way. He had to be the number one suspect.

Ray thought that he and Karl had better go and have a talk with Barry and Hilda.

Teddy and Barry met up at a pub in Port Melbourne. They were sitting quietly, having a beer and talking about the interest Karl was showing in Barry and the disappearance of Jack.

'Mate, they can't know anything at all,' Teddy stated.

Barry looked at his friend and said, 'That fucking Slither was asking questions about when Jack's car was parked in the car park of the marina.'

'There could have been a number of reasons that the car was parked there, mate,' Teddy said, smiling, 'Jack might have left it there to do a bit of snooping around. He could have parked it there and got on the piss somewhere. There are a million possibilities.'

Barry happily agreed, 'We are the only ones who know what really happened, so if we don't say anything, then all is well.'

Teddy looked at Barry and said, 'Mate, you are 100 per cent correct. We don't know anything.'

Karl and Ray made their way around to Barry's place.

Ray knocked on the door.

Hilda saw the two men standing there and decided not to answer it.

She and Barry had made a rule for her not to open the door to anyone if Barry wasn't home.

The two detectives talked for a couple of minutes and left.

They headed down to the marina.

Slither was emptying the rubbish bins when the two detectives walked into the marina.

Karl introduced Ray to Slither, 'This is Jack's and my boss. Tell him what you told me about Teddy and Barry going out to sea for a couple of hours the other day around the time when Jack went missing.'

Slither repeated that he thought that he noticed Jack's car in the parking lot around the time he went missing. He couldn't be sure, but he reckoned that it was there all day, and when he came in the next day, it was gone. He explained how Teddy and Barry took Barry's boat out for a run and how he was there when they returned. He didn't know what they were doing, and they didn't say.

Ray asked Slither a few questions about what day it was, and Slither couldn't put his finger on exactly the day.

He said that he had asked Barry and he wasn't sure either, but he thought that Teddy would know.

Ray saw that he wasn't going to get any more out of the old drunk, so he and Karl walked back to their car. Ray decided that he should go and see this Teddy and see what he had to say for himself.

They drove over to Teddy's place and knocked on his door.

Teddy opened it and asked, 'What do you want?'

Stepping forward, Ray said, 'My name is Ray Boyd, and I'm here to ask you some questions about the disappearance of Detective Jack Andrews.'

'What exactly do you think I know about where some dumb copper is?' Teddy questioned.

Ray ignored the insult and went on, 'Jack's car was seen down at the marina the day when he disappeared. You and Barry went out in Barry's boat and came back a couple of hours later. You two could have easily dumped his body at sea.'

'Did anyone actually see Jack, Barry, and me together?' Teddy asked.

'No,' stated Ray.

'So there you fucking well have it. We didn't see Jack. We didn't speak to Jack. We didn't murder him and dump his body. We didn't do any fucking thing. So fuck off and leave me alone. You are wasting your time and you're wasting my time. Get the picture!'

With that, Teddy closed the door in their faces.

The two detectives looked at each other, and Ray said, 'What do you reckon? Do you think that these blokes had anything to do with Jack's disappearance?'

Karl shook his head, and they walked back to their car. 'I reckon that there is something going on. That Teddy is a cool customer. I reckon that Barry is the weakest link. The more pressure that we put onto him, the more we might get out of him.'

They returned to their office.

The tracking system that they employed to locate Jack's phone led them to believe that Jack's phone had been taken to Tullamarine airport, and so whoever took the car out to the airport must also have taken the phone.

That made sense.

Ray figured that they probably dumped the phone when they dumped the car.

Barry was thinking hard.

The weakness in the whole deal was Slither. If that idiot kept asking everyone questions about when Jack's car was at the marina, then sooner or later, the two detectives would catch on to the fact that something had happened there.

Barry thought, *If Slither keeps sticking his head into the investigation, then he will have to be dealt with.*

The weather started to improve, and Barry and Teddy spoke about a run out into Bass Strait. They decided that Deal Island would be the place to go. There was plenty of abalone out there, and it was so far away that the chance of the fisheries getting onto them was minimal.

Barry fuelled up his boat and got all the supplies on board for a week away.

Teddy discussed bringing Barry's old deckhand Des along as someone who could run the abalone meat across of a night.

Des on hearing that he was to be included was really happy.

Barry and Des were old mates, and when Hilda arrived, Des had been left out, and it had hurt. He had made the mistake of ringing the fisheries when Teddy and all the crew went hunting for the Japanese submarine and he had dobbed them in.

Luckily, everyone thought that it was Slither who did the deed.

Des thought that Jack, the detective, had an idea that it was him who made the phone call.

He hoped that the despicable act would never see the light of day.

All the boys were alerted, and their gear was taken down to the marina.

Slither watched as Barry and Hilda loaded the provisions onto Barry's boat.

He rang detective Karl and told him that Barry was loading up his boat once again and was getting ready for a trip away poaching abalone.

Karl rang the fisheries, and Wallace P. Trotter was happy to hear that Barry was getting ready for a trip away. Wallace asked after Jack and was mystified when told that Jack was missing.

Wallace readied himself and a team of fisheries officers.

He would stake out Derek's processing factory once again, and he would alert the Tasmanian Fisheries Department of the possibility that a group of poachers would be working out in Bass Strait.

Des was down at the marina well before Barry and Hilda arrived.

Barry introduced Hilda to Des, and they all got ready to ship out.

The boat was almost to the heads when Des announced that Teddy and the boys were fast approaching.

The Shark Cat sped past them.

All the boys waved, and soon they were almost out of sight.

Teddy brought the Shark Cat into the area of Deal Island. He manoeuvred it into position above a shallow reef.

They had decided to work well away from where Barry's big boat was going to anchor.

The boys were soon all wet-suited up and ready to go. Teddy liked the attitude of his mates. There was no standing around and talking.

It was as if they were here to work, and that was exactly what they did.

He started the compressors, and the three divers went over the side.

They swam down in the crystal-clear water and started to chip abalone off the reef.

Soon Dean had his net bag full, and Tom swam over and took it to a position on the sandy bottom. This was going to be where the first stockpile of abalone would be.

Tom had swapped his half-full net bag with Dean's full one. Tom then swam over to Curly's side and swapped his net bag with an empty one and swam Curly's net bag back to the stockpile.

This continued, and, after about an hour and a half, the divers surfaced for a bit of a rest.

There were eight net bags at the bottom—about 250 kilos of meat after the abalone were shucked.

Teddy saw the boys were in good spirits.

Dean asked, 'Is Barry here yet?'

Teddy replied, 'No, mate, he won't be here for a while yet.'

Tom joined in, 'Those big boats are pretty damned slow.'

'They are slow and easy. Just like me,' Curly offered.

Everyone laughed.

The divers ate some high-energy protein bars and got ready for another session.

Teddy took the boat over to another spot.

The boys went over the side and swam down.

Barry, Des, and Hilda were steaming towards the Deal Island group.

Everything was going well. They all seemed to be getting on well together.

They started to talk about Slither and what a contemptible bastard he was.

Barry said to Des, 'If you hadn't rung us and told us that Slither was on the piss with a pocket full of money, and that it wasn't pension day, then we might have walked into the fisheries when we dropped off the abalone at the processors. That fucking Slither has been giving us up every time we go out. I bet the bastard has rung through to whomever and told them we are away as we speak.'

'Someone should knock the shithead,' Des commented.

Hilda said, 'That's a bit drastic, isn't it?'

'It's not the first time that such action has been taken down on the water front,' Des murmured.

Barry and Des both laughed.

Des said, 'What's the old Painter and Dockers saying?'

'We catch and kill our own,' Barry said, laughing.

'Them good old boys didn't fuck around,' Des commented. 'If you messed with them, you ended up very unwell.'

Both the men laughed again.

Hilda wasn't sure what was funny.

Hours later, Barry pulled his boat in under the lighthouse on Deal Island.

He said to Hilda, 'This is the highest lighthouse in Australia. It's built on an elevated piece of land, so although the light-house is only 22 metres high, its total elevation is 305 metres.'

Hilda looked at the lighthouse and said, 'I wouldn't mind living on a lighthouse. I reckon that the isolation would be wonderful.'

Barry looked at Hilda and said, 'It wouldn't be much fun to be isolated with Jack.'

Hilda felt a wave of repulsion run through her body.

'You're dead right there,' she answered.

Barry dropped anchor, and Hilda started to get some tea ready.

Barry said, 'I hope the boys bring up some crayfish.'

He explained to Hilda that after tea for a bit of a snack, they normally had garlic crayfish before they hit the sack.

'Sounds good to me,' Hilda offered.

Des said, 'That's my job, cooking the crays. I'll show you how to do it, if you like.'

Hilda said, 'Thanks, Des, that would be great.'

Barry noticed that they were both doing all that they could to get on together.

He felt that things would work out all right; he hoped so.

Piggy had alerted the Tasmanian Fisheries that Teddy and Barry were out amongst the islands in Bass Strait. They assured Piggy that they would look into it and send a boat out to investigate. Piggy offered to fly over and be of some assistance, but the offer was declined. They were sure that they could do all that was needed.

In Melbourne, fisheries officers were on stake-out duty, watching Derek's factory.

All that could be done was being done.

Teddy and the boys were getting ready to call it a day.

They had about eighteen bags at the bottom, and, as usual, they wouldn't process any of the first day's catch until they were ready to take all the abalone meat back to Melbourne.

They steamed over to Barry's boat, and all the boys climbed up.

Des started to organise filling up the Shark Cat's two long-range fuel tanks.

He told Teddy to go and have a shower and get ready for tea.

Teddy smiled to himself. It was good to see Des back and doing his bit.

Soon all the boys were showered and ready for tea.
Hilda had done roast lamb with all the trimmings.
Everyone started eating.
Hilda felt a great sense of contentment, watching them all eat. She really felt as if she was part of it all.

Senior Sergeant Ray Boyd and Detective Karl sat in front of the white board.

They had written up all the names of who they thought might be of assistance to them in searching for clues about the disappearance of Detective Jack Andrews.

Ray said, 'On the day when Jack's car was spotted down at the St Kilda Marina, no one had any contact with him. And no one is admitting seeing him there or anywhere since. Slither saw the car there all day, and it wasn't there the following day. He would be a hopeless witness whom the opposing council would rip to shreds when we go to court. He will fall apart like a house made of playing cards.'

Karl proposed, 'This is what I reckon might have happened. Jack made his way down to the wharf to talk to the old fisherman Barry. They got into a fight, and somehow Barry belted the shit out of Jack. He killed Jack either by accident or because he meant to. He called Teddy in for some advice. Between them they decided to dump Jack's body out to sea, where no one would find it.'

Ray thought for a moment and said, 'You might be correct in assuming that's what happened, but how can we prove it?'

'What we need is a confession from either Teddy or Barry about the deed,' Karl said.

Ray added, 'I can't see either of them falling over and confessing to something that we can't pin onto them. They both have been around too long to be tumbling into that.'

The pair of detectives studied the list of names.

'Do you think Jack's wife knows anything about Jack, maybe ending up in the bay?' Karl asked.

Ray said, 'It's a win-win situation for her. She has got rid of Jack and landed on her feet.'

Karl slowly nodded, 'Our only hope is that Slither, the odd-job man can remember what day he saw Jack's car in the car park.'

Ray shook his head, 'I don't reckon that prick knows what day it is.'

'We should put pressure on Barry and Hilda, squeeze them, and see what comes out,' Karl said.

'We can't do anything until they come back from their trip,' Ray said.

Karl nodded, 'I'll put some pressure on Slither.'

Murphy, the security guard, came on duty and noticed that the favoured spot for the fisheries was taken once again.

'Looks like our friends are back again on stake-out, watching Derek's factory,' he quietly said to himself.

He gave Derek a ring and told him that there was some action once again. Derek as usual promised him a crayfish, and Murphy once again made a token of refusing it but, as usual, Derek won the battle.

Derek rang Teddy and told him that the fisheries were watching Derek's factory.

Teddy laughed and said, 'Well, at least we know what they are up to. We have got nothing doing tonight, so we can rest easy. Go back to bed and relax. I'll give you a ring tomorrow night and let you know what's going on.'

Derek laughed and said, 'Thanks, mate, I'll talk to you soon.'

Piggy settled his large bottom more comfortably into the 4WD's front seat and prepared himself for a long night. Luckily, he had bought along plenty of high-energy bars to help keep him awake.

As the night drifted along, so did Piggy. He was woken by the crash of a garbage truck, loading a bin of rubbish into its rear.

He got out and had a piss against the rear wheel. Derek's factory was quiet and in darkness. Piggy jogged on the spot for a couple of minutes to get the blood flowing and then got back inside the 4WD.

There was nothing at all to report.

He watched as the girl who worked in the fish and chip shop opened up, and he saw Derek arrive and open up the factory.

He thought about an egg and bacon McMuffin for breakfast.

The divers were all sitting out on the rear deck, and Des had organised the crayfish. He had drowned them in fresh water and split them down the middle.

He then spread some garlic butter onto the cut side of the crayfish and poured a little white wine into the open shells. He then placed them onto the barbeque, cut side up, and put a large steaming lid over the top of them.

After about half an hour, he lifted the lid and saw that the meat of the crayfish had turned an opaque colour. They were cooked, and the smell was wonderful.

All the boys cheered, and Dean said, 'Good on you, Des. Mate, you win "Our Kitchen Rules".'

Everyone laughed, and Des proudly handed out the sides of steaming crayfish.

Hilda tasted them and said, 'This is the best crayfish that I've ever eaten.'

Tom said, 'It takes the shine off ordering crayfish at a restaurant when you can get this at work.'

Everyone laughed and agreed.

When Teddy had finished his crayfish, he said, 'That's it for me. I'm hitting the fart sack.'

They all turned in for a night's sleep.

Piggy was on the phone to his counterparts in Tasmania.

He was amazingly alert for a man who hadn't slept a wink the previous night.

He explained to them that the factory that the abalone would be delivered to was under surveillance. If the Tassie team missed them, then they would be apprehended his end.

The Tasmanian Fisheries decided to send a boat over to the islands in the middle of Bass Strait to check things out.

The next morning, Teddy and the boys were hard at it. They had got an early start and were well under way by 10 a.m. They had a number of bags stockpiled in a heap on the sandy bottom.

Barry watched as the fisheries vessel came around the northern tip of Deal Island.

It was a forty-five-foot launch and probably had a top speed of twenty knots.

He said to Des and Hilda, 'Here come the cavalry. Rest easy as we haven't got any abalone on board.'

Barry phoned Teddy to say that the fisheries were about and they would be on board with him in ten or so minutes.

Both the men agreed that the Shark Cat had better stay out of sight over the horizon.

The fisheries vessel pulled up and a smiling fisheries officer asked, 'Who's the skipper and what port did you come from?'

Barry smiled and gave his name and address.

The Tasmanian fisheries officer asked if he could come on board.

Barry knew that he couldn't refuse as the fisheries have more power than the police.

'Yes, mate,' Barry said. 'Tie up and bring your whole crew over for a cup of coffee and a lamb roll.'

He said to Hilda, 'Love, and make up a couple of hot lamb rolls for the boys. They will be hungry as they must have left early this morning.'

The fisheries officers all came aboard, and Barry introduced them to Des and Hilda, first names only.

The officer in charge of the fisheries, Stan Bates, said to Barry, 'Mate, what are you doing out here?'

Barry smiled and said, 'Me and the crew are just having a couple of days off. We do it quite a bit. We just get away from the hustle and bustle of Melbourne and relax.'

Stan laughed, 'Mate, your reputation precedes you. We got a call from the Victorian Fisheries, and they reckon that you are out here poaching.'

Barry smiled, 'Do we look like poachers? Can you see any diving gear or anything else that we might use for poaching on board? And have a look at us. We are a bit long in the tooth to be poaching. Getting out of bed at our age stuffs us, let alone diving for abalone.'

Everyone in the cabin laughed.

Then Stan showed a different side as he continued, 'I remember you and Des from the old days and the Orange Ruffy caper.'

Barry said, 'Yes, those were the days, my friend. I thought that they'd never end,' quoting a Petula Clark song from the Sixties.

Stan commented, 'We got a couple of you. Some skippers ended up doing time.'

'Well, I suppose that it proves that we were innocent and did no wrong. So we weren't affected,' Barry offered.

Stan quipped, 'More by good luck than anything else.'

'But as I say, we didn't get prosecuted,' Barry reminded him.

Stan didn't say anything, just nodded.

'Would you like another lamb roll?' Hilda asked.

Stan shook his head, 'No, thanks, Hilda. We will be getting going. We will have a look around and see what's about.'

With that, the fisheries got back onto their launch and slowly headed away on a search-and-arrest mission.

Stan said to the other fisheries officers on board, 'We will wait and see what they are up to. We will see if they hook up with the rest of their team. It will be a wait-and-see operation.'

Barry rang Teddy and let him know that the fisheries were about and that they remembered that he was involved in the Orange Ruffy business a few years previously.

Teddy took stock of the information.

They were well into their second day. There was a good load for the Shark Cat.

All it needed was for them to be shucked out.

That was a problem with the fisheries on the lookout.

They would have to load the abalone, still in the shell, onto the Shark Cat and then everybody get in and shuck as much as they could and as quick as they could.

They would bag it up in the Shark Cat and then run it across to the mainland under the cover of darkness.

Teddy said to himself out loud, 'That fucking Slither, he keeps giving us up whenever we make a move. Something will have to be done about him.'

When the divers had made another stockpile of net bags of abalone, they came to the surface.

Teddy told them what was going on, how the fisheries had been aboard Barry's boat, and how there was every possibility that they were lying in wait for them to team up. They probably would wait in the darkness and pounce on them when they had some of the abalone on board.

Tom asked, 'Why don't we shuck out some abalone here and now and then just drop us off onto Barry's boat and let Des take the Shark Cat over to the mainland while we relax on board?'

Teddy admitted that was as a good plan as he could come up with.

He took the Shark Cat over to the GPS position where the first stockpile of abalone had been stacked the previous day.

Tom swam down and started to swim up the net bags.

Teddy rang Barry and told him what he had in mind.

He told Barry that they would shuck out all the abalone from the previous day's diving and then they would come over to Barry's boat and the divers would get off.

They would fuel up the Shark Cat and then Des would run the abalone meat to Melbourne. That way, it would be almost impossible for the fisheries to grab them when they were in possession of the abalone meat.

Barry positioned his boat in such a way that it would be impossible for the fisheries to sneak up and catch them unawares.

As darkness descended, all the boys were busy shucking out the abalone.

Soon it was all in clear plastic bags with the tops tightly closed with wire ties.

Teddy rang Barry and asked if the coast was clear.

Barry gave the OK, and they steamed towards where Barry was waiting.

As soon as the Shark Cat was beside Barry's boat, Des started to refuel its long-range fuel tanks.

The divers climbed up, and Des made his way down into the boat.

Teddy gave Des a mobile phone and said, 'Tony will ring you and let you know what boat ramp to meet him at.'

With that, Des drove the Shark Cat into the darkness.

All the divers had showers and got ready for another fabulous meal of roast chicken prepared by Hilda.

Des drove the Shark Cat into the night.

He was really happy that Teddy had given him the chance to be an active part of the team. This would cement his place in the group.

He prayed that the truth would never come out about him ringing the fisheries and dobbing in his mate Barry.

Fucking idiot, he thought to himself.

The powerful motors were pushing the Shark Cat through the water at a great rate of knots.

It was amazing just how far you could see at night.

Des didn't see another boat.

He hoped that he wouldn't run across any illegal drug runners or anything. He wondered what those two drug running bastards whom they bumped into a few months before were doing. That had been fucking scary.

Tony's phone rang.

He was expecting a call from Teddy.

'Teddy mate, what's up?'

'Hullo, mate,' Teddy said. 'The Shark Cat has just left. Des is on his own. Do you want to take someone with you to unload?'

Tony thought for a moment. 'Well, if I have someone with me, it will cut the time down by half. I can get one of my cousins and pay him $100. He will be happy with that.'

Teddy replied, 'Sounds good to me. Give Des a ring and tell him where you will meet him.'

Teddy gave Tony the number for the phone that he had given Des and hung up. He knew that Tony would ring Derek and organise for a place and a time for them to unload. He had a quick shower and joined the boys for a beer and got a bit of tucker into him.

Tony rang a cousin of his. He knew that this bloke wanted the money and would keep his mouth shut. He was big and strong and didn't mind doing a bit on the side every now and then. He arranged to pick him up a couple of hours later.

Tony then rang Des and asked how far away he was from the heads.

Des replied that he was about an hour away as they spoke. Tony directed him to the same boat ramp that they had used another time when Des was with them. It was always better to go to some place that they already knew.

Tony decided that they would go to a different place the next night.

He next rang Derek and told him that there was a load on the way and all was going well.

They arranged to meet in a couple of hours.

Derek explained to Tony that the fisheries were staking out his factory as they spoke, so he would have to go to another factory.

This one was in Footscray and was the place where he got his pre-cut chips from.

Derek explained that he and the boss would weigh up and freeze the abalone at that factory and then ship it over to his factory disguised as potato chips.

Everything was ready to go.

All they were waiting for was for Des to arrive.

Tony and his cousin Mario were waiting in the chill of evening at the allotted boat ramp.

They heard the sound of the Shark Cat coming towards them. Tony took out a powerful LED torch and shone it towards the noise.

Des immediately saw the light, slowed the Shark Cat down, and made his way to the boat ramp.

He jacked up the motors, and the Shark Cat grounded on the sandy bottom of the boat ramp.

Mario strode purposely up to the diver's door, and Des passed a clear plastic bag of abalone through to him. Mario put it on his shoulder and walked quickly up to the van. Tony did the same, and soon all the bags were off the Shark Cat.

Tony and Mario made ready to head back into Melbourne.

Des shook hands with Tony, and Mario pushed the boat backwards into deeper water. Des lowered the two motors and started them up.

He swung the boat around and headed off the way he had come in.

Tony drove across to Footscray to the side loading door at the chip factory.

Derek was waiting there with the owner Bob.

They quickly unloaded the bags of abalone meat into the cool room.

The whole unloading took only a few minutes.

Tony drove his cousin back to where he had picked him up and gave him a $100 note.

Mario laughed and said, 'anytime that you need a hand, please give me a ring.'

'Sure thing, mate, I'll be seeing you,' Tony said with a smile.

With that, Tony drove home.

'Mission accomplished,' he said to his wife, and they both went to bed.

Stan Bates, the Tasmanian fisheries officer, readied his men aboard the fisheries vessel.

He had moored away from where Barry and his crew could see them. He was of the opinion that with Barry just out of sight, he could run around the corner of the island and be onto the boat before Barry was aware that they were coming.

Stan raised the anchor. It was dark, about four hours after sunset.

He pressed the throttles down to full speed ahead, and the forty-five-foot vessel surged forward.

They swung around the corner where they thought that Barry's boat was anchored and saw that it was in fact well out to sea.

Stan had been outsmarted.

It would take them half an hour to get out to them.

But Stan decided to press on.

Barry saw the fisheries boat steam around the corner of the island they had been anchored close to.

He reckoned that there would be half an hour before they could get to them.

When the fisheries boat pulled up alongside, Stan and his crew jumped up onto Barry's boat.

Stan asked Barry, 'Why did you move out so wide?'

Barry answered, 'To avoid the backwash from the shore. One of the crew is new to boating, and she was feeling a bit seasick, so I moved out to calmer waters.'

Stan realised that he had been outsmarted.

He and his crew had a bit of a look around, but they could see that there wasn't any abalone on board.

They climbed back down to the fisheries launch.

Stan said as a parting gesture, 'I'll be keeping my eyes on you lot.'

Barry replied, 'Good on you. Keep up the good work.'

Barry turned to Hilda when the fisheries officers had gone and said, 'That fucking halfwit couldn't catch me years ago, and he's got no hope of catching me now.'

Hilda asked, 'How come you are so friendly with the Tasmanian Fisheries and not the same with the Victorian Fisheries?'

So Barry explained, 'Over here, it is different. Everyone on the water relies on each other for their safety. Out on the water, there is no "them and us". We are all in the same boat. You can walk into any of the waterside hotels in Hobart and see fisheries and fishermen having a drink together. We are all the same. It is different with the Victorian Fisheries.'

Hilda thought. *Men are strange creatures.*

Barry rang Des, 'How are you making out, mate?'

Des answered, 'Mate, all's unloaded, and I'm out past the heads. So far, everything is going fine.'

Barry said, 'Well done, mate. We'll see you in a couple of hours. The fisheries have been in to see us again. They surprised us. Of course there wasn't anything around that would interest them.'

'See you soon,' Des answered.

When Tony dropped off the abalone to the chip factory, Derek and the owner were waiting for them.

They tipped up the plastic bags and poured the abalone meat into draining trays. The clear blood ran across the floor and into the drains. They started boxing them up.

A fair bit of cleaning had to be done to clean off bits of guts that were still attached to the meat.

They also had to separate the blacklip abalone from the more popular greenlip abalone.

It all took time.

After a couple of hours, all the abalone was boxed up and in the blast freezer. Derek was pleased with himself.

He took a quick look at the tally and worked out that there were 120 boxes. Multiply that by ten, and that's how many kilos were in the blast freezer.

Derek felt happy that there was a lot of green lip abalone. That was what everyone wanted; he felt on top of the world.

He was sure his little mate whom he exported to in Japan would be happy. He reminded himself to give Akinobu

Okumura a call in the morning when the times matched up a bit better.

Teddy and the boys all stayed in their cabins.

There was no need for the fisheries to know that they were there. If possible, they would stay out of sight.

The morning sun was just peeking over the horizon, and they were all up and about.

Hilda was cooking up breakfast.

Des had brought the boat back to the Barry's big boat in the early morning, had quietly tied it up, and had gone to bed.

The divers were ready to go and get back into it.

Barry was worried about the possibility of the fisheries making a surprise visit. So once again, Teddy and he decided not to bring back any abalone for processing on board Barry's boat.

It would all have to be done at sea. That was a nuisance, but sometimes things just work out that way.

When they got to the new diving site, the boys went over the side and started doing what they did best, chipping off abalone.

Piggy was almost alert.

It had been a long, uneventful night. Nothing at all had happened at the factory.

He was sure that if Teddy and the boys were out poaching, then they would have to bring in their abalone at some time soon.

A theory slowly began to take shape in Piggy's brain. *What if we are at the wrong factory? What if Teddy is running his fish into another factory?*

Piggy's head began to spin. It seemed that he would never get on top of Teddy.

Detective Karl and his boss Detective Inspector Ray Boyd knew that they didn't have any real evidence. They thought that they had worked out what had happened to Detective Jack Andrews.

It was clear to them that Jack had driven his car down to the marina.

Somehow he and Barry had got into a fight, and Barry had done away with Jack.

Then he and Teddy had taken Jack's body out to sea and dumped it in deep water.

Slither was their sole witness, and, untasteful as it might be, he was their ace up the sleeve. They would have to make sure that Slither was looked after in every possible way that he could be looked after.

When Barry came back from sea, they would arrest Barry on suspicion of murder and take him away.

They would persuade him to plead guilty of manslaughter as it wasn't premeditated, and he would only do a short term. He would be out before he knew it. He might even avoid jail. Who knows? Anything was possible.

Karl had an idle thought that he might have a chance with Hilda if Jack and Barry were out of the picture.

Stan and his fellow fisheries officers were up and about.

They had discussed what was happening with Barry and the abalone poachers. They hadn't encountered the others as yet.

They must be out there somewhere, but where? That was the question.

It was obvious that they must be working miles away and using Barry's boat for refuelling and supplies.

It was going to be a real cat-and-mouse operation.

They would wait and see what happened next.

Meanwhile, the divers were going well.

They were on a rich reef that had abalone back-to-back.

Tom was stockpiling net bags full of abalone in a pile, and there was no sign of them slowing down. They were on a roll.

Teddy kept an eye out for the fisheries, but for them to come across the boys was like trying to find a needle in a haystack. There were miles of water out there.

When the time came for the divers to come up and start shucking out the abalone, the sun was sinking in the west.

Teddy drove the boat over to the stockpile that they had deposited earlier, and Tom started to swim up the bags two at a time. The other divers started shucking out the abalone.

Soon the deck of the Shark Cat was awash with the clear abalone blood.

It took a couple of hours for the boys to shuck out all the abalone—some from the previous day's work and some from today's effort. By the time the abalone was all done, they were pretty well bushed.

Teddy rang Barry who said that the coast was clear.

He would have Des ready to fuel up the Shark Cat. As soon as the divers got on board, Des would run the abalone meat back to Melbourne.

Teddy took the Shark Cat over to where Barry's boat was lying.

It only took a couple of minutes for the Shark Cat to be refuelled and for the divers to get off.

Des took off into the darkness towards Melbourne with the load of abalone meat.

The boys had their showers and relaxed.

Hilda had dinner prepared—roast pork with all the roast vegetables. It had taken her most of the afternoon. She felt that every meal had to be better than the previous one.

The boys started eating, and there was silence in the galley.

Teddy asked Barry, 'Mate, do you think the weather will break soon?'

Barry took time with his answer.

He said slowly, 'There is a low approaching. It should hit us in about a day's time. We should get tomorrow in. I reckon an early start for you blokes. Des, Hilda, and I will head off towards Port Phillip Bay after breakfast. We should be almost home when you catch us up.'

'That sounds pretty good to me,' Teddy answered.

They finished their dinner, went out to the rear deck, and relaxed.

Teddy gave Des a ring.

He was almost at the heads of Port Phillip Bay.

'How is it going, mate?' Teddy asked.

Des was happy and said, 'Mate, its going good. I'll be at the new boat ramp in less than half an hour.'

Teddy replied, 'No worries mate. Tony will have a bloke with him to give you a hand.'

'Thanks mate,' Des said.

Tony and his cousin Mario waited at the boat ramp in silence.

Soon they heard the noise of a boat coming towards them at high speed.

Like the day before, Tony shone his torch out at Des.

Des slowed the Shark Cat down and cruised into the boat ramp.

Mario waded out, grabbed the bow, and gently eased the twin hulls onto the sand.

Des grabbed a plastic bag of abalone meat, and Mario put it on his shoulder, ran it up the ramp, and stacked it into Tony's van.

Tony did the same.

Soon the Shark Cat was unloaded, and Des was being pushed backwards out into the bay. Mario spun the boat around. Des lowered the pair of powerful motors and started them up. With a final wave, he accelerated out into the darkness.

Tony and Mario went back to the van and drove off towards the chip factory where Derek and Bob were waiting.

When they pulled into the factory, Derek and Bob helped them unload the abalone.

Soon it was all in the cool room, and Tony and Mario drove away.

Derek started to weigh up and box the abalone. Soon they were all in the blast freezer.

Derek drove home, happy with the night's work.

He rang Teddy and gave him the weights.

Teddy was happy with the results.

Piggy was as vigilant as ever.

He and another fisheries officer had taken over from the previous fisheries officers, and as there wasn't anything to report, he felt sure that this would be the night.

Sooner or later, Teddy and them bastards would roll up at the factory, and guess what? There would be Wallace P. Trotter waiting to greet them.

He started to tell the younger fisheries officer tall tales about how he had outsmarted dozens of illegal fisheries operations. The poor younger officer gritted his teeth and thought; *It's going to be a long night.*

Stan Bates wasn't a fool.

He realised how easy it would be for Barry to be the mother ship for an illegal abalone poaching operation. He knew that sooner or later, the poachers would have to be on or near the mother ship.

He made it clear to the other fisheries officers that if they kept at it, sooner or later, they would catch the lot of them together.

He rang Wallace Trotter.

When Piggy's phone rang, he was halfway through talking about his ability to shadow a F100 from Melbourne to Eden completely unobserved.

He stopped talking and answered his phone, 'Wallace Trotter, how can I help?'

The voice on the other end said, 'Good evening, Wallace, this is Senior Officer Stan Bates. I'm ringing to let you know that I and my crew have been aboard Barry's boat and found no sign of anyone else. Apart from his two crew members. There were no poachers aboard.'

'The bastards are about somewhere,' Piggy fumed.

Stan replied, 'They might be shucking out the abalone at sea and running them across, but we haven't seen hide nor hair of a Shark Cat like you described.'

Piggy looked at the young officer whom he was sharing the stake-out with and shook his head.

'Mate, it's got to be there,' he said. 'I bet they are working in it of a day and then getting someone to run over to the mainland with it full of abalone meat of a night.'

Stan realised that what Wallace said was probably correct.

How was he going to be there when Teddy and the divers came back? And where was the Shark Cat now?

Piggy said, 'Stan, if that's the case, then they will have run a load over last night and also a load tonight. They haven't unloaded them here, so they must be unloading them somewhere else. That would make our stake-out here a complete waste of time.'

Stan agreed, 'Yes, mate, it looks like they are dumping it elsewhere.'

Letting that sink in, Piggy said, 'Where the fuck could they be unloading them?'

Stan replied, 'Well, it would have to be a seafood-processing plant, wouldn't it?'

Piggy replied, 'Yes, it would have to have a freezer to get the abalone down to minus 30 degrees.'

Stan asked, 'what other types of factories have got the facilities to do something like that?'

'Almost all types of food-processing factories would have that ability to freeze stuff quickly, and there must be a hundred of them in Melbourne,' Piggy surmised.

'So they could be unloading anywhere then?' Stan queried.

Piggy thought for a moment and said, 'I don't know what to do. Should we stay here in case they drop off a load here? Or do we go home and see what happens?'

Stan replied, 'Wallace, I can't give you any advice. But what I'm going to do is wait and see if I can grab them when they come in to unload or fuel up.'

'That's all you can do,' Wallace said, sounding dejected.

Derek spoke to Tony and said, 'Mate, we are ready for you when you arrive. How far away from here are you?'

Tony said, 'Mate, we are about thirty minutes away, maybe less.'

'Good stuff,' Derek said. 'We are waiting for you.'

As soon as Tony and Mario pulled up at the side door of the potato chip factory, the door was opened, and Derek and Bob gave them a hand to get the abalone into the cool room.

Within minutes, Tony and Mario were driving away from the factory.

Mario said, 'Hey, Tony, you blokes have really got things worked out well.'

Tony felt a sense of pride and replied, 'Yes, mate, me and Teddy have got everything worked out. The whole operation runs like clockwork.'

Tony dropped Mario off after giving him his $100 and made his way home.

This is easy money, Mario thought.

Teddy rang Des and asked, 'How far off are you from us?'

Des looked at the GPS and answered, 'About three hours away, I reckon. Is everything OK?'

Teddy replied, 'Mate, the fisheries are in the area. They are likely to pop up at any time. Just be on the alert.'

Des responded, 'No worries, the boat is empty, so we haven't got a problem.'

'Right,' said Teddy. 'I'll see you when you get here.'

With that, Teddy disconnected and decided that it was time to hit the sack.

Stan and his crew waited until it was well past midnight and slowly motored out from their anchorage.

With all running lights off, they silently made towards Barry's seventy-foot boat.

He cut the motors and drifted up to Barry's boat.

All was silent; the boat was in darkness.

Stan jumped aboard, and his crew lashed the two boats together.

Armed with powerful torches, they walked down the sides of the boat.

Stan shone his torch into the wheelhouse.

As soon as the fisheries men jumped on board, Barry was awake.

He hoped that Teddy would have been awakened by the noise.

Barry started to get out of bed.

The door to his cabin was opened.

Stan was there, saying, 'Barry, we are making a search of your vessel. Please come with us and offer no resistance.'

Barry smiled and said, 'No worries, mate. Let me show you all around.'

Together they went from cabin to cabin, waking everybody up and asking them to assemble in the galley.

Soon everyone was there.

Stan looked at the group, 'Well, well, what have we here? This looks like a crew of abalone poaches if ever I've seen one.'

Teddy and the boys looked back in silence.

Stan asked, 'Which one is Teddy?'

Teddy smiled and said, 'I am. Who are we talking to, and why did you wake us all up?'

Stan said, 'I am Senior Fisheries Officer Stan Bates, and I've been told by fisheries officers in Victoria that you are over here poaching abalone.'

'Well, as you can see, we aren't,' Teddy said. 'We are just out with our mate Barry having a bit of a spell and catching a couple of crayfish for our dinner.'

Stan looked at Teddy, 'My information is that you and your crew are poachers.'

Teddy smiled and said, 'You must be listening to that fat-arsed Piggy Trotter. He is always trying to get us for poaching, but because we aren't poachers, he can never catch us with abalone, just like you. Now fuck off and leave us in peace.'

Stan said, 'We want to have a look around before we go.'

Barry said, 'Do what you like. There are no illegal fish on board.'

Stan and his fellow fisheries officers started to look around.

Barry lit up the decks with the bright overhead lights.

Tom said, 'Now that I'm awake, I'm going to have a shit, if that's all right with you lot.'

He made his way to the toilets.

He silently mouthed the words to Teddy, 'I'll tell Des.'

Teddy gave a slight nod.

Des was making good time when his borrowed phone rang.

He answered, 'Hullo?'

Tom spoke quietly, 'Des mate, it's Tom.'

'Hullo, Tommy mate, what's happening?' Des asked.

Tom answered quietly, 'The fucking fisheries are on board and are searching the boat. It would be wiser if you didn't arrive here until they are gone.'

Des knew the rules.

He said, 'Sweet mate, I'll hang back until I get the word to come in. I'll lay out here. Maybe I'll put my head down and have a snooze.'

Tom said, 'Right mate, I'll get back to you.'

Stan and his officers had a good look around. They didn't find anything that shouldn't have been there.

They slowly got onto the fisheries launch and Barry bid them goodbye.

Everyone went back to bed.

Tom said to Teddy, 'I told Des to lay low for a while until the fisheries fucked off.'

Teddy smiled and said, 'It would have been a bit embarrassing to have Des pull up alongside when the fisheries were looking around.'

Barry agreed that they were correct.

Detective Karl and his boss Ray Boyd kept their ears to the ground as to the whereabouts of Barry and the rest of the poachers.

They had kept in touch with the fisheries and knew that all the team were out in the middle of Bass Strait. They knew that it was only a matter of time before Barry had to come into port. They were prepared to wait.

Karl kept in constant communication with Slither, the odd-job man at the marina.

Slither had no idea he was their star witness in the prosecution of Barry for the murder and disappearance of Detective Jack Andrews.

Karl walked down onto the jetty at the marina and said to Slither, 'Gidday, and mate. No sign of Barry as yet?'

Slither shrugged and said, 'No, mate, he's due back any day now.'

The detective palmed Slither two $20 notes.

And he made the money disappear.

'Mate, give us the mail the minute he lobs. We want to talk to him as soon as possible.'

'What do you want to talk to him about?'

'Ah . . . ' Karl said, 'just a bit of this and that. We are trying to fill in a few blank spots as to the whereabouts of Jack when you saw his car down here all day.'

'Do you reckon that Barry and Teddy had something to do with his disappearance?' Slither asked.

'What can I say? His car was down here, and Jack must have driven it here. He must have got out of it, and we don't know what happened after that. Maybe Barry can fill us in on a few details. Who knows?'

Slither suddenly started to show some interest. 'Is there a reward?'

Karl looked at him and said, 'Mate, I don't have to tell you how important it would be for us to find out just what happened. If we could discover exactly what went on, then I'm sure that there would be something in it for you.'

Slither had a quick flush of excitement run through him.

He asked, 'Would it be in the hundreds of dollars?'

Karl smiled and thought, *got you! You fucking drunk!*

'It might be in the thousands,' he informed the eager Slither.

This was a whole new ball game as far as Slither was concerned.

Suddenly he was in the team a 100 per cent.

Everyone on board sat at the galley table.

Teddy said, 'It looks like our race here is nearly run. We have got the fisheries waiting to pounce, and as soon as Des lobs here, they will be on to us. I think that it's time to cut and run. We have a couple of tonnes of meat onshore already. If we got another day in, it would be great, but I reckon that the risk is too great. I think that Barry and all of us should head home. What do you all think?'

There was silence around the galley table.

Tom spoke first.

He said, 'If we have got a couple of tonnes in the factory, that's worth about $80,000. That's a good cop for a few days' work. I'm happy with that.'

The others nodded in agreement.

Dean said, 'Yer, fuck it. If there's a chance of us getting sprung, we'll call it a day. I'm cool with that.'

Teddy looked at Barry and said, 'Well, that's about it. Let's get the fuck out of here.'

Barry smiled and said to Hilda, 'Start breakfast, love. I'll get the anchor up, and we'll haul arse out of here.'

Teddy rang Des and said, 'Mate, it's all over for us. We are starting to head back home. Meet up with us, and we'll refuel the Shark Cat. You can jump on board, and I, Tom, Dean, and Curly will take the Shark Cat back to port.'

Des was happy.

He said, 'Tell Hilda to save me a bit of brecky, and I'll come towards you.'

With that, Des set a course towards Barry's big boat.

Senior Fisheries Officer Stan Bates saw that Barry's boat was heading off towards the mainland.

He said to one of his crew, 'Looks like they are doing a runner. I'll ring Wallace Trotter and let him know what's happening.'

Piggy's phone vibrated in his pocket.

All good surveillance officers knew that a noisy ring could give you away.

Piggy looked at his underling and hoped that he noticed that his phone was on vibrating, not ring.

It's all wonderful experience for the young falla, Piggy thought.

'Wallace Trotter,' he answered.

Stan Bates said, 'Wallace, I think that your poachers are heading away back home. I feel it's due to the relentless surveillance that we have had them under. The rest is up to you.'

Piggy smiled into the phone and said, 'Thanks, Stan, we can take it from here, mate. I'll give you a ring and let you know what's going on.'

Stan disconnected.

He turned to his crew and said, 'Let's head for home. It will be good to sleep in my own bed.'

Barry and Teddy spoke quietly.

Teddy said, 'It's a good thing that we shucked out all the abalone that was at the bottom. I reckon that we have over two tonnes of meat in the freezers.'

Barry said, 'Yer, mate, not a bad result for a couple of days' work.'

'The good thing is that we are empty of abalone meat,' Teddy said. 'I reckon that there will be a reception committee waiting for us when we get back into the bay.'

'Yes, mate, you're probably right,' Barry commented.

Piggy was all go. He figured out that Barry would leave with the slower boat and Teddy and his crew would get going in the Shark Cat.

Well, one Wallace P. Trotter would be waiting for them as they appeared.

He would get a fisheries launch and a water police boat.

There was no way of escaping.

He thought that the Shark Cat would come through the heads of Port Phillip Bay first.

Piggy arranged for the water police to be on full alert. Their sleek mono-hulled thirty-footer with the twin 300-hp motors was ready.

The water police and the fisheries officers waited in eager anticipation.

Out at sea, Des checked the radar and saw Barry's boat heading his way. He sped towards the big boat as he was getting low on fuel.

When he pulled up beside Barry's boat, Dean and Curly had the 200-litre fuel drums waiting. The fuel was quickly transferred via a hose from the deck of Barry's boat into the long-range fuel tanks of the Shark Cat.

Within minutes, Des was up on the deck of Barry's boat, and Teddy and the boys were in the Shark Cat.

Teddy pushed the throttles down, and the Shark Cat quickly sped into the distance.

Des went into the wheelhouse and said to Barry, 'Another day in the office completed.'

'Well done, mate,' Barry acknowledged. 'Have a spell and get some brecky into you. Hilda will have knocked up something for you.'

Des walked into the galley, and Hilda said, 'Hi, Des are you hungry?'

He laughed and said, 'It must be the sea air. I could eat a horse.'

Hilda smiled and said, 'Let's hit you with a combination omelette and some bacon and hash browns and see how that sits with you.'

She slid a cup of steaming coffee across to Des.

'Thanks, love,' Des said.

He felt like he was one of the team.

It was funny he thought, but as a bloke gets older, he values being wanted, and Des felt he was wanted on board.

He felt a sense of closeness towards Barry and Hilda, and he wished that this feeling could last forever.

Teddy steered the Shark Cat into Port Phillip Bay through the heads.

All the boys watched as the water police boat exploded through the water towards them.

Tom said, 'Fuck me dead, that boat can move. I reckon that it's doing about eighty miles an hour.'

Dean said, 'Maybe it's going faster than that.'

Teddy asked, 'I wonder what size props it's swinging?'

'Maybe twenty-three-inch stainless steel,' Curly offered.

The police boat sliced through the water. The officer driving the boat waved his hand sideways through the air in a gesture that meant 'Stop your boat'.

Teddy did just that.

Piggy, face flushed by the wind rushing past him, strode to the side of the boat closest to Teddy's boat and yelled, 'Pull up! We want to have a look at you and your boat.'

With that, the two boats came together.

One of the police officers put a couple of soft rubber buffers between the two boats to stop the boats bashing together.

Piggy took over the investigation.

He loudly said, 'What have you lot been up to?'

Teddy answered, 'We've been through all this before, Officer Trotter. You are always making accusations about how we spend our days off, and we always say that we have been out sports diving, looking at wrecks, taking it easy. Why don't you believe us?'

Piggy said to the water police on their boat, 'Bullshit, they are abalone poachers. I can see that there isn't any abalone on board, but I bet that it's on the other boat. Yes, that's where it will be, on the other boat.'

The water police looked at a dishevelled Piggy and started to wonder, *Maybe this bloke is a little off his head.*

They all could see that there wasn't any illegal abalone on board or anything else. There was nothing else that they could do.

The skipper of the police boat said to Piggy, 'There's nothing here. Let's go home.'

There wasn't anything else left for Piggy to do but go and sit down the stern of the boat and sulk.

The water police quickly headed back to where they had come from.

Teddy pointed the Shark Cat towards the St Kilda Marina.

He rang Tony who said he was ready and waiting.

When the Shark Cat came into view, Tony backed the trailer into the water.

Teddy drove it up onto the trailer, and he and all the boys climbed down.

'Let's grab a taxi and get home and relax. It will be a couple of hours until Barry and the crew get in and dock,' Teddy suggested.

Slither could see the boat ramp from the marina.

He saw that Tony had backed the trailer for the Shark Cat into the water, and he saw Teddy drive the boat onto it and the boys all get out and stretch and limber up their bodies.

He noticed that they all looked relaxed and were happy. Slither thought, *Yes, you pricks are happy now. Just wait until Detective Karl and his boss find out that you are back in town. They have a nasty surprise in line for Barry and Teddy.*

Slither smirked to himself. He had better make himself scarce when Barry came in.

He wondered just how big the reward would be.

Things were looking up.

He made his way to the payphone on the marina and dialled Karl's number.

Karl's phone rang.

A voice on the end said, 'It's me. I'm ringing to tell you that Teddy and the divers are back in port. They have just put their Shark Cat onto a trailer and have headed off in a taxi. Barry should be in shortly. I'd give him a couple of hours.'

Karl thanked Slither and turned to his boss Ray Boyd and said, 'That was the odd-job man down at the marina. He said that Barry would be in port in a couple of hours.'

Ray answered, 'Well, I reckon that it's only fair that we arrange a welcoming committee to meet them.'

Karl laughed and said, 'I bet we scare the shit out of Barry. Let's hope we can convince him that it will be the best to come clean, for his own sake.'

Both the men smiled.

They were confident that they would soon find out what had happened to Detective Jack Andrews.

Barry steamed through the heads of Port Phillip Bay.

He said to Hilda and Des, 'Teddy rang and told me that the fisheries had stopped them and had a look in his boat. He said that we should expect the same treatment.'

Des laughed, 'I hope that it's Piggy. It will give him the shits when he sees we are empty.'

Barry smiled and said, 'Mate, he has got to get out of bed a bit earlier than he has been to tackle us.'

Hilda asked, 'Has he ever sprung you or Teddy?'

'No, love, not yet,' said Barry, 'but it's not for the want of trying.'

Both he and Des laughed.

Barry told Hilda that it had been close when they went out and had a jump on the New Zealand Star Bank. If it hadn't been for Des bumping into that bastard Slither, then they might have been in the shit big time.

Des laughed and said, 'You know the rules, mate. You have got to keep your ear to the ground at all times.'

Barry muttered, 'that fucking Slither, someone is gunna have to shorten him up, for all our sakes.'

A thoughtful silence descended on the wheelhouse.

The water police in their sleek pursuit craft came out of nowhere and were beside Barry's boat in what seemed like an instant.

Barry throttled back and allowed the police craft to be tied up alongside.

Piggy was in his element.

'Ahoy there,' he yelled, 'prepare to be boarded and searched.'

With that, a couple of fisheries officers clambered aboard Barry's boat.

Piggy walked up to the wheelhouse and said to Barry, 'We are going to search your boat for illegal abalone.'

'Help yourself,' Barry offered.

Piggy instructed his members to do a search of the vessel.

They looked from end to end, but all to no avail. There was no abalone on board.

Barry looked at a crestfallen Piggy and asked, 'Why do you keep picking on us? We are law-abiding citizens, just taking the boat out for a run and enjoying ourselves.'

Piggy started to go red.

He slowly said, 'You lot are poachers. I know that you are poachers and you know you are too. One day I will catch you red-handed and you will all go to jail. You wait and see!'

Barry said, not unkindly, 'Mate, take your hand off it. We are not poachers. We are honest fun-loving sportsmen and woman just enjoying the autumn of our lives.'

Piggy looked at the water policemen and said, 'Get back into the boat. Today's not our day.'

With that, Piggy and the others made their way back aboard the police vessel.

Within minutes, they were a speck on the horizon, heading back to Geelong.

Barry pushed the throttle down and steered towards the St Kilda Marina.

Ray Boyd and Karl watched from afar as Barry steered the seventy-footer into its mooring space. They watched as the boat was expertly positioned in place.

Des tied up the bow, and Hilda tied up the stern. Des ran a stringer line from the stern to the wharf. This would help keep the boat away from the wharf.

Barry said, 'Let's just get home. We can take everything off the boat tomorrow.'

Des and Hilda went up the wharf, and Barry followed.

Suddenly Ray and Karl appeared.

Ray said, 'Barry, we want to ask you a few questions about the disappearance of Detective Jack Andrews. Come down to the station where we can talk to you in private.'

Barry hesitated, 'What the fuck do you pricks want from me?'

Karl said, 'Mate, just come down so we can have a talk with you. We have got some questions for you to answer.'

'What if I refuse?' Barry asked.

'Then we will formally charge you with the murder of Jack Andrews. My advice is to accompany us now and let us talk to you,' Karl answered.

Barry looked at Des and said, 'Make sure Hilda gets home and ring Teddy. Tell him what is going on.'

Des nodded and said to Hilda, 'Come on, love, we will get you home, and Barry will be back before you have got the fire going.'

Hilda looked at Barry and asked, 'Are you OK?'

Barry said, 'Yes, love, toodle off home with Des, and he will make sure that you are safe and sound. I'll be home before you know it.'

She said, 'OK if that's what you want me to do. I'll call Teddy as soon as I get home.'

Barry walked away with Ray and Karl.

Teddy had had a shower and changed into clean clothes.

Then his phone rang, and he saw it was Barry's landline.

He answered, 'Hullo, Barry mate, long time, no see!'

Hilda was on the other end, and she said, 'Teddy, its Hilda. Barry has been taken down to the police station. That Karl and his boss were waiting for us when we tied up at the marina. They took Barry away for questioning about Jack's disappearance. I'm sure that he doesn't know anything about that. What should I do?'

Teddy took in all the information and said in a calm voice, 'Don't worry. The cops go a bit crazy when one of their own goes missing. They start to pull rabbits out of hats. Don't worry, I'll go in and see if Barry needs a solicitor. Everything is under control.'

With that, Teddy disconnected.

He said to Rita, 'You won't believe this, but the coppers have got Barry in for questioning about the disappearance of that detective.'

'Well, he is living with the detective's missus,' Rita commented.

Teddy seemed to pause for a moment, 'Yes, there is that to it, I suppose. You just don't know what them coppers think.'

Teddy hadn't had anything to drink, so he decided to go to the police headquarters where they had taken Barry and see what was going on.

On the way in, he rang Derek and told him he would be a bit late as there was a problem with Barry. He briefly explained what had happened and said he was going to try and sort things out.

In the police headquarters, Ray and Karl sat across the interview desk from Barry.

The room was Spartan, a desk and three chairs, just like you see on the TV.

Barry looked calm. He looked like a man with nothing to hide.

They started by doing the good cop/bad cop regime.

'Look you fucking idiot,' Karl said. 'We have a witness who saw Jack drive into the marina and wait for you. He said that when you came into the marina, you both went onto your boat, and Jack wasn't seen again. Mate, I'm not Sherlock Holmes, but for fuck sake, one and one make two. It's that simple.'

Ray came in with a soothing voice and said gently, 'Barry we know that you didn't mean to kill Jack. He was a bit off the planet and was probably looking for a fight. He really had the shits about his missus fucking off. And, mate, we weren't there, but you've been around. If someone comes at you, you're gunna belt them. It's that simple.'

Barry looked at the two detectives and said, 'You've got someone spotting me and Jack meeting in the car park, have you?'

Karl said, 'I'm afraid so. It was someone who knows the both of you.'

Barry thought, *that fucking Slither. He's sold me down the drain for the price of a fucking drink.*

Ray said, 'Barry mate, it's open and shut. As far as we are concerned, with the sworn statement from our witness, you'll end up doing fifteen years. Mate, I can tell you that Hilda won't be hanging around. She'll grab some other mug, and while you're sitting in jail, playing with your dick, she'll be out, rooting and having a ball.'

Ray knew that the way to get a mug worried was to say about their partner playing up while they were locked up in jail.

Barry said, 'You blokes should get a job as fiction writers. You make up better stories than anyone whom I've read lately. Like I told you, I've never set eyes on the bloke. I wouldn't know him from a bar of soap. You're looking at the wrong bloke this time and wasting your time. Can I go home now?'

Ray said in a friendly voice, 'Barry mate, we know that you didn't mean to kill him. It was just an accident. It was just one of those things that happen. Listen, mate, you can plead down to manslaughter and fair dinkum you will only get a couple of years. You will be out before you have got used to your bed in jail. These days if it's not premeditated, then you can nearly go home on the same day. Mate, they are as soft as soft once they find out that it wasn't intentional.'

Karl and Ray both knew that if Barry showed the slightest response to the fact that he could get a lesser sentence by pleading guilty to manslaughter, then they had their man. Heaps of crims gave themselves up in this manner.

Barry relaxed and said, 'So you want me to plead guilty to manslaughter to a crime I didn't commit? That doesn't sound too smart to me.'

Ray, who secretly enjoyed sparring with an old-time criminal, said, 'Mate, we are only trying to help. We know you meant no harm to Jack. It wasn't your fault he ended up dead. It was just one of those things that happen sometimes to good people.'

'Well, I'm sorry to disappoint you, but it didn't happen to this good person. Can I go home now?' Barry asked.

Both Ray and Karl knew that they didn't have enough on Barry to hold him.

They also knew that if Barry got legal advice, he would have to be released.

Ray said, 'Barry, we are on to you and your mate Teddy. We are going to build a case against you and you will end up with your arse in jail.'

Barry smiled and said, 'Oh, don't scare me to death. Like a mate of mine says, all jail means to me is three meals a day and my dick sucked whenever I want it. I'll get my teeth fixed and lose some weight. It will be cheaper than a holiday.'

With that, Barry stood up and asked, 'Whose gunna show me out?'

Ray nodded to Karl. He opened the door and directed Barry out to the front reception area.

Teddy stood up as Barry walked through the door.

'Hullo, mate, can't I leave you alone for ten minutes. The minute I let you out of my sight, you get yourself into trouble.'

Barry gave a shrug, smiled, and said, 'Let's get a pot into us.'

Teddy smiled and said, 'My shout.'

Teddy and Barry drove to a pub in Port Melbourne, and Barry went through all that had happened in the police station.

When he had finished, Teddy said, 'Mate, it's just as we thought. They know fuck all. I'm not a Rhodes Scholar, but I do know that you and Jack didn't meet in the car park. He was waiting for you when you got on board.'

Barry shook his head and said, 'I bet it's that fucking Slither. They are giving him money, and he's leading them on. Telling them what they want to hear. He would be their star witness.'

Teddy shook his head, 'I bet they are promising him the world, and he's dumb enough to go along with them.'

They both looked up as Des walked into the beer garden, and, on spotting them, he came over to their table.

'Hullo, boys,' he said. 'I knew you would be out and about. They haven't got anything on you, have they?'

Barry shook his head, 'Des mate, they reckon that they have got a witness who can put me at the marina talking to Jack and then apparently we went onto my boat and he wasn't seen after that.'

Des said in disbelief, 'A fucking witness. Who would that be?'

Barry and Teddy looked at Des.

'That fucking Slither. He would give his mother up for a warm slab of beer,' Des said, shaking his head.

Barry said, 'Des, I didn't see or talk to Jack in the car park. It didn't happen.'

Des said what they were all thinking, 'Someone's got to do something about Slither before he says or does something stupid.'

The three friends all nodded grimly.

Detective Inspector Ray Boyd looked at Karl and said, 'We need a statement off that drunk down at the marina. We want him to say that he saw Jack talking to Barry on the morning that Jack went missing. We need him to say that he then saw Jack get onto Barry's boat, that he saw Teddy arrive, and that they all went out to sea and only two came back.'

Karl smiled and said, 'That shouldn't be too hard. I'll tell him that the reward will be $10,000 or $20,000. That should get his juices running. I reckon that he would give up Christ himself for that sort of bonanza.'

Ray smiled at Karl and said, 'You had better go down and keep him sweet. Give him a $100 to show we really care about him.'

When Karl walked along the wharf, Slither was as usual, looking like he was busy cleaning up and sweeping.

'Gidday, mate,' Karl said. 'How are things? My boss is over the moon with you and the assistance that you are giving us in solving the disappearance of Jack. If it wasn't for you, we wouldn't have a clue about Jack's car being here all day. You have been a real help, and we don't forget our friends. The boss wants you to have lunch on him. He gave me this $100 to give you for a counter lunch.'

Slither looked hungrily at the green note.

He thought, *Counter lunch, my arse. I'll spend it on the drink and buy a pie on the way home.*

Home to Slither was a room in a run-down boarding house in the back streets of St Kilda. It was run by an obese woman who was a bad-tempered ex-whore.

She could swear like a man, and, when necessary, she could fight like a man. She was vile of both nature and temperament.

The name she went by was Rosie Box.

When she introduced herself, she would say, 'I'm Rosie Box and that's just what it smells like, roses.'

With that, she would throw her head back and roar with laughter, leaving no doubt that she was a woman of very low moral standing.

It was thought that she was the one who christened Slither with that nickname.

A rich Jew in Melbourne owned the boarding house, and he had given Rosie the job of managing it for free accommodation and a per cent of the rental income. So Rosie was very particular that the rent was always paid on time.

Slither was frightened of her as were most of the tenants.

Teddy rang Derek and said, 'Mate, we are over all our problems. Where shall we meet to pick up the money?'

Derek said, 'It looks like the fisheries have stopped their stake-out, but I'm still not too sure about you being seen here. So what do you say that we meet in a couple of hours at Curly's shed and you can whack the money up there?'

Teddy smiled and said, 'Sounds good to me, mate. We'll be there then.'

He rang all the boys, and they agreed to meet at Curly's shed.

Teddy asked Barry, 'Are you going to grab Hilda and bring her along?'

Barry nodded his head and said, 'There's no show without punch.'

Teddy smiled. He was pleased for Barry that he and Hilda were getting along so well.

All the group were at Curly's shed when Derek arrived.

Derek had with him the standard Target shopping bag full of money.

He tipped it onto the pool table and said with a grin, 'First in best dressed.'

Teddy was the only one who moved towards the money.

Derek said, 'First load was 1,200 kilos and the second load was 1,150 kilos. We ended up with total of 2,350 kilos. At the going rate of $40 a kilo, that equals to $94,000.'

Teddy did the sums.

He scribbled down a few things and said, 'Twenty per cent for Barry equals $18,800. $1,000 for Tony, and he has to pay Mario out of that. We didn't get any abalone for Henry. So that means we have got to split up $74,200. If we divide that into four even parts, we all end up with $18,550. Is everyone happy with that?'

All the boys laughed and agreed that it wasn't a bad earn.

Barry and Hilda took their $18,800, and Barry said, 'I'm going to pay Des $3,000. We used about $4,000 in fuel and provisions so that leaves you and me to split up, leaving us with $5,900 each.'

Hilda was more than happy with that.

She tried to tell Barry that he was far too generous, but Barry just laughed it off and said, 'It's a joy going to sea with you and all the boys. I don't need the money, and I really enjoy taking out the boat and smelling the clean fresh air.'

He looked at Hilda and said, 'You know I'm really happy.'

Hilda smiled and said, 'Barry, I'm really happy too. My life has changed completely since I've met you and Teddy and all the boys. I couldn't have dreamt of being this way.'

Barry smiled, but he knew that dark clouds were gathering.

He had to do something about the witness who claimed that he and Jack were together on the day of Jack's disappearance.

Des was at his local hotel.

Barry had rung and said that there was $3,000 waiting for him.

Des said that he would be around the next day to pick it up and asked if Barry wanted a hand to clean up the boat. Des thought that Barry was as happy as Des had seen him since his wife had passed away. He felt glad for his old friend.

Des was thinking about going home when Slither walked into the pub where he was having his drink.

Slither made his way over to the bar, sat down beside Des, and said to the barman, 'Two pots and two rums. Thanks, mate.'

Des looked at Slither and said, 'You seem to be killing the pig these days. You always seem to have a pot of beer and a rum chaser at the ready.'

Slither looked drunkenly at Des and said, 'Yes, mate, a bloke and I are doing a bit of business. I've got what he wants, and he's got plenty. Soon I'll be in the big time. I'll have money to burn. All I've got to do is keep my eyes open, and everything will be sweet.'

Des said, 'Good on you, mate. You deserve a good run. You've been doing it a bit tough the last couple of years.'

'Well, all that will be over shortly. I'll be in front and living the good life,' Slither said.

'Good on you, mate,' Des said. 'I wish you all the best.'

Slither gathered himself and got closer to Des.

'I'm not all that smart, and I can't read tea leaves, but I reckon that Barry and maybe Teddy are gunna be in the shit over that Detective Jack's disappearance.'

Des pretended not to take a lot of notice.

He laughed and said, 'That Barry is pretty smart. He and Teddy are too smart to make any stupid mistakes.'

Slither touched the side of his nose with a straightened finger and said, 'They aren't that smart. There are people who know what happened to that Jack. And there are people who could be of a great assistance to them.'

Des smiled and said, 'What do you mean?'

Slither was suddenly reluctant to say anymore.

He simply said, 'Wait and see, my friend. Wait and see.'

Des's mind was racing.

He knew that Teddy and Barry were aware that Slither had been giving up to Detective Jack Andrews when they went away. Now that Jack was missing, Des reckoned that Detective Karl had taken on Jack's snouts.

It all became clear to Des.

Slither was the witness for the coppers.

He was spilling his guts, and he had told them that Jack had been seen talking to Barry on the morning of his disappearance. He had told them that Jack had gone onto Barry's boat and was never seen again.

Des realised that Slither was the copper's strongest witness, and so he made a decision.

He said to Slither, 'Mate, why don't we go down to Barry's boat. There is a bottle of Bundy Rum on board. We can have a drink in peace and get away from all these people.'

Slither was almost broke.

He thought, *Why not? Me and Des will go and have a drink on Barry's boat. Fuck him, he's got plenty.*

With that, the pair made their way down to the marina.

Des jumped on Barry's boat and felt for where Barry left the key.

The marina was swathed in darkness, and there was no one around. Des turned on some lights, and the two men sat in the wheelhouse and started drinking straight rum.

'That Barry is a good bloke. He is the first to hit his kick if someone needs a hand up,' Des said.

'Yes,' said Slither, 'he always makes sure that I'm right for a drink. He wouldn't leave anyone out.'

'I remember him and me fighting side by side in many pubs in Tasmania,' Des recalled.

Slither was close to tears, 'Yer, he's been good to me over the years. He always made sure that I had a drink each Christmas. He never forgot me, not once.'

Des sadly said, 'There is some bastard out there who reckons that he saw Jack and Barry talking together the day that Jack disappeared. That can't be true.'

Slither was quiet.

He gently said, 'Des mate, I had to give him up. There's a $20,000 reward. Mate, it's a fortune.'

Des said in disgust, 'How could you do that? How could you put in a mate?'

Slither looked Des square in the eyes and said, 'How could you do what you did? You gave Barry, Teddy, and the boys up when they left you out of that trip up to the NSW border. Jack told me he listened to the tape and that it was your voice on it.'

Des was shattered.

He stared at Slither.

Slither drunkenly sneered at Des, 'I'm gunna tell them it was you. You think that you are so fucking smart, hanging out with Barry and Teddy. They won't want you cleaning their shithouses after they find out that it was you who shelved them to the fisheries.'

Something snapped in Des's head.

He lunged at Slither who was taken completely off guard.

Des started to choke Slither.

His arms flayed around, but he was no match for Des.

Des held Slither in a vice-like grip.

Slither made a gurgling sound.

He passed out, and Des let him hit the floor of the wheelhouse.

Des collected his thoughts, *what to do? What to do?*

A thought came to Des, *There's only one place for him, and that's over the side.*

Des half-carried Slither out of the wheelhouse and lowered his head and shoulders down towards the dark waters.

He held onto his feet and let his head submerge into the water. Nothing happened for a brief period.

Suddenly Slither started to kick his feet and tried to swim, but Des had a firm grip onto his legs.

Slither slowly stopped all movement.

Des hung onto the legs until he was sure that Slither was still.

He slowly let go of Slither's legs, and he floated face-down in the water.

Des was sure that his secret was safe.

He went and got another drink, and when he came out, he could make out Slither's body in the water still lying face-down.

'You're a fucking dog,' Des said to the lifeless Slither. 'You got your right whack. You won't be telling any more coppers what my mates are up to.'

Des decided to get going.

He turned off the lights on Barry's boat and made his way from the marina.

Slither's body lay still in the cold water.

Piggy was in a quandary. He knew that Teddy and his divers had got past him and the fisheries.

He screwed up his forehead and rubbed his hand through his hair.

There must be some way of working out how Teddy was getting the abalone past them.

He thought that he had everything covered.

The arresting at sea hadn't worked, and staking-out the factory hadn't worked.

Maybe Derek's factory wasn't the one that they were processing their abalone in. He only had Jack's word about that, and now Jack had vanished.

Piggy slowly shook his head. He didn't know what to do next.

He was out of ideas, and he knew that his bosses were getting agitated at his lack of performance.

He had to come up with a plan—one that would work, and he needed to do it quickly.

The two detectives were looking at the white board the next morning.

Ray said, 'I reckon that we should put some pressure onto Teddy and Hilda. Let's see if we can squeeze something out of them.'

Karl suggested, 'We can tell Teddy that we want to arrest him for the illegal disposal of a body. And we can tell Hilda we are going to charge her with being an accessory to murder.'

Ray shook his head, 'That Teddy is too smart to tumble to something like that. He will just ask where the body is. And we are stuffed, as we can't come up with a body. If we are right, we will never recover the body from the bay. It will be impossible to find, and depending on how long it has been in the water, there may be nothing left.'

Karl was convinced.

They were in a hopeless situation.

Sometimes amateur fishermen fish around the jetties at the marina.

Although the gates are locked, now and again, boat owners will leave the gates ajar, and fishermen, mostly young lads, sneak through and have a fish.

Two such amateur fishermen were casting soft plastic lures around the pilings.

Little Robbie and Johnny were having the time of their lives. They were casting out and retrieving their lures in an action that made the lure look like a fish that was wounded.

Then Robbie cast and let his lure sink to the bottom. As he flicked the end of his rod, he felt the lure snag onto something.

In an excited voice, he said to Robbie, 'Fuck mate, I think I've snagged something.'

His fishing rod bent almost double.

'Don't lose the lure,' Robbie warned. 'They are almost $10 each.'

'Whatever it is, it's slowly coming to the surface,' Johnny laughed.

'Be fucking careful,' Robbie cautioned.

They were both looking into the water when all at once a body appeared through the murky water.

The two friends were speechless. The lure was hooked into Slither's arm, and as they watched, his hand slowly came out of the water in a reaching movement towards them.

'Fuck me,' Robbie screamed and bolted up the wharf.

Johnny dropped his fishing rod and followed him.

The rod jammed itself behind an upright fender on the wharf, leaving Slither's open hand out of the water as if he was asking for assistance.

The two terrified lads ran up to the office and told a startled receptionist that they had hooked onto a dead body.

The boys explained where the body was, and the receptionist called for a senior member of the boat sales team to go and have a look.

He made his way importantly down the wharf.

When he saw the fishing rod, he looked over the side. Slither's hand was moving slightly in the water.

The salesman had a crazy thought. He had once heard the Queen saying that when she waved to the crowds, she made a gesture as if she was replacing a globe.

Slither's hand was slowly moving from the ripples and currents in the water just like that. It was unnerving.

He quickly made his way back to the office, and, in a shaky voice, he asked the receptionist to call the police. She immediately dialled triple zero and asked for the police.

Two young constables, both female, pulled up at the marina. The salesman walked up to them and said, 'There's a body in the water down jetty number two. Two young boys found it a couple of minutes ago when they were fishing.'

The two constables walked quickly down the jetty.

When they got to the fishing rod, they looked over the edge and saw the grotesque hand seemingly reaching out to them.

The older of the police women looked at the younger one and said, 'Whoever it is. They are dead. We will ring it through and get the meat wagon here.'

The younger constable looked a bit green. The older one asked, 'Is this your first floater?'

'Yer,' the younger one said, nodding her head.

The other replied, 'Just wait until they have found a body that's been floating in the sea for week in the middle of summer. That puts you off your tea.'

The younger constable said, 'I can hardly wait.'

They rang it through, and news soon got to Ray and Karl, who jumped into a car and made their way down to the marina.

A small crowd had gathered around the office.

Someone had bought the young boys a can of drink. But they both refused the offer of a pie.

The police divers went in and retrieved the body. Soon it was on a stretcher, and someone from the sales office identified it as Slither.

One of the sales people volunteered, 'He was a good sort of a bloke. He drank a bit, but he was always friendly. You could find him down here seven days a week. I don't know where he lived.'

Karl and Ray looked at the lifeless body, and they both thought to themselves, *there goes our only chance of getting Barry for Jack's murder.*

Ray looked at Karl and said, 'Well, Barry has to be our number one suspect.'

'Do you reckon that Barry knew that Slither was going to testify against him?' Karl asked.

Ray responded, 'We have to assume that he was in the know and got rid of our number one witness.'

'There is a possibility that Slither got pissed and fell into the water and drowned by himself, without anyone's assistance,' Karl suggested.

'We will have to wait for the autopsy to come through. Let's get a statement from the young blokes, who hooked him up,' Ray said.

The two young fishermen had gotten over the shock of Slither's hand reaching up for them and were enjoying their five minutes of fame.

Karl asked them what their names were.

Ray smiled to himself at the eagerness of the young boys to tell all. It would only be a matter of time, and they would grow to hate the coppers. *Goes with the territory, I suppose,* he thought.

The body was taken away for an autopsy, everyone went about their business, and the boys retrieved their fishing rods and went home to tell everyone about their adventure.

Barry and Hilda made their way down to the marina.

On the walk to their boat, another boat owner said to Barry, 'It was bad luck about Slither, wasn't it?'

Barry didn't know what he was talking about.

'What do you mean?' he asked.

The boat owner was happy to be the bearer of the news, 'Well, they fished him out of the water this morning. He must have got pissed and fell in and drowned. Poor bugger.'

Barry looked at Hilda and said, 'Well, I'll be stuffed. Imagine that. Those coppers will be on to me about my whereabouts last night anytime now.'

Hilda looked at Barry. 'Dear me, it's sad the poor, poor man. I feel sorry for him all the same.'

'Yer, he didn't have much going for him, poor bastard,' Barry conceded.

Barry rang Teddy, 'Mate, I'm at the marina. They just fished Slither's body out of the drink. It looks like he fell in and drowned. A couple of kids fished it out this morning.'

Teddy answered, 'Shit, that's bad luck. I wonder what happened. I'll come down for a look.'

'See you soon,' Barry said.

Barry rang Des, 'Mate, that bastard Slither was found in the water. He must have slipped and fallen in, poor bugger.'

Des sounded amazed, 'Holy shit, I only had a drink with him last night. We had a couple of pots with a rum chaser. I'm on my way down. I'll see you in a couple of minutes.'

Barry hung up and said to Hilda, 'Both Teddy and Des are on their way down. We'll put on the kettle and have a cuppa with them when they arrive.'

Hilda busied herself, getting the kettle ready.

Teddy and Des walked down the jetty together to Barry's boat and climbed aboard.

'Gidday, Hilda. Gidday, Barry. Hey, that was bad news about Slither,' Teddy said sadly.

Barry replied, 'Mate, you don't know when your time is up.'

'I had a beer with him only last night,' Des said. 'He was happy as Larry. We had a couple of pots, and both left at the same time. I went home, and I thought that he was heading home as well. He must have come down here for a look-about first.'

Teddy replied, 'Yes, he was a bit of a gig.'

Des thought, *If I act surprised, then nobody will put me with him when he met his doom.*

'He was pretty pissed when we parted,' Des said to no one in particular.

Barry asked, 'Does anybody know where he lives?'

Des said, 'He lives in a boarding house just around the corner. It's run by Rosie Box. She is one tough motherfucker.'

'Someone had better let her know,' Barry said.

'I can do that on my way home,' Des offered.

Barry handed Des a roll of notes and said, 'Thanks for your help on the trip. It made a real difference having someone whom we can trust running over the abalone meat.'

'No worries,' said Des, 'I'm available whenever you need me.'

Barry answered, 'Thanks mate.'

'I'll go around and tell Rosie that her star tenant has given up smoking,' Des said. 'I hope that she doesn't want to shoot the messenger.'

Teddy said, 'She might want to root the messenger.'

Des looked at his mates, 'I reckon that I would prefer getting shot.'

Everyone smiled.

Des made his way around to Rosie's boarding house.

It was a run-down mansion, and Des knew that it was always full of deadbeats.

There was an abundance of this sort of people who filled in a group just above the homeless.

He knocked on the door that had a sign 'Manager' on it.

It was about lunchtime, and Rosie was cooking up some lamb chops to eat.

She turned off the gas and waddled out to see who it was.

When she opened the door, she recognised Des.

'Hullo, Des love, how have you been keeping?'

He smiled and said, 'Oh, I'm all right, but I've got some bad news. Slither was found dead in the water down at the marina this morning.'

Rosie took a step back.

She said, 'Really. Oh, that's so sad. How did it happen?'

'No one really knows,' Des said. 'They reckon that he might have been drunk and tripped and fell into the water.'

Rosie smiled sadly, 'Poor bugger couldn't swim. Did you know that?'

'He couldn't swim?' Des questioned.

'No,' Rosie said. 'The poor bastard couldn't swim a stroke to save himself.'

She took a step back and said, 'Come in, and we'll drink to his memory.'

Des couldn't refuse.

Rosie made her way into the good room of the apartment and indicated where Des should sit. She opened a cupboard and got out a bottle of brandy and a bottle of port. Then she got two beer glasses, half-filled them with brandy, and then topped them up with port.

Rosie said, 'Port wine and brandy, nectar of the gods.'

They touched their glasses together in a salute, and Des said, 'Here's to Slither. May his journey to wherever he is going be swift.'

With that, they both swallowed almost all their drinks.

'Whoa!' Des gasped. 'That's pretty potent.'

Rosie had tears in her eyes. 'He was a good man with a lot of good points. He always paid his rent on pension day, never missed.'

Des finished his drink, and Rosie emptied hers.

She made an effort to renew their drinks.

He said, 'I had better get going as I've got to do a bit with Barry.'

'You're not going to leave me on my own to grieve a dear friend, are you?' Rosie asked sadly.

'Well, I suppose another little drink won't hurt,' Des conceded.

Rosie had the glasses filled in a second.

She handed one to Des.

He raised it and said, 'Here's to the girl who lives on the hill. If she won't, then maybe her sister will.'

Rosie threw her head back and roared with laughter.

Des started to warm to her.

They both threw their drinks down, and Rosie refilled them again.

'I hate to think of Slither dying on his own in the cold water,' Rosie said.

'Well, I was with him just before he went in,' Des said. 'We were having a drink at the local. Then I went on my way home, and he went his way. I thought that he was heading here to his room, but he must have gone down to the wharf for some reason.'

Rosie asked, 'Why the fuck would he go down to the marina that late at night?'

She shook her head and swallowed the rest of her drink.

'Whose gunna bury him?' Des asked as he reached for his glass that Rosie had refilled again. The drinks were getting stronger, but Des had always enjoyed a strong drink.

Rosie said, 'I suppose that I will have to as he didn't have any family, least none who he spoke about. He seemed to be a bit of a loner, stayed to himself, and didn't welcome family or friends.'

Des spoke sadly, 'I didn't even know his right name. I just stuck with Slither.'

'William James McKenzie was his proper name,' Rosie said. 'He told me that one day. We were having a drink, and we started talking about old times. He told me his name and how he never got on with his family. He had always been a big drinker, and his family was some strange religion that was against the drink, so they drifted apart. Some nights when he wasn't too drunk, he would call in to see me and have a drink. We had some fun together.'

Des finished his drink and said, 'I bet you made him happy. You were probably the only friend whom he had.'

Rosie said, 'He used to talk about you a bit. He seemed to like you. He always used to say, "Des wouldn't let me go without a drink. He always looks out for me".' Des felt guilty and a little drunk.

He reached into his pocket and pulled out the $3,000. He separated $1,000 and said to Rosie, 'Put this towards his funeral costs. I'm gunna miss the little fellow.'

Rosie thought, *That was easy.*

The fact that Slither had never mentioned Des to her at all made no difference.

Rosie had always believed in the old saying, *why muck up a good story with the truth?*

It had been her plan all along to make Des feel as though he should contribute to the cost of Slither's funeral.

She would get the salvos to bury him. It wouldn't cost her a cent, and she would pocket any money that was put up for the funeral.

Rosie adjusted her blouse to let her ample bosom reveal a lot of cleavage.

She noticed Des taking an interest.

So she leaned across the table, took Des's hand, and put it on her breast.

Des looked at her and said, 'How about it?'

Rosie smiled and said, 'How about what?'

He simply said, 'A root.'

Rosie said, 'It will cost you a hundred.'

'Cheap at twice the price,' he answered.

Rosie got out of her chair and walked Des to the bedroom.

She thought to herself, *you've still got it, girl.*

Ray and Karl knew that the only hope was that somehow Barry would buckle under pressure, but they both also realised that now they didn't have a lot to pressure Barry with.

They made for the local pub and asked the barman, who looked as if he was on the verge of dying from high blood pressure, if he had seen Slither the night before.

Dan, the barman, recognised Karl from a previous visit. His head pounded. *Fuck the piss,* he thought.

He answered Karl's question, 'Yer, he was in most of last night. He and another bloke left just before closing time. They were both pretty pissed.'

'Isn't there a law about serving drunks?' Ray queried.

In an act of defiance, Dan said, 'I've served plenty of drunken coppers.'

'Be that as is it may be. You said that Slither went home with someone?' Ray asked.

'Him and Des went out the door together,' Dan said. 'I don't know where they went or what they did after that.'

Ray looked at the drink-sodden barman and said, 'Well, Slither ended up dead.'

'Fuck me,' Dan said. 'How did it happen?'

Karl butted in and said, 'We reckon that he went down to the marina for a look about and fell or was pushed into the water and drowned.'

Dan looked a bit shocked, 'Well, bugger me, who would have thought? Shit, he was only here last night. I served him and Des pots with rum chasers. Well, I'll be stuffed.'

Ray asked, 'When will Des be in?'

Dan screwed up his face and said, 'Later on today, that's if he's not working. He sometimes goes away for a couple of days.'

Ray didn't bother to tell the barman that, in fact, Des had just returned home and he wouldn't be going anywhere for a while.

He turned to Karl and said, 'Let's get going.'

With that, both the detectives walked out of the pub into the bright sunlight.

When they got into their car, Ray said, 'We had better check out where Barry was last night and then catch up with Des.'

Teddy and Barry had a quiet chat. They both realised that it was a stroke of good fortune that Slither had met his end.

They both knew that he was selling them down the drain to the police and from there the fisheries were being notified.

'This should make things a bit easier for us when we go diving,' Teddy said.

Barry nodded his head and said, 'Yes, the old bastard must have rung the coppers every time we made a move.'

'And still the fisheries couldn't get near us,' Teddy commented.

'Well, that's one problem fixed,' Barry said. 'I wonder how Des got on with Rosie at the boarding house.'

Des slowly regained consciousness.

He was in a massive bed and was lying beside Rosie who was naked.

It slowly came back to Des.

No more port wine and brandy before lunch.

Cursing himself, he made a vow not to tumble into that again.

He slowly moved, and Rosie was instantly awake.

Years of training had taught her that if you didn't get your money before they rooted you, you had to get it off them as soon as they woke up.

'Ah, you're back with us, Des love. Did you have a good sleep? You're pretty active for a bloke your age.'

Rosie rolled over and pushed her breasts into Des.

'Do you want to go again?' she asked hungrily.

Rosie had seen the wad of money and thought that she had a chance of getting more of it.

'Shit,' Des exploded. 'Is that the time? Barry will be wondering what has become of me. I've got to get back.'

With that, Des got out of bed and started to get into his jeans.

'Sure you don't want desert?' Rosie asked.

Des laughed and said, 'I'm an old man. I'll have to take a rain check on that.'

Rosie realised that it was over.

She got up and wrapped herself in a dressing gown.

'Don't forget you owe me a spot,' she said.

Des quickly got out the $100 and gave it to Rosie. 'Thanks, love, you're terrific.'

Rosie answered, 'I'm always here if you feel like a drink and a bit of fun.'

Des bolted out the door and headed towards the marina.

Rosie returned to the stove and took over from where she had left off with the lamb chops $1,100 richer.

She was a good earner.

Ray and Karl were talking.

'I'm betting that he was pissed,' Ray said. 'If we speak to Des, we'll find out just how pissed he was.'

Karl commented, 'He's probably pissed all the time, the old "I've never had a hangover" type.'

Both the detectives nodded. They made their way down to the hotel and waited for Des to appear.

After he got away from Rosie, Des hightailed it to the pub.

When he walked inside, he immediately saw Karl and Ray waiting for him.

They walked over, and Karl said, 'We want to ask you some questions about your mate Slither.'

'I don't know anything about Slither,' Des replied.

'You were with him last night until closing time, and then you both went home,' Ray stated.

Des looked at the two detectives. 'I didn't go home with Slither. I left him in the street outside. I thought that he was going home.'

Karl said, 'So you didn't go anywhere else for a drink?'

'No, mate,' Des said, 'I went my way, and he went his way. Like I said, I thought he was going home. We had had plenty by then.'

'You didn't get into a blue over something?' Ray asked.

'No, mate,' Des answered, 'we got on all right. I was probably his best friend. We always had a drink together.'

Ray looked Des straight in the eyes and said, 'We'll be looking further into this. We'll get to the bottom of it.'

Teddy and Barry were having a drink and talking about the timely demise of Slither.

Barry said, 'It was a blessing in disguise, mate. If Slither hadn't ended up in the drink, then we would have had to do something about the useless prick.'

Teddy slowly shook his head and said, 'He let himself down by ringing up and putting us in for every move that we made. He was walking a fine line.'

Both the men took a drink from their pots.

Barry said, 'If he is the only witness that the coppers have got, then we are sweet.'

'Yes, it looks like we are all clear. We shouldn't hear from the coppers again,' Teddy said.

Detectives Ray and Karl were waiting for the autopsy.

When it came, Ray looked at the amount of alcohol in Slither's blood.

'Fuck me dead,' Ray said. 'I'm surprised that he didn't spontaneously combust. He was about ten times over the legal limit.'

Karl said, 'He drank every day. Or I should say that he got into a drunken condition every day, week in, week out. If he didn't have the money for beer, then he would drink wine. If he couldn't afford wine, then he would drink anything that he could lift up to his lips as long as it was alcoholic.'

Ray said, 'It says here that his liver and kidneys were shot. They had completely had it. It's funny, but those old drunks just keep on keeping on.'

'What else does it say?' Karl asked.

'Well, it looked like he had given up eating as there was hardly any food in his stomach. He must have just lived off the drink,' Ray said.

Karl was starting to feel a bit sad about Slither's condition. 'Poor bugger. We should have taken him out for a meal sometime.'

Ray commented, 'I reckon that he was too far gone. After subjecting himself to years of alcohol abuse, he probably couldn't eat any more than a handful of food at a time.'

'A bit like those prisoners of war after the Japs had starved them for years,' Karl said.

Ray nodded. 'He probably only had a couple of years, or maybe even months, to live at the rate he was drinking.'

He went on to say that there were marks around his throat that could indicate he was strangled a bit before he ended up in the water.

But there was salt water in his lungs, so that meant that he was alive and breathing when he entered the water.

There was also some slight bruising around his ankles. That might indicate that he was strangled and then put head first into the water and held in an upright position until he drowned.

This could be the work of Barry, Teddy, or Des.

Karl screwed up his face and said, 'Let's start with Barry. He is the one under the hammer. We reckon that he killed Jack and he and Teddy dumped the body out in the bay. Slither was the only one who noticed that Jack's car was in the car park all day. So he is the one most likely to have been able to put Jack and Barry together. Next there is Teddy. Slither reckoned that Barry and Teddy took the boat out for a run. When they came back, there was no sign of Jack and he hasn't been seen since. Next, we have the last known person to see Slither, Des. He was with him on the night that he died. Maybe they had an argument, as drunks do. It could have been about anything. Maybe Slither owed Des some money and wouldn't or couldn't pay it back and Des got a bit stroppy. They started to argue, and Des choked him and hung his body in the water until Slither stopped breathing.'

Ray said, 'All highly likely. But we have no proof. All we know is that Slither was drunk and drowned. The marks around his throat could be there due to any reason. It might be a coincidence that he had bruises around his ankles.'

Rosie Box had told all her tenants that her dear friend Slither had unfortunately passed away and his funeral was coming up soon.

She made it known that she was going to have to pay for the funeral as she was under the impression that Slither didn't have any family and the only friends whom he had were his 'new family' where they all lived.

Rosie wiped a tear as it slowly ran down her fat cheek.

She said in a trembling voice, 'If any one of you could please put in a small amount to help with the funeral costs, it would be greatly appreciated. I'm sure that Slither would do the same for you. Tomorrow is pension day, so if you all could put in an amount, I'll pass it on to the undertakers.'

There was silence in the room as all the down-and-outs wondered just how they were going to dodge their landlady between tomorrow and the funeral.

But they assured each other that it was the least that they could do, especially seeing that Slither was a wonderful human being and generous beyond belief.

They told stories amongst themselves about how he would never see someone without a drink and how he would go without if his friends ever needed something.

Each one boasted how they had helped Slither over the years that they had known him and how he had helped them and never asked for anything in return.

Yes, he was a saint and a person who would be sadly missed.

They would make sure that his funeral was a big one and that there was plenty of food and drink so Slither could be sent off in the manner fit for a champion of the people.

Rosie watched her tenants talking and making claims, each one bigger than the last.

She thought there might be a bigger earn than she had thought.

She had already spoken to the Salvation Army, and a pink-cheeked officer had assured her that they would do all they could for her dear friend and, of course, they would bury him in a proper grave, not some mass burial plot.

Rosie had wept and kissed the officer's hand.

The trusting salvation officer shook his head and was saddened for Rosie at her loss.

This is what he had joined the Salvation Army for—to help the needy and support the poor.

He spoke to his superior and was a little taken aback by the attitude of his senior as he didn't seem to be as enthusiastic as he was.

The older man remembered years before a similar incident when he himself was approached by a woman who needed support to bury her friend.

It came out after the funeral that the woman had raised funds for the funeral and hadn't passed the money raised on to the Salvation Army.

Was this history repeating itself? He wondered.

Ray and Karl decided to get Barry, Teddy, and Des in for questioning. Ray said he would ring them up and ask them to come in for an interview.

If they refuse, then he would tell them that he would send out a divvy van with a couple of officers and bring them in that way.

Ray explained to Karl that this was an easier way of getting them in.

The crims felt a bit more in control of the situation if they brought themselves in.

Sometimes they brought along their solicitors. If they did, it was a sign that they were guilty or were worried that something might come up.

Ray got to the phone and rang Teddy.

After a bit of discussion, Teddy agreed to come in.

Barry was reluctant, but when Ray explained that he would organise a divvy van to pick him up, he also agreed to come in.

When Ray spoke to Des, he found Des reluctant to be of any assistance at all and was very abrupt. Alarm bells started ringing in Ray's head. This was what he had hoped for—someone to show their hand.

He thought to himself, *this is interesting. Maybe Des has something to hide. After all, he was possibly the last person to talk to Slither.*

He and Karl schemed up a series of questions to ask the trio.

Barry arrived first and was taken to an interview room where Ray and Karl were waiting.

In one wall was a mirror, it appeared to be a normal mirror.

In fact, it was a two-way mirror, and on the darkened side was a table and chairs.

There were three people sitting at the table, facing the two-way mirror.

One was a police man, a young constable, and the other two were a husband and wife team of criminal investigators.

The investigators, Walter and Patty McQueen, were in their forties and were well known throughout the Melbourne court fraternity. They specialised in body language.

Ray thought that they were a joke, well meaning, but a joke.

He asked himself, *How can they think that someone is guilty by the way he sits? For fuck sake, what next?*

Karl was confident that these two investigators would be a great help.

He said to Ray, 'Mate, these people have studied what body language means. It's like when you know in your head that someone is guilty. You can't put your finger on it, but you know in your heart that he's guilty.' Karl was becoming more and more familiar with Ray since they had started working together and had started to call him mate.

'Yer,' said Ray, 'it's called experience. When you've been around as long as I have, you seem to get second sight.'

Karl started off with the good cop/bad cop routine once again.

He was the bad cop and said, 'Barry, for fuck sake, we know that you killed Jack. You may not have meant it, but he ended up dead. You and Teddy dumped his body out in the bay, and when you realised that Slither had put two and two together, you acted without thinking. You knocked the poor bastard for being in the wrong place at the wrong time.'

Ray entered the conversation and said gently, 'Barry mate, we know that you are under pressure and we realise that Jack's death was an accident. You're really in the shit at the present time. Mate, we can help you, but you've got to come clean. The sooner you admit to your crimes, the sooner we will be able to help you.'

Barry leant back in his chair. He seemed to be on the verge of confessing all.

He asked in a questioning tone, 'So you blokes want me to confess to a murder that I didn't commit. Then confess to another murder to silence a witness who couldn't possibly have seen Jack and me together in the car park to stop him from giving evidence against me. I reckon that you two are clutching at straws. You are just hoping that I'll panic or something. Fellas, I had nothing to do with the murder of Jack or the drowning of

Slither. You are wasting your time and mine. Can I go home now?'

Ray looked at Barry, he said, 'Barry, you are not telling us anything new. We can't help you if you don't help yourself.'

Barry smiled and said, 'Then there is nothing more for us to talk about. Charge me, or else I'm off out of here.'

Ray got out of his chair and opened the door.

Barry walked out of the office and walked outside to the car that he and Teddy had come in.

The McQueens, Ray, and Karl sat down and discussed the interview.

Walter said, 'We both think, through his body language, that Barry had something to do with the disappearance of Jack Andrews. But we don't think that he had anything to do with Slither's death.'

Walter looked at his wife. She nodded and added, 'He is a man who isn't intimidated by the presence of police. He obviously has had a fair bit to do with you at some time. He seemed to relax more and more as the questioning went on. When you got past Jack's disappearance, he relaxed.'

Karl looked at the McQueens and said, 'Yes, that's how I read it also.'

Ray thought, *Fuck me dead, what hope have I got?* He shook his head.

Karl said brightly, 'Next cab off the rank is Teddy. Now we don't reckon that Teddy had anything to do with Jack's demise, but we reckon that Barry and Teddy dumped the body at sea.'

The McQueens and the constable retook their positions behind the two-way mirror.

Teddy entered the room and had a hard look at the mirror.

He thought, *I wonder who is behind that, watching*

Karl started with, 'We reckon that you didn't have anything to do with Jack's death. But you shit yourself when you realised that Slither had clocked you and Barry coming into port after you dumped the body in the bay. So rather than have the old drunk give you two up, you decided to take things into your own hands and you got rid of him. There were marks on the body to indicate that he was strangled and then drowned.'

Ray came in and said, 'Teddy, we know that you were only trying to help a mate out. If you had any idea of what was going on, you would have kept out of it. Mate, we know that Barry is a criminal and a nasty character. We know that you're not frightened of him, but we realise that you have to treat him with respect because he's a tough old bastard. The sad thing is, if he goes down, then he will drag you down with him.'

Teddy looked at the two detectives. 'What you're saying is that you've got nothing on anybody. You reckon that there are two murders and you only have one body. The question on everyone's lips is, if we killed and got rid of Jack's body, why didn't we do the same for Slither?'

There was a stunned silence from the two detectives.

'Can you answer me that?' Teddy went on.

Ray was the first to answer, 'Maybe you didn't have time.'

He was floundering; neither of them had thought of that. It was the obvious question.

Teddy said, 'The way you two geniuses describe it, the bay is full of bodies. They are stacked ten high. You two really have to think a bit harder than what you are doing. That's all the advice that I can give you so I'll be off. OK?'

Ray and Karl admitted to themselves that there was nothing that they were going to get out of Teddy.

This wasn't working out as they had planned at all.

After Teddy had gone, the McQueen's sat with the two detectives.

Once again, Walter led off the conversation, 'As far as we can ascertain, that man is not involved in any of the things that you are interested in charging him with.'

Patty went on to say, 'We don't think he has any involvement at all. It was rather clever of him to say what he did about dumping Slither's body out at sea, because when you think about it, that would have been the obvious thing to have done. If they did it once and got away with it, then what's stopping them doing it again?'

Ray could have kicked himself.

That fucking Teddy had made him and Karl look stupid.

Karl took up the running and said, 'Let's have a look at Des and see what you think.'

Des came into the interview and looked at the mirror.

The thought didn't cross his mind that there could be people behind it, looking at his body language.

Karl started with his bad cop regime. 'We know that you and Slither were as drunk as twenty men when you left the pub. We reckon that you followed him down to the marina and got into an argument over money or something. It got a bit heated, and he ended up in the drink and drowned. You probably did all you could to save him, but in your drunken state, there was nothing that you could do.'

'Mate,' Ray soothed, 'we've all been in that situation. Things get out of control. You've had a little too much to drink, and before you know it, the bloke is dead.'

Des said, 'What? Are you confessing to murdering someone?'

'Don't be a fucking idiot,' Karl said loudly.

Ray suggested, 'Mate, tell us what happened. If it wasn't premeditated and it was a spur of the moment thing and you admit to it, mate, the judge will go easy on you. You'll get a couple of months on a prison farm in the bush.'

'What like Club Med?' Des asked hopefully.

'You know what I mean,' Ray said.

'Fuck off,' said Des. 'I didn't follow Slither down to the marina, and I didn't have an argument with him. I didn't kill him, and I didn't dump his body in the water. Did you know that the poor bastard couldn't swim to save his life? How do you know that he didn't trip and fall into the water of his own accord? It's been known to happen every day. People with too much grog in them end up in water above their heads, and they drown.'

Karl said angrily, 'There were marks on his body that indicated that he had been in a fight before he died.'

Des said, 'Bugger me dead. Slither couldn't fight his way out of a wet paper bag. The wind could blow him over. You may not have noticed, but he wasn't a fitness fanatic.'

Ray and Karl were in a bad space. They could feel their whole case slipping away.

These three men had been around, and they were tight. There was no way they could put a wedge between them.

Des asked, 'Can I go home now?'

Karl in a beaten voice said, 'Fuck off. We know where you are if we need you.'

Des walked out of the room and started walking back towards his local hotel.

Teddy and Barry were waiting outside the police station when they saw Des walk down the front steps. Teddy pulled out and drove up beside him.

'Hullo, sailor, want a lift?' Barry asked with a grin.

Des got into the rear seat. 'Thanks for waiting for me. I could do with a beer.'

'Let's get somewhere quiet and have a pot or two,' suggested Teddy.

'Great minds think alike,' Barry laughed.

Soon the three friends were sitting in a pub.

Barry asked, 'What did they ask you about, Des?'

Des put down his half-empty pot and said, 'All they wanted to know about was, did I follow Slither down to the marina and have a blue with him? I told them that I left Slither at the front door of the pub and I walked one way and he walked the other way.'

Teddy laughed. 'They wanted to know if I had something to do with Slither's death. I told them that they already had me and

Barry dumping Jack's body out in the bay. If either of us had done Slither, then we would have done the same thing to his body. We would have dumped it at sea. I don't think that they had thought of that.'

'They tried to get me for killing Jack and Slither. Fuck me dead, they have got me pictured as a mass murderer,' Barry complained.

Barry said to Des, 'Mate, I see that you had a drink on board the night that Slither went missing.'

Barry knew that someone had been on board as there was rum missing out of the bottle and things had been shifted in the wheelhouse and galley since he had left the boat. He took a chance on it being Des and Slither.

Des looked a bit uncomfortable. 'Yer, I must have gone on down after I left the pub. I can't remember much of what happened.'

'Did you take Slither down for a drink?' Barry asked.

It wasn't uncommon for Des to go and have a drink on Barry's boat.

The boat was always well-stocked with booze, even though Barry hardly ever drank at sea.

Des was in a spot, and he knew it.

'We might have gone down for one or two,' he said.

Barry said, 'Mate, it won't leave this table. Whatever you tell us will stay between the three of us.'

Teddy nodded.

Des went on to say, 'It's a bit of a blur. I remember Slither saying that he was going to make up a story about him seeing you, Teddy, and Jack going out to sea and only the two of you coming back. I don't know what happened. I just snapped, and I grabbed him by the throat. Next thing I knew he was in the water, and I had hold of his feet. He was dead when I left him.'

Barry nodded slowly and said, 'Well, mate, like I say, this information will go no further than this table. The problem is that, as those two coppers say, you were the last to see him.'

'That doesn't mean anything,' Teddy commented. 'Someone had to be the last to see him.'

Teddy walked up to the bar and said to the barmaid, 'Three of your finest, thanks, love.'

She smiled and got the pots.

When Teddy returned with the beers, Barry said, 'It's pretty clear to us all that we are the usual suspects. But there is nothing that the coppers can prove. There were no witnesses, and no one here is going to say a word to anyone. I reckon that we are in the clear. We are innocent men wrongly accused.'

That brought a smile to everyone's face.

The next morning, Ray and Karl went around to Rosie's boarding house.

They knocked on the door with the 'Manager' sign on it.

Rosie came to the door, and, as it was before lunch, she was still in her dressing gown.

She opened the door and, on recognising Ray, said, 'What do you want?'

Ray smiled and said, 'Hullo, Rosie, how's business?'

'Hullo, Mr Boyd, long time, no see. I'm not on the game anymore. I've retired and just run this boarding house. I've made an honest woman out of myself.'

Ray said, 'Good for you, Rosie. We have come to ask about one of your tenants who unfortunately has passed away.'

'Oh, yes,' Rosie said. 'Mr McKenzie, he was a wonderful man. He was such a joy to have around the place.'

Karl asked, 'Are we talking about the same bloke Slither?'

Rosie said, 'I believe that some people called him that. But he was always Mr McKenzie to me. He was always on time with his rent and kept a very clean room.'

'Can we have a look at his room, please?' Ray asked.

'I haven't been into his room as I was waiting until his family or someone else came to collect his possessions,' Rosie said mournfully.

The truth was, as soon as Rosie had done her business with Des, she had scampered up the stairs and gone through everything that was in Slither's filthy room.

She had claimed a few things that she thought she could possibly sell, but it was a worthless pile of possessions. Hardly anything in it was worthwhile saving, let alone selling.

Rosie opened the door, and the smell of dirty socks and sweaty underwear assailed their nostrils.

'The room needs a bit of airing out,' Rosie explained.

Ray and Karl had a look around. They didn't know what they were looking for.

They hoped to find something that would give them a clue on the life of Slither. But there was nothing of any value either price-wise or evidence-wise.

Walking out, Ray said to Rosie, 'Thanks, love. I reckon that you can store what's worth anything and give the rest to the salvos.'

'That's if they will take it,' Rosie commented.

'It's left up to me to bury him,' Rosie added as the two detectives walked away. 'He must have been one of your snouts. Is there any way that the police force could help out in the way of a few dollars for his burial?'

Ray laughed and said, 'Next, you will want a police escort for the funeral.'

Karl reached into his back pocket and pulled out a $50.

'Here, take this. It might help a bit,' he said.

Rosie smiled her sweetest smile and said, 'You've got a good heart, love. Why don't you drop around sometime for a drink?'

Ray said, 'You aren't soliciting, are you, Rosie? I thought that you said you were off the game.'

'Just being friendly, Mr Boyd.' Rosie lent forward a bit to show off her ample bosom.

Karl's eyes were on her breasts.

He said, 'See you around.'

Both the detectives walked to their car and drove off.

Rosie was happy with the way the day had turned out.

She had got another $50 towards Slither's funeral fund, and there was a chance that the younger copper would be back one night when he had a belly full of beer.

Rosie walked into the kitchen and decided what she would have for lunch.

Meanwhile, at the time all this was occurring, Wallace Piggy Trotter had resigned himself to the fact that Teddy and his band of poachers had gotten away with another raid.

He was at his desk when an urgent message came through to him that he was required to attend a meeting with his superiors immediately. Piggy rose to his feet, flattened a few wrinkles out of his uniform, and headed into what could only be a bad meeting.

Piggy walked into the office of the head of the regional fisheries.

There were four men sitting at a table.

His boss motioned him to sit in an empty chair.

Piggy recognised all but one of the men. He had spoken with them before.

His boss introduced him to the stranger.

'Wallace, this is Senior Fisheries Inspector Brian Walsh.'

Brian made no attempt to shake Piggy's hand; he just looked straight through him.

Piggy felt a bit uncomfortable for some reason.

His boss said, 'We have brought Brian in to lead the pursuit of the abalone poachers who seem to have eluded you time and time again.'

'What makes you think that he will do any better than I have been doing?' Piggy asked.

Brian spoke for the first time, 'Well, I certainly couldn't do any worse than you. You have blundered about for ages, costing the department thousands of dollars with no result.'

Piggy had little to defend himself with.

Brian went on to say, 'You have huffed and puffed your way across the state in a mindless attempt to catch these illegal poachers. I've read your reports, and as far as I can see, you have done everything the wrong way. I've had plenty of experience with abalone poachers in South Australia, and I stop them in their tracks. I arrest them and jail them. I confiscate all their gear and take their cars. I hit them hard, and when I hit them, they stay hit.'

Piggy hardened his resolve, 'In all fairness, you haven't seen any poachers like the poachers I'm up against. These blokes aren't weekend warriors. They are dedicated professionals. The ring leader Teddy is a pro, and he's never had a conviction against him.'

'Please don't make him out to be some sort of super poacher,' Brian went on to say. 'He's just a man who, in my opinion, hasn't had a lot to deal with fisheries-wise.'

Piggy's boss then said, 'Wallace, we have got Brian on a temporary loan from the South Australian Government. Well, actually we have got him for as long as we like. Or until we get those poachers in jail.'

'What am I to do?' Piggy asked dismally.

Piggy's boss smiled and said, 'we want you to keep on doing what you are doing, but leave all the abalone poachers to Brian. We feel a new broom sweeps cleanest.'

All the fisheries officers nodded.

Piggy said, 'So I'm to let Teddy and his band of poachers run riot.'

'No, no,' soothed Piggy's boss. 'We want you to concentrate on the amateur fishermen and leave all the abalone business to Brian. He will spend a week with you, going through your reports and preparing himself, and then he will roll up his sleeves and get stuck into those poachers.'

With that, Piggy was excused from the meeting. He got up and walked away from the table his head held high.

He could hear the senior fisheries talking to Brian, their new boy.

Piggy walked back to his desk and sat heavily down.

Bastards, he said to himself.

This had taken the wind out of his sails.

He had toiled long and hard to catch those bastard poachers. He was eager to see just what this Brian was going to pull out of his arse.

Ray and Karl were dead-ended.

Jack was gone.

They both believed that Barry had killed him in a fight and that Teddy had a hand in getting rid of the body.

Slither, well, that was anybody's guess.

The marks on his body indicated that he was killed, but by who? That was the question.

Both Teddy and Barry had alibis with their partners; admittedly Barry's alibi was Jack's estranged wife Hilda, but it was still an alibi.

Teddy's partner was a librarian, so she would be a solid dependable witness as far as a jury was concerned.

Des was the last person to see and talk to Slither, but he had sworn that he left him at the pub and they went different ways.

There was nothing else that they could come up with.

They were stumped.

All the boys were all in Curly's shed having a drink and a game of pool.

Teddy said, 'Well, me hearties, I reckon that we should go and get wet in the next couple of days. What do you reckon?'

They were all eager to get back into the water and away from all the hassle being caused by murder and mayhem.

Epilogue

As the Sun Set
Teddy and Rita
As the sun set over Williamstown, Teddy poked at a large T-bone steak on the BBQ grill and rolled his gold chain between his fingers. He was happy with how things were going. Rita carried out a fresh salad and placed it on the table.

'Looks like those steaks are just about done,' she commented.

Tom and Sandy sat in the cool of the evening and slowly sipped a glass of wine.

Dean and Leckie were at an upmarket Chinese restaurant in the city. Dean looked at Leckie and marvelled at how beautiful she was.

Curly pocketed the black ball on his pool table in his shed.

'That's another slab you owe me,' he said to his mate Jim.

The young humpbacked whale was pulled by instinct back from the warmer northern waters at the top end of Australia. He slowly started to make his way back to the southern waters of the deep southern ocean past Tasmania.

He was content and felt happy. He had spent most of his time up north with other young humpbacked whales.

Unhurriedly he swam past Bondi Beach and headed south towards Gabo Island, following that instinctive route.

The huge moray eel was resting inside the once again undisturbed Japanese mini submarine, waiting patiently for its next victim to pass by so it could satisfy its voracious hunger.

Gazza and Louie were stringing an illegal net across the river. They would wait until the tide turned and then come back the following day to hopefully fill a couple of bins with bream, luderick, and maybe a couple of flathead, a nice little earner.

They hadn't been able to catch their usual number of fish since the whale became entangled in and destroyed their big net a few months previously.

The white pointer was cruising on his usual path along the reef. This was the same reef where he had attacked the abalone diver, and he still avoided divers because they tasted of rubber.

He sensed movement in the water and recognised it as too big to be considered for attacking, so he ignored the humpbacked whale and continued with his constant searching for food.

Muddy, the Bikie, was feeling unsettled and uncomfortable. Although his wounds had healed and he was back to his miserable old self, he was constantly concerned that some dickhead would damage Billy Boy's daughter's cafe and that once again he would be on the receiving end of vengeance dished out by the poachers and the Japanese martial art experts.

He believed them when they had said that if anything else happened to the girls, they would come back and kill him. He decided he should up the protection on the cafe, just in case.

Olivia and Danni were running a fine business. Their cafe was a great success, and now there wasn't any threat of trouble from the bikies, they were relaxed and doing it easy. Baby Darcy was doing well.

Detective Jack Andrew's disappearance still wasn't sown up. His boss Ray Boyd thought that he would have to promote someone up from the junior ranks to partner Detective Karl.

Jack's body was now just a few bones rocking gently in the currents at the bottom of the bay. The sea lice and other bottom feeders had successfully destroyed any evidence of the crime.

Henry and his father continued to work hard in their thriving restaurant. His sisters seemed to have forgotten all about the problems caused by the Silver Eagle.

They remained constantly on the alert for any further trouble.

The Silver Eagle's gang had elected another leader and were still making their presence felt by committing petty crimes and standing over some of the vulnerable Vietnamese community. They had decided that the illegal abalone business was just too difficult to break into, for the present time.

Slither's funeral was a great success.

Teddy and Bass Strait Barry had a word with Dan, Slither's regular barman and the last one to serve him. They had managed to acquire a couple of barrels of beer to contribute to Rosie who held the wake at her establishment.

Free beer was on hand, and the locals ensured Slither was well sent off on his final journey. Wherever he was going, he would need as much goodwill as possible. Stories abounded both tall tales and true.

The minister from the Salvation Army was taken aback by the drunken expression of grief shown by the mourners, but Slither was a close and personal friend to all those present and deserved a liquid send-off.

Rosie was in her element; she was running the show and making sure that everyone was being looked after. It was great to be surrounded by so many drunken men. She knew that sooner or later, some of them would end up in her bed. She planned to take advantage of those with money before they became too pissed for her to move on and needed to stay in her bed to sleep it off.

Des had his eye on Rosie. He thought that if there was a break-in proceedings, he might have the opportunity to slam one into her. It was a bargain at only $100.

He felt like a young man again.

Tony, Teddy's run-around bloke, was as usual on the alert. He knew that in a couple of days or weeks, he would be called on to assist Teddy and the boys again.

He told his cousin Mario to be ready to help him again and be able to leave at the drop of a hat.

Piggy Trotter was sitting in his office, looking over his files. What was the next move?

Even though he wasn't supposed to be doing any work on the 'Teddy and the poachers' file, he just couldn't stop thinking about the bastards.

He knew that the weather was improving and that those bastards would be getting ready to have another go.

Ronny, Teddy's next-door neighbour was content. He had done a deal with the local Chinese restaurant to swap the abalone that Teddy bought him for meals, and he was in credit. So he thought that he might take his wife out for a special treat.

Derek, the processor, was happy with the way things were working out. He had recently checked with Akinobu, his abalone importing friend from Japan, and everything was going fine. Derek was in his office at the rear of the factory when he heard Carol shutting up the fish and chippery. He thought that he might go home to his wife.

Carol closed down the front shop and went and said goodnight to Derek.

She felt her heart quicken when she saw him. He was such a wonderful man.

Dave and Lee sat on chairs out the back of Lee's place in the quietness of the bush, sipping out of beer cans. Lee said, 'Mate, we've got a fair dinkum furniture trip coming up in a week.' Dave laughed and said, 'It would be funny if Piggy searched us right through, and all we had on board was furniture.'

They both laughed at the thought.

Hilda settled into her chair in the good room, watching TV with Barry. She sipped on a glass of port and realised just how happy she was in herself and with her current situation.

She wondered where Jack was and if she would ever be bothered by him again. She hoped with all her heart that he would never show up at her door again.

Barry helped himself to another port. He knew where Jack was and knew why Hilda shouldn't worry.

Chikara looked out at his family's restaurant and saw that it was busy. He had thought, for some time, that he should approach Teddy about some abalone, preferably green lip. His father wouldn't want to have any part of anything illegal, but there was a lot of money to be made. He looked at his staff handling the customers and pondered.

Murphy, the security man, was happy with his lot. He had a large crayfish in his Esky.

He could see the look on his wife's face when she saw it.

The sun set again over the bay and Teddy's mob.
Life was good, but who can tell the future.
Dark clouds always blot out the sun.